Dorathea Brunker

The new Zebra Regency Romance logo that you see on the cover is a photograph of an actual regency "tuzzy-muzzy." The fashionable regency lady often wore a tuzzy-muzzy tied with a satin or velvet riband around her wrist to carry a fragrant nosegay. Usually made of gold or silver, tuzzy-muzzies varied in design from the elegantly simple to the exquisitely ornate. The Zebra Regency Romance tuzzy-muzzy is made of alabaster with a silver filigree edging.

A MOST UNSETTLING ENCOUNTER

Caught up in the heady excitement of her first kiss, Maryann wrapped her arms around Stephen's neck and hung on for dear life as she sank into a whirlpool of pleasurable sensations.

When he pulled away, she murmured a protest. His arms tightened around her, but he did not kiss her again.

"Are you aware," he asked gruffly, "that I am committing the ultimate folly for a man of my questionable position?"

"No. What is the folly?"

"I fear I am falling head over heels in love with you."

"You . . . are?" she asked, even more flustered by his words than by his kiss. . . .

N

THE BEST OF REGENCY ROMANCES

AN IMPROPER COMPANION (2691, $3.95)
by Karla Hocker

At the closing of Miss Venable's Seminary for Young Ladies school, mistress Kate Elliott welcomed the invitation to be Liza Ashcroft's chaperone for the Season at Bath. Little did she know that Miss Ashcroft's father, the handsome widower Damien Ashcroft would also enter her life. And not as a passive bystander or dutiful dad.

WAGER ON LOVE (2693, $2.95)
by Prudence Martin

Only a rogue like Nicholas Ruxart would choose a bride on the basis of a careless wager. And only a rakehell like Nicholas would then fall in love with his betrothed's grey-eyed sister! The cynical viscount had always thought one blushing miss would suit as well as another, but the unattainable Jane Sommers soon proved him wrong.

LOVE AND FOLLY (2715, $3.95)
by Sheila Simonson

To the dismay of her more sensible twin Margaret, Lady Jean proceeded to fall hopelessly in love with the silver-tongued, seditious poet, Owen Davies—and catapult her entire family into social ruin . . . Margaret was used to gentlemen falling in love with vivacious Jean rather than with her—even the handsome Johnny Dyott whom she secretly adored. And when Jean's foolishness led her into the arms of the notorious Owen Davies, Margaret knew she could count on Dyott to avert scandal. What she didn't know, however was that her sweet sensibility was exerting a charm all its own.

Lady Maryann's Dilemma

Karla Hocker

ZEBRA BOOKS
KENSINGTON PUBLISHING CORP.

ZEBRA BOOKS

are published by

Kensington Publishing Corp.
475 Park Avenue South
New York, NY 10016

First printing: August, 1990

Printed in the United States of America

To Mary McLeod

Chapter One

Lady Maryann Rivington heard the door close behind the footman who had delivered the summons from her mother.

Pray don't let Mama be ill. Not tonight. Not on the night of my betrothal ball.

"Hurry, Jane!" In a flurry of skirts, Lady Maryann rose from the dressing table. "My gloves. And where did you put the rose Lord Tammadge sent?"

"One miserly flower." The maid, a sharp-featured young thing whose head was stuffed to overflowing with romantic notions, gave a disparaging sniff as she pinned the white bud in its pearl-encrusted silver holder to her mistress's ball gown.

"Should 'ave been red roses. A dozen of 'em."

"The rose is perfect." Absently, Lady Maryann adjusted the folds of gold silk draped over an underskirt of heavy white satin.

The gown was perfect; the flower was perfect; and the ball promised to be the perfect conclusion to long and tedious negotiations of a marriage contract between Lady Maryann, youngest daughter of the Earl of Rivington, and Francis, Eighth Viscount Tammadge.

If only Mama has not fallen victim to one of her sick headaches.

Irene, Lady Rivington had been in high spirits all morning, but Maryann knew she had been closeted with her husband in the small ground-floor study for quite half an hour during the afternoon. Maryann had heard the roar of her father's voice on the floor above, where she was adding the final touches to the floral decorations on the dining table.

Well, procrastination paid no toll; so she had best see what the summons was all about. Her future was settled. Even a canceled ball could not spoil her plans.

Maryann's slippered feet fairly flew along the corridor to her mother's chamber at the opposite end of the magnificent London town house. Once, she tripped, but instead of slowing, she merely tugged her skirts a little higher. Breathless, she burst into the familiar room with its pretty rosewood furniture and draperies of Brussels lace.

"Mama—"

Maryann came to an abrupt halt. She tilted her head this way, then that, for a different perspective of the elegant woman gowned in a creation of mauve silk, diamonds sparkling on her ears and neck, her luxuriant honey brown hair swept up in an elaborate coiffure.

"Mama, you look lovely. No one will believe you're the mother of five grown children and a grandmother of eight."

"Thank you." Irene Rivington smiled faintly, remembering when a three-year-old Maryann had first copied the head tilting from her German grandmother, the Baroness von Astfeld und Hahndorf. It was a habit the girl had never discarded.

"You don't have a headache, do you, Mama?" asked Maryann, closing the door. "That's what I feared when James brought your message."

"I feel perfectly well, dear." Irene replaced the stopper on a flacon of perfume, rose from her dressing table, and moved briskly to the brocaded day bed beneath the window.

"Come and sit with me, Maryann," she said, wishing her voice were as brisk and purposeful as her movements. "There is something I want to discuss."

She watched her daughter cross the room. Her youngest child, the one most like her in appearance, Maryann was small and lithe as Irene had been before she became a wife and mother. Now Irene was small and plump. Maryann had also inherited her mother's wide gray eyes and rich, honey brown hair, wearing it in short, riotous curls framing her face.

"Mama?" Maryann said softly. "What has happened? You said there's something to discuss."

Irene gave a start. She had a duty to perform. Despite Rivington's prohibition.

She met her daughter's steady gaze. "It is about your betrothal."

Maryann went cold inside. Surely Tammadge had not cried off on the eve of their betrothal ball! She counted on getting married; only a husband could remove her from her father's house.

"Child, are you sure you wish to go through with it?" Irene asked anxiously.

"But of course!" In her relief, Maryann broke into a peal of laughter. A proper fool she'd been to think Tammadge would cry off. He was a gentleman; he'd never commit such an outrageous faux pas as jilting a lady.

"It is all arranged, is it not, Mama? The announcement was in the papers, tonight is my betrothal ball, and in five months I shall be a married lady and reside over my own establishment."

"Yes, but—" Irene looked at her daughter helplessly. She'd had her words all planned, but in the face of Maryann's complacency the carefully rehearsed warning stuck in her throat.

"Maryann, you are not yet nineteen. Lord Tammadge is five and forty if he is a day."

"You saw no problem with the age difference when Lord Tammadge asked for my hand."

"Are you in love with him?"

Her daughter's gray eyes widened. "Were you in love

9

with Father?"

Irene hesitated, her gaze fixed on the white rose pinned to Maryann's ball gown.

"I hardly knew Rivington. The marriage was arranged. But," she added almost inaudibly, "when I was eighteen, I still dreamed of falling in love."

"I, too, dream of love." A smile teased the corners of Maryann's mouth. "I believe a girl cannot help dreaming. And that's all right as long as she doesn't allow it to cloud reality."

"You're thinking of Elizabeth."

"Poor Bess. If ever a bride was in love, it was she. And what did it get her? A husband who squanders his money on mistresses and opera dancers while Bess sits at home and cries."

Irene knew it was true. None of her elder daughters had found happiness with their spouses.

Correctly interpreting her mother's silence, Maryann drove home her point. "And look at Emily, Gussy, and Margaret. They were in such a hurry to escape Father, they married the first men who showed an interest in their dowries. Now they're stuck in the country with their dour-faced, penny-pinching husbands. They merely exchanged one kind of tyranny for another."

"It doesn't have to be that way," Irene said, ignoring the voice of reason pointing out the shortcomings of her own marriage. "If you were to meet the right man . . ."

"Lord Tammadge is most eligible. He is well mannered, personable, respected and admired by his peers. He has a large house in Grosvenor Square, and he certainly does not have a need of my dowry. He proved that when he agreed to have the money placed in an account in *my* name."

Lady Rivington made no reply, and Maryann shifted restlessly. Sitting still was a penance. She preferred to be up and pacing, but it made her mother nervous. She compromised by tapping a foot.

"This is my second season, Mama. No one half as

eligible as Tammadge offered for me last year, and besides, Father gave me no choice. He refused all offers I did receive. And next year," Maryann added in a voice of doom, "I'll be considered on the shelf with little prospect of contracting a marriage."

"At times, I wonder if spinsterhood is indeed the awful fate it's said to be."

Maryann suppressed a shudder. Spinsterhood meant living under her father's thumb, or a lifetime devoted to nieces and nephews. She rose, shaking out her skirts.

"Mama," she said firmly. "You have no need to worry about me. Marriage to Lord Tammadge will suit me just fine."

"There have been rumors about him . . ."

"I have yet to meet a man—or a lady for that matter—who hasn't caused some kind of stir or other." Maryann cocked an eyebrow at her mother. "Dearest, even you are no exception."

"What?!" Irene Rivington sat bolt upright, flecks of color burning on her cheeks. "I have never done anything—"

"No, of course not," Maryann assured her. "It's not *your* doing that your friends speculate on the cost of your gowns and hats. It is Father's awful roar, which can be heard from here to Blackfriars."

"Oh." Lady Rivington's indignation died. "I didn't think you noticed. You're forever in the Sloane Street gardens, muddying your hands and skirts."

Maryann's daily visits to Mr. Salisbury's Botanic Gardens had long been a bone of contention between mother and daughter. Maryann ignored the remark.

"How can I not notice when I see you laid up on your couch? Father's shouting always gives you a headache."

"But to accuse my friends of taking an interest in my bills! Maryann, that is unkind of you."

"Oh? Only last week, when you were indisposed after Madame Blanchard sent the bill for the mauve silk you're wearing, bets were offered that Father would

11

cancel the betrothal ball."

"Nonsense. Rivington has too much pride to cancel the ball for any reason but the king's demise."

"And what's more, Father has no call to lose his temper over a gown. You don't spend extravagantly, and he is far from being purse-pinched."

Irene, who had cause to know the workings of her husband's twisted mind, had for some time suspected that the Earl of Rivington was not as well off as he led others to believe. But if she dared economize by wearing last season's gowns, his anger, fed by an inordinate pride and what he considered his duty to his name and standing in society, would be worse than when she presented him with a dressmaker's bill.

"I think," she said, "we are straying from the point. Speculation about gowns and hats is not the kind of gossip I meant."

"You meant rumors about Lord Tammadge and his ladybirds." Maryann gave her mother a wise look that sat oddly on her youthful features. "I, too, have heard the gossip, and it doesn't worry me a bit. It's not as though I expect Tammadge to live in my pocket once we're married."

Irene swallowed. The rumors were worse, much worse. She had changed her mind a dozen times whether or not to tell Maryann since, earlier that afternoon, her maid reported the sordid tale. Irene had even consulted her husband, something she rarely did and which had done no good.

Rivington's face had turned purple as he berated her for listening to servants' gossip. He had forbidden her to mention the matter to Maryann. Lord Tammadge, he had reminded his wife furiously, was a gentleman of impeccable birth and breeding.

Chastened, Irene had nodded and promised to put the gossip out of her mind.

Three hours later, she had sent for Maryann. But as she studied her youngest daughter now, she changed her mind once again. The rumors—which, as Rivington pointed out, circulated only among the servants—might be false after all. She prayed they were.

Repeating the wicked tale to Maryann would serve no purpose but to upset the girl. She would not be allowed to break the engagement if she wanted to. Aside from the fact that a lady did not jilt a gentleman without suffering dire consequences, Rivington had made it clear his youngest child *would* marry Viscount Tammadge. And no argument about it!

I ought to count my blessings, Irene told herself. *For once, Maryann has the same goal as her father.*

"Mama, let's go downstairs. The dinner guests will arrive presently, and you know how Father hates to be kept waiting."

Irene sighed. Clasping her gloves and reticule, she slowly got to her feet, assuring herself that she was doing right by not disturbing Maryann's peace of mind. An integral part of her daughter's charm was her innocence, her frank and open manner, which would surely suffer, and perhaps wither away, if she learned about the rumors. Her bubbly, irrepressible nature, though, was slowly stifled by Rivington's harshness.

But that was something she must not dwell on. Not tonight. It always made her ill because she was powerless to do anything about it.

She looked at her daughter, who met her gaze with perfect calm.

"I swear," she said, glad to focus her worries on something relatively innocuous. "It is not normal for a young girl embarking on such a serious step as matrimony to be as calm and placid as you are."

"I have every reason to be placid." Maryann led the way from the third floor to the first, where the reception rooms and the formal dining room were located. "When I marry Lord Tammadge, I'll not only have my dowry but also the income from consols he settled on me."

She stopped on the landing. With the air of a contented kitten, she looked at Lady Rivington. "Mama, do you realize that I shall have four thousand pounds income at my disposal annually?"

"Heavens, child! You sound like a banker or a solicitor. Neither your sisters nor I understood or cared anything about marriage settlements."

And that, thought Maryann as she continued downstairs, *is the reason why Bess, Margaret, Emily, and Gussy are miserable, and why Mama has headaches and is obliged to spend many a beautiful day on her couch when Father flies into a rage.*

Languishing in her rooms was not a life Maryann could tolerate. Neither was silent suffering acceptable — nor was the harshness of an unloving father who would permit no character trait in a daughter but meekness and passivity.

Maryann was far from meek, but in order to do all the things she wanted to accomplish, she must have a certain measure of freedom and money. Viscount Tammadge would give her both. The freedom of a married lady to move about as she pleased, and the money to indulge her most ardent desire.

In return, Lord Tammadge had promised, she need do no more than give him her wifely support when he entertained and, in due course, present him with an heir to his vast estates.

Well satisfied with the arrangement of her future, Maryann joined her father and her sister Elizabeth with her unfaithful spouse in the salon to wait for Lord Tammadge and those of the guests who had been asked to dine before the ball. It was not until much later, during the sixth course of the lavish dinner, that she wondered once again about the interview with her mother.

They had talked at great length, but somehow, Maryann suspected, they had not touched upon the meat of the matter. The summons, her mother's agitation, all hinted at some weightier problem than a difference in ages or gossip about Lord Tammadge's fair paphians.

She shot a speculative look at her betrothed, but could see only his classic profile as he listened to the lady on his left. Well, if Mama was troubled about something, there was time aplenty to discuss it. The wedding and her removal from Rivington House were still five months away.

But nothing Mama might say would sway her from the course she had set. Maryann was done with her father's rule, done with being shouted at, or locked into a dark cellar room for some alleged wrongdoing.

The elaborate meal was finally over. Flanked by her parents on one side and her fiancé on the other, Maryann greeted the endless stream of guests filing up the wide staircase and into the ballroom that took up the full length of the second floor.

She prayed for the ceremony to end. Her glove felt sticky from countless handshakes. Her mouth was beginning to tremble from the effort of maintaining a smile. And a feeling of listlessness that attacked her with increasing frequency since the onset of her second season threatened to claim her once again.

She peeked up at Lord Tammadge. As usual, his thin, long face showed traces of boredom. The expression in his pale eyes was bland. Despite herself, Maryann was piqued. True, there was not a shred of affection between them. Neither one pretended otherwise. But this was the night of their betrothal ball. Surely *some* show of feeling, a gleam of interest, would not come amiss from the man who had won Lady Maryann Rivington's hand.

Glancing to her left, she noted that her mother was pale, the smile forced. Her father seemed to be the only one enjoying himself. Always of a taciturn and sour disposition, he actually beamed at each of the arrivals.

Fate had not presented Reginald Rivington, Sixth Earl of Rivington, with the son he desired, only with five very unsatisfactory daughters. Now, with the arrangement of a contract of marriage between his youngest, most troublesome, daughter and one of the most eligible men in the country, he had done his duty by them.

"My lord," Maryann whispered between curtsies to a beturbaned dowager countess and the wife of an M.P., one of Tammadge's friends, "the orchestra has warmed up long enough. Do you think we should go in and open the ball?"

Viscount Tammadge raised a hand, languidly fanning himself with a scented, lace-edged handkerchief. "If you like, my dear."

He did not look at Maryann but scanned a party just ascending the stairs. A spark of interest lit his pale eyes, and he tucked the handkerchief into his pocket.

"Wait just a moment, though," he said with more fervor than he had expressed when he formally proposed to Maryann. "I should like to welcome a friend. I particularly asked your mama to invite him."

Maryann had wished for interest—but not in some bore of a friend.

She watched her betrothed more closely. He would always be a distinguished-looking gentleman with the shock of silver-speckled dark hair above a high forehead, the elegant clothes that sat without a crease on his slender frame. But when his face came alive, he was handsome.

If he looked at *her* like that, with an air of anticipation, even eagerness, Maryann thought wistfully, their marriage might turn out less of a business arrangement than she expected.

Every girl, as she had pointed out to her mother, allowed herself to dream.

Curious as to who had brought about the transformation in her fiancé, she studied the newcomers. Not

Lady Jersey or Mrs. Drummond-Burrell, or the stunning blonde accompanying the two patronesses of Almack's. Lord Tammadge had spoken of a "him." Extending her hand to the formidable Mrs. Drummond-Burrell, she turned her gaze to the two men following at some distance.

The older, a portly, florid-faced gentleman, was about the viscount's age. He grinned from ear to ear as he approached the receiving line and shifted small pig's eyes from her to Lord Tammadge.

No doubt about it. He was the friend, although why he should elicit anything but irritation, Maryann could not begin to guess. She found his gaping quite repulsive.

She directed a cursory look at his companion — and caught her breath as listlessness and annoyance vanished with incredible speed. She looked again; she could not take her eyes off the stranger.

Chapter Two

A first impression of the stranger was one of vitality and strength. His presence shrank the lofty space of the second-floor landing. He walked with a jaunty step; broad shoulders strained to burst the seams of his coat; keen, dark eyes took in everyone and everything at once, observing, evaluating.

If Bella were here, Maryann thought, *the minx would be swooning at his feet, or, more likely, into his arms. My dear friend has, if her letters are not pure invention, a knack for swooning into a handsome gentleman's arms.*

He greeted her parents, then stood before her, bowing over her hand. She marveled at the rugged features—skin deeply tanned, hair a dark brown with sun-bleached streaks. Fine lines radiated from the corners of his eyes, as though he had spent years squinting against a bright sun. Tammadge said a name, but Maryann paid no heed. She stared up at the bronzed gentleman, and a long way up it was to the dark eyes that looked more black than brown. She might be imagining it, but she thought they were frowning at her.

"Lady Maryann," Tammadge said with an edge to his voice. "Have you no word of welcome for my friend?"

She blinked and drew a deep breath. So this was the man who had wiped the look of boredom from her fiancé's face. Caught up in her study of him, she had quite missed the name.

"I beg your pardon," she said. "We have not met before, have we? I am so glad you could come."

"Enchanté," he murmured. A smile softened the chiseled contours of his face and dispelled the frown in his eyes. "I, too, am glad that I came. Very glad."

Maryann inclined her head. She felt rather odd. Light headed, tingly, breathless, alive — the way she had felt when she had stolen away to go up in a hot-air balloon and she had soared high above the world.

The stranger moved on to speak to Tammadge, and the portly gentleman with the pig's eyes, who introduced himself as the Marquess of Woverley, squeezed her hand in a manner she could not like.

Maryann murmured something she hoped sounded polite while she watched Tammadge's friend pass through the double doors into the ballroom.

She still did not know his name.

Maryann did not ask her fiancé for enlightenment. She herself wanted to discover the gentleman's identity and lots more about him besides.

It was easier said than done. First she must dance with her betrothed, then with dozens of gentlemen clamoring for the privilege of leading her out. Lord Tammadge's friend, she noted, was not among those claiming a dance.

Maryann saw her chance after midnight when a sumptuous supper had been consumed in the salons and the guests began to drift back upstairs to the ballroom. While she and Lord Tammadge stood talking with Lady Jersey, the Marquess of Woverley, and several sharp-tongued matrons, the stranger parted the heavy velvet curtains on one of the floor-length salon windows. Moments later, he disappeared onto the small balcony hanging like a bird's nest above Mount Street.

Murmuring an excuse to her companions, Maryann slipped away and crossed the room toward the gently billowing drapes. She did not stop to consider the wisdom of her action. She was consumed by curiosity about this man, whose arrival at the ball had penetrated her fiancé's indifference and dispelled her listlessness.

Letting the curtains close behind her, she stepped out onto the balcony. It was a balmy night for April, and for once the choking mixture of fog and smoke from thousands of coal fires was blessedly absent. She clearly saw the sunburnt gentleman in the silvery light of an almost full moon. He stood not three feet from her, leaning over the wrought-iron railing, his gaze on the glowing tip of a cigarillo.

She must have made some small sound, a movement, for he turned and tossed the slender cigar into the street below.

"Lady Maryann," he said without surprise, or, if he were astonished, he hid it well. "Have you come out to scold me for bringing my filthy habit to your ball?"

She shook her head. "I wish you hadn't done that, sir. Toss away your cigar. Now I feel guilty for having followed you."

"I believe you mean that. Most ladies would grasp the opportunity to read me a lecture on the evils of smoking."

"Humbug to most ladies. And for your information, I always say exactly what I mean."

She did, indeed. Despite her father's attempts to teach her otherwise.

Maryann tilted her head to one side. "Don't you?"

He pushed away from the railing. Since the balcony was tiny, one long step toward her reduced the distance between them to a mere nothing. His dark visage with the narrowed eyes suddenly looked dangerous, even threatening.

Maryann shivered as a light breeze stirred the silk of her shawl.

"W-well, sir? *Don't* you say what you mean? If you

were not sincere, you need not have emphasized that you were glad you came to the ball."

His brow smoothed; a corner of his mouth twitched upward. The air of danger was dispelled.

"Lady Maryann," he said softly. "I must confess that most of the time I lie and deceive for all I'm worth. But when you looked at me with those wide gray eyes and greeted me so charmingly, I could no more have told an untruth than I could have deserted at Waterloo."

"Oh." The monosyllable slipped out, but Maryann instantly recovered her poise. After all, it wasn't her first encounter with flattery.

"You were an officer," she said, steering the conversation in the direction she wished to explore. "That explains much. Your coloring, the way you look about you. What was your regiment?"

"Seventh Light Dragoons."

"A hussar regiment." She nodded approvingly. "You must have met a number of your old friends tonight. Philip Wainwright and young Mablethorpe, they were in the Seventh. John Smythe in the Fifteenth—"

"No," he interrupted. "I'm afraid I don't know a soul but Tammadge and a few of his friends. And now, of course, I know you."

Maryann rested her back against the window frame. "But how is that possible? You must be acquainted with some of your fellow officers."

"I was on special assignment since Vimiero. That was in '08—a long time ago. You were still sewing samplers in the schoolroom."

"Indeed," she said with dignity. "But that doesn't mean I don't know about the battle of Vimiero. It was Wellington's second engagement in Portugal. Only then, of course, he was still plain Sir Arthur Wellesley. Tell me, what does an officer on special assignment do?"

"He lives behind enemy lines and takes care not to be seen by friend or foe."

"You were a spy! One of the invisible heroes." *How envious Bella will be when I write to her!*

"I knew the moment I saw you that you were . . . different," she finished lamely, for he was watching her with an avuncular tolerance that made her feel three years old.

But it took more than an amused look to stop Lady Maryann from asking questions.

"And what do you do now? I cannot believe you'd be content to live the life of a society fribble after years of danger and excitement."

Something in his face, a fleeting look of alertness, or merely his silence, gave her a feeling of unease. She could not understand why he did not answer. They had never met before; surely, her curiosity was not extraordinary.

"You're a strange child." His gaze was inscrutable. "I wonder—"

"What do you wonder?" Maryann drew herself up. "I assure you, sir, I may be small, but I am not a child. This is my second season, and I shall be nineteen in December. Is that what has you puzzled? My age?"

The disquieting stillness about him, that air of watchfulness, disappeared.

"Nineteen in December. By Jupiter!" he said, marveling. "And this is April. Let me see. That makes you just four months over eighteen."

"You are laughing at me. I don't like that."

"I beg your pardon." He bowed, then resumed his former stance at the railing.

"Tell me, Lady Maryann," he said, looking at her over his shoulder. "How long have you known Tammadge?"

"For ages," she said breezily. "The Countess Lieven introduced Lord Tammadge to Mama and me last year."

Again, she had the impression that he was amused. She gave him a reproving look. A year *was* like ages, and that she had spoken to Tammadge on a mere half-dozen occasions didn't change the length of their acquaintance.

Impatiently she said, "And you? How long have you known my betrothed?"

"Since February."

Maryann frowned. "I thought you must have known each other much longer. Tammadge asked Mama to invite you. He said you're his friend."

"I'm honored."

The dry statement made her remember his earlier assertion that he often lied and deceived. She could not see his face, for he chose that moment to turn and look down into the street where the clatter of hooves and the rumble of carriage wheels proclaimed the departure of the first guests, but she did not believe he was honored by her fiancé's friendship.

How curious.

Maryann stepped toward the railing—toward him. "You are not a very skillful liar, you know. I don't believe you feel honored at all, and I wonder how you convinced Tammadge that you are his friend."

She had only been her forthright self, but he flung around so quickly that she knew she had hit upon a sensitive nerve. She had no chance to evade him. His hand closed on her wrist. He gripped firmly, not causing her pain, but forcing awareness of her own frailty and helplessness against his superior strength.

"And I wonder what it is about you that makes Tammadge willing to jump into parson's mousetrap," he said. "From all I've learned about him, his preferences are better accommodated outside the marriage bed."

Maryann was speechless with shock. She twisted her arm free, her face aflame with indignation.

"Sir, you are offensive!"

"I beg your pardon." Face pale and grimly set, he looked less remorseful than angry. "I truly am sorry, Lady Maryann. I had no right to speak to you thus."

23

Coldly, she said, "I must see to my guests. Pray excuse me, Mr. . . ." She turned from him, adding a final snub, "I'm afraid I wasn't attending when my betrothed introduced you."

"I am Stephen Farrell."

She gave no sign of having heard but slipped through the draperies and disappeared from his view as quietly as she had approached.

Stephen swore under his breath, yet neither the eloquence of the outburst nor the violence inherent in the colorful words brought relief. Seething with frustration and anger at himself, he lit a cigarillo.

He'd botched it. He had allowed emotions to get the better of cool reason. Instead of gaining the Lady Maryann's trust, he had offended and alienated her.

Liar. The word mocked him. He had planted it in her mind and she had tossed it back at him. Rightly so. Even the name he'd given her was a lie.

Stephen *Farrell*. Pshaw! He didn't want to be Farrell, but as Stephen Fant—Maj. Stephen Fant—he'd never have gotten anywhere near Tammadge.

Or near Tammadge's betrothed.

To meet her had been his reason for attending the ball. Only, he had expected a sophisticate, a lady of experience.

A pixyish face framed by an abundance of short honey brown curls rose before his mind's eye. Bloody hell! When he first laid eyes on her as he ascended the stairs to the ballroom, he had come damned close to a stumble. She was an innocent. An enchanting child. He'd give his last sovereign to keep her out of the mess in which he had involved himself.

The cigarillo followed the course of the first, the one he had tossed over the balcony railing when Lady Maryann joined him. An oath from below warned him that his second missile had found a target.

Stephen leaned against the window frame where Lady Maryann had stood such a short while ago. Having spent the past nine years on the war-torn Peninsula and in France, with four or five brief furloughs at Fant Court in Sussex, his acquaintance with young ladies of the *ton* was of a recent order. Even so, he judged Lady Maryann refreshingly different from the young misses he had met since February.

He certainly had not expected to find a girl like her affianced to Viscount Francis Tammadge, a lecher, a cheat, and worse.

The man who had robbed his brother of dignity and fortune. The man responsible for William's death.

If Stephen had followed his inclination, Tammadge would have come to his deserts by now. Maj. Stephen Fant, traveling posthaste from Paris to London after reading his sister-in-law's distraught message, had been prepared to issue his challenge. He would have killed Tammadge. It didn't matter that he would have been forced to flee the country.

But he had promised when he conveyed the widow and her three young daughters to her parents' house in Hertfordshire, that he would go to Bow Street and lodge a complaint against Viscount Tammadge.

He had anticipated only polite interest from Sir Nathaniel Conant, the chief magistrate at the Bow Street court, and regret that without evidence or witnesses of Tammadge's cheating nothing could be done. He had not expected Sir Nathaniel's disclosure that Bow Street had started an investigation of a white slavery charge against the viscount.

Sir Nathaniel had convinced him that a conviction and Tammadge's death by hanging would be more satisfying than a gentleman's death in a duel. Maj. Stephen Fant had resigned from his regiment and entered the circle of Tammadge's intimates under the name Stephen Farrell.

"Farrell, my dear fellow." Wearing his habitual look of boredom, Lord Tammadge stepped onto the balcony. "Lady Maryann told me you were hiding out here. She seems to think you're shy and in need of a friend's support before you dare brave the ballroom again."

Stephen gave him a sharp look. So the Lady Maryann had seen fit to keep their contretemps from her betrothed. Unexpected, but most fortuitous.

"As a matter of fact, I came outside to blow a cloud and to escape the boring chatter. I assure you, my friend, for none but you would I have attended a gathering like this."

The viscount's thin mouth twisted. "Indeed," he drawled in the soft, expressionless voice that was one of his peculiarities. "I, too, would prefer a game of dice or cards, or any of the various entertainments offered at Moll's establishment."

"In that case, shall we retire to Soho Court?"

"I fear that until my wedding day I'm expected to fulfill my duty toward my dear betrothed."

"Pay the piper, eh?"

"You can call it that. May I count on your support, Farrell?"

Stephen shrugged. "Could have knocked me over with a feather when you told me you're planning to get riveted. Why bother? A wife will only crimp your style."

"She won't."

Lord Tammadge parted the curtains and cast a quick look into the salon. "Once I've planted my seed in her," he said softly, "Lady Maryann will reside at Sevenoaks, my estate in Northumberland."

"Northumberland can be a lonely place for a young lady."

The viscount stared at Stephen. His pointed brows, which, in combination with his narrow, high forehead, gave him a satyric look, rose a fraction.

"Compassion from *you*, Farrell?"

"Not compassion." To cover his blunder, Stephen put a sneer on his face. "I fear your wife will look for other diversions if you deprive her of your companionship."

Tammadge examined the handkerchief in his left

hand, then gave it a flick as though removing a speck of dust.

"She won't," he said softly.

"Come now! When you have no further use of her, she'll feel free to —"

Tammadge cut him off with a look that held no trace of blandness or boredom — only a cold, deadly anger. "Lady Maryann is mine. I don't share my property."

Stephen found himself gritting his teeth. He didn't know whether the cold fury was directed at him for suggesting it, or at the prospective bride who might contemplate cuckolding the viscount, but the thought of Lady Maryann as Tammadge's property turned his stomach.

Gripping the balcony rail, he said, "I shouldn't have thought you'd go for her kind of innocence. A lady of experience would be more to your taste."

A slight quirk of the tight-lipped mouth indicated that the moment of anger had passed.

"Every once in a while, my dear Farrell, you drive it home that I'm your senior by more than a decade. 'Experience,' as you call it, is only a night removed from the freshness and innocence that now make Lady Maryann desirable."

"And, possibly, an experienced lady would not be easily ruled or banished to the wilds of Northumberland?"

"Exactly, my friend."

Stephen pushed away from the window frame and gestured the older man to precede him into the deserted supper room. He must leave. He couldn't bear the viscount's company a moment longer. And since the scheme of using Tammadge's betrothed in the Bow Street magistrate's investigation must come to nought, he had no need to stay.

Not if success depended solely on Lady Maryann's cooperation would he drag her into the dirty, dangerous game he was playing with the aid of Sir Nathaniel

Conant. In fact, if he could help it, he wouldn't see her again.

It shouldn't be difficult to avoid her. Despite Tammadge's request for support, Stephen had no intention of attending a number of society functions. He had no friends in London, but there was still the off chance that he might be recognized by someone who had known him as a youngster in Sussex.

At the foot of the stairs leading to the ballroom, Stephen halted. "Allow me to take my leave. I have a mind to visit a tavern I discovered in Seven Dials."

A gleam lit the viscount's pale eyes. He moved aside to allow passage for a dozen or so departing guests.

"That's what I like about you, Farrell," he said when they were once more alone. "You have a knack for finding unusual entertainment. If you wait a half-hour, I'd be pleased to go with you."

"Sorry." Stephen assumed a look of regret. "A cavalry regiment couldn't drag me back upstairs. Let me take you to the Fighting Cock tomorrow."

The viscount's mouth compressed into a tight line. Then he smiled.

"Begad! For a groat I'd forget about politeness and leave with you right now. But with advancing age, man gains a modicum of wisdom and caution. Thus, for the next five months I shall watch my step."

"Five months? The wedding date is set, then?"

"October the tenth, Lady Maryann will be mine."

Chapter Three

Lady Maryann's betrothal ball had taken place on a Saturday. When the last guest finally left well past two o'clock Sunday morning, she had been only too glad to fall into bed and close her eyes without a thought to spare for either her betrothed or his friend, Mr. Stephen Farrell.

But all day Sunday, Maryann was at leisure to consider Mr. Farrell and his reprehensible and utterly tasteless remark. She wished she had never heard his name. She certainly, definitely, would not smirch the pages of a letter to her friend Bella Effingham with the name Farrell.

How faulty one's judgment could be. The man had impressed her with his vitality, his earthy looks and keen, clear gaze. She had been intrigued and curious. And when she learned he had been a spy during the war, she had been utterly fascinated.

Some Englishmen, her father for instance, held spies in contempt, judging them lower than the smugglers who had filled Bonaparte's coffers with British gold. Maryann admired the courageous men who had, unprotected by government or army, gathered intelligence in enemy territory. They were her heroes.

Yet this hero had proven beyond a doubt that he was a cad.

He had offended her and insulted the man who regarded him as a friend by speaking of Tammadge's preferences in the marriage bed. Or was it outside the marriage bed? It mattered not; one was as unseemly as the other.

And why she hadn't alerted her fiancé to his friend's disgustingly loose tongue was more than she could understand. It certainly wasn't because she feared to be overcome by missishness.

Neither did she understand why, above perfectly justified anger, she should feel sadness and disappointment at Mr. Farrell's perfidy.

All in all, on Sunday, April 14, Lady Maryann's emotions more closely resembled those of a woman left waiting at the altar than those of a young lady whose betrothal to Viscount Tammadge was considered the coup of the season. But Monday morning, as Maryann got ready for her stint in Mr. Salisbury's Botanic Garden, she dismissed all negative thoughts.

She had rose bushes to mulch, wilted tulips and narcissi to clip. Mr. Farrell was of no importance compared to the work that lay ahead. As she would pluck a weed from the soil, she'd pluck him from her mind and toss him out with the rubbish.

Having made up her mind not to think of Stephen Farrell again, she was more than a little irritated to find a curricle drawn up behind her carriage when she stepped outside, and the detestable man himself in conversation with her groom at the foot of the marble steps, where she could not help but take notice of him.

If it had been the old coachman speaking to Stephen Farrell, she might not have minded. But Robert was her friend, her childhood companion, and even though he could not know that Farrell had insulted her, his chatting with him was like a betrayal.

"Robert," she said, addressing the groom in an unprecedented imperious tone. "I am ready to leave."

Blushing to the roots of his sandy hair, the strapping young fellow pulled off his cap and jumped aside to let her pass. Maryann intended to sweep past Mr. Farrell with no more than a cool nod, but, whether he anticipated her move or whether by accident, that gentleman suddenly stood directly in her path.

"Lady Maryann, please allow me to apologize for my inexcusable behavior Saturday night."

She wanted to ignore him but refused to resort to cowardly sidestepping. Instead, she fixed her gaze on a point just off his sun-streaked hair.

And why the dickens did he not wear a hat like other men?

"You did apologize, Mr. Farrell. Nothing more need be said."

"You're wrong. Much more must be said, but words are inadequate to convey my regret for having caused you distress."

She tilted her head, focusing fully on his face. "Mr. Farrell, I assure you, I'll gladly accept your apologies, inadequate or otherwise, if you will only step aside. I am pressed for time, and besides, I don't like to keep the horses standing."

"Neither do I. Why don't you ask Robert to return your carriage to the mews, and we'll exercise my horses while I explain what prompted me to go beyond the pale."

He clasped her elbow, clearly expecting her to accompany him. But Maryann was not easily persuaded. He couldn't possibly have an explanation for his offensive behavior. Or could he?

Unmoved by the gentle pressure of his hand, she contemplated the set of his jaw while contrariness and curiosity fought a brief if violent skirmish in her breast.

Curiosity won. She started walking toward the curricle.

"Since it's such a lovely morning," she murmured, giving him a sidelong look.

His dark gaze touched her hair, her nose, lingered on her mouth, as he assisted her into the seat. "Too lovely

31

to waste in a closed carriage."

Her face grew warm, but nothing would induce her to admit she was flustered and felt unsure of herself in the presence of this unpredictable man.

Arranging the folds of her skirt about her feet, she called out to her groom. "Robert, you may fetch me at the usual time."

Farrell climbed up beside her, and with a flick of the reins they were off. For a while they drove in silence, Maryann determined not to betray by word or look that curiosity had prompted her to accept the invitation. By the time they turned into Park Lane, she was ready to toss resolve to the wind. Would he never get around to the promised explanation? Or to saying anything at all?

Uneasy, she shifted on the seat. Her foot touched something soft. "Ho," she said, leaning down to feel behind her skirts. "Are we carrying a stowaway?"

"Dash it! If I didn't forget."

Farrell slowed the horses to a walk. His long arm shot out, and after a brief tussle with an ankle and her hand, he came up with a posy of violets rather the worse for wear.

"For you," he said, giving her a crooked grin. "Thought you might need some inducement to drive out with me."

She accepted the limp blooms, cradling them in her hands. Poor things. They needed water. She looked at Farrell. His expression, an odd mixture of uncertainty and boldness, made her sit up straighter.

"You offered an explanation, sir. That was inducement enough. Pray get to the point."

"Yes, my lady."

But Stephen took his time. When he made the sudden decision in the wee hours of Sunday morning to see the Lady Maryann once more, to drop a word of warning about Tammadge in her ear, it had seemed a simple task. He'd hint with a delicate phrase or two at the viscount's unsuitability as a husband and be off the

32

hook, his conscience salved.

To get Tammadge was his primary concern. He would say or do nothing to jeopardize his position of trust in the viscount's circle of intimates. During the eight weeks since his brother's suicide, he had pretended to be a Captain Sharp, an adventurer, a ruthless opportunist in search of easy money. Instinct told him that Tammadge was on the point of offering a cut in his dirty deals.

And that would be the end of Tammadge, cheat, despoiler, peddler in human flesh. With Stephen's evidence, the magistrate of the Bow Street court could place the noose around Tammadge's neck.

But, then, there was Lady Maryann, Tammadge's betrothed. Perhaps by the time Sir Nathaniel was in a position to act, she'd be married to the viscount — a thought that tore at Stephen's guts, toughened as they were by his experiences in the Peninsula.

The scandal, justly or unjustly, would annihilate Lady Maryann. Unless he warned her away from Tammadge. Unfortunately, the young lady beside him did not look as though she'd listen meekly to whatever he might say, thank him, and take her leave — or that she would heed his warning.

Under the guise of negotiating the heavy traffic at Hyde Park corner, Stephen studied her closely, taking note of the primed mouth, the haughty tilt of the nose, which would have delighted him if it hadn't added to the aura of determination surrounding her. Inquisitiveness as well as intelligence shone from her wide gray eyes, and instinct told him to tread with the utmost wariness.

"Lady Maryann," he stated cautiously. "You must understand that I was quite bowled over when I learned such a very young lady is betrothed to Lord Tammadge. Too bowled over to choose my words with care."

"Young? Or do you mean naive? The two don't necessarily go hand in hand."

33

"But perhaps they should?" he countered, irked but not surprised that she would immediately split hairs.

With an impatient gesture, she brushed aside the question. "You must think me very naive, indeed, if you believe I'll swallow that yarn about being bowled over. It wasn't until I said you weren't a skillful liar and asked how you convinced Tammadge of your friendship that you made your vile remark. You hit back like a villain unmasked."

Not a fool, the Lady Maryann. He had indeed felt unmasked, but he would not be caught off guard again.

And neither would he allow her to distract him. If Tolly's directions were correct, they'd reach Mr. Salisbury's Botanic Garden in another block or two. Even at a sedate walk, the distance did not allow time to pussyfoot around a warning.

"Well?" Her clear voice mocked coldly. "Are you a coward as well as a liar?"

"Neither coward, nor liar." At least, no more a liar than when he pretended to be a Portuguese or Spanish peasant in order to gather vital information for Wellington. "But I fear I may be the world's biggest fool."

"And how is that, Mr. Farrell?" she asked sweetly.

"Because I'm risking Tammadge's friendship by meddling." That sounded good. Even noble. Encouraged, he spun the yarn further. "I'm trying to warn you, to save you embarrassment, Lady Maryann. And I'm trying to spare your betrothed the pain of hurting you later on."

She made a sound that was not quite a sniff nor a snort, but conveyed a wealth of meaning — disdain, irritation, and utter disbelief.

"Warn me? Is that what you meant to do when you flaunted propriety and decency and spoke to me of Tammadge's preferences in the marriage bed?"

"I didn't want to repeat the offense," he said mildly. "But since *you* mention it . . . Lady Maryann, I spoke of preferences better accommodated *outside* the marriage bed. You see, I don't think your betrothed is cut out to be a husband."

Her small hand balled into a fist, and he feared he might get his ears boxed for his pains.

"You take great pleasure in trying to put me to the blush," she said angrily. "But let me tell you, Mr. Farrell, I am not so innocent that I am unaware of Tammadge's interest in the muslin company. Nor am I too missish to acknowledge it."

Tammadge's high fliers weren't quite what he meant, but they must do for now.

"And you don't mind?"

Under his gaze, a blush seeped from the neck ruffle of her spencer to her hairline, making her look just like the innocent young maiden she had hotly denied.

"I think we had best part company," she said with icy dignity. "Pray stop the carriage, Mr. Farrell."

Ignoring the request, Stephen speculated about the kind of marriage she anticipated. Was she resigned to a husband who'd seek his pleasures elsewhere?

Sharply, he called himself to order. What he ought to tell her had as little to do with extramarital affairs as a Covent Garden nun had to do with a convent. But he could not, must not, let on that Bow Street was investigating her betrothed.

He could, however, frighten her just a little by using some of the brutal facts he had learned in his association with the viscount.

"You *are* naive." He spoke bluntly, harshly. But, then, there was no other way of saying it. "Preferences outside the marriage bed refer to cravings, as sadistic as they are perverted, to which a wife or even a lady of easy virtue would not willingly submit. Tammadge is known to—"

"Stop! I won't listen to such filth."

Oblivious to danger, Lady Maryann scrambled to her feet and would have jumped from the moving vehicle had he not clasped her arm and forced her back on

35

the seat.

Wrath blazed from her eyes. "Let me go! How dare you speak to me of matters no decent man would broach to a young lady! How dare you approach me with lies about my betrothed!"

Tightening his grip on her arm, Stephen pulled up in front of the Sloane Street gardens. He wanted to shake her. He had risked all to spare her the humiliation of a marriage to a swine, and she wouldn't listen. She'd probably cast herself on Tammadge's bosom and complain bitterly about his false friend.

"Why the deuce should I lie, knowing you only have to ask Tammadge to expose me? Go ahead," he urged, hoping the bluff would save his groats. "Go ahead and speak to him."

"I will!" she spat.

Taking him by surprise, she tore free and sprang to the ground. She ran a few steps in stumbling hurry, then turned to look back at him.

"You are despicable. Tammadge holds you in high esteem, and you stab him in the back. Just tell me this! Did you bribe my groom to ferret information about me?"

Stephen kept an eye on the restive horses and a firm grip on the reins. "I had no information from your groom."

"*I* did not tell you where to drive me this morning, yet you took me straight to the gardens."

Another slip. Damn, but the girl was a distracting peck of troubles.

"Don't blame the groom," he said gruffly. "I have other sources."

Tolly, his brother's faithful butler, who had dragged his arthritic bones into every church, park, and public house where one of Lord Rivington's servants might while away an hour on a Sunday. Tolly, who had learned that Lady Maryann left at nine sharp every morning for Mr. Salisbury's Botanic Garden—come

36

rain or shine, Monday through Friday.

"I forbid you to question our staff about me!"

"I have no need of your servants, Lady Maryann. Already I know more about you than *you* know about your betrothed."

A sound like a sob tore from her chest. "I despise you!"

He hardened his heart against compassion for the slender girl, hat askew, fury and defiance blazing from her eyes. But he could not steel himself against the whiplash of her voice. Her disgust cut too deep.

"I know, for instance, that you're a hard-headed bargain driver, Lady Maryann. That you wouldn't consent to wed Lord Tammadge until a fortune was settled on you."

"You're scum, Mr. Farrell! Hateful, detestable scum."

Stephen watched her run until a hawthorn hedge swallowed her from view. His hands clenched on the reins, but he did not give the horses the office to go.

He shouldn't have added that rider. He had accomplished his purpose, had delivered a warning, perhaps planted a seed of doubt in her mind. Reminding her that her betrothal was a business arrangement as much as, or more than, a pledge of affection, had probably done more harm than good.

Bloody hell. Once again he had botched, had discarded logic and reason to indulge in an emotional act. Because her accusations and disgust had cut him.

Fool! Emotion, he reminded himself bitterly, was a dangerous encumbrance he could not afford to lug around. He was already burdened with bitterness against William, who had thrown away his life; he must not add to that weight by letting Lady Maryann get under his skin.

He should have stuck to his decision to stay away from her, but he had to follow his blasted conscience and bloody well jeopardize the whole investigation.

Forget her now. She had parents, hadn't she? Let the all mighty Earl of Rivington protect his precious daughter.

But in case, just in case she should have a need of him, he had given that strapping young groom of hers the name of the Fighting Cock tavern.

Stephen sent a last glance at the spot where Lady Maryann had stood and called him scum; a few feet away, on the flagged walk leading into Mr. Salisbury's Botanic Garden, he saw the posy of violets — more wilted, more battered than before.

He hesitated only an instant, then got down from the curricle and picked the flowers up.

Chapter Four

"Bounder! Scum! Muckworm!"

Dandelion, clover, Queen Anne's lace, proud survivors of a time when Sloane Street was still wide open pasture land, fell victim to Lady Maryann's punishing hand as she weeded in a secluded corner of the gardens.

"Cad! Back stabber! Blackguard!"

And if tender shoots of anemone, columbine, or daisy were uprooted in Maryann's quest for violence, it was nothing to be wondered at. She shook in the grip of red-hot fury, a rage such as she had not experienced since Cousin Reggie, her father's heir and a pesky brat spoilt by misguided and indulgent parents, had guillotined her favorite doll. Ten years younger, more than two heads shorter than Cousin Reggie, Maryann had flown at him and engaged him in a battle that required the combined forces of her father and a footman to break up.

The only reason why she had run away from Farrell instead of flying at him with balled fists, was that she had learned the hard way it was all right, even laudable, for boys and gentlemen to engage in fisticuffs. Girls and young ladies, however, were locked into windowless cellars if they so much as boxed a deserving ear.

But how she wished she had aimed a jab at the square jaw, or a punch at the nose with its proudly aquiline curve.

She had admired that nose and jaw when Farrell walked toward her in the receiving line. She had believed him the most fascinating of the guests. She had liked him — perish the thought! — until he stepped beyond the bounds of decency. And when she expected an explanation, he compounded the offense with more foul remarks and lies about Tammadge.

"Confound it! I'll make him pay," she grimly assured the plants. "He'll pay for embarrassing me. Pay for spreading lies about my betrothed. He'll rue his words to the end of his days."

Maryann abandoned weeds and trowel. Dropping gloves and sacking apron along the way, she hurried to the Sloane Street entrance of the gardens. She *would* speak to Tammadge. She'd tell him about the viper he had nursed in his bosom.

As she approached the gate, Maryann's steps slowed. She remembered that it was far too early for Robert to be waiting with the carriage.

And it occurred to her that even the most indifferent of fiancés might ask why she had been in Mr. Farrell's company today — in which case she'd have to confess that the viscount's "friend" had already slandered him at the ball. She'd have to admit that not only had she allowed Farrell to get away with slander, but had accepted his invitation this morning in the hopes of hearing a redeeming explanation.

Considering the matter, Maryann was not at all certain how much of what had transpired she was prepared to disclose to her betrothed. Even Tammadge with his habitual air of indolence and boredom might feel obliged to call Farrell out if he were to learn the whole truth.

Not that she'd mind if Tammadge shot Stephen Farrell, Maryann thought bloodthirstily. But she couldn't be certain that her betrothed was a good marksman — or a fencer. It seemed to her that the choice of weapons was up to the challenged party. Farrell, no doubt, was expert with either, the pistol or the sword.

It was with less fervor than she would have displayed a few minutes earlier, that Maryann hailed a hackney.

"Rivington House. Mount Street."

The least she could do was bathe and change before calling on her elegant betrothed. The sturdiest apron, the thickest gloves, did not stop a gardening enthusiast from getting dirty. And besides, the long, sphinx-footed tub, installed two years ago in the former powder closet, was her favorite thinking place. By the time she was clean, she'd know exactly what to say to Lord Tammadge.

Whether the magic of the tub had worn off, or whether Maryann's mind was in too much of a turmoil, when she was freshly gowned and coiffed, she still had not come up with a satisfactory argument why, on the one hand, she didn't want her betrothed to do something rash, and why, on the other hand, she wanted him to do *something* to punish Farrell for his despicable behavior.

It did not occur to her that she might, to avoid uncomfortable questions, back down from her decision to see Tammadge, or, at least, postpone the visit. Maryann was a doer. She wanted to warn her betrothed about his false friend, and she'd warn him *now*. She wanted to make Farrell pay, and she'd instigate his punishment *now*.

Mouth set, step firm, Maryann swept into her mother's chamber to beg the chaperonage of Hedwig, Lady Rivington's formidable German maid, who had left Lower Saxony with her young mistress thirty years ago to accompany her to a new home in England.

"Of course you may have Hedwig." Irene Rivington put down the novel she had been reading and removed the spectacles no one but Maryann and Hedwig knew about.

Adding more cushions to the stack supporting her back on the day bed, she asked, "But why, dearest?

41

Where on earth are you going that your own Jane is not sufficient protection? And why are you not in Sloane Street?"

"I must speak with Tammadge."

Irene raised a brow. "I take it you plan to pay him a visit in Grosvenor Square. It would be more proper to send a note asking him to call on *you*."

"I know." Maryann started to pace. "The thing is, Mama, I don't want to sit around waiting for him. I have something unpleasant to disclose, and I'd rather get it over with."

"Child!" Spectacles, book, and the lace shawl covering her legs, dropped to the floor as Irene Rivington sat up. "You're not—not breaking the engagement, are you?"

Startled, Maryann came to a halt in front of the dressing table. Break her engagement? Give up the marriage that would provide the means for financial independence from both, father and husband?

"No, Mama. I'm not crying off."

In the mirror, Maryann saw her mother's agitated face. Their eyes met, and she remembered the interview before the ball. Her mother had voiced sudden doubts about the betrothal. About Tammadge's suitability.

As had Farrell.

Her mother had mentioned gossip about the viscount. Maryann had assumed the gossip referred to Tammadge's mistresses—just as she had assumed Farrell's vulgar remark was about her fiancé's ladybirds.

She felt cold. She saw her mother's eyes, wide with distress, and it was as though she were looking into her own eyes, seeing her own growing apprehension.

"Mama? Those rumors you mentioned. About Tammadge. They were about his mistresses, were they not?"

Irene opened her mouth as if to speak. But she said not a word, only shook her head.

"What sort of rumors, then? And where did you hear them?"

"Hedwig told me."

Hedwig was outspoken and blunt, but Maryann had never known her to indulge in idle gossip.

"What did she say?"

Irene hesitated, then, with an air of resignation, reached for the bell pull behind her. "Let Hedwig tell you herself. I cannot bear to."

After one more glance at her mother's wan face, Maryann turned from the mirror. Once again she took up pacing, as though the exercise would help stave off the questions she burned to ask.

"I tried to make myself tell you," Irene said. "Even though your father forbade me to do so. And then I simply couldn't. Since you are committed to Tammadge, I thought you'd be better off not knowing. Especially since Rivington assured me that there's no basis to the rumors."

Maryann kept pacing. She knew, if she pressed her mother for answers, she'd get them. But she also knew that somehow her father would learn of his wife's disobedience. He would shout at her until she took to her couch with a sick headache; or, his favorite method of punishing Irene, he would hurt her through her daughters.

Since the older girls were married, Maryann had for a year and a half borne alone the brunt of Rivington's malevolence. She would marry soon, and thus escape her father's tyranny, but for Irene there was no such easy way out. A woman who left her husband was considered no better than a fallen woman.

Hedwig did not keep them waiting. Wasting no time on a knock, the gaunt German woman marched into the chamber. She was dressed in gray. Her gown and stockings were a light silver gray, her apron a dark charcoal—the only colors Hedwig considered suitable for a lady's maid, colors that should have made her inconspicuous.

But Hedwig had a weakness for caps. Pretty, frilly, lacy caps of gigantic proportions, which, set atop a head of fiery hair that refused to be confined by any number of hairpins, made her as inconspicuous as a peacock among a flock of hens. On this morning, Hedwig sported a lavish creation of Nottingham lace and pink satin bows against which strands of escaped hair flamed brightly.

"And why are you not sleeping as you promised, my lady?" Hedwig demanded as she picked up shawl, book, and spectacles. "Reading has never cured a headache yet."

Unlike Irene, who was educated by an English governess, a French mademoiselle and a German *Fräulein,* the maid had spoken only her native tongue when she arrived in England. Now, her English was as correct as that of any upper servant, but she had never lost the guttural German accent.

"Please lie down, my lady. Let me bathe your temples with lavender water. And you must take a drop of tonic. You're too pale and your hands are like ice. You know you shouldn't be sitting about without a rug to cover you."

"Don't scold." Lady Rivington allowed Hedwig to plump cushions and to replace the shawl over her legs, but shook her head when the maid reached for the tonic bottle and glass on a table nearby. "Leave that for now. I need you to tell Maryann what you learned about Lord Tammadge."

"Well now! If those aren't the first sensible words I've heard you speak since Saturday. *Gott sei Dank im Himmel, kann ich da nur sagen. Es wird höchste Zeit.*"

Only when she was deeply moved did Hedwig resort to German, and Maryann was startled to hear the familiar words. But she knew better than to follow up in that language.

"What is it that I must be told without delay?" Maryann pulled two rosewood chairs closer to the day bed. She sat down, offering the second chair to the maid. "Why do you make it sound as though my life depended on it, Hedwig?"

"Perhaps not your life. But your sanity."

Maryann saw that her mother had started to tremble and reached out to clasp her hand. "Hedwig, please don't tower above us. And for goodness sake, don't talk in riddles."

"Very well." Hands folded on her knees, back poker straight, the maid perched on the edge of the chair. "It is said that Lord Tammadge's wealth comes from brothels he owns in Seven Dials and on the waterfront."

The words delivered in Hedwig's harsh, guttural voice had barely sunk in when Maryann cried out in protest.

"Brothels! That's preposterous. Not Tammadge!"

Hedwig said nothing.

"Tammadge is an honorable man!" Maryann tightened her grip on Irene's hand. "One of the most respected peers in the country."

"Dearest," whispered Irene. "Dearest child."

"Stop shaking, Mama. Hedwig made a mistake. There's nothing to those outrageous lies. Nothing to worry about."

"It is *you* who is shaking, my love."

Maryann stared at the hand lying atop her mother's, a hand bearing on the fourth finger a sapphire-and-pearl betrothal ring. Her own hand, firm and strong from gardening, but trembling like that of a palsied octogenarian.

Stephen Farrell's words echoed in her mind. "You *are* naive! Preferences outside the marriage bed refer to cravings, as sadistic as they are perverted. . . ."

She shuddered. What else did Farrell say before she interrupted him? She couldn't remember. She had shut her mind against the horrid implication of his words, then cut him off. Would he have told her what Hedwig said? That her betrothed owned houses of ill repute? That the money he planned to settle on her came from the filthy brothels of Seven Dials?

"Drink this." Hedwig put a glass to Maryann's lips and coaxed a sticky-sweet, potent draught down her dry throat.

Gagging, Maryann pushed the glass away. She would not believe Hedwig's tale. It was totally and absolutely incredible, as farfetched as it was revolting. Tammadge and whores? Impossible. He might have a mistress, a ladybird or two. But he was a gentleman. He was respectable. Honorable. He wouldn't go near a brothel, let alone own and profit from one.

Chapter Five

"Where did you hear that filth, Hedwig? That . . . slander."

"Do you remember Rose, who was upstairs maid, then married the butcher?"

"Vaguely," Maryann said impatiently. "She burnt the stair carpet once when she dropped a bucket of hot ashes. What does Rose have to do with this?"

"Rose has a friend whose cousin, Lucy Weller, is kitchen maid in Grosvenor Square, next door to Lord Tammadge. Lucy is walking out with one of Lord Tammadge's grooms."

Maryann's mouth twisted contemptuously. "So the groom told Lucy, Lucy told her cousin, the cousin told Rose, and Rose told you."

Her stomach settled, and the trembling of her limbs ceased. "Servants' gossip! Hedwig, you know better than to listen to such spiteful, contemptible talk. Or repeat it to Mama!"

"Yes, I know better." Hands on bony hips, Hedwig met Maryann's angry look. "But where there's smoke, there's fire. And you, Lady Maryann, are about to wed the man."

"Then why didn't you come to me directly?"

The maid opened her mouth, but Maryann was in full spate. She did not stop to draw breath, or to listen to an answer.

"And why, for pity's sake, did you wait until the betrothal ball to speak up? I feel sure everyone below stairs, from the boot boy to the butler, knew that Tammadge had asked for my hand before I did. Why didn't you go to my father? *Before* the announcement appeared in all the papers."

"I did."

Having run out of breath and further reproaches, Maryann could only blink at Hedwig's terse reply.

"You did?" cried Irene. "But you didn't tell *me* until—oh, now I understand why Rivington was so angry when I mentioned the matter to him on Saturday! He never likes it when something is brought to his attention more than once."

"What did my father say, Hedwig?"

"Called it servants' gossip, like you did, Lady Maryann. Told me not to stick my nose into the affairs of my betters unless I was prepared to look for another position."

A martial glint appeared in Maryann's eyes. Despite her instant denial of the rumors, she had been shaken, confused—until Hedwig repeated her father's threat. It had given her thoughts direction, had given her an aim.

She rose, planting a kiss on her mother's icy forehead, then strode purposefully to the door.

"Where are you going, Maryann?" asked Irene, a note of alarm in her voice. "Surely you won't call on Lord Tammadge now?"

"I think not. I believe it's time I requested an interview with my father."

"Maryann!" Irene looked close to fainting. "Both Hedwig and I brought the matter to his attention and got our noses bitten off. If you approach him as well . . ."

Silence fell. Nothing more need be said; the three women knew what would happen if Maryann aroused Rivington's ire. He had always been a harsh and unloving man, particularly when dealing with his daughters, as though it were their fault that they had not been born male.

Maryann's chin tilted mulishly. "Since Father was aware of the rumors, he should have told me."

"Yes, love. But he is convinced there's no basis for the gossip."

Hand on the doorknob, Maryann said, "Mind you, I don't believe a word of this rubbish either. Tammadge and brothels! It is too preposterous. Servants' gossip, nothing more. But you know how quickly tales spread from maid to mistress, from valet to master, and sooner or later all the *ton* will be abuzz with whispers. The least Father can do is to investigate the matter and set my mind at ease."

Both Lady Rivington and Hedwig heard the contradiction of not believing a word of the rubbish and Maryann's demand for peace of mind. Both knew there was little or no chance Rivington would pay heed to a request for an investigation.

When the door closed, Irene rubbed her temples. She knew how much Maryann counted on the freedom and independence marriage to the wealthy viscount would give her. Surely the girl was right; the rumors simply could not be true.

"Maryann returned from Sloane Street early," she said, accepting a cloth soaked in lavender water from Hedwig. "She was all set on seeing Tammadge. She said she had something unpleasant to disclose to him."

"Perhaps someone else blackened his character. If you ask me, Lady Maryann recovered too quickly—as if she'd heard the rumors before. As if she'd decided, already before she listened to what I had to say, not to believe anything she was told about him."

Irene closed her eyes. "Do you know, Hedwig? I cannot believe it either. Tammadge is of an old and noble family. Why would he engage in activities that must ruin his position? His good name?"

"I couldn't say, my lady."

"Everyone says Maryann has landed the catch of the season. The betrothal is talked about as much as Princess Charlotte's upcoming marriage."

"Yes, my lady." Hedwig covered her mistress with a light quilt. "Go to sleep now. There's nothing to be done until Lady Maryann makes up her mind whether to believe Lucy Weller's tale or not."

Lady Rivington's maid came closer to the truth than she could have suspected. Maryann *refused* to believe anything as preposterous as Lucy Weller's tale. She *refused* to believe that Farrell might have motivation for approaching her other than the cheap thrill of putting her to the blush.

She would not, could not, admit to the slightest doubt about Tammadge's integrity. To do so would be to admit that her carefully planned future might be in jeopardy. And yet she marched downstairs fully determined to get to the root of the matter, to ask her father that he dig for the source of the outrageous rumors.

Maryann had all but descended to the ground floor when the knocker sounded at the front door. She stopped, undecided whether to retreat upstairs, or continue and be seen and possibly intercepted by the caller.

Harv, the younger of the two Rivington footmen, approached at a dignified pace from somewhere beyond her view of the foyer. He flung the door open, and a young lady, daintily raising the ruffled hem of a green-and-white striped walking dress, tripped across the threshold.

"I've come to see Lady Maryann," she told the footman with a winning smile on her dimpled face. "Oh, please, do say she's in!"

"Bella!"

Maryann flew down the last of the steps. No longer was the interview with her father of paramount importance. Her dearest friend had come to town; all else must fade beside the unexpected delight.

She enveloped Bella in a hug, and only then, her arms around Miss Isabella Effingham, did Maryann see her betrothed standing in the doorway.

Her heart hammered wildly, and Hedwig's teutonic voice echoed in her mind. "It is said that Lord Tammadge's wealth comes from brothels he owns . . ."

How utterly absurd!

Slowly, Maryann disengaged herself from Bella and took a step toward the viscount. She might be selfconscious, confused, but breeding and social training helped her over the awkward moment.

"What a pleasant surprise," she murmured, giving Tammadge her hand.

"My dear."

As he bowed, stopping short of kissing her hand, she thought again how preposterous the rumors were. A glimpse of the thin, aesthetic face with the classic profile, an encounter with one of the bored and indescribably haughty looks, and any vestige of doubt must dissipate.

But, then, she had never doubted him at all.

A smile, spontaneous and heartfelt, lit Maryann's face. "I did not look to see you before the Crabtree rout on Wednesday, Lord Tammadge."

"The occasion to call on you presented itself thanks to the kind offices of Miss Isabella's mama. And, naturally, I could not resist."

The voice was as bland as ever, and yet Maryann was conscious of sarcasm, a fault of which she had never suspected him before.

She stepped aside so he might hand hat and gloves to Harv. "Then you and Isabella arrived together. And here I was about to introduce you to each other. I thought you had merely chanced to meet on the doorstep."

"Oh, no." Bella linked an arm through Maryann's. "It

51

was like this, you see. Lady Jersey, who's one of Mama's bosom bows, called this morning because Mama had sent a footman to her the moment we arrived last night. And Lord Tammadge came with Lady Jersey."

"How nice," murmured Maryann, still trying to unravel the involved speech.

"It was most fortuitous! All the maids and footmen were busy, and Mama insisted I must have an escort to your house. So she harpooned Lord Tammadge to fill the post of chaperon."

"Of course," said Maryann, who remembered Lady Effingham as a sweet-tempered lady whose vast store of patience was topped only by her resourcefulness in dealing with her daughter.

"Yes. You see, I am quite dreadfully in disgrace. So totally in disfavor that Papa bundled dearest Mama and me off to London without delay. And now we must come up with some entertainment for me."

"What horrid punishment!" Maryann's eyes twinkled. "Especially for a girl who swore to go into a decline because she was to wait another year for her come-out."

"Yes, isn't it absolutely ghastly?" Bella's dimples flashed. "Are you punishing me further by keeping me standing in the hall? Not a word either, how thrilled you are to see me!"

"How could I say *anything?* I was and still am overcome by astonishment."

"At least," said Lord Tammadge, "my arrival was a pleasant surprise. Or so I understood you to say."

Again, Maryann was aware that his blandness covered a sting. But she immediately reprimanded herself for finding fault. A little sarcasm, after all, did not hurt anyone.

She led her visitors into the small downstairs parlor. It seemed impossible that she and Bella hadn't seen each other in over two years, she thought, watching her friend sink into the most comfortable chair and sprawl there in the same hoydenish manner she had employed as a fifteen-year-old schoolgirl.

They had met during Maryann's brief stay at a select seminary for young ladies in Bath. The Earl of Rivington had ruthlessly terminated his daughter's association with the school when he learned that she was encouraged to read and, God forbid! *debate* philosophies he deemed eminently unsuitable for a young lady. But the friendship with Isabella had survived separation and blossomed with the aid of extensive and frequent letters.

Listening to the involved tale how the enterprising damsel had ended up in the briars, Maryann poured a glass of Madeira for her betrothed and carried it to the window where he stood, idly drumming his fingertips against the glass pane.

"And so you see, dearest Maryann," Bella concluded triumphantly. "When I was caught at midnight in the gazebo with that rattle, Barney Epsom, there was nothing Papa could do but send me to London."

Maryann saw innumerable possibilities for a father set on reforming his daughter. None of them included a stay in town at the height of the season. But she did not mention any of the various methods; Bella would accuse her of dipping too deeply into Mrs. Radcliffe's gothic novels.

She looked at Bella and said lightly, "What a pity you weren't bundled off two days earlier. You might have come to my ball."

"Yes, but it didn't occur to me until it was too late. But at least I shall be in town for Princess Charlotte's wedding!"

The ingenuous admission of deliberate misbehavior drew a chuckle from Maryann. She glanced at Tammadge, but his back was turned, and she couldn't tell whether he shared her amusement. She doubted it.

"Won't you join us, my lord?" she asked, rendered uncomfortable by his silence.

53

"It will not strain me unduly to stand while Miss Isabella gives you the reason for her surprise visit," he said, directing a colorless look over his shoulder at the young lady. "She assured me it wouldn't take long."

"Gracious!" Dramatically clapping a hand to her forehead, Bella got to her feet. "I can't believe I'm sitting here gabbing, when we should be on our way. Mama sent Lord Tammadge and me to fetch you to my alfresco luncheon."

In Tammadge's presence and with Bella's expectant blue eyes on her, it seemed absurd even to consider declining the invitation merely to face her father over some ridiculous rumor.

"What a delightful notion! I haven't been to an alfresco luncheon since last summer." Maryann dipped into a curtsy. "Excuse me while I tell Mama. I shan't be but a moment."

Chapter Six

The Effingham town house was built to the design of Sir Edwin Effingham, Miss Isabella's great-grandfather, who had made a fortune in the Indies. Situated in Adelphi Terrace, the mansion's imposing colonnaded front and curving carriage drive looked toward the Strand, while a second porticoed entrance at the rear of the building faced the Thames.

Graveled paths wound past flower beds and through immaculate lawns extending from the house to the riverbank, where, the baronet had insisted, he must have his own private water stairs. Even in this year of 1816, when more bridges spanned the Thames than in Sir Edwin's day, a number of wherries and sculls bobbed in the water near the stairs.

It was in this lovely garden on the Thames, in the shade of some fine old elm trees, that Miss Isabella's luncheon was set out. All morning, the Effingham chef had slaved and driven his minions to despair in an effort to overcome the handicap imposed by mistress and daughter of the house: shortage of time. All morning, footmen and maids had delivered invitations for the impromptu party Miss Isabella insisted she must have.

Only Lady Maryann had been personally invited and fetched. Isabella knew of Maryann's obsession with gardening, and she had suspected that an invitation delivered to Mr. Salisbury's Botanic Garden might end up unread—though, perhaps, watered and lovingly tended—in a garden urn or a flower bed.

About a dozen young ladies and as many young gentlemen sat on cushions and rugs spread on the close-cropped turf and within minutes demolished the delicacies created by the chef in hours of agony.

Ladies of more mature years, like Lady Effingham and mothers of Isabella's friends, a governess or two, a poor relation serving as companion, were more formally seated in chairs around a cloth-covered table. Four gentlemen also formed part of that group, and after a look at the youthful males surrounding Lady Maryann and Miss Isabella beneath the elms, Lord Tammadge murmured something to his betrothed, bowed, and took himself off to the table and chairs.

Maryann showed no sign of surprise or distress at her fiancé's desertion, but chatted happily with Bella and responded to comments and questions addressed to her by the young people.

Most of the remarks had to do with her engagement to Tammadge and were of a congratulatory nature. A few young ladies sounded cattish, commenting on Tammadge's advanced age, his blandness, and making sly references to the fact that he was as rich as Golden Ball. Maryann shrewdly put these barbs down to envy.

She did, however, send surreptitious glances in Tammadge's direction, observing as she did so that the silver in his hair was no more and no less pronounced than the gray in Mr. Folsett's beside him, and whom she knew to be of her father's generation.

Tammadge was five-and-forty, her mother had said. Maryann had not given the matter much thought, but wondered now if the difference in age would have a bearing on their marriage. His sitting down at the table, for instance. Would he expect her to join him with the matrons and elderly gentlemen when they were married?

And suddenly, for no reason that she could fathom,

56

Mr. Stephen Farrell came to mind. She tried to dismiss the detestable man from her thoughts, but his image kept popping up — among the young people who, replete now, were more aptly described as lounging rather than sitting on the rugs. She also pictured Farrell with the group at the table, between Tammadge and Mr. Folsett. And the strangeness of it was, Farrell seemed to fit into both parties with equal ease.

He might not be a true gentleman; he might be a false friend, a back stabber, but he was a man who would draw notice. There was nothing bland about him. His tone as well as his words were forceful. Physique and the keen, dark eyes betrayed a latent power, a sense of purpose and determination.

Maryann could not possibly imagine Farrell leaving his betrothed for a comfortable chair.

When Tammadge arrived at her side after the repast and invited her for a gentle walk along the riverbank, she assented readily enough. She might as well make use of the time and ask questions about her fiancé's friend. If she satisfied curiosity as well as made up her mind whether or not there was still any purpose in warning Tammadge, it wouldn't be a bad thing at all. Once she knew more about Farrell, she would have no need to be preoccupied with him.

Since most of the party appeared too lazy or too stuffed with food to leave cushion, rug, or chair, Maryann and Tammadge soon found themselves out of earshot but well within sight of Lady Effingham and the eagle-eyed matrons who had come to assist in the task of chaperoning.

It was a golden opportunity for questions, but Maryann, after several false starts, was about to give up. How did one interrogate a husband-to-be about another man without giving the impression of being unduly interested in said man?

Stopping to admire some especially fine specimen of fern growing where the graveled path met with the stone and rock of the embankment, Maryann finally spoke of the betrothal ball and what a great success it had been. The subject might give her an opening to bring up Farrell's name.

"Then you don't find that sort of social do a bore?" asked Tammadge, standing dutifully at her side and even casting a cursory glance or two at the gently waving fronds. "Your father gave me to understand you're more interested in gardening than in dancing."

"Oh, I admit I am passionately interested in gardening."

And I shall get to work on my own botanical gardens as soon as I am in possession of my dowry and the consols you settled on me, my lord.

She had always loved the outdoors, the home woods and gardens at Rivington Hall in Kent. But gardens had taken on a special meaning since her father started to lock her into a windowless cellar room when he wished to punish her. Only he held the keys to that remote part of the cellars. It was where he stored his wines, and it was impossible for Irene and the servants to smuggle food, books, or a candle to her as they had done when she was confined to her bedchamber.

Maryann hated darkness and confinement. She needed the kiss of sun, wind, and rain on her skin; needed to smell and touch flowers, grass, earth; needed to sit under trees and hear the song of birds.

When she went to live in London the first time, she had discovered Mr. Salisbury's Botanic Garden and the pleasure it gave thousands of Londoners, trapped as they were in dark, overcrowded lodgings, in narrow streets shadowed by the towering facades of gray brick houses.

It was then that her dream had crystallized. She wanted gardens not just for herself, but to be enjoyed by others. She wanted to give color and brightness to families whose lives were as drab and gray as the London streets.

She wanted her own botanical gardens.

Maryann became aware of her fiancé's prolonged silence. Perhaps she had been too fervent in her assurance that she liked gardening. Perhaps he assumed her passion would distract her from her wifely duties.

She studied his face, but as usual, it told her nothing.

"As long as I don't have to attend a ball or rout every night," she assured him, "I do enjoy the diversion of going into society. You need not be afraid I shall shirk my duty as your hostess."

Gently fanning himself with the scented, monogrammed square of lawn that was never long out of his hand, Tammadge said, "As long as we remain in London, there will be one or two occasions when I require a hostess, but once we remove to Sevenoaks, your duties will not be too arduous. You may devote as much time as you please to the gardens."

"Sevenoaks?" she asked faintly. "That is your estate in Northumberland, is it not?"

"Indeed. You will find it a challenge for a gardener."

Maryann stared at the ferns. She could only agree with him. Northumberland with its raw climate, its hills and moors, was indeed a challenge — one she could do without.

"I wonder," he said, "what is so intriguing about a fernery?"

Murmuring an apology, Maryann started walking. "I presume, my lord, we shall not spend all year in the north? You would wish to live in town — during the season at least — to enjoy the company of friends?"

He did not reply right away, but took her elbow as they turned onto the embankment with its uneven surface of rock and stone.

"What I wish," he said, "is that you will stop calling me "my lord." If you feel it is premature to address me by my given name, you might at least call me Tammadge."

"Thank you. I think it will be best if I call you Tammadge. For now," she added diplomatically. "But we were speaking of your friends and that you would miss them at Sevenoaks."

"*You* were speaking of them, my dear."

There was no mistaking the sarcasm in the low voice, but Maryann plunged on with barely a check. "Tell me about your friend Mr. Farrell. He does not seem to have been in town before. How did you meet him?"

Tammadge released her arm. Carefully folding the handkerchief, he slipped it into the pocket of his coat.

"I made his acquaintance through Woverley. You must remember the marquess who arrived at the ball with Farrell?"

She remembered pig's eyes darting from her to Tammadge and the grin splitting Woverley's round face. She remembered that she had found him repulsive.

"Does Mr. Farrell attend many of the social functions?"

"Why do you ask?"

"Well, he did not seem to enjoy our ball. I did not see him dancing once."

They were approaching the property of Effingham's neighbor to the west and turned to retrace their steps.

"Mr. Farrell," Maryann persisted, "strikes me as a man who'd be more at home in a country setting."

She could see him leading the local hunt, organizing a steeplechase, but she could not, as she had told him to his face, see him in the role of a Bond Street beau, a society fribble.

"I believe Farrell once mentioned a farm in Cornwall." Tammadge gave her a look Maryann could not possibly call bland.

A farming gentleman? She knitted her brow in an effort to visualize Stephen Farrell striding across fields or listening to a tenant's needs. It was not impossible . . .

"And before you ask," Tammadge said with a definite edge to his voice, "no, I don't think he is married. And I believe his fortune to be nil."

"I had no intention of asking any such questions," Maryann said indignantly. She hoped her face did not look as hot as it felt. What awkward business this prying was.

"But I admit to some curiosity about him. He—well, he is quite unlike any man I've met."

They both stopped, as though the arrival at the water stairs signaled the end of their stroll. Tammadge kept his gaze on the murky waters of the Thames and looked like a man lost in deep thought. Maryann had her eyes on her betrothed and wondered if, possibly, her curiosity in Farrell had been misunderstood.

"Tammadge," she said hesitantly. "I did not mean to make it sound as if Mr. Farrell were someone special or extraordinary when I said he's unlike any man I've met. But he explained, you see, that he'd been a spy during the war—"

She faltered when Tammadge turned and looked at her through narrowed eyes.

"I only meant," she said, growing rather desperate in her effort to stress a natural and quite disinterested curiosity, "that he is not an ordinary man. He's—well, different."

Tammadge returned his gaze to the river, and Maryann reflected wryly that explanations were not her forte. She seemed to have made matters worse.

Considering the experience a lesson well learned, she wisely kept quiet.

"Perhaps it would be advisable," Tammadge said, "if we spent more time in each other's company before the wedding. It is borne home to me that I do not know you as I thought I did. I understood from your father that you would have no objection to living at Sevenoaks. He also stressed that you have a somewhat, shall I say, passive? Yes, a passive nature. That you have no curiosity, no interest outside your gardens."

Maryann blinked. This was the longest speech Tammadge had ever directed at her. And there was much food for thought.

"How could you possibly believe me passive when I interceded in the negotiation of the marriage contract and asked not only that the dowry be mine outright, but also that you settle money on me to be spent at my own discretion?"

Tammadge did not turn from the prospect of the Thames. He pulled out his handkerchief but, without once fanning himself, crushed it into a tight ball and crammed it back into the pocket.

"I had no notion the clause was inserted at your insistence," he said so softly that she barely heard. "I was given the impression it was your father's doing. That he was looking out for your interest."

Maryann denied herself a sniff of disdain. Her father knew only one interest — his own.

"And what about curiosity?" she asked with some asperity. "Is it such an intolerable trait in a wife?"

His back went rigid.

"To me, yes." There was anger in his voice and something else, a razor's edge that threatened . . . menaced. "I absolutely do not tolerate curiosity in those around me."

Maryann caught her breath, as much at the menace in his voice as at the reply itself.

She would readily admit that curiosity was not always a virtue, and she had quite expected Tammadge to say something along those lines — since he had all his ladybirds to hide — but to hear him, one would think he was a man obsessed.

Or a man who hid worse than a mistress or two. A man who feared his wife would pry into the dark secrets of his life.

A chill brushed her skin, and neither the long sleeves of her spencer nor the April sun could warm her.

The rumors! Lucy Weller's tale must be true after all. Fear of discovery would explain the threat underlying Tammadge's words. A man making his fortune off prostitution would find himself ostracized by the *ton,* blackballed by the members of his club.

But then her betrothed turned, smiling at her with such tenderness that she wondered whether she suffered from the madness afflicting the poor king, whether she had been hallucinating when she heard menace in his voice and believed him capable of dishonorable activities.

"My dear Maryann." His voice was quite definitely gentle, wistful. "You are so very young, so sweet, so innocent. But I'm afraid there may come a time, after we've been married awhile, when you will be curious about other men. Can you blame me if I regard curiosity as a husband's bane?"

She stared at him and saw a man whose narrow, handsome face showed fine lines of age around the mouth and nose, a man who worried about a young wife wanting to take a lover. How could she have believed he feared discovery of a dark secret? How could she have let Farrell's and Hedwig's tales poison her mind?

He took her hand, touching it to his lips, and she felt the tingling warmth of his mouth against her wrist — just the way a hand kiss felt when she allowed herself the luxury of daydreaming about an imaginary lover.

"No," she said. "I mean, yes, I can blame you."

Confused, embarrassed, and feeling about herself as she felt about a slug in a bed of strawberries, Maryann tried to pull her hand away. But his slender white fingers held with unsuspected strength and drew her closer.

"Tell me what you're thinking," he said caressingly.

"First of all, you have no cause to believe any such thing. I assure you, Tammadge, I shan't be interested in another man."

"And secondly?"

His breath stirred tendrils of hair against her temple,

and his arm wound with disturbing intimacy around her waist. She could not deny that the sensations evoked by his touch were quite thrilling. Never before had she been held by a man, not even while dancing, because her father had unequivocally forbidden her to participate in the waltz.

"Won't you look at me, Maryann?" Tammadge said coaxingly.

She kept her eyes on the sleeve of his coat, where a ladybird, the small orange-red bug with black-dotted wings that shared its name with ladies of easy virtue, had alighted and was exploring the blue valley created by a crease in the cloth.

"And secondly," Maryann said softly. "Should a gentleman who keeps as many ladybirds as another might keep hounds, be quite so vehemently opposed to a woman's curiosity in the opposite sex?"

The arm around her waist tightened like a steel band.

"Yes!" His voice was harder than his arm. "If the woman is *mine.*"

She pulled away, and this time he let her go at once.

"My dear, forgive me," he said, gentle once more. "No doubt you think me harsh, but believe me, I will not be a husband who'll look the other way should my wife wish to take a lover."

"Ah, well." Flustered, Maryann turned to gaze at the small boats tied to hooks high on the embankment. "I believe I already assured you that I shan't be contemplating such a step."

"Sweet, innocent child. You blush now at the thought of a lover. But, you see, I do not subscribe to the theory that a lady of quality does not have the desires and passions society takes for granted in a woman of the lower orders. I believe it is the course of nature that you will develop an interest in other men."

He placed a finger under her chin and tilted her face until he could look into her eyes.

"But I will never tolerate it if you take more than a casual interest. He would face me across the distance of twelve paces, your would-be lover. Do you understand, Maryann? He must die so that my wife may remain faithful and pure."

Chapter Seven

He must die so that my wife may remain faithful and pure.
Tammadge's impassioned pledge hammered in Maryann's head until she could bear it no more.

She paced the length and width of her bedroom, as she had done since she returned from the alfresco luncheon in the late afternoon. She had stopped pacing to change into a nightgown when her mother looked in on her before retiring, then resumed the restless prowling. But the activity did not have the soothing effect she had come to expect.

She had been overwhelmed by the depth of emotion in her formerly indifferent fiancé, flattered and thrilled by the change in attitude. But she was also disturbed.

And why the dickens was she so affected by the words that she couldn't get them out of her mind? There was no man in her life who might die because of Tammadge's vow. And there wouldn't be.

As on previous, most unsuitable occasions, Stephen Farrell invaded her thoughts. This time, he was speedily and ruthlessly dismissed. He might fit in at a garden party, but he definitely had nothing to do with the matter occupying her mind.

Maryann lengthened her stride, the voluminous folds of her nightgown snapping against her ankles as she relived the scene on the Thames embankment when Tammadge had turned to her with a tender smile and gentle, wistful words.

This first show of emotion from the man who had asked her to be his wife had deeply touched her. It had warmed her and wiped out the moment of horror when she believed him capable of profiting from the reprehensible business of prostitution.

How ashamed she had been; and how bedazzled by his loverlike attentions.

When he escorted her back to the party, she had noticed the envious looks of young ladies who formerly pointed out Tammadge's advanced age and blandness of demeanor, and she had smiled to herself. Tammadge was an attractive man when his face came alive and his eyes held a glint of emotion.

Even Lady Effingham had allowed herself to comment on the viscount. Drawing Maryann aside, she said, "Tammadge is always so stiff and correct. You could have knocked me over with a feather when I saw him slip an arm around your waist. Now, mind you, he shouldn't have done it—even in full view of the chaperons. But it did my heart good to see him so attentive to you, and I knew, of course, that he can be trusted not to go beyond the line of what is proper."

Maryann had lived through the afternoon as if in a dream. Never had the air smelled sweeter, refreshments tasted more delicious, lawn games been more fun. It had been a golden afternoon when hope had blossomed that her marriage need not necessarily be the cold, businesslike arrangement to which she had resigned herself.

But it had been a dream, Maryann acknowledged with a kick at the constricting folds of the nightgown. One of those romantic daydreams she occasionally indulged in.

The moment Tammadge had left her in the foyer of her own home in the early evening, the moment his caressing voice no longer befuddled her mind, she had started to wonder about the sudden change in his attitude. Had he used his vast experience with females and set out deliberately to charm her?

He had called her an innocent on several occasions. Since she had brought up the subject of his ladybirds, he must have known she wasn't innocent as in "sheltered."

Tammadge could have used innocent the same way Stephen Farrell had used naive.

In that case, both men believed her a silly female with no more brains than an earthworm.

She very much suspected she was indeed a silly widgeon to have been so moved by Tammadge's show of emotion. Away from him, she remembered—and could no longer dismiss as hallucination—the menace in his voice when he said he absolutely did not tolerate curiosity in those around him.

That, in retrospect, did not sound like a man speaking of a fiancée's or wife's curiosity about another man. Not even her very obvious interest in his friend Farrell could have triggered such vehemence.

Tammadge's words, in retrospect, once again sounded like the words of a man afraid to have his dark secrets unveiled.

Since she had closed the door of her chamber behind her, Maryann had argued back and forth with herself, saying one moment that the rumors might be true, and assuring herself the next that they could not possibly be. But now she was tired of arguing with herself, tired of pacing, tired of shilly-shallying. No longer would she deny the unpleasant truth.

It was entirely possible that the servants' gossip about Tammadge was true.

The candle on her dressing table guttered, and she went over to blow it out. As she bent to the task, she caught her reflection in the mirror. She stared at herself, curiously searching the wide eyes, the mouth, for signs of distress after the momentous admission.

But the mouth was not pinched; it was full and relaxed. The eyes, instead of a tragic look, held a look of determination.

Maryann blew out the candle.

"Admit it!" she told the dimmed and shadowed image in the mirror. "If there is a particle of truth to Farrell's or Lucy Weller's tale, you won't want to marry Tammadge. Thus, the sooner you see Father and demand an investigation, the better."

With this resolve in mind, Maryann dropped into bed and was asleep before she could turn down the wick of her bedside table lamp.

The next morning, she left word with Mr. Winsome, the very efficient bookkeeper-cum-secretary, that she must see her father on a very urgent matter, then drove as usual to Mr. Salisbury's Botanic Garden. Past experience had taught her that Rivington took a certain pleasure in making her wait as long as possible.

When she was told on her return from Sloane Street that she could not see her father that day, she was annoyed but not surprised. She even managed a smile for Mr. Winsome, who, after all, could not help being the bearer of unwelcome news. And he was such a thin, nervous man who appeared to suffer from a chronic cold, that Maryann felt sorry for him. In all the years he had served the earl, she had not once encountered him when his eyes were not red rimmed and watery or his nose was not chapped and twitchy.

"I'll be sure to ask Lord Rivington again tomorrow, Lady Maryann," the secretary assured her, punctuating his words with a dry cough that could be a nervous habit or another symptom of the perpetual cold.

The next day, Wednesday, Maryann arrived home later than usual and was once again informed Lord Rivington was unable to see her. He had driven to Oxford, a journey he made once or twice every month, and was not expected to return to Mount Street until late that night.

She was civil to the apologetic, coughing secretary,

but when she reached the privacy of her rooms and soaked in the lovely sphinx-legged tub, she voiced a string of very uncivil thoughts before settling down to enjoy the bath and to devise a strategy that would make it impossible for Rivington to evade her again.

Her father took breakfast and lunch in his study, and dinner at his club—unless guests were expected or he and the family had been invited out. It was therefore not unusual if she did not see him for days on end, a situation that normally suited her just fine.

But now she *must* see him, and she had counted on an interview before Tammadge would escort her and Irene to the Crabtree rout later that evening. Had she been asked to explain why it was important, she would have been hard pressed to put her feelings into words. In either case, whether she saw her father first, or after the next meeting with her betrothed, facing Tammadge with all her doubts must be an awkward business.

Dripping scented water—quite cool by now—Maryann emerged from the tub. Her mind was made up. She wouldn't be put off much longer. If she must, she'd surprise her father in his sanctuary, the library, before setting out for Sloane Street in the morning.

She took so long over her choice of a gown for the rout that Jane, her maid, asked tersely if, mayhap, Lady Maryann didn't want to go at all.

"Dinner's been set for'ard, an' it'll be served in 'alf an hour. An' milor' Tammadge will be comin' for ye at eight-thirty."

A look at the clock on the mantel shelf confirmed that it was six-thirty.

"Gracious," Maryann exclaimed. "I didn't realize I was in the bath close on two hours. You should have made me get out, Jane. It totally slipped my mind that the Crabtrees have that new house way out of town—toward Richmond, is it?"

"Chiswick, milady."

"Yes, that's it. And we'll have to set out at an hour

when civilized people sit down to dine."

Maryann pulled a gown of stiff blue silk from the closet. Since this was her second season, she need no longer wear white or pastel shades. Royal blue with a narrow trim of midnight blue, the French dressmaker had assured her, was a perfect foil for a creamy golden complexion and honey brown hair. The colors added an intriguing touch of *je ne sais quois* to her gray eyes.

Just the thing, Maryann decided, to give her confidence.

Despite the long day at the Sloane Street gardens, she had no appetite for dinner, which, of course, did not escape her mother's eye.

"Are you unwell, dearest? Do you wish to beg off from our engagement?"

"Oh, no, Mama. I am perfectly well," Maryann assured her, even while recognizing that she suffered from the effects of cowardly reluctance to face her betrothed.

She forced herself to take a few bites of roast duckling and, during the second course, to eat a prawn or two, a mouthful of peas, and a sliver of gooseberry tart, all of which gathered in her stomach like lumps of lead.

And then, when Tammadge arrived, the meeting was quite painless. He punctiliously handed first Irene, then Maryann into his elegant carriage and eased himself into the opposite seat. With no more than a gentle smile did he remind Maryann of the emotional scene at Bella's alfresco luncheon. His conversation was addressed exclusively to Irene—until the carriage made an unexpected turn into Curzon Street.

He looked at Maryann. In the light of the lanterns affixed above the carriage doors, his eyes seemed cold and colorless, but his mouth shaped once again the tender smile that had so moved her when she saw it for the first time. It did not move her now.

"My dear, I hope you'll forgive me if I delay our drive to the Crabtrees by a few minutes. There's a house here in Curzon Street which I have recently acquired. I'd like you to see it."

"Yes, of course." Boldly, Maryann looked into those pale eyes. "But why?"

"It occurred to me that you might feel uncomfortable in my Grosvenor Square house. It is old and vast and, I admit, quite dark and gloomy. This house is smaller, but since the interior was done by Adams, you can be assured of light and loftiness and elegance. The perfect setting, I thought, for a perfect bride."

But would she be his bride? Maryann lowered her gaze lest he see her doubts.

The carriage came to a stop just then, and she said, "Yes, I should like very much to see the house. Wouldn't you, Mama?"

Irene pulled aside the thick velvet curtain and peeked out the window. "Oh!" she exclaimed, startled. "It is the Fant house! That's where William Fant shot himself this past winter."

One of Tammadge's footmen opened the door and let down the steps, but Maryann hesitated.

"Shot himself in the house? I'm not sure —" Uncertainly, she looked at Tammadge. "Won't it be rather strange . . . ghoulish, going through the rooms? Or living in them? I'd be wondering all the time where and why the poor man did such an awful thing."

Tammadge looked annoyed. "There was some sort of accident with a gun, but I wouldn't go around saying it was suicide, Lady Rivington. There was no proof of that."

"He lost all his money gaming," said Irene. "And a property in Sussex. It is so sad. He had three little girls."

"Rumors!" Tammadge said harshly.

"No rumors, my lord. I had the news from Fant's sister-in-law, who's a neighbor at Rivington Hall." Irene turned to her daughter. "It was just before we left for town in early March. Surely you remember Lady

Oglesby's visit?"

"I missed the visit, Mama. But I remember you telling me that her sister and her three young nieces moved back into her parents' house in Hertfordshire. It is strange, though, isn't it, that there has been no talk here in town?"

Tammadge interrupted the ladies. Any gentleness or tenderness he had displayed earlier was wiped out when he addressed Maryann. "Ma'am, will you take a look at the house, or will you not?"

Maryann blinked. "I think not."

"Very well." Tammadge glared at the footman standing silently to attention outside. "Shut the door, fool! We're driving on."

For quite half an hour, no one spoke inside the carriage, but when they had passed through Kensington village, Tammadge apologized very handsomely, saying that he had been disappointed to have his gift to Maryann rejected unseen.

Good manners dictated that Maryann beg pardon as well, but although Tammadge's words made her feel guilty, she was also resentful, and her apology for having hurt his feelings did not carry conviction.

Irene Rivington did her best to bridge the awkwardness with a flow of small talk, but it was a rather subdued party that arrived at the Crabtrees' beautiful home set in several acres of timbered land. Neither did it help that Maryann's first sight upon entering the vast drawing room was Stephen Farrell in animated conversation with Bella Effingham.

Chapter Eight

Irene had gone straight to their hostess, but Tammadge heard the gasp Maryann tried in vain to suppress, and followed her gaze.

"Ah," he said softly. "I see my friend has found a new flirt. But you need not worry about Miss Isabella's safety, my dear. Mrs. Effingham has her eagle eye on the pair."

"I'm not worried." Indeed, she was not. But in that instant of recognition, she had wished her friend to the dickens and herself in Bella's place.

Slightly flustered, she met Tammadge's sardonic gaze. "I'm merely surprised that Mr. Farrell should have received one of Mrs. Crabtree's coveted invitations. After all, he hasn't been in town very long."

"If you remember, I mentioned that Woverley is Farrell's friend as well as mine. And Woverley is Mrs. Crabtree's nephew."

"And why," Maryann demanded, "did you say that I need not worry about Bella? Is Mr. Farrell so dangerous to a young lady, then?"

"Farrell is a good fellow," Tammadge said lightly. "But something of a rake."

"He is?"

Maryann studied the rake through narrowed eyes. She had thought him many things, but never a man with libertine propensities. Even now, seeing him

74

chuckle at something Bella had said, she tended to believe that Tammadge was wrong.

"He can't help it, I suppose," Tammadge said. "Young ladies are inevitably drawn to a dark, mysterious stranger who tells them that he was a spy."

"Who *tells* them?" She did not take her eyes off Farrell and therefore did not see the look of satisfaction crossing Tammadge's face at her obvious chagrin. "Farrell is lying? He wasn't a spy at all?"

The viscount knew a moment's temptation to simply say, "Yes, he is lying." But the records at Whitehall, as accessible to Lady Maryann as they had been to him, showed clearly that Farrell had spent most of his career on special assignments. The specifics of those assignments, however, were still kept under lock and key. Even his friend at Whitehall had been unable to take a look at the secret files.

"I know Farrell's story," Tammadge said suavely. "He does not tell an outright lie, but, I fear, he does exaggerate the importance of his role as a spy. Not that I blame him. It makes him a hero in the eyes of romantic young ladies—and an acceptable suitor for a wealthy cit's daughter."

Maryann gave an imperceptible start at the mention of a spy-hero and romantic young ladies, but the face she turned to her betrothed was calm. "Are you implying he is a fortune hunter?"

"No, sweet, innocent Maryann. I am simply saying that he may pick his flirts where he wishes, but must consider fortune if he wants to marry. Will you come with me to tell our hostess how happy we are to have received her coveted invitation?"

She permitted herself one more glance at Stephen Farrell—the broad shoulders, the proud tilt of his head, sun-streaked hair gleaming in the candlelight, rugged features softened in a smile at Bella.

He turned his head slightly, and across a distance of some twenty feet, his eyes met and held hers.

As on the night of the betrothal ball when she saw him the first time, she felt the power and strength Farrell emanated, and she could not believe that he would exaggerate the part he had played in the war.

Neither would he broach certain taboo subjects to a young lady unless he had a very good reason.

Maryann took an involuntary step toward him, but Tammadge touched her arm.

"My dear," he said silkily. "I beg you to remember that Farrell is *my* friend. If I wish you to speak with him, I shall let you know."

"You jest! Surely I may speak to whom I like."

"In general, yes." A touch of steel crept into his voice. "But, as *you* pointed out, Farrell is different."

Maryann thought she saw Farrell raise a brow at her and Tammadge. He bowed and, saying a few words to Bella Effingham, accompanied the girl to her mother.

She might have reason to be irritated with Tammadge, but none at all to feel disappointed, Maryann told herself when she went with her betrothed to make her curtsy to Mrs. Crabtree, a plump, garrulous lady of some fifty years or more. She hadn't really wanted to speak with Stephen Farrell.

Throughout the evening, Tammadge stayed at Maryann's side, even when Bella joined her. Bella was in raptures over the many conquests she had made that evening, including Mr. Farrell—Wasn't he simply divine? A *real* man!—and chattered like a magpie about the sumptuous parties Lady Effingham had planned for her.

Tammadge plied Maryann with ices, champagne, and tidbits from the buffet supper set out in one of the adjoining rooms. He showered her with tender attention, and everyone, from the Dowager Duchess of Thorpe to the latest debutante, assured her what a lucky girl she was to be the chosen bride of such a gentleman.

And yet Maryann could not shake the conviction

that Tammadge was merely playing the part of the devoted fiancé. She felt uncomfortable in his company and made no demur when Irene rejoined them to suggest they start the long drive home. It was not yet midnight, but for Maryann the evening could not end soon enough.

Tammadge left to order the carriage brought around, and Maryann used the opportunity to step out onto the Crabtrees' magnificent terrace paved with ivory and black marble. Paper lanterns had been strung, and a number of guests had wandered outside to admire the mosaic in the center of the terrace or to exclaim over the potted Mediterranean plants coaxed through the English winters in succession houses by a small battalion of gardeners.

On this night, Maryann had no eyes for plants or flowers. The moment she passed through the French doors, she saw Stephen Farrell standing near the steps leading down into the gardens.

He was half turned away from her and seemed lost in grim reflections. His face had a tight look; his brow was furrowed. She walked toward him, not knowing what she would say when she reached his side. Their last meeting had been painful, embarrassing, and she might owe him an apology.

"Good evening, Mr. Farrell."

He gave a start and swung around as though she had fired a cannon to get his attention, and that was indeed the effect her clear voice had on him.

Stephen, who had sworn to wash his hands of Lady Maryann, to let her father look after her interests, had gone to the Crabtree rout against his better judgment. He should not care what became of her. She was not his responsibility. Yet he had come to the rout hoping to see her, hoping to see some evidence that she had taken his warning to heart.

He did see her, entering the drawing room on Tammadge's arm. As to heeding his warning—pshaw! She

77

had allowed her betrothed to sit in her pocket all evening. It had been a slap in the face for Stephen.

And then she had made him jump like the veriest green-head when she finally spoke to him.

"I am sorry if I startled you," said Lady Maryann. She tilted her head and looked at him in that serious manner she sometimes had. "Or is it that you do not want to speak with me?"

"Not at all." Drawing on his vast experience at dissembling, Stephen summoned a grin. "I feared I'd *never* get a chance to greet you. Tammadge was like a guard dog, yapping at your heels all evening and making sure you didn't stray."

She immediately perceived the truth of the observation. There were no more than sixty or eighty guests at the rout, an intimate gathering by any hostess's standards, and the odds were that at some time or other, they should have met face to face. But they hadn't, due to Tammadge's clever maneuvering.

"Well, Lady Maryann? Does your betrothed forbid you to speak to me?"

"Of course not," she said haughtily. He had, quite unwittingly, hit on the truth. But Tammadge's unreasonable attitude was not a subject she cared to discuss with Farrell. "If you remember, we parted under somewhat, ah, strained circumstances, and I don't quite know what to say to you."

He remembered their last meeting well, her cry, "I despise you!" And he promptly read disdain in her manner.

"Strained, indeed," he said coldly. "No one can accuse you of exaggeration. But don't fret, I shan't hold it against you that you lost your temper and flew at me like a little shrew."

"Of all the odious—" Indignation took her breath away. "If you had not been so provoking and absolutely detestable, I should never have given rein to my temper."

"Pray, my love"—Tammadge's soft voice behind her made her start and spin, as Farrell had done a short while earlier—"do not give rein now. I do not care to see my betrothed in the role of a Billingsgate fishwife."

"Never fear!" She bestowed a scathing look on each of the two gentlemen. "I have nothing else to say to either of you."

She would have walked away, but Tammadge's fingers closed around her wrist. Short of making a scene, she had no option but to stay at his side.

Drawing a handkerchief from his pocket, Tammadge fanned himself gently. "Farrell, my good fellow. I must thank you for keeping my betrothed amused while I was absent."

The gentlemen engaged in a low-voiced conversation, in which Maryann took no part. She stared with distaste at the lace-edged square of lawn in her fiancé's hand. Carrying a handkerchief was a foppish affectation, and one she found she could not like. It certainly was not a fashion she could imagine Stephen Farrell adopting.

And what the dickens did that have to say to anything? she asked herself irritably. She had always acknowledged that Farrell was no fop, and simply because she was now willing to believe his warnings about Tammadge did not mean she must compare him favorably with the viscount.

Trying to contain her irritation, she counted the embroidered oak leaves on the gently rippling cloth. There were seven leaves—for Sevenoaks, Tammadge's estate in Northumberland.

"Farrell, you must come and dine with me some evening," said Tammadge, and the casual pleasantry toward the man with whom he had forbidden her to speak only served to increase Maryann's annoyance. "There is something I wish to discuss with you."

"Pleasure. Just send me word when you want me to come."

Tammadge nodded.

Turning to Maryann, he smiled without warmth and drew her arm through his. "Come, my dear. We must not keep your mama waiting."

Even the travesty of a smile vanished as soon as they had taken leave of their host and hostess.

"Why did you, against my express wishes, seek out Farrell?" Tammadge demanded.

Still incensed by his high-handed treatment of her on the terrace, Maryann fired up with deplorable heat.

"Because I am not to be ruled by you, my lord. Not unless we're married may you tell me what to do. And perhaps not even then! If I wish to speak with Mr. Farrell, I shall do so with or without your leave."

"You are mistaken, ma'am. When we are married, you shall be governed by my every wish."

Maryann made no reply, and neither did she initiate conversation during the drive to town. She pondered Tammadge's assertion that a wife must be ruled by her husband—as a daughter was ruled by her father until she married. A bleak expectation. Shivering, she drew her silk cloak tight around her shoulders.

Tammadge kept an excellent stable, and the team of matched grays took them back to Mount Street in little more than an hour. Having seen Maryann and her mother into the foyer, the viscount took his leave, bowing gracefully first over Irene's, then over Maryann's hand.

The footman was about to close the door when Tammadge turned back. Light from a lantern affixed above the stoop fell on his face. He was smiling, but Maryann had learned to look at his eyes rather than his mouth for an indication of his mood. And his eyes were cold.

"Dear Lady Rivington," he said. "Pray forgive me for harping back to a distasteful subject, but I cannot advise you strongly enough *not* to repeat the gossip you heard about William Fant. Think of the poor widow's feelings—she'd be devastated if any such rumors came to her ears."

"Thank you for your advice, my lord, even though it was unnecessary," Irene said repressively. "Lady Oglesby told me that her sister, Mrs. William Fant, does not want it known her husband committed suicide. I would not have mentioned the matter at all had you not proposed that my daughter take up residence in the house. I must ask *you* not to repeat what I said."

Maryann silently applauded. Every now and then, her gentle mother showed a refreshing tartness.

Tammadge's pale eyes came to rest on Maryann.

"It was to prove my concern for your comfort that I invited you to inspect the Curzon Street house. I apologize for causing you distress. You may rest assured that I shall direct my man of business to put the house on the market," he said curtly, turned on his heel, and departed.

See if I care! Maryann thought defiantly as she started up the stairs.

"Mama, what else do you know about the Fant affair?"

"Nothing, my love. I believe Lady Oglesby was sorry she told me as much as she did. But she was so overset, the poor dear. Not a penny was left for her sister, and with three little girls to provide for!"

"I think it is strange that no one in town heard about it. Usually, when a gentleman loses his fortune and estate gambling, the *ton* is abuzz with the news."

"Well, there is, of course, the upcoming royal wedding, which keeps the gossips occupied. And, I suspect, the Fant affair happened at a private card party, and the gentlemen involved are keeping it quiet."

"Indeed! Who'd want to boast that he had driven a man to take his own life?"

"Or else," said Irene, stopping on the third-floor landing to kiss her daughter good-night, "it happened in one of those gaming hells where they are not above using pinked cards and loaded dice. And no one would want to talk about *that*."

When Maryann entered her bedchamber, William Fant and the Curzon Street house receded from her thoughts as she remembered her resolve to seek out her father in the morning. Nothing that happened this evening between her and Tammadge had been an inducement to change her mind.

The rumors about her betrothed *could* be true, and there was only one reason why she had refused to acknowledge this earlier: confirmation would mean total disruption of her plans for the future.

For as long as she could remember, she had wanted to be free of her father, but not, as her sisters had done, to become the chattel of a miserly husband. She had not been upset when her father refused several proposals of marriage during the past season. The young men had been eligible, but without prospects.

Not until the wealthy Viscount Francis Tammadge offered for her hand had she seen her way to freedom, and she had grasped her chance, insisting on a generous marriage settlement.

Maryann pulled off the ring Tammadge had given her and looked at it for a long moment before placing it in her jewelry box. She had not known when she accepted the ring that Tammadge, always so bland and indifferent, also had a possessive, tyrannical side to his nature.

Still, the possible loss of everything she had aimed for was not a prospect she could face with equanimity, and as she slipped between the sheets, she determinedly directed her thoughts away from an uncertain future.

That her thoughts would turn wayward and lead to Stephen Farrell, was none of her doing. She did *not* want to think of the man who made her bristle with indignation every time they exchanged words.

Chapter Nine

"Your daughter is a jade!" Tammadge said later that night in one of the reading rooms of White's Club where he encountered Lord Rivington relaxing with a glass of cognac.

The earl had just returned from Oxford. He'd felt tired, but pleasantly so, and his mood had been mellow. Tammadge's words, however, brought on a sharp stab of anger, as did any reference to Maryann, and the inevitable prickle of apprehension caused by Tammadge's obvious displeasure.

With forced casualness, he asked, "What's she done?"

"Done? Nothing . . . yet. But she's rebellious, disobedient, and forward. On top of that, she made me feel a complete and utter fool. Why the devil didn't you tell me it was *she* who'd been the driving force behind that ridiculous clause in the marriage contract?"

"Keep your voice down, for heaven's sake." The Earl of Rivington's florid face turned a shade darker. "Do you want every dammed soul in the club to know you have a problem with Maryann?"

"*I?*" Tammadge's pointed brows rose. "It is *you* my friend, who has the problem. I admit, since I've made up my mind to marry and beget an heir, I'd as soon marry your daughter as anyone else's. But if she doesn't suit, I won't hesitate to call an end to the betrothal."

"And our partnership? You said it was contingent on the marriage."

"Naturally, our partnership will be dissolved. It's not important to me."

Lord Rivington gulped. He could *not* afford to dismiss their arrangements lightly.

"Maryann's a beautiful girl," he said. "The spit 'n' image of Irene when she was younger, and you always said you couldn't tolerate anything but exquisite beauty around you."

"She is a delicious morsel, but you assured me she's the meekest, most timid creature on earth. Just the kind of wife I was looking for."

"Can I help it that you didn't bother to exchange more than two words with her since the engagement?" Rivington demanded belligerently. "She'd have told you about the bargaining for the dowry and consols readily enough."

"Then you admit you misled me?"

Rivington flinched at the silky note in the viscount's voice. Running his fingers through the remains of hair that sat like a dull gray crown on his head, he reflected bitterly that the only reason he had allowed Maryann a say in the marriage contract was to ensure she was well disposed toward Tammadge. And the one time he had given the girl her head, his leniency worked against him.

"She is biddable," he said, grimly determined to make her so.

"She's damned impertinent! Objected to living at Sevenoaks."

"Opposition has never stopped you from staying the course."

"She's inquisitive to a fault. Questioned me about Farrell. How I met him, why he doesn't seem at home in society."

"I don't tolerate it when she questions me," said Rivington, his eyes hard and cold. "You shouldn't either. But, about Farrell—who is he? His family?"

"He's a down-at-the-heels adventurer and, I admit, quite out of place among the members of the *ton*. But if *I* sponsor him," Tammadge said softly, "what reason or right do you and your daughter have to pry into his history?"

"Stap me, Tammadge! Can't a man be curious?"

Tammadge ignored the outburst. Rising, he bowed with just the correct degree of deference and familiarity to old Lord Ponsonby shuffling into the reading room. The venerable gentleman had been a very good friend of his grandfather.

"Good evening, sir. I hope I find you well."

"Is that you, Tammadge, my boy?" Leaning heavily on his cane, Lord Ponsonby peered short-sightedly into the viscount's face. "Aye, and looking and acting every day more like your father and grandfather before you."

"You are too kind, sir."

"They would've been proud of you, my boy. Mighty proud. That speech you gave last week on the hardships of climbing boys—just what your grandfather would have said. You're a chip off the old block."

Nodding to himself, the old gentleman shuffled toward the far corner of the chamber where the most comfortable chairs and a set of footstools were reserved for him and three or four others of his generation.

Tammadge's thin mouth twisted cynically. His sire and his grandsire, under the influence of his Quaker grandmother, had expended time, energy, and vast amounts of money on such projects as foundling homes, orphanages, charity schools, and asylums for fallen women who wished to change their way of life. Thank goodness, they had both succumbed to a virulent fever, picked up while sticking their long, pious noses into various prisons and the prison hulks on the Thames, before they could totally deplete the family coffers.

Young Francis Tammadge had realized at an early

age that he had absolutely nothing in common with his father and grandfather. At the age of five, he had known that his own inclinations were best served if kept hidden, unless he wished to spend his childhood kneeling and praying for his salvation on the hard floor in his grandfather's room. By the time he attended Oxford, he was a master of dissimulation, and when he came into his inheritance shortly afterward, he was regarded by the *ton* as a pattern card of rectitude and respectability.

He was at liberty to make his fortune whichever way he chose and, after conscientiously discharging his obligations to the charities set up by his forebears, he chose to spend it on the opulent beauty of Eastern treasures, on paintings by masters of the Italian and Dutch schools, on exquisite furniture unearthed in some tumbledown French chateau. Never again would he live in the austerity introduced by his Quaker grandmother.

He was considered a great matrimonial catch, and while insipid daughters were paraded before him by starchy matrons of the *ton,* he could satisfy his less orthodox cravings in the flesh houses of London's slums and stews.

Tammadge prided himself on having led a double life for nigh on twenty years. To work for him, he had chosen men whose primary drive was greed. Avarice was as effective in ensuring a man's silence as a gun held to his head. And if he became too grasping — or careless, or curious — he was eliminated. London held an endless supply of men and women clawing for an opportunity to escape poverty, and never, until Rivington, had Tammadge chosen a partner for one of his ventures from among the *ton*.

Giving the earl a covert look, Tammadge resumed his seat. He hadn't been surprised when Moll, who ran one of his gaming establishments in Soho Court, had told him a year ago that Rivington cheated. Nothing much astonished Tammadge, and he himself enjoyed every now and again the fleecing of a gullible sprig of noble family or winning the property of some country bumpkin. However, he did not tolerate anyone but the dealers to cheat in *his* gambling salons.

Ordinarily, he would have instructed Moll to issue a warning to the Earl of Rivington. If that didn't do the trick, well, all of his gaming hells employed a set of strapping fellows capable of persuading the most recalcitrant client to do as he was bid.

But Tammadge had been bored at the time, bored with life and effortless, unchallenged success. He had for some time toyed with the notion to expand his gambling facilities — right into the heart of the *ton*. Rivington's house in Mount Street, he knew, already had a room ideal for his purposes.

And so he had merely watched Rivington, had noted the earl's distaste for scandal, the obsessive pride in the Rivington name. He'd had him followed on frequent journeys to Oxford, where — strangely, he had believed at first — Rivington was honored as a benefactor at Christ Church. He had bided his time while the earl plunged deeper into debt, losing at the races, dropping a bundle on the Exchange, and, despite his cheating, losing at the gaming tables.

Then providence in the shape of Countess Lieven at Almack's had introduced him to Rivington's youngest daughter, the Lady Maryann. He had known instantly that he must possess her.

She was not voluptuous like the women he picked as his mistresses. Maryann's beauty was as delicate as the beauty of carved jade. And although freshness and innocence were not qualities that appealed to him in general, they were a prerequisite for the future Viscountess Tammadge.

But now, it seemed, the Lady Maryann had feet of clay.

Remembering her in the Effingham garden, the blush and stammered explanation that Farrell was, after all, very different from other men, remembering her dismay when she saw Farrell with her friend Bella, he scowled at Rivington.

"On top of showing her curiosity, your daughter makes no bones about it that she's intrigued by Farrell."

"Maryann?" Rivington gaped in astonishment. "You're barking up the wrong tree. The chit's never shown an interest in any man. Five suitors I sent off with a flea in their ears last season, and not so much as a sigh from her."

"Undoubtedly they were all young, and none of them had a guinea to his name, or any immediate prospect of inheriting."

"So? Neither, apparently, has this Farrell fellow."

Tammadge beckoned to one of the menservants hovering near the door of the reading room and ordered more cognac. He silenced the earl, when he opened his mouth to speak, with an impatient flick of the ubiquitous handkerchief. Only when the glasses had been placed on the table between them and the waiter had returned to his post by the door, did Tammadge address his companion again.

"Neither was your daughter safely engaged to be married to a very wealthy man last year. Don't you see, Rivington? She's already on the look-out for a lover."

"Come now!" Offended by what he considered a slur cast upon *his* name, the earl felt obliged to protest. "You're doing it too brown! I think you're misreading what she said, judging her by the women you've known so far."

Tammadge shot him a look of disdain.

"Maryann *is* a Rivington," the earl blustered.

As though it were yesterday, he remembered that night in March of '97 when he had planted the seed of their fifth child in Irene. He had caught Irene with the four older girls and that infernal German wench sneaking out through the garden. Irene was taking the children to Germany, she said. Just because he'd given the puling Augusta a cuff on the ear.

Well, he had made sure his wife wouldn't run off again. He had seen to it that she never had so much as a shilling in her purse, and he'd made it clear she wouldn't see any of her daughters again if she tried to leave him. He had been certain the child conceived that night would turn out a son—his heir. But it had been another girl, Maryann, and Irene had not conceived again. Damn them both!

"Maryann is a Rivington," he repeated grimly. "On that I'll swear my oath. And she'd never—"

"Rivington or not, her blush gave her away. She is as transparent as glass, and I know she has a fancy for Farrell. I had to stand there and patiently make her believe I'm besotted enough to blow her lover's brains out when I'd as soon tell her I'll strangle her if she attracts so much as a breath of scandal to *my* name.

"Are you saying you *wouldn't* blow the fellow's brains out?"

"Rivington, you are a fool. I'll see to it that she'll forget about Farrell. I have plans for him. He's too good a man to waste on a woman's fancy."

Swirling the cognac in his glass, Tammadge sat staring at the amber liquid. His expression was such that the Earl of Rivington deemed it prudent not to break the silence.

Tammadge raised his eyes. "But if he dares approach Maryann, you may be sure I'll kill him. Not, my dear Rivington, because I'm besotted with your daughter. I'd kill him because he aspires to what is mine."

Rivington suppressed a shiver. "Then why the devil did you go through that rigamarole with Maryann, trying to convince her you're taken with her?"

Tammadge raised the glass and drank deeply. "I'll woo and pacify her if I must," he said softly. "It is unwise to frighten a young girl before the nuptials."

Rivington glowered. "It may be unwise for you, my friend. But if she encourages Farrell, I'll have her hide."

"I hope you jest," Tammadge said coldly. "She's mine, and it is up to me to chastise her. If, when, and how I think best."

"She's not yours until the knot is tied."

The viscount's pale eyes narrowed. "You see to it that she stays in line until the wedding. But put one blemish on her, Rivington, and the marriage is off. And when the marriage is off, our deal is off."

Chapter Ten

Early Thursday morning, well before it was time for the groom to bring around the carriage that would take her to Sloane Street, Maryann approached the closed door at the back of the ground floor.

She raised a hand to knock, and let it fall again. Never before had she invaded the library—or been asked to enter it. In fact, the orders were that no one, not family or the king himself, was to be admitted without first making an appointment through Mr. Winsome.

Squaring her shoulders, Maryann rapped on the solid oak panel, and entered.

"Good morning, Father. Pray forgive—" Maryann stared at her father—what she could see of him—in utter dumbfoundedness.

Years ago, she had speculated about Lord Rivington's secret activities in the forbidden room; she had, depending on her own personal fancy of the moment, envisioned him snatching treats between meals, playing with some out-of-bounds animal, or reading a piece of banned literature. She had realized when she was about six or seven, that none of these activities were in character with the harsh, unloving man who was her father, and she had dismissed the closed library door as one of the vagaries of adulthood.

One other possibility had occurred to her, later on, when she had grown well into adolescence. She had briefly wondered if her father were seeing a woman in the library.

But never had she imagined she might find him prone beneath a table, whose baize cloth had been tacked up and in whose center reposed a roulette wheel.

"Get out!" Reginald Rivington, sixth earl of a distinguished line, emerged red faced, his wreath of grizzled hair disheveled, from beneath the table.

Maryann looked at the tool clutched in his hand. It was, she thought, the same kind of instrument used by the head gardener in Sloane Street to tighten the metal wheels turning a miniature windmill. A screwdriver the gardener had called it.

"Father, I must speak with you." She firmly closed the door and advanced on him.

She had herself well in hand now. Not so much as the flicker of an eye betrayed her curiosity in the various baize-covered tables, the packs of cards and the dice set out on a sideboard.

"I must speak to you about Tammadge."

Rivington shot her a baleful look, but, hearing the viscount's name, apparently thought better of ordering her from the room.

"What about Tammadge?" he demanded. He dropped the screwdriver into a case filled with similar instruments and snapped the lid shut. "Did he jilt you?"

"No."

"Then there's nothing to talk about."

"Father, I have heard disturbing rumors about Tammadge. So disturbing, I think they must be investigated."

His red face turned a mottled purple. "Oh, you *think*, do you?"

He took a threatening step closer, and Maryann acknowledged the inevitability of punishment for what she was about to ask at the same time as she recognized there might be no escape from marriage with Tammadge.

"Let me tell you what *I* think," he said, his mouth tightening in anger. "That conniving, lying, interfering wench your mother brought from Germany has overstepped herself this time! She'll be out in the streets, and I'll make dammed sure she's never employed in an English household again."

"If you're referring to Hedwig, she has nothing to do with this," Maryann lied coldly.

"Don't lie to me! Could have been no one but your mother's woman. Or your mother herself."

"It was one of Tammadge's friends."

As she had hoped, the pronouncement robbed the earl, at least temporarily, of speech.

"I was warned," she said quickly, before he could recover, "that Tammadge is not at all suitable as a husband. That he is sadistic and has perverted preferences."

"Why, you baggage! That a daughter of mine," said Rivington, breathing heavily, "has the indelicacy to discuss her betrothed with one of his fancy pieces! And has the impudence to brag about it!"

She did not correct her father's misapprehension, but tilted her head in unconscious imitation of her proud German grandmother and gave back stare for angry stare. There might be no point to keeping Farrell's name from him, but withholding it gave her a sense of victory over Rivington's unreasonable demeanor.

"Then it is true that you knew of the rumors?" she asked. "Perhaps knew of them well before Tammadge offered for my hand?"

Something flickered in the depths of Rivington's eyes and disappeared just as quickly, to be replaced by a blaze of wrath. But Maryann had not missed that moment of hesitation, the strange look, and she felt very cold.

"You are wicked and unprincipled!" Her father's fleshy countenance turned a shade darker. "How dare you question Tammadge's honor? You're a baggage, a trollop! No better than a piece of Haymarket ware."

He drew a shuddering breath. "The sooner Tammadge takes you in hand, the better. You'll be married as soon as the banns are read."

Maryann flinched as though he had struck her. "But that would be in three weeks!"

"And not a moment too soon." Rivington's eyes narrowed. "God knows I did my best to break you of the bad habits encouraged by your mother's indulgence. I can do no more, save turn you over to a husband. It'll be up to him to teach you the delicacy of mind you so obviously lack."

"No!" Panic drove her to bold opposition. "I cannot marry Lord Tammadge until I know there's no truth to the rumors. Three weeks is not time enough to —"

"You'll do as I say, miss!" Hands clenched, head lowered like a charging bull, Rivington advanced on his daughter. "I wasted my blunt on you last season. This year, I'll see you wed."

Maryann's thoughts raced. She knew that stance, the tone of his voice. He'd never listen to reason now that he was in a rage.

But if her betrothed were the unscrupulous man Lucy Weller said he was, she would not marry him for all the wealth of Midas. She'd rather give up her dream of escaping her father's house — and of having her own botanical gardens.

"I'll brook no opposition. No argument." Rivington's hand shot out to grab her. "You'll marry Tammadge . . . if I have to lock you into the cellars until the wedding day."

Dizziness engulfed Maryann. Her father never uttered an idle threat. The cellars had a nasty way of sapping her courage; at any cost, she must avoid getting locked up.

Bowing her head as a meek and obedient daughter should, at the same time hiding the betraying flash of rebellion in her eyes, she made a daring decision. She'd stay betrothed to Tammadge. But she would investigate the rumors herself.

"I am sure you know best, Father. I only fear three weeks do not allow for preparations . . . gowns . . . catering arrangements . . . invitations . . ."

She risked a peek and, encountering a suspicious, glowering stare, added, "You wouldn't want Lord Tammadge to think us shabby."

Rivington flung her from him. "Don't bother me with trivia. I am a busy man." His gaze, as though drawn by a magnet, darted to the roulette table. He muttered, "I've waited long for this moment. Too long."

"Waited for what?"

"Get out!" he shouted.

Free! Maryann obeyed with alacrity. Picking up her skirts, she ran, barely hearing above the pounding of her heart the bellowed command to help her mother with wedding preparations.

Pulse racing, she hurtled down the hallway, out the front door.

Three weeks' liberty to probe into Tammadge's life!

She ran blindly, without thought of where she was going. But when she darted past the mews, she caught a glimpse of her groom mounting the carriage box. It was nine o'clock, the time she usually drove to the Sloane Street gardens.

She remembered the morning Stephen Farrell had driven her to the gardens and started to shake the foundation of the future she had so carefully designed. Stephen Farrell, who was a friend of Tammadge, and yet called her betrothed a sadist and, last night, likened him to a guard dog yapping at her heels.

The beginnings of a plan came to her, and she retraced her steps to the corner of the mews.

Robert's jaw dropped when she hailed him. "Lady Maryann," he stammered. "I was just about to fetch ye."

"Drive!" she ordered, scrambling into the carriage. "Not to Sloane Street. Just anywhere."

She leaned against the squabs and sat there, eyes

closed, her thoughts tumbling, until she had worked out exactly what she must do.

It wouldn't be easy, but nothing ever was. And if she could be assured of Robert's cooperation . . .

She looked out the carriage window. They had driven farther than she realized, approaching the Strand. From there, it wasn't far to Bella's house. Her friend would be the first to want to help, but she could not go to Bella. The girl had come off lightly when her tryst in the gazebo was discovered, but she was still in disgrace and must be kept out of trouble.

Maryann slid open the communications panel behind the coachman's box. "Robert, pull up when you find someone to mind the horses."

"That'll be near Somerset House. There's always someone waitin' on the nobs who come to see them paintin's." The young groom half-turned on his perch. "Where is it you'll be wantin' to go, Lady Maryann?"

"Just down to the river."

Maryann sat on the edge of the seat, her foot tapping impatiently until the carriage came to a halt. She jumped out before Robert could let down the steps and set out with the long stride she had acquired in the country. With the groom at a respectful distance behind her, she turned into narrow Arundel Street leading to the Thames. It would be quiet there at this time of day. Anyone wishing to be ferried across the river would use the Somerset or the Temple Stairs some distance away.

Arundel Stairs were crumbling and overgrown with lichen, but to Maryann that only meant she would be undisturbed. She was about to sit on the top step when Robert caught up to her.

"Mind yer gown, Lady Maryann. At least sit on my coat if ye must sit here."

"Thank you." Craning her neck, she smiled up at the young man. "Won't you join me, Robert? We have known each other too long to stand on ceremony, and I have something to discuss with you."

He hesitated only an instant before taking the step below hers. Still, she was not quite eye level with him.

He was as tall as Farrell, she thought. Perhaps taller, and definitely more powerful in the shoulders. In fact, Robert's unquestionable physical strength gave her the boost of assurance she needed.

"Are ye in a scrape, Lady Maryann?"

She drew a deep breath. "Yes, Rob."

With the use of her childhood name for him, Maryann in one fell swoop bridged the gap forged by years of strictly enforced mistress/servant relationship. He was once again the friend and companion who had roamed the fields and meadows of the Kent estate with her, who had shared his fishing gear, his kittens and puppies.

Removing his cap to expose a freckled forehead and a mop of sandy hair to the breeze blowing off the river, he met her gaze with the frankness she had expected and relied on all her childhood years.

"Ye know I'll do anything to help, lass. But if it's about that fee-an-say of yourn, that Viscount Tammadge, there ain't much I *can* do against yer father."

"You heard the rumors?"

" 'Course I heard."

"Do you believe what Lucy Weller says?" Maryann watched him with painful intensity. "That Tammadge owns . . . disreputable houses?"

The freckles all but disappeared in a sudden rush of color to his face, but he did not tell her this was no subject a lady might discuss with her groom.

"Aye, lass. I believe it. And I heard at the Wheel an' Axle—"

"A tavern!" She could not resist teasing him just a little, and raised a reproving brow. "You shock me, Rob."

"A public house," he said firmly. "I ain't a lad no more, an' it's in the Wheel an' Axle that I sit in me spare time an' swap tales with ostlers an' coachmen."

"And what did you hear?"

"That his lordship ruined his share of young bloods in gamin' hells where they're not above usin' nicked cards or loaded dice."

The library at Rivington House, devoid of desk, book shelves, or other furnishings one might expect, but filled with baize-covered tables, flashed before her mind's eye. She pushed the intrusive thought away. It had nothing to do with gaming hells or with her predicament.

But there was something about gambling, about nicked cards, loaded dice, and financial ruin she ought to remember. . . . Yes, Mama had mentioned gaming hells, and William Fant, who shot himself.

And Tammadge had acquired his house. Had he won it from William Fant or had he purchased it from Fant's widow? Another question to add to the store she was piling up.

She frowned. "There seems to be talk and gossip aplenty among servants. I cannot understand why the rumors haven't reached the *ton*."

A look of astonishment crossed Rob's face. "Think on it," he said gruffly. "Even if *you* was to go around, hintin' at some of these goin's-on, who'd believe ye?"

"You're right. I'm not certain I should believe them myself."

Maryann looked downriver, well past Strand Bridge, but the stairs to the Effingham property and the embankment where she and Tammadge had strolled were hidden by a hump of riverbank that protruded like a spur into the water.

"Tammadge is too dashed respectable. Or, rather, is *believed* respectable."

"It'd be riskin' his bloody position if a servant was to blab to his master about the viscount."

Robert did not add that one of Tammadge's own footmen, who had "blabbed" to a friend, had been found a few days later floating in the Thames. He'd been stabbed before he ended up in the water.

And a twelvemonth ago, a gentleman's gentleman

had disappeared without a trace after telling some colleagues that his late master's death on the hunting field had been suicide, not an accident. According to the valet, the reckless young lordling had staked family jewels, to which he had no right, in a card game in some hell in Soho Court. He'd lost, and, the valet said, the jewels had ended up in Lord Tammadge's possession. And then the valet had vanished.

'Twas enough, Robert thought, to make a fellow damned cautious. And if it weren't for Lady Maryann . . .

"My father has set the wedding date forward, Rob. I am to be married as soon as the banns are read."

"Blimey!" The groom forgot himself enough to grab her arm. "Ye mustn't do that, Lady Maryann!"

"You're a one to talk! You knew Tammadge had asked for my hand, but not once did you warn me about him."

"But I thought . . ." He started to fiddle with his cap. "I hoped there'd be time to do somethin' to stop the weddin'."

"The wedding cannot be stopped. A lady of quality does not jilt a man without good reason," Maryann said sternly.

Shifting restlessly, Rob dislodged several bits of loose masonry with his large boots. He waited until the clatter subsided and the last pebble plopped into the murky water.

"But if someone was to keep an eye on Lord Tammadge? And was to bring proof of how he makes his fortune?"

"Then, I think," Maryann said slowly, deliberately, "no matter how much my father may desire the connection, fear of a public scandal would force him to end the betrothal."

"Aye, that's what I figgered. He's that proud of his name, he is."

"Will you help me, Rob?"

He gave her a sidelong look. "Can't do it alone. Not

enough free time to follow the man. Harv and James are fillin' in for me whenever they can," he said, taking Maryann by surprise.

"Our footmen?" she asked faintly. "The three of you are spying on Tammadge?"

She tried to imagine the two stately footmen creeping after their quarry, and failed. "Why, I am touched, Rob. And very grateful."

Rob looked bashful, but also downcast. "Only thing is, his lordship's been avoidin' gamin' hells and the bad parts of town since the betrothal was published."

Maryann sighed. "And there's so little time."

She allowed a moment or two to pass before she peeked at the groom with the air of one just making a discovery.

"We must find Mr. Farrell. You remember, Rob! The gentleman who drove me to Sloane Street on Monday. He, too, warned me against Tammadge, and I feel certain I can enlist his help."

Maryann was not certain of anything regarding Stephen Farrell, except that he had tried to warn her about Tammadge and that he must know more about her fiancé's activities than anyone else of her acquaintance — must know firsthand rather than by hearsay.

He had warned her, but could she trust him, his motivation for involving himself?

When she saw him at the Crabtree rout, she had once again sensed his power and strength. Yet, when all was said and done, she knew nothing about him, save what he himself had told her — and what Tammadge had said, none of which inspired confidence.

She did know that, if she were prudent, she'd think twice about placing herself in the hands of a stranger. But she had no option. Even if Rob and his assistants spied on Tammadge every night, they might not find the evidence until it was too late. Until she was wed.

She must get in touch with Stephen Farrell.

Maryann was about to repeat the suggestion to the

strangely silent Rob when she noted his heightened color and remembered that Farrell had engaged the groom in conversation on Monday morning.

"Do you by any chance know where Mr. Farrell can be found?"

Rob gave a start, and the look he shot her was both indignant and self-conscious. "D'ye think me all-knowin' then? The man passed the time o' day with me. He never said a word about where he might be lodgin'."

Maryann watched Robert twist and turn the cap in his hands, a habit she remembered from the past when he was debating the right and wrong of a difficult decision.

"But you know something about him?" she prodded.

"Aye."

"For pity's sake!" Exasperation crept into her voice. "Tell me what you know."

Encountering her fierce look, he grinned sheepishly, then slapped the cap at a rakish angle atop his sandy hair.

"He did let on that messages can be left for him at the Fightin' Cock tavern in Seven Dials. In case," Rob added with emphasis, "ye ever have a need of him."

Chapter Eleven

"Leave a message at a tavern if I have a need of him?"

It was Maryann's turn to frown. Farrell had expected her to come to him for help? How strange. But he had spoken with Rob *before* she accused him of being a back stabber, scum, and possibly worse. She remembered the look on his face when she said she despised him and could not doubt that he did not intend to ever see her again.

But he had seen her, last night, and he had assured her, albeit coldly, that he didn't hold her loss of temper against her.

And she . . . With a sinking heart, Maryann remembered that she had promptly lost her temper again.

Trying to hide her misgivings in a flurry of activity, she rose and shook out the coat Robert had loaned her.

"What are we waiting for, Rob?" Flinging the coat at the groom, Maryann marched off. "Let's be gone to the Fighting Cock and send for Mr. Farrell."

"Go to Seven Dials? Are ye daft?"

There was nothing of the respectful groom about Rob as he strode at her side up Arundel Street, into the Strand where the carriage waited. He painted for her in gruesome detail the horrors of Seven Dials—lair of thieves and murderers, home of pimps and whores. No reasoning, no cajolery, could move him to change his stubborn mind. He would not drive Maryann to the

Fighting Cock.

In fact, he insisted with maddening superiority, he *could not*. He didn't know the exact location of the tavern, and he was not about to stop and ask directions in a district notorious for mobbing any carriage that moved at too slow a pace to be a danger to would-be robbers.

"Very well!" Ignoring the invitingly open carriage door and the gaping, peg-legged ex-soldier who had taken charge of the horses during their absence, Maryann made a last attack on Rob's defenses. "I'll take a hackney."

For a moment it was touch and go whether she'd be picked up and tossed into the carriage or put across his knee for a deserved spanking. A *well*-deserved spanking. She knew she was treating him abominably. But too much was at risk to wait for him to take her home, find the tavern, deliver a message, and hope for the best that Farrell had not decided to ignore a request for help.

The soldier said eagerly, "Oi can show ye to the tavern. Oi's been there many a time."

"There, you see!" Maryann gave Robert a challenging look. "That's settled, then."

He scowled at the soldier, then at his mistress. "An' ye would take a hackney if I said no, wouldn't ye?" he said bitterly. "I've never known anyone so mule-headed. Well, get in, then. I'd rather take ye meself than let ye go off with no more'n a jarvey to protect ye."

While Rob, with the soldier beside him, drove her northeast through a rabbit warren of ever-narrowing streets, Maryann found herself once again sitting on the edge of the carriage seat. This time, her foot was tapping not in impatience, but to relieve the tension mounting in her.

Despite Rob's graphic description of the horrors to be found in the disreputable slum area, Maryann was unprepared for the reality of naked children playing in the kennels, of men and women comatose on the steps of taverns and gin shops, of the stench penetrating into the

103

carriage and making her gag.

Not in her wildest imagination could she have pictured such squalor, such filth as she saw in the alleys crisscrossing the seven converging streets that gave the district its name. If the groom had stopped and offered to take her to Mount Street, Maryann might have agreed to turn back and wait for Farrell in her father's house.

But the carriage rolled on at a smart clip, turned sharply, and swept through an arched gateway. Before Maryann could see more than a cobbled yard walled in by stables and a coach house on two sides, Rob hustled her through the back entrance of a tall, narrow brick building.

Darkness and a foul, yeasty odor engulfed her as he guided her along a passageway. Somewhere ahead, she heard the din and racket, the raucous laughter, the shrill screams that had marked taverns and public houses throughout the carriage ride here. Behind her, the soldier's peg leg stumped on the wooden floor.

This could not possibly be the Fighting Cock, the place Stephen Farrell had chosen as a repository for messages. Surely no gentleman would know such a squalid tavern. If it hadn't been for the groom's reassuring hand on her arm, she'd have taken to her heels and run as fast as she could.

"An' what can I do for ye?" The male voice coming from the deepest gloom of the passage conveyed irritation and suspicion rather than willingness to serve.

"A private parlor for the lady," said Rob with the aplomb of a duke. "And send a message to Mr. Farrell to come hither *instantly.*"

Another voice, a voice Maryann recognized, demanded impatiently, "Who's that, Fletcher? Who's asking for me?"

Maryann shook off Rob's hand and stepped forward. As her eyes adjusted to the dark, she distinguished a rotund, apron-clad figure, presumably Fletcher, the publican of the Fighting Cock, and next to him, the tall, powerful shape of Stephen Farrell.

They stared at each other.

There was something about Farrell, a certain raffishness, a look of devil-may-care, which Maryann had not been aware of during their prior meetings. Perhaps it was the effect of the sun-streaked hair that was especially unruly this day, the coat of excellent cut and material, but very much in need of pressing, the Hessian boots that would benefit from an application of blacking. Whatever it was, it did nothing to soothe her growing unease.

"The deuce," Farrell muttered. "What are *you* doing here?"

Maryann drew herself up. "You did tell my groom I might send for you."

"That, Lady Maryann, was before I decided to wash my hands of you. And sending for me is a far cry from showing up yourself."

Daunted but determined not to show it, she measured Farrell with a look Queen Bess could not have surpassed in hauteur. "Is there a room in this — this hostelry, where we might speak in private?"

Farrell and Fletcher exchanged glances. What message passed between the two men, Maryann could not tell, but the publican's suspicious mien changed to an ingratiating smile.

"To be sure, yer ladyship! I can offer a very fine private parlor. If yer ladyship will step this way?"

Bowing and scraping, he gestured to a staircase that so far had escaped Maryann's notice. She eyed the worn, dirty steps, the greasy handrail missing several banisters.

"I shall follow you, Mr. Fletcher."

With a speed and agility amazing in one so round and heavy, the publican mounted the stairs. Gingerly, Maryann ascended behind him and was in turn followed by Farrell and Rob. She did not hear the soldier's peg leg and was thinking that she wouldn't have minded if he had come along and offered his services and protection, when the stairs gave a sudden twist and she was distracted by the feel of carpeting beneath her feet. The handrail still felt slick, but she doubted grease was the cause. The unmistakable smell of beeswax tickled her nose.

The change in atmosphere was so startling that even in her state of apprehension she could not help but wonder about it. She glanced at Farrell close behind her, but the reserved, even cold, expression on his face changed her mind about asking questions.

She trod higher and reached the upper hallway. Light streamed through windows that had recently been washed, exposing clean white walls, polished woodwork, a gleaming brass fixture or two.

Fletcher opened a door not too far removed from the stairs. "Here ye be, yer ladyship. Best private parlor in the house."

Maryann entered a chamber furnished with an oak settle against one of the walls, and a large table and chairs in the center of the room. Worn but spotless rugs covered the wooden floor; starched curtains of bright green cotton graced two mullioned windows. A fire was laid in the fireplace, but when Fletcher reached for the tinderbox on the mantel, Farrell waved him away.

"Does this meet with your approval, Lady Maryann?" Farrell's voice mocked, but his dark eyes betrayed a trace of concern.

"It will do."

Maryann nodded dismissal to Fletcher and, when the door closed behind the publican's bulk, took a seat at the table.

"Will you join me, Mr. Farrell?"

He perched on a corner of the table, placing her at the disadvantage of having to look up at him.

"Coming here for the sake of a chat was ill-advised and foolish, Lady Maryann. You saw me last night.

Why didn't you say then whatever it is you wish to say to me?"

Maryann looked at the groom standing stiffly to attention. "You'll be more comfortable, Rob, if you pull a chair up to the door."

"Blocking entrance or exit?" asked Farrell. "Don't you trust me, Lady Maryann?"

She returned his mocking stare gravely. "Are you telling me I may trust you?"

His face went still, expressionless. Even the booted leg swinging jauntily a moment ago, hung motionless.

"If you weren't so young, you'd know not to ask a man whether you may trust him. You'd follow your instinct. What does your instinct tell you, Lady Maryann?"

She'd had so many doubts about him, such grave misgivings about asking his help, but, facing him now and looking into his eyes, she could not recall a single one. Even his rakish looks did not alarm her any longer. She rather liked them.

Instinct told her to trust him — but could she trust her instinct?

"I've learned a lesson about blind trust, Mr. Farrell. And I'm convinced that common sense and an application of prudence and caution never hurt anyone."

"Just so. To be discovered tête-à-tête with a man other than your betrothed might be difficult to explain away."

She would not rise to provocation. Not today. Determinedly, Maryann took the plunge. "It is about my betrothed that I wish to speak with you."

Farrell raised a brow and waited politely.

"You made certain remarks, sir."

"Indeed. You found them offensive."

"Mr. Farrell, will you listen to me? It is difficult enough for me to broach such matters without the benefit of your comments."

He bent his head to examine the border of white linen extending beneath the sleeve of his coat, but Maryann felt certain he was watching her.

"Then you have not come to make up for your omission on Monday?" he asked. "You've not come to box my ears?"

In a flash, she remembered that moment in the curricle when her hands had balled and she had wanted to hit him. "You *knew* I wanted . . . ?"

She bit her lip, annoyed with herself. If he could catch her off guard so easily and distract her from her purpose, she'd be no match for him in the tricky business about Tammadge.

She swallowed. "I accused you of lying about my — about Tammadge."

"You accused me of worse, Lady Maryann. You accused me of taking pleasure in putting you to the blush."

She felt the telltale surge of warmth to her face, and rushed on, not considering whether she ought to apologize or explain, but merely wanting to get her point across.

"I meant to go to Tammadge. To tell him about you. How you blackened his character. But then I did not."

"What happened to make you change your mind?"

"I heard . . . rumors. How Tammadge is acquiring his wealth. I could not ignore the tales. They made me look at your words in a different light."

Farrell flicked a glance at Robert sitting stolidly in front of the door. "Your man," he said. "Do you trust him?"

"With my life."

His mouth twitched. "Obviously. You *must* trust him with your life if you allowed him to drive you to this place. But I meant, are you afraid he'll gossip? You seem reluctant to come to the point of your visit."

"Lady Maryann got no cause to think I'll carry tales about her," Rob cut in angrily. "And don't ye go puttin' foolish notions in her head, Mr. Farrell. Like havin' me wait outside, 'cause I won't leave her alone with anyone for any reason."

"Very laudable," Farrell said drily. "I'm glad to know

108

you have *some* sense."

Robert's face burned with mortification, and Maryann was quick to jump to his defense. "Robert has a lot of sense. He didn't want me to come here, but he could not go against my orders."

She turned to the groom. "You needn't fear I'll ask you to leave."

"Now that it is settled that your groom has shown admirable good sense and you, apparently, possess a modicum of it—after all, you did choose someone as your guard who'd show off to advantage in a boxing ring—let me have the word with no bark on it. Why did you come to see me, Lady Maryann?"

"I need to find out if that tale—that rumor—is true. Will you help me?"

Farrell did not speak right away, and the dark eyes fixed unblinkingly on her did not tell Maryann anything. He slid off the table. His back to her, he stood looking out the window.

"I don't see what purpose it would serve if I involved myself further in your affairs, Lady Maryann. As you pointed out Monday morning, I *am* considered Tammadge's friend."

"But you dislike his habits enough to warn his betrothed!"

He stood unmoving, silent.

"Mr. Farrell, you specifically told me that he is not cut out to be a husband. That he has cravings—" She took a deep breath, wondering if it was easier or more difficult to speak to that stiff back. "Cravings to which a wife would not willingly submit."

"If you believe me, why are you still betrothed?"

"I cannot break the engagement without good cause! Everything you said to me may be true. None of it can be proven, however, until too late. But the rumor about these other activities could be substantiated, if only you would help."

He made no reply, did not have the courtesy to face

109

her.

After a moment, Maryann rose, too. There had always been a possibility he might refuse his help, but she had not let the prospect daunt her. Now, faced with silence and an implacable back, her self-control slipped.

"You must help me!" Desperation added a hoarse note to her voice. "I'm not asking you to get involved, but you're familiar with Tammadge's habits. You know Seven Dials and, I doubt not, the waterfront as well. You could so easily lead me to the houses he is supposed to own!"

He swung around, and once again, as on the night of the ball, she noted the look of total alertness in his eyes, the tautness of his stance.

"So that's it," he said softly. "You heard about the brothels and the gaming hells."

"Yes."

She watched him curiously, for she had the impression he was relieved, as though he had expected her to disclose something even worse.

"If you believe Tammadge is involved in prostitution and gambling," he said brusquely, "why are you here? Why aren't you at the offices of *The Times* and the *Gazette,* with a notice ending the betrothal?"

"But there's no proof! If they exist, I must find those houses and take the information to Bow Street."

Behind her, Robert stirred restlessly. Maryann found herself wishing he'd get up and pound some sense into Farrell's head. Why didn't Farrell want to help? The odious man simply stood there, staring at her as though she were a freak at Bartholomew Fair.

At the end of her wits, Maryann decided to brazen it out. "If you don't want to assist me, say so. I'll find someone else."

"I doubt it."

She not only doubted it, she knew there was no one else who could lead her to the proof of Tammadge's nefarious activities in the time she had left. Hedwig's friends, Lucy Weller and Rose, knew only secondhand rumors. Rob, Harv, and James were spying on Tammadge, but they might not have any greater success in the future than they'd had in the past.

Farrell was her only hope. He was close to Tammadge. He must know where to look for the brothels and the gaming hells.

"Will you help me?" She swallowed her pride. "Please?"

Chapter Twelve

Stephen could not believe his ears. The same girl who had tried to jump from the rolling curricle to avoid listening to his warning, now pleaded with him to show her proof. And how the devil had she learned of the viscount's investment in brothels?

Stephen observed Lady Maryann closely, her desperate "please" still ringing in his ears. He'd like to help her, but he didn't see why she must have proof of Tammadge's activities.

In fact, any nosing around she might do, questions she might ask, would endanger his own mission. Under no circumstances must she be allowed to stir up dust, especially now when Tammadge seemed on the point of discussing business. That, Stephen hoped, was the reason Tammadge wanted him to dine in Grosvenor Square.

But there was that look in Lady Maryann's eyes—a silent plea. Perhaps even fear.

"Lady Maryann, did Tammadge approach you in an improper manner?" Stephen spoke gently, as he would to a terrified child even while his hands curled as if to close around the viscount's neck. "Did he force himself on you?"

"No!" Hauteur and anger wiped out the pleading look he had caught. "Do you think I'd need help if that were my problem? Confound it, Farrell! I'd box his ears and draw his cork as well."

Her language would have amused him if he weren't exasperated. Perhaps nettled was the better word.

"So you don't need me to protect you. Very well. Then why the deuce did you come to me?"

"I told you! To help find the brothels."

"Fustian. If you've finally come to your senses and want to end the betrothal, all you need to do is tell Tammadge that you've changed your mind. Or tell your father."

"My father wouldn't tolerate my crying off," she said stiffly.

"Indeed. No doubt he's looking forward to the day he can hand you over to a husband."

He had spoken sarcastically, wanting to show her that he was not taken in by the implication of a harsh, un-yielding father. But to his astonishment, Lady Maryann nodded.

"Yes. For some reason he's determined that I marry Tammadge."

Stephen's keen sense of hearing alerted him to some slight sound in the room next door. There was no time for long, soothing reassurances. He must convince Lady Maryann that it was time to leave. Quickly.

"Ye gads!" He took her by the shoulders, steering her toward the door. "What a to-do you make over a simple matter. After all, your father cannot force you to marry Tammadge, especially if you tell him why you've changed your mind."

She said nothing, but something in the way she looked at him, gave him pause.

He moderated his tone, forcing himself to show patience. "Lady Maryann, I want you to go home now. I shall call on you in a day or so, and we'll discuss the matter again. If," he amended, "you still want to."

She looked at him stonily.

Now, when exasperation would have been of help in propelling her out the door, he could not rekindle that emotion. He turned to the groom instead.

"Ask Fletcher for a pistol before you leave. And do not bring your mistress into Seven Dials again. I need not tell you how unsafe it is. You were lucky you weren't mobbed in the carriage."

Responding to the voice of authority, Robert rose. "Aye, sir. Just what I told her, too."

Robert pushed aside the chair, opened the door, and stood waiting for Lady Maryann to precede him.

At the same moment, the connecting door to the adjoining chamber opened. A young woman, clad only in petticoat and shift, long hair the color of burnished copper rippling down her back, stepped across the threshold. Thrusting naked arms above her head, she stretched with careless abandon while giving Farrell a smile that widened into a yawn.

"Tolly's come with the message ye was waitin' for," she mumbled, yawning again.

She stretched once more, showing off a generous swell of bosom above the low-cut shift, spun on her bare feet, and with graceful, fluid movements returned to the bedchamber. For such it was, confirmed by the tester bed with its mussed sheets just beyond the open doorway.

Stephen tugged at his collar, which was far too tight all of a sudden. Damn the timing of the message! Damn Meg and her uninhibited ways. She ought to know better than to exhibit Drury Lane manners in the presence of a lady.

He directed a covert look at Lady Maryann, then boldly faced her wide-eyed gaze.

They looked at each other, she as determined as he to betray no feeling, to show no reaction to the incident. But Stephen had a reason for pretense. He must protect the secrets of the Fighting Cock, and his own. He wished Lady Maryann would show some emotion, even if it were contempt or disgust. Anything would be easier to bear than her carefully blank face.

Abruptly, she turned and walked away.

"Something is bound to happen before your wedding day," he felt compelled to assure her.

He stood in the door watching the straight, slender back, the proud carriage of her head—willing her to look at him. But she did not.

Good! said the cold, logical part of his brain that had served him well in the Peninsula. *Without her presence cluttering the issue, you'll work much better.*

But some other, more chivalrous part of him had to have the last word.

"Urgent business will take me out of town for a day or so, but I'll call in Mount Street as soon as I return. Promise me not to go off on your own to look for the brothels."

She had reached the stairs.

"Lady Maryann! I assure you, by October Tammadge will be in no position to marry anyone."

Foot poised above the step, she looked at him over her shoulder.

"The wedding, Mr. Farrell, is May the sixth. In three weeks."

A blow in the gut could not have affected him more powerfully than her words. *Three weeks.*

He stared after her, feeling winded and sick as on the morning the message of William's death had reached him in Paris, and watched her disappear down the stairwell. Three weeks . . . but unless Tolly's news from the Wapping docks was a whole lot better than he expected, there was nothing he could do to stop Tammadge from claiming her.

Lady Maryann, another victim . . . as William had been.

Anger and bitterness threatened to choke Stephen as he remembered his arrival at Fant House in Curzon Street on a raw February morning. Tolly had opened the door and led him straight to the study.

"This is where I found him, Master Stephen." The old butler's voice had quavered as he pointed to the leather chair behind the desk. "Already cold and stiff, and the blood drying on his face and hair. And on the good Axminster carpet, too."

Bleary-eyed, his mind reeling with fatigue, for he had not slept since he left Paris, Stephen had looked at the chair where his brother had taken his own life. Blown his brains out.

Why? he wondered numbly.

If anyone but William's wife had sent the news, he wouldn't have believed it. William had been timid and retiring, but never too timid to face responsibility and obligations. Of course, he could have changed during his younger brother's absence. Stephen had been gone nearly nine years—fighting Napoleon Bonaparte.

But now Bonaparte was banished to St. Helena in the South Atlantic, and although Wellington was still in Paris as commander of the joint army of occupation, Maj. Stephen Fant regarded his own usefulness at an end. He had planned to leave Paris on the first day of March, resign his commission, and enjoy the diversions of London until he could decide what to do with his life.

William had expected him. Although he hated London, William had traveled up from Sussex to put the Fant town house in order for Stephen.

And then? What had happened to force William to take the desperate step?

"Why, Tolly?" Stephen's face showed a grayish hue beneath the Peninsular tan and the shadow of a day-old beard. Weariness and pain twisted his mouth into a thin, crooked line.

"Why did he shoot himself? My sister-in-law wrote that the estate, this house, the money, are gone. But that's no reason to—Dammit, Tolly! We would have come about. William had a wife and children to think of."

"I don't know what the master said in the note to Mrs. Fant." Tolly fumbled in the pocket of his coat. "But he wrote to you as well, Master Stephen."

116

He took the crumpled missive the butler handed him and broke the seal. His brother's neat, precise pen strokes danced before his eyes. Neat and precise, that's what William had always been—until death spilled his blood.

Blinking away moisture and travel grit, Stephen concentrated on William's last words.

Stephen, my dear fellow—

By the time you read this, you'll have damned me roundly for gambling away everything we owned between us—save for your Cornwall property, which I forgot about. You'll have damned me for being such a blasted fool as to fall in with Viscount Tammadge, and, mostly, for being a coward.

Stephen's hand shook. William knew—had known him well. After reading Susan's message, he had indeed cursed his brother for being a coward.

I was introduced to Tammadge at my club. He is respected and well liked, and while we played at White's, nothing could have been more correct than his game. But then I was fool enough to accompany him to some private establishment, a gaming hell I suppose you'd call it. And there I found out that Tammadge cheated.

I confronted him. He laughed. I mentioned the matter to members of White's and Brookes's clubs. They looked at me as though I were out of my mind. The curst thing is, everybody regards Tammadge as a pattern card of respectability.

You know me, Stephen. I am not an aggressive type of fellow, but I do not like to be led by the nose. I played with Tammadge again, and again. I believed I could expose him as the cheat he is. He won my money, Fant Court, this house, and—you may curse me for a villain, Stephen; I have already done so!—the investments you entrusted to my care and management.

"A fool, yes," Stephen muttered under his breath. "A villain, never."

I accused Tammadge again. He had me thrown out of that accursed gaming hell. It was more than flesh and blood could stand! As though I were the Captain Sharp!

I told him to name his seconds lest he wanted to have his name blackballed at every club in town. He set some half-dozen ruffians on me with cudgels. That I might have borne, but Tammadge threatened to abduct Susan and my little girls if I said a word against him or persisted in challenging him.

I'm afraid, Stephen. I'm afraid he'll harm them whether I say anything against him or not. He is dangerous, and I am not the man to protect my family.

I have foolishly thrust them into danger. I cannot live with that knowledge. . . .

Stephen crushed the letter in his hand. William was right. He had not been the man to protect anyone against anything.

But why the devil did he think he must be dead for his brother to come and offer assistance?

"He was a very sensitive man," said Tolly, as though reading his mind. And probably he did read it. He had known the Fant boys when they were still in short coats.

"The coroner found he'd been severely beaten. It's not something the master would have borne lightly."

Stephen tasted bile. "Damn Viscount Tammadge!"

"I think you'd better leave now, Master Stephen," the butler said gently. " 'Twouldn't do if his lordship were to find out you've been here. His man of business gave strict orders not to let anyone into the house until he has taken inventory."

A nerve twitched in Stephen's cheek. "Are you the only one of the staff who came to town with my brother? What about his valet?"

"Chance left on the first instanter. The master planned to engage a new man along with the staff you would require."

"And you have entered Tammadge's employ?"

A tinge of color rose in the butler's sunken cheeks. "No, Master Stephen. As soon as his lordship's man of business has found a caretaker, I shall have to leave."

"I am sorry, Tolly. I wasn't thinking straight."

Stephen turned on his heels and marched down the hallway to the front door. His brother's death—a senseless, unnecessary death—not only touched the immediate family, but servants and tenants as well. Tolly, who must be on the shady side of seventy, would not find a new position waiting for him.

He looked over his shoulder at the frail old man. "I'll send for you when I've found lodgings."

"Thank you, Master Stephen." The butler wiped a sleeve across moist eyes. "Are you planning to stay in town, then?"

Staring at the gleaming brass of the front door handle, Stephen willed his mind to function with the cold, emotionless precision that had governed his missions into enemy territory. Pain, bitterness, and anger must be banished. Feelings, as he knew only too well, were dangerous encumbrances when a man set out to do what he must.

"I'll drive down to Sussex to convey Mrs. Fant and the girls to her parents," he had said, stepping out into the damp, chill February morning. "Then I'll come back and go after my lord Tammadge."

And he had come back to London. But instead of facing Tammadge across twelve paces on some lonely stretch of common, he had pledged himself to Sir Nathaniel Conant, the chief magistrate of the Bow Street court, who wanted to see the viscount convicted and hanged for the crime of white slavery.

He could not go back on his word. He could only do his damnedest to deliver Tammadge to the gallows, thus, at the same time, avenging his brother's death and saving Lady Maryann.

Chapter Thirteen

Maryann sat at the pretty rosewood desk in her mother's room. She was supposed to be writing invitations that afternoon for a reception given by the Earl and Countess of Rivington in honor of their daughter's marriage to Viscount Francis Tammadge. But the ink had dried on the nib of her pen, and the stack of gilt-edged cards ready for delivery was suspiciously low. Maryann did not want to send out invitations to a wedding she hoped would never take place. Just as she did not want to order champagne and ices, or be measured for a wedding gown.

It wasn't that she felt guilty spending her father's money, but she knew that her chances of being released from her promise were nil while he, or rather Mr. Winsome, was already paying the bills.

Maryann thrust back her chair and rushed to the window. She knew it offered no view of Mount Street and the carriage that might, finally, bring Stephen Farrell, but the sight of a narrow strip of garden and a brick wall was a good deal more pleasing than those dratted invitations.

Four days since she had made herself walk away from Stephen Farrell! Days of mulling over his vague promises, of trying to convince herself that he meant to help her find Tammadge's brothels after all. Days and nights of regret that she hadn't turned back to plead her case once more.

"Dearest," said Irene Rivington from the day bed nearby. "You're making yourself ill with needless fretting.

Maryann flung around. "I must do *something*, Mama! I cannot bear this sitting around and waiting."

She had told her mother enough of the exchange with Stephen Farrell to give her hope the wedding might be called off. She had not disclosed where the interview had taken place, nor had she mentioned a certain young woman in undress.

And now it looked as though Farrell had no intention of keeping his word. Four days had passed, and he had not called on her.

"You've not been sitting still." Irene removed her spectacles and gave Maryann a quizzical look. "Besides doing your best to wear down the rugs, you've spoken with Rose and with Lucy Weller."

"What good did it do? I wish I could speak to Lucy's young man. Tammadge's groom. I feel certain *he* could tell enough so that I would not need Mr. Farrell at all."

Pencil and various lists painstakingly compiled for housekeeper, caterer, florist, and wine merchant, dropped from Irene's fingers.

"Oh, but you must not approach him!" she cried. "You know what Lucy said—"

"Yes, I know. The groom is too afraid to talk." Maryann's hands clenched in frustration.

"And no wonder! Just think what happened to that other servant. One of Tammadge's footmen, I believe."

" 'Stabbed and drownded 'cause he talked too much,' " Maryann said under her breath. Those had been Lucy's words, and the little maid had shuddered with horror.

Maryann tried to tell herself that the death of a servant need not necessarily be attributed to the man's master, but she, too, felt a chill on her flesh. The man's master was her betrothed.

She regretted, however, that in her burning impatience to be doing something she had invited Lucy Weller to Mount Street and interrogated her in her mother's presence, for now Irene was suffering sleepless nights worrying about Maryann's safety.

Neither were Maryann's nights restful. Physical exhaustion alone should have guaranteed slumber, for she still attended to her self-imposed chores in Mr. Salisbury's Botanic Garden every morning, ran errands for her mother in the afternoons, and at night accompanied Bella and Lady Effingham to some party or other. But she could not sleep.

Instead, she mulled over the meeting with Stephen Farrell. In the first place, he shouldn't have been at the Fighting Cock. Messages could be left there, he had told Robert; but it looked as though he *lived* there — with a woman, who was obviously no better than she should be.

Maryann would hastily skip over that moment when the bedroom door opened. Her emotions when she saw the half-clad female, the uninhibitedly sensuous stretch, the careless intimacy of address to Farrell, were too mixed and confusing to deal with.

She had, however, Maryann acknowledged modestly, shown great presence of mind by ignoring the whole incident. She had concentrated on recovering the pride she had lost while pleading with Farrell. And it hadn't been an easy feat after his question whether Tammadge had approached her in an improper manner, which had, unfortunately, reminded her of Tammadge's lovemaking on the Effingham embankment.

Then, when Farrell spoke to her in that odious, patronizing manner, telling her something was bound to happen before the wedding, it had seemed an excellent notion to simply walk away. Silence, she had reasoned, would show him how wrong he was. A dignified exit would prove she was not a child who exaggerated her problems.

But as one day passed after another, she lost faith in her judgment. It was impossible to read Farrell's character.

At this point of her nightly ruminations, Maryann would get out of bed and start pacing. Trying to understand Farrell made her restless. He was an enigma. He spoke and—at times—acted like a gentleman born and bred. Yet he could not be a gentleman. If he were, he'd know a lady did not jilt a man because servants gossiped about him. Nor would a gentleman keep her waiting four days when he said he'd be gone a day or so only.

She'd wonder if she should ignore his orders and revisit the strange tavern in Seven Dials with its noxious downstairs and well-kept upper floor.

Or she might send the soldier. His name was Rush, and he had lost his leg at Waterloo. He had been waiting at the carriage when Maryann left the Fighting Cock and had begged for work. Using her meager pin money, she had hired him to assist Robert and the footmen in trailing Tammadge. Rush was eminently suitable as a shadow. With his peg leg and his tattered clothing, he was indistinguishable among the many unemployed ex-soldiers roaming the streets.

But Tammadge was behaving in an exemplary fashion, attending only the respectable gentlemen's clubs of St. James's, and on Friday a dinner at Carlton House, her spies had reported.

He had not called on Maryann since the day of the Crabtree rout, but Rivington had confirmed that Tammadge knew of the changed wedding date, and, in fact, declared himself delighted. Maryann did not know whether to be glad of Tammadge's neglect, or whether to add it to her other worries.

Her plan to use Farrell in the discovery of Tammadge's slum houses had come to nought, and she knew of no one else who might help her. Inexorably, the wedding day was rushing closer. On Sunday, the banns had been read the first time. Struggling against discouragement and growing panic, Maryann thought that this must be how the fox felt when the hounds closed in.

"Maryann dearest! I've been trying these past five minutes or more to get your attention."

Her mother's softly reproaching voice brought Maryann back to the present with a start. She realized that she had automatically started to prowl while she was thinking, but she did not stop now. She increased the pace.

"I am sorry, Mama. It's just that—" She broke off, searching for the right words to explain her feelings. But it didn't matter *how* she expressed herself. She just had to say it to someone.

"Mama, I feel trapped. I am frightened. I don't want to marry Tammadge. I don't think I want to marry him even if he has nothing to do with brothels or cheating young men out of their fortunes."

Caught by surprise at her own words, Maryann stopped in her tracks.

When had she decided she didn't want to marry Tammadge at all? She didn't know and had no time to worry about it, for her mother once more claimed her attention.

"Maryann, I know you don't." Irene swung her feet off the day bed. "Come and sit with me. We need to talk."

Mutely, Maryann obeyed. Her mother's words reminded her of the night of the betrothal ball. Then, she had felt a stir of disquiet lest her betrothed had cried off. Now she was in such a dither that only the news Tammadge was waiting below with a special license in his pocket could have put her in a worse state.

"I want to help you." Irene looked agitated, her face flushed.

Maryann reached for her mother's hand, patting it.

"Please, Mama. There's no need for you to worry or to do anything. It is up to me to find a solution. And I shall," she said, ebullience and youthful optimism reestablishing themselves as she spoke. "I still have two weeks. *Something* will occur to me."

"You don't understand. I'm not worried. I'm excited!" Irene lowered her voice to a whisper. "I received a letter from your grandmother this morning, and by chance or oversight—I do not care which—Mr. Winsome gave it to me unopened."

"Yes?" Intrigued, Maryann copied her mother's hushed tones. "I hope *Grossmutter* is well."

"She enclosed seven hundred pounds, Maryann! Said she was in Bad Homburg to take the baths, and some Englishman lost the money to her. She says she has no use for it."

"Gambling in the baths?"

Maryann stifled a giggle as she pictured her haughty grandmother up to the chin in a smelly sulphur bath and raking in her winnings from a floating card table.

"If it isn't just like her! Oh, I wish I might have seen it. I wish," she added wistfully, "I might visit *Grossmutter* again."

"But don't you see, Maryann? That's just what you will do. I've been thinking about it all morning, only I wasn't certain you'd agree to go."

"Mama, you cannot believe that Father would allow me to travel now."

"Of course not." Irene sounded almost impatient. "You'll take the money and go to Germany. You won't be here for the wedding, and we shan't tell your father where you are."

Maryann's look of wistfulness changed to awe. Her sweet, gentle mother suggesting an act of defiance! It was incredible.

It was ingenious.

"Do you mean it?" she asked in growing excitement. "You want me to go to Schloss Astfeld and stay with *Grossmutter?*"

Smiling, Irene nodded. "Your father won't look for you there. He'd search all England for his missing daughter, but he'd never suspect you had the means to go to Germany."

"Even if he did," said Maryann, giving the day bed a bounce, "he wouldn't come to fetch me back. He stands too much in awe of *Grossmutter.*"

"Yes, he does, doesn't he?" Irene looked pleased. "He once said a scold from her has more sting than a swarm of bees."

"Father doesn't like to be paid in his own coin. *He* likes to be the tyrant," said Maryann, not mincing matters.

"Surely you're not saying your grandmother is a tyrant? A bit strong-minded perhaps. She's such a dab of a woman — like you — but she is indomitable."

A frown appeared on Maryann's forehead and she stared with great concentration at the far wall.

"Well." Irene rose, shaking out her skirts. "Now that we have the matter settled, we had best get to work. We'll tell Hedwig. She must find out for us how to make the travel arrangements. And then there is the question of a companion for you. Jane is too young and a flibbertigibbet besides. Would you like to take Hedwig?"

"Mama, you go too fast!"

Irene was not to be stopped or slowed. "That soldier you engaged should go as well," she said briskly. "He'll be handy with a pistol, and I could be sure, at least, that you're well protected."

"An armed guard?" A gleam of amusement lit Maryann's eyes. "The war has been over for ages, Mama. No longer are bands of bloodthirsty French menacing the German countryside."

"There might be highwaymen, brigands. You never know until it is too late to do something about it. But you'll be prepared, my love."

Maryann watched her mother's glowing face. "And you? Will you come with me?"

The glow faded.

Irene stared at Maryann, but she did not see the girl. A memory she had locked away in the deep recesses of her mind pushed and prodded its way to the forefront.

Memory of the night she had tried to escape to Germany with the four older girls. The night she conceived Maryann.

Rivington had been livid with rage when he caught her and had dealt with her in a manner she could only pray to forget. He had not abused her since, but when he turned on her in anger and shouted, she became violently ill.

And she hated the nights he came to her room and demanded his husbandly rights.

She had given him five daughters. Rivington did not want daughters; he wanted an heir. Irene was aware that he had mistresses, but did not know if one or the other had borne him a son. Not that it would matter. No male offspring, unless it was a child of a legal marriage, could inherit title or the entailed estates.

"Mama, come with me," Maryann said insistently.

"No, child." Briefly, Irene closed her eyes. It was too late for her. "Much as I hate to lose you, I have to face the fact that you're grown now. Sooner or later, we must part."

"If I were to go," Maryann said slowly, "I wouldn't be able to return until I reach majority — in over two years. And even then, unless I were married, I'd still be dependent on Father."

"Elizabeth's husband might help you then. He can do nothing now, but when you're one-and-twenty . . ." Irene's voice trailed off uncertainly.

"My brother-in-law would not lift a finger for me. He needs all the money he can lay his hands on for his expensive mistresses."

Irene gave her outspoken daughter an anguished look, but did not reprimand or contradict her.

Maryann would have paid no heed in any case. She was lost in deep thought.

"It is beyond comprehension," she exclaimed suddenly, "that I should consider running away as a means to escape marriage!"

Ignoring her mother's startled face, she jumped to her feet. Posture and stride betrayed determination as she set out to pace the length and width of Irene's chamber.

"As Mr. Farrell said, Father cannot force me to marry Tammadge."

"But he will lock you into the cellars!"

Resolutely, Maryann suppressed a shudder. "If he does, I'll say no at the altar."

"Child, you don't know what you're saying. You're unwell. Please lie down and let me make a cooling compress for your head."

"I have never felt better." In passing, Maryann swept written and unwritten invitation cards off the rosewood desk.

"But why are you so upset about going to Germany? You told me you wished you could visit your grandmother. You were happy and excited when I said you should."

Maryann whirled and started back toward Irene. "Oh, indeed. But that was the coward in me. It seemed such a simple solution. I run away and — poof! — no wedding. But what you said about *Grossmutter* gave me pause. You said she's a dab of a woman like me, but indomitable."

Irene sank onto a chair. "Dearest, so are you! Indomitable. I cannot count the times your father tried to—"

"Mama, I won't run away."

There was a moment of silence, then Irene said quietly, "Rivington will not allow you to cry off."

"I shall find those brothels and gaming hells Tammadge owns. I do not need Mr. Farrell! I can do it alone, and I shall lay the proof before the Bow Street magistrate. And when Tammadge is arrested, I shall be free."

"But the scandal — if you're still betrothed at the time, the scandal will touch you, too. Your father—"

Maryann gave a short, harsh laugh. "As though there wouldn't be a scandal if I ran away. But that's beside the point. Scandal won't hurt me. And I will approach Father before I go to Bow Street with the proof. Surely, when he knows Tammadge will be exposed, he'll call the wedding off."

"Child, I don't know if I can stand it. What if your probing shows Tammadge innocent?"

Maryann hesitated. She didn't believe there was a chance of that happening. But if it did—

"I still wouldn't marry him. Don't ask why. I don't know the answer. It's another thing I must find out."

Maryann knelt at her mother's feet. "You'll stand by me? You won't let on to Father that I'm deceiving him? That I'm merely biding my time by staying betrothed?"

"Must you ask?" A spark lit in the tired gray eyes, making them mirror images of Maryann's. "I may not be as courageous as you, but I would never betray you to Rivington."

Maryann flung her arms around Irene and held her close, but before long, their embrace was interrupted by a scratch on the door.

Maryann scrambled to her feet. Face still flushed with emotion, she admitted James, the older of the footmen, whose stateliness was surpassed only by the butler's.

"Mr. Stephen Farrell to see you, Lady Maryann."

Chapter Fourteen

Confusion rendered Maryann speechless. She had been upset, angry, frustrated that Farrell hadn't called. Now she was conscious only of relief and gratitude. Surely there was no reason to feel that way since she had just decided that she did not need him.

Her mother telling James to show Mr. Farrell into the drawing room brought Maryann to her senses.

"No, James," she said firmly. "I will see Mr. Farrell in the downstairs parlor. Alone."

Shutting the door, she hurried to Irene. "Don't say it's improper, Mama! I must see him alone." She must believe that his visit meant he'd do as she had asked.

"But why? It *is* improper, and surely you need have no secrets from me."

"You worry already, and I'm afraid you may not want me to do some of the things that must be done if I want to learn the truth about Tammadge. So I'd rather you didn't hear whatever plans Mr. Farrell has made."

"Because—" Irene held Maryann's gaze. She was close to tears, but swallowed and said flatly, "Because if I forbade you to go certain places, you'd disobey me."

"I would have to."

Resigned but with a great deal of reluctance, Irene said, "Very well, child. Do what you must. I shall do my best to convince Rivington that you're out running errands for me."

"Wedding arrangements," Maryann suggested and was pleased to see a smile in return.

Blowing a kiss to her mother, she hurried off. She felt weightless, lighthearted, and her feet flew down the three long flights of stairs.

She expected to see James near the downstairs parlor in readiness to usher her in with ceremony. Instead, on her approach, he opened the front door.

"I took the liberty," he said stiffly, "of suggesting to Mr. Farrell that you preferred the outdoors, and he kindly offered to take you for a drive."

Maryann blinked. It was difficult to imagine the stately and very correct footman on his nights off sneaking after Tammadge.

"James," she said, trying to look stern. "You may safely leave worrying about the propriety of my meeting with Mr. Farrell to Mama."

"Yes, Lady Maryann. Perhaps I should explain that I was moved to change the arrangements because of Lord Tammadge's presence in the house."

"Lord Tammadge?" she echoed faintly as lightheartedness flew out the open door.

"He is with Lord Rivington in the study, and was overheard to say that he wishes to speak with you before he leaves."

"I see."

She remembered her flippant thought of Tammadge with a special license in his pocket. The feeling of lightness might be gone, but determination to escape marriage to Tammadge was as strong as ever.

She stepped past the footman. "I daresay he'll be sorry to have missed me."

"Shall I pass on your regrets, Lady Maryann?"

"By all means."

She started down the front steps. "James?"

"Yes, Lady Maryann?"

"You're a jewel of a footman. I wouldn't be surprised

if you ended up butler in Windsor Castle."

She thought she heard him chuckle, but she was approaching the familiar curricle, and weightier matters than James forgetting his dignity occupied her mind. Stephen Farrell, for instance, who watched her with a look that reminded her strongly of his displeasure at the Fighting Cock.

What reason did he have to look so dour? She had not kept *him* waiting four days.

He did not get down, but reached out a hand to help her onto the seat beside him, then drove off at once.

"Good afternoon, Mr. Farrell," Maryann said briskly. "I hope your urgent business went well."

"No." He flicked the whip above the horses' heads, urging them into a fast canter.

"Well!" Taken aback and strangely hurt by the harshly delivered monosyllable, she said tartly, "You needn't take your disappointment out on me or the horses. None of us had anything to do with your stupid business."

"I did not say or imply that you did."

She was only slightly mollified. "And you probably had a perfectly splendid time—gentlemen usually do when they are away from home—while I was kept wondering whether you'd ever call."

Some of the harshness left his face. "Lady Maryann, I went without sleep these past four days, only to realize I was sent on a wild goose chase. I raced back, bathed and changed, and went straight out to call on you. You have my sincere apology for any inconvenience I may have caused you."

She gave him a sidelong look. "What a strange business you must be in that it keeps you up day and night. If I didn't know for certain that Bonaparte is safely on St. Helena, I'd think you were still a spy."

He grinned, but it was a weak attempt. She noticed grooves along the side of his mouth that hadn't been there when she saw him last.

"Don't talk nonsense. Let us instead discuss *your* business. Do you still insist you need proof of Tammadge's nefarious activities before you can break the engagement?"

"Yes. Have you found the brothels or the gaming hell?" She noted that they were driving toward Covent Garden, the direction her groom had taken from the Strand. "Is that where you are taking me? To Seven Dials?"

"I would not take you to Seven Dials for any reason. No man, woman, or child is safe in that breeding ground of crime. Even the Bow Street runners don't venture into the district unless they absolutely must."

"Indeed."

She shifted in the seat to confront him squarely. "In that case, Mr. Farrell, it is just as well I made up my mind to proceed on my own. I have realized, you see, that I don't need you."

"No doubt you've talked your groom into being your guide."

A haughty look and an upturned nose were his answer.

He was bone weary, but making the misguided young fellow see sense was obviously another matter he'd have to take care of.

"Mr. Farrell, will you be so kind as to take me back to Mount Street?"

"No, Lady Maryann, I will not."

"What?!"

"If you had fur, you'd bristle," he said callously and quite unmoved by her look of outrage. "I suspected you might have the vapors if I refused to take you to Seven Dials. But need you confirm my fears?"

"I do not indulge in the vapors, Mr. Farrell. I am upset that *my* fears have been confirmed. You are *no* gentleman. Else you would not break a promise."

"But I am keeping my word. You may recall I never promised to help you find Tammadge's brothels. I said I'd call on you, and we'd discuss your problem if you still wanted to do so."

"I don't want to discuss anything with you," she said coldly. "Just take me back to Mount Street."

"I'm afraid that won't be possible. You see, Sir Nathaniel Conant, the Bow Street magistrate, is expecting us."

Maryann gave Farrell a scornful look. "A likely story!"

"I am devastated," he said, sounding utterly crushed. "You still don't trust me. You still believe I'd lie to you."

The reproachful tone was at odds with a teasing gleam in the dark eyes. No longer did he look fatigued, but he was once more the man who had impressed her with his vitality when she first saw him, a man who stood apart from the bored and boring gentlemen of the *ton*, a man in whom, her intuition told her, she might safely place her trust.

Once again, she felt lighthearted—as she had felt when James announced him, and she was hard put not to respond to his quizzing with a smile. This seemed to be her morning for drastic mood swings, she reflected wryly. As though she had a pendulum inside her that had gone out of whack.

But why his teasing should make her feel thus, she did not understand or question too closely. After all, a girl as inextricably entangled in the briars as she was had more pressing questions to solve.

"Come now, Mr. Farrell. Surely you don't expect me to believe you did indeed arrange a meeting with the Bow Street magistrate? What would be the purpose? And how would you have had the time? You just arrived in town—or so you said."

Taking the reins in his right hand, he held up the left as though to ward off a physical attack. "Too many questions at once. Have pity on my tired brain."

"Are you, perchance, stalling for time?"

"I should think not. Would I attempt something so foolish, so close to our goal?"

They turned into King Street just beyond the Covent Garden markets, and Maryann knew they would shortly pass the theater and arrive in Bow Street.

"Tell me quickly, then. What is the purpose of seeing the magistrate since we have nothing concrete to lay before him? I warn you, I won't be made a laughing stock or be pitied as a hysterical female."

"Sir Nathaniel won't laugh at you." Grave now, he faced her. "Lady Maryann, after your visit at the Fighting Cock, I took the liberty of discussing the matter with the magistrate."

Her eyes widened. "Without consulting me? But never mind that. If you already told him everything, why do you want me to see him now?"

"It is Sir Nathaniel who wants to see *us*. When I returned, I found his note at my lodgings. And before you ask, no, he did not say what—if anything—he discovered during my absence."

Stephen did not tell her about the second note Tolly had handed him, a command rather than an invitation, to dine with Tammadge at the Grosvenor Square mansion that night. Neither did he speak of his conviction that one or both of the notes portended the progress denied him during the wearying days and nights he had spent on the docks of Wapping.

And it was just as well he kept a guard on his tongue, for Lady Maryann, the little skeptic, questioned too much as it was.

"Sir Nathaniel knew you'd be back in town today?"

"No. While I set out to fetch you, my man went to inform the magistrate of our impending visit."

"Then that is why you so *kindly* agreed to take me for a drive." She smiled impishly. "And James, our footman, believed it was due to his skillful persuasion."

"Hmm. Did he now?"

Watching her, Stephen reflected that the expressive little face had never looked more pixyish than now. He had seen her serene and composed at social functions, and sparkle with interest when she learned of his military past; more than once he had seen her bristle with anger or turn stiff and cold with disdain; but the mischievous look was rare.

Odds were, if she ended up married to Tammadge, that look would never be seen again. Intolerable, he acknowledged. Both, her being wed to the cad, and the loss of a pixie imp.

Her expression changed to one of puzzlement. "But how could you have been so sure to find me at home? I might have been out. This is the fashionable hour for walking or driving in Hyde Park, you know."

"I am somewhat familiar with the custom," he said drily while giving his attention to the turn into Bow Street. "I drove through the park on my way to Mount Street, but my main concern was that you might be out on some foolhardy enterprise, such as exploring more of Seven Dials."

Keeping her eyes demurely lowered, she folded her hands in her lap. "I suppose I should sit at home weeping softly like a damsel in distress of the olden days?"

"I wouldn't like to see you weep, but I've no fault to find with the first part of your illustration."

"Alas," she said. "I lack the faith a damsel of old had in miraculous rescue."

He cast her a rather startled look. She seemed to be flirting with him, yet he could not credit it was her nature to do so.

"You see, I do not believe," she said, suddenly meeting his gaze, and her voice devoid of playfulness, "that a knight will charge into St. Margaret's church to carry me off in the nick of time."

Their eyes held, held no longer than the span of a heartbeat or two while the rumble and clatter of traffic, the buzz and shouts from the nearby market, receded to the very horizon of consciousness and they were alone in a deep silence. For just the span of a heartbeat.

Stephen's hands were not quite steady when he pulled up in front of the drab, gray building that housed the Bow Street courts. He could not offer himself for Lady

136

Maryann's rescue, a realization that bit deeper than it should.

He had no time to play knight in shining armor. Like revenge for William's death, Lady Maryann's predicament must take second place to his commitment to the Bow Street magistrate. Tammadge had spread a web of evil and depravity throughout the city. He must be caught, convicted, and hanged.

Tossing the reins to a scrubby boy of twelve or thirteen years, he got down from the box and reached out to assist his companion.

"How can anyone so young be so disillusioned?" he asked when she stood beside him on the flagged walk. "You should not let disenchantment with Tammadge rob you of belief in man's chivalry. You have a father and, most likely, several other male relatives. Have you no faith in them or in any man at all?"

She turned and started for the entrance of the Bow Street offices.

"I trust Rob."

"Your groom?"

Lady Maryann must have read criticism or snobbery into his astonishment, for she gave him a reproachful look over her shoulder.

"Rob has been my champion since he dragged me out of the duck pond when I was four. He is a mere two years older than I, and we grew up together in Kent."

Stephen opened the heavy door for her. He had not meant to imply the groom was unworthy of her trust; rather, the silent dismissal of her father had astounded him. It had been more damning than a negative remark.

She swept past him, her eyes bright with curiosity in her surroundings, which were quite innocuous this morning. No manacled prisoners lined the benches in the hallway and no one more alarming than Jeremy Swift, the old and far from speedy clerk, peered at them from his pigeonhole office.

"Go right on up, Mr. Farrell. He's been expectin' you and the young lady this past quarter-hour."

Stephen glanced at Lady Maryann, but if she were surprised that the old man recognized him instantly after his supposedly first and only visit to Bow Street several days ago, she did not show it. Without demur or hesitation, she accompanied him to the first floor and entered the private office of Sir Nathaniel Conant, who rose and stepped around his desk to greet her.

The busy and often impatient chief magistrate put forward his best social manner in an attempt to smother any fears or inhibitions the young lady might harbor. He courteously offered tea, which was declined, and a comfortable chair, which was accepted. Stephen had stayed near the door while Sir Nathaniel was thus occupied, and he was not surprised to see Lady Maryann needed no such bolstering of her courage.

Waiting only until Sir Nathaniel had resumed his seat behind the desk, she said, "I understand Mr. Farrell acquainted you with the rumors I heard regarding my — regarding Lord Tammadge."

"Well, now!" Bushy gray brows rose a fraction, and the hint of a smile softened the magistrate's stern features. "A lady after my own heart. Straightforward and to the point."

"Do you have proof, sir, that Lord Tammadge owns gaming hells and brothels?"

Prepared to savor the unusual interrogation in which the Bow Street magistrate would have to answer the questions, Stephen leaned against the doorjamb, a position that allowed him to observe Lady Maryann in profile and Sir Nathaniel full face.

His alert gaze on Lady Maryann, Sir Nathaniel said, "We are investigating the matter. I have assigned men to watch certain notorious houses. One in the Dials and one in Soho Court."

Lady Maryann tapped a foot. "Indeed, sir, I am very glad to hear your news. However, at the risk of seeming horridly stupid—what is the purpose of watching the houses? I should have thought you'd close them and arrest Lord Tammadge."

"First, we must watch for evidence. So far we know only that the viscount owns the properties. We have no proof that he is involved in the, ah, business conducted on the premises."

Lady Maryann's foot tapped faster.

"The business, sir, is prostitution," she said calmly while the soft apricot tones of her cheeks turned the color of peonies. "I really am the straightforward girl you complimented earlier and not such a poor, missish creature that I would blush at hearing a spade called a spade."

The case-hardened magistrate, staring at the young lady's deep pink cheeks, was momentarily at a loss for words. He could only mutter, "Admirable. Ahem, quite admirable."

Apparently unaware of her high color, Lady Maryann asked, "But when you have the proof, you will arrest Lord Tammadge?"

"At the moment I have no such intention. He'd merely pay the fine and go on as before."

Lady Maryann looked bewildered. "If you cannot or will not do anything, why did you want to see me?"

Crossing his arms on the desk top and leaning toward his visitor, the Bow Street magistrate said, "My dear, it was not to distress you or to crush your hopes that I asked you here. The fact is, I need your help. I have something which I believe you can identify."

Stephen tensed. Quickly, he crossed the short distance to the desk. When he last spoke with Sir Nathaniel, they'd had nothing, their hopes centered on what he might discover in Wapping. Apparently, the magistrate had been more fortunate than he.

"I would like you to look at this, Lady Maryann." Sir Nathaniel pulled a folded, lace-edged square of lawn from underneath some papers, flicked it open, and spread it out on the desk. "Have you ever seen the like before?"

Her eyes widened and a gasp escaped her. She had recognized it instantly. As had Stephen.

"It is one of Tammadge's handkerchiefs, is it not? The monogram, the seven oak leaves—" She stretched out a hand but pulled back before her fingers touched the cloth. "There's blood on it!"

Stephen, too, had seen the reddish brown stain. His pulse raced, as it had in Portugal and Spain when he was close to some vital bit of information.

"When was it found, sir?" he asked hoarsely.

"Three nights ago, a young female was discovered on the waterfront near Parson's Stairs. She was clubbed and, apparently, left for dead. The girl clutched this handkerchief."

"She's alive?"

"She is, but—"

"Then we can question her?"

"The girl is no longer unconscious, but she has not spoken a word. Her parents refuse to have her interrogated while she is in shock."

Stephen smacked a fist against his thigh. Bloody hell! They had finally reached a turning point in the investigation, and now they couldn't talk to the girl.

He saw that Lady Maryann stared at the handkerchief with an expression of horror and revulsion. He wanted to reach out to her, but told himself not to be a fool. Above all, he must remain aloof. Too many times had impulse led him to make a grave mistake where she was concerned. And if the set of her jaw and the kindling look of determination in her eyes were any indication of her feelings, she was in no danger of swooning.

"Lady Maryann," Sir Nathaniel said at his most persuasive. "It is imperative that I find the proof linking Viscount Tammadge to heinous crimes . . ."

Stephen slid off the desk and started pacing, lost in angry thoughts of frustration. He paid no attention to

Lady Maryann's reply or to the question she posed shortly afterward. But Sir Nathaniel's next words brought him up sharply.

"Mr. Farrell has been assisting me since February in the investigation of a white slavery organization, which, we have reason to believe, is led by your fiancé. If and when the young girl is willing to talk, I feel sure we'll have the information necessary to put the noose around my lord Tammadge's neck . . ."

Whether Lady Maryann listened to more of Sir Nathaniel's disclosures after learning that Tammadge's supposed friend worked with the Bow Street magistrate, Stephen did not know. He heard no more. His attention was focused on a pair of wide gray eyes that looked at him in utter incredulity.

Chapter Fifteen

"So you work for Bow Street." Maryann's voice was expressionless, giving no hint of the confusion in her mind, the chagrin that Farrell had deceived her. For deceit it was that he had not told her his profession when she begged him for help.

She measured him with a cool look. "You might have trusted me. I would not have given away that you are a — what *are* you? Not, I presume, a runner."

"You might say I am a Bow Street spy." His voice matched hers in flatness, but the dark eyes compelled and would not let her look away.

"Lady Maryann, you once asked me what I do now that I no longer spy for army and government. You said you could not see me in the role of a society fribble after years of danger and excitement."

"I remember."

She had called him one of the invisible heroes. But there was nothing heroic about spying on members of the *ton*. True, Rob was spying on Tammadge. But that was different. Farrell had deceived her. He had not told her who he was even after she sought him out in Seven Dials.

She felt letdown, disillusioned, and suddenly, it was not at all difficult to break the hold of his eyes, to look at the magistrate.

"You mentioned white slavery, Sir Nathaniel. How

could Tammadge be involved in the hideous practice engaged by the Barbary states?"

Sir Nathaniel leaned back in his chair. "In this case, I am not speaking of the seizure of ships and the capture of crew and passengers by Barbary pirates. The term white slavery also applies to the sale of young Englishwomen to brothels on the Continent — or in the markets of Tunis, Tripoli, and Algiers."

"Your betrothed owns three ships," Farrell interposed. "The *Venture*, the *Good Fortune*, and the *Daring Maiden*, all engaged in trade with India and China."

Maryann kept her eyes on the magistrate. "A route that does not lead past the Barbary Coast."

"Exactly." Farrell would not be ignored. He perched on a corner of the desk, disturbingly close to her.

"Unless the shipper had arranged for a special cargo to be loaded or unloaded," he said, "a vessel sailing for Calcutta or Canton would not deviate from its route and stop in Algiers."

"But Tammadge's ships do?" She glanced at him then, hurt and disappointment carefully disguised by an edge of irony. "You have seen them?"

Farrell's mouth twitched. "No doubt you think my spying better employed among the Corsairs than among the elite of English society."

"It seems to me you have not accomplished very much here in London," she said witheringly. "If you tried to catch Tammadge carrying human cargo, and failed, then you ought to have gone to Algiers to witness the unloading."

Sir Nathaniel cleared his throat. "There are reasons why I cannot send Farrell to Algiers. I shall not bore you with arguments that are mere points of law, but, you see, I have specific orders from Whitehall not to do anything that might disrupt or endanger treaties under negotiation with the deys of the three Barbary states."

"Oh." Maryann knitted her brow. "I think I understand. I remember reading — but this was some time

143

ago, during the congress in Vienna and again last fall—that an appeal was made by one of our naval commanders to stop slavery in the Barbary states."

"Admiral Sir William Sidney Smith," said Farrell. "He founded an organization, 'The Knights Liberator of the Slaves of Africa.' In September of '14, the Knights Liberator held their first meeting—in Vienna—and demanded that Castlereagh stop preaching on the subject of white slavery and take action."

"It was through Smith, who has contact with many escaped and ransomed slaves from Barbary," Sir Nathaniel interjected, "that Whitehall learned of three English vessels stopping regularly at the port of Algiers."

Maryann stared at the handkerchief spread across the desk. "The *Venture,* the *Good Fortune,* and the *Daring Maiden,*" she murmured, then met Sir Nathaniel's keen gaze. "So Whitehall charged you to look into the matter, but, at the same time, tied your hands by ordering you not to kick up a dust in Algiers."

"Precisely," said the magistrate, the hint of a smile briefly lighting the austere features.

"Do you know when you can expect the negotiations to be completed?"

"No. This is a delicate affair and, I need not add, quite secret."

"I understand, sir. But since I am one of those creatures known to delight in tattling and gossiping, you *do* need to add it."

This time, the smile lingered. "I tell you this much, young lady. Admiral Lord Exmouth has been put in charge of the Barbary affair. He sailed from Leghorn on March 4, and we've had word that he arrived in the Bay of Algiers on the first of this month. The admiral is not only empowered to negotiate new treaties with the three deys, but also to ransom British, Sicilian, and Sardinian subjects in captivity."

"An awesome responsibility. And in the meanwhile, you can do nothing but hope that Tammadge will give

144

himself away to Mr. Farrell."

"Well —" Sir Nathaniel shot a look at Farrell, but received only a shrug in return.

Tilting her head to one side, Maryann eyed the Bow Street magistrate severely. "Why," she asked, "since Mr. Farrell was at such pains to conceal his . . . profession from me, have I been told today that he is in your employ?"

"Because of this —" Sir Nathaniel flicked a finger against the lace edging of the handkerchief. "And because I hoped you might assist us in the investigation."

"Devil a bit!" Farrell said sharply. "Not if I can help it."

Maryann and Sir Nathaniel looked at him in some surprise as he pounced off the desk and, fists planted on the paper-scattered top, thrust a grim face toward the magistrate.

"For goodness sake, sir! You cannot involve the child. Telling her of the white slavery charge was risky enough, but, at least, it should convince her that she must end the —"

"As I have told you before, Mr. Farrell," Maryann interrupted coldly. "I may be small, but I am not a child. And I cannot end the betrothal until I prove to my father that Tammadge is a scoundrel."

Both men ignored her.

Farrell stared at the magistrate. "It's dangerous, dirty business! She must not be embroiled. Besides, she'd more likely prove a hindrance than a help."

"Don't be a fool," the magistrate said not unpleasantly. "It is through Tammadge's betrothed that we can learn of his engagements ahead of time. We can then assign two or three men to follow him if it seems likely he'll slip out a back door once he's safely inside his supposed destination."

"Indeed!" Maryann's breath came faster as she remembered Rush's report of Friday night. "Tammadge was at Carlton House the night the girl and the handkerchief were found. He left his carriage in The Mall at

145

seven-thirty and did not call for it until the early morning hours. But there are innumerable ways of leaving Carlton House and slipping back in unobserved. And hackneys are readily available in Warwick Street, Pall Mall, or St. James's Square."

Sir Nathaniel chuckled. "Seems to me, you've joined ranks with us already, my dear lady."

Farrell was not so reasonable in his attitude. "Spying on your betrothed?" he asked in what seemed to Maryann a decidedly nasty manner. "Perhaps you think it is more honorable than crying off—or my spying on him?"

Her face grew warm, but she would not concede the point. In fact, she decided, she'd do her best to make him pay for deceiving her about his profession.

Farrell turned to the magistrate. "Any information we need about Tammadge, I can supply. After all, I worked hard these past months to gain his confidence."

"He trusts you sufficiently to request your company in the slums and gaming hells, but will he inform you of his social engagements?"

"He asked for my support while he is 'fulfilling his duty,' as he phrased it, 'toward his dear betrothed.' "

If Farrell meant to annoy Maryann, he had failed. She did not rise to the bait.

"Sir Nathaniel," she said, "I shall do everything in my power to assist you. Please tell me what to do."

"Whenever you can, inform Farrell of Tammadge's plans."

All innocence, she widened her eyes at the magistrate. "Should I leave the message at the Fighting Cock?"

"If I catch you near the place," Farrell cut in, "I'll personally administer the spanking you so richly deserve."

"Will you? But as you said, you'll have to catch me first."

"Farrell will get in touch with you," said the magistrate, frowning impartially at them both. "Do you have a servant you can trust, Lady Maryann?"

"Yes, indeed." She ignored Farrell's thunderous brow and named her champions with aplomb. "There's Robert, my groom, then our footmen, James and Harv, and I have recently engaged Rush, a very capable old soldier."

"A veritable army of confederates. Have one of them take a list of your engagements to Farrell's lodgings in Ryder Street."

"Ryder Street! How disgustingly respectable." She observed the tightening of Farrell's jaw, and added audaciously, "However, I daresay it's all in the line of duty."

"May I be permitted to make my point?" Sir Nathaniel asked sternly and proceeded to do so without delay. "Once Farrell has your agenda, he will be able to attend the same nightly functions you do and hear your report or give you instructions from me."

"Oh, I *will*, will I?" Farrell looked even grimmer than before. "Have you considered the consequences, sir, if I am seen by someone returning from Paris, or by an old acquaintance from Sussex?"

Enjoying herself more and more, Maryann gave him a saucy look. "Outrunning your creditors? Yet you were not too frightened to attend my ball or the Crabtree rout."

"And a bloody fool I was," muttered Farrell.

He was about to say more. Whether on the subject of his being a fool or to convince the magistrate not to involve her in their schemes, Maryann could only guess, for his opportunity to voice an opinion was lost as a sudden clamor arose downstairs.

"What the deuce?" muttered Sir Nathaniel. "Can we not keep peace and order at least in the Bow Street offices?"

He looked at Maryann, who could scarcely conceal her satisfaction at having scored a number of points over Stephen Farrell.

"One more thing, my dear. If you have news and cannot get in touch with Farrell, go to my old friend

147

Samuel Crabtree. It is best that you do not come to see me again — except in a dire emergency."

Maryann nodded. Mr. Crabtree, of course! He would have introduced Farrell to his wife, who had in turn introduced him to her nephew, the Marquess of Woverley — a close friend of Tammadge.

The ruckus on the lower floor had not subsided. On the contrary, it grew louder and was coming closer. Above the clatter of high heels on the stairs, Maryann heard a strident, tantalizingly familiar voice order someone to "let go o' me, old spindly-shanks! I know he's up there, an' I promise ye, he'll be ever so glad to see me."

Maryann cast a startled, questioning look at Farrell. Beneath the tan, his face turned a dull red as light footsteps approached the magistrate's office at a run. He looked as though he would have liked to barricade the door, but before he could move, it was thrust open to reveal the young woman of undress Maryann had seen at the Fighting Cock.

"Stevie, love!" she cried, at the same time swinging her reticule at Mr. Jeremy Swift, the Bow Street clerk, who was doing his puny best to prevent her precipitate entrance.

"Tolly said ye was back, an' I couldn't wait ter see ye!"

Chapter Sixteen

Maryann felt as though the rug had been pulled from beneath her feet. *Stevie, love. Indeed!*

The flamboyant, copper-haired woman was not, of course, in dishabille this afternoon. Nothing could have been more proper than her walking dress of deep amber poplin and the long-sleeved spencer striped in amber and green. The neckline was no lower than Maryann's, nor was the cut of the gown in any way outrageous or spectacular. But, oh! What a goddess shape was displayed by this quite ordinary bit of clothing.

"Afternoon, Sir Nathaniel." The goddess blew a kiss to the magistrate, aimed another swing of her reticule at the clerk, and stepped nimbly across the threshold.

Maryann watched her walk up to Stephen Farrell and acknowledged sadly that the churning in her breast was not indignation, which would have been the right and proper reaction for a young lady of sensibility thrust a second time into the presence of Mr. Farrell's dasher.

No, Maryann admitted. She was burning with envy.

She had always been fiercely proud of her small, trim figure, of her slender arms and hands that could toil as hard as those of the brawniest gardener. But suddenly she felt scrawny; she would have suffered incarceration in the cellars if it would gain her extra inches. Not only to add to her height, but to circumference as well.

"Stephen!" The woman placed a hand on Farrell's arm. Green eyes glittered in excitement, and the smile she gave him was as generous as were her curves.

"Ye won't half believe what I've got ter tell. That viscount ye brought to the tavern a sen'night ago, well, he—"

"Meg," Farrell interrupted quietly but firmly. "Your tongue is running on like a fiddle stick. Allow me to introduce you to Lady Maryann Rivington."

While Miss Meg stood speechless—mayhap she was unused to interruptions, or she was struck dumb at the prospect of an introduction to an earl's daughter—Farrell gave Maryann a quizzing look.

His face was no longer flushed, and without a trace of embarrassment or apology, he said, "Lady Maryann, allow me to make known to you my good friend, Miss Meg Fletcher."

Maryann rose and extended her hand. "It's a pleasure, Miss Fletcher."

She should be offended, yet she was not. She was annoyed with Farrell, but could not determine the source of her irritation. It was certainly not the brazen introduction of Meg. Had he slighted the young woman or shown himself ashamed of her, Maryann would have despised him.

"Are you related to the publican of the Fighting Cock, Miss Fletcher?"

"Aye, indeed, my lady. Fletcher's me father."

Green and gray eyes met with equal curiosity and in frank appraisal of the other.

Maryann's heart sank. Contrary to what she'd heard—that ladies of easy virtue looked hagged when observed in close proximity—Miss Fletcher was beautiful. She had a flawless complexion; white teeth that might not be quite even but added a certain charm to her smile; and the hair piled artfully beneath a green silk hat was as naturally fiery and curly as Hedwig's.

Suddenly, Miss Fletcher sighed. "Lord love ye," she

said wistfully. "What I wouldn't give ter be a tiny sprite like yer ladyship!"

The artless disclosure so warmed Maryann that she smiled at Meg. Before she could speak, however, Stephen Farrell intervened.

"We must not detain you any longer, Lady Maryann. A thousand pardons that I cannot take you home personally. But Sir Nathaniel, I am sure, will put his carriage at your disposal."

"Well! Of all the—" Indignantly, Maryann turned to the magistrate. "Sir! Miss Fletcher spoke of a viscount. If, as Mr. Farrell's hasty interruption leads me to suspect, she is about to make certain disclosures about Lord Tammadge, I want to hear them."

Sir Nathaniel raised a brow and looked at Farrell.

"If it concerns Lady Maryann, I'll be happy to keep her informed of any new development," Farrell said curtly. "But it is best that she leave now. We must consider her position. And besides, it's growing late."

"Very well. Lady Maryann will understand, I'm sure."

Lady Maryann would not. A certain mulish look that would have alarmed anyone who knew her well, settled on her face. But Sir Nathaniel did not seem to notice.

With his usual air of imperturbability, he addressed the clerk still hovering in the doorway. "You will see to it, Jeremy. In fact, I think it best if you accompany the young lady to Mount Street."

Maryann was about to protest with renewed vigor when Farrell clasped her shoulders and turned her toward the door. He used no force, but the firmness of his grip doused rebellion, and she went meekly enough.

She fought an irrational desire to lean back against the shelter of his broad chest and to turn her affairs over into his capable hands.

What madness is this? she thought, shaken.

For as long as she could remember, she had resented

151

her father's right to arrange her life. She had not wanted Tammadge to be in control of her and had schemed for financial independence. And now she would consider handing the reins to Stephen Farrell? Madness!

"Where shall I find you tonight, Lady Maryann?" he asked. "Will you be at Miss Effingham's dance?"

His voice, self-assured and impatient, exercised a bracing effect. It was too late to put up a fight. Already Jeremy Swift proffered his thin arm, and she'd look a recalcitrant child if she refused his escort now.

There was nothing to be done but confirm that she would be at Bella's dance. She added, a militant spark in her eye, "And I am looking forward to seeing you there. No doubt you'll have much to tell me."

"It'll be my pleasure."

Maryann took her leave with the curtest of nods to the gentlemen and a very friendly smile for Miss Fletcher.

Stephen shut the door with unnecessary firmness. Since he had himself performed the introductions, he had no reason to feel piqued by Lady Maryann's calm acceptance of Meg. He told himself it was relief he felt, and suspicion at her docility. He had not missed the flash in her gray eyes.

"Meg, my love," he said with forced cheerfulness. "What the deuce possessed you to barge past poor old Jeremy? I could wring your neck."

Meg threw back her head and laughed. "Ye're welcome ter give it a try."

"Later, if you please," Sir Nathaniel said testily. "Let's hear the report first."

Taking the chair Lady Maryann had formerly occupied, Meg Fletcher stripped off her kid gloves and lovingly arranged the folds of her skirt.

"Ye tol' me at the tavern," she said, giving Stephen a long, thoughtful look, "that Lady Maryann's wishful of breakin' her pledge to the viscount. An' why is it, I wonder, that ye didn't want me ter talk about him while the poor wee thing was here?"

Sir Nathaniel's fingers beat a rapid tattoo on the desk top. "Just what I ask myself. But it's water under the bridge. So let's get on with the report."

Meg, however, persisted. "Eh, Stephen? Why?"

Except that he strongly felt Lady Maryann already knew too much for her own good, Stephen had no answer. He did his best to stare Meg down, following his old rule of the Peninsula, that silence is the policy of the wise.

Meg returned his look with one promising he hadn't heard the last on the subject of Lady Maryann, then turned to the magistrate.

"Sir," she said, a note of excitement sharpening her voice. "Tammadge is about ter walk into the trap. He came to the tavern Friday night, an'—"

"What time?" Stephen cut in sharply.

"Must ye shout?" Meg wrinkled her nose at him. "Fussin' and shoutin' drives the thought clean out o' me head."

"Meg, it's important," said Sir Nathaniel. "We believe that Tammadge organized the abduction of a young girl Friday night. We must know what time he appeared at the Fighting Cock."

"Well, I'd say 'twas close to Saturday mornin'. I'd just been thinkin' of puttin' up the cards an' goin' to bed when he came in. So, then, I settled down to another game, but he just sat an' watched me wi' those pale eyes o' his."

"Go on," prompted the magistrate.

She rubbed her arms as though she were cold. "Made me feel like a goose walked over me grave, it did!"

Stephen gave her a reassuring pat on the back. "I know, love. But I won't let any harm come to you, I promise. His looking at you wasn't all, though, was it?"

"Came back this mornin', he did. Invited me to sup with him an' play a game of piquet in Grosvenor

153

Square come Thursday night."

Stephen and Sir Nathaniel exchanged looks.

"Bloody hell," Stephen said softly. "Is that how he operates? From his own house?"

"We'll surround the place. He won't be able to make a move without our being aware of it. You'll be quite safe, Meg." Sir Nathaniel's voice was firm, but he looked troubled. "However, if you're frightened—"

"I'm quakin' in me boots, an' that's the truth. But," said Meg, drawing herself up, "that ain't never stopped me yet."

An image flashed through Stephen's mind of Lady Maryann in Seven Dials. She, too, had been shaking in her elegant little shoes, but it had not stopped her from entering the Fighting Cock and demanding a private room so she might speak with him.

An intrepid little thing, the Lady Maryann. Not a whit less courageous than Meg. Thank goodness convention made it impossible for them to be friends; they'd get on like a house on fire.

"Ye needn't grin!" Meg said indignantly. "Just because I said I'm scared!"

Stephen hastily begged pardon. He fetched the tinderbox from the narrow mantel shelf above an old-fashioned wood grate and busied himself lighting the lamp on Sir Nathaniel's desk.

The next few minutes were spent discussing safety measures for Thursday night when Meg would sup at Viscount Tammadge's Grosvenor Square mansion and, they suspected, would be drugged and taken to the *Venture* lying at anchor in Wapping.

Stephen paced restlessly. "The more I think about it, the less I like it. The *Venture* has been overhauled, victualed, and ready to sail since last Thursday. Pimms and Townsend swear nothing was loaded, save for the grain and tools listed on the bills of lading."

"If Pimms and Townsend swear to it, you can be sure no females were smuggled aboard before you arrived," said Sir Nathaniel. "This is not the first time they've worked for me on the docks. What about the days and nights you watched the *Venture?*"

"Oh, I let a whole troop of wenches slip by me," Stephen replied. A corner of his mouth twitched upward. "Eight to be exact. They boarded Thursday night, left at sunrise, returned Friday eve, and went ashore again shortly past midnight."

"Pinch-pricks and tar-molls." Meg was as blunt as she was contemptuous. "They always board the night afore sailin'. Some o' the lads don't get shore leave, ye see."

"The night before sailing," said Stephen. "Yes, that's what I thought, too. Yet the *Venture* lies at anchor still, and this morning all but three of the crew went ashore."

"And on Friday night, the girl was found. More dead than alive and clutching Tammadge's handkerchief." Sir Nathaniel looked at Meg. "I understand she has hair like yours. A shade or two lighter perhaps."

Again Meg rubbed her arms as though she were cold. "That's why ye picked me," she said brightly, but her smile was forced and tremulous. "Ye said yeller or red hair do fetch more 'n mousy hair on the Barbary Coast."

The magistrate nodded, but it was clear that his mind was already off the subject of hair color.

"Tammadge's ship is ready to sail," he muttered. "From Sir Sidney Smith we know that no less than half a dozen girls are put ashore in Algiers on each trip. If the young woman we found was part of a shipment, what, I ask, did Tammadge do with the others?"

Stephen stopped in his tracks. "Are you saying I could have been duped? That some of the women who boarded the *Venture* . . . ?"

For a gut-wrenching moment, it seemed entirely possible that some of the bedraggled troop of waterfront whores who had trudged aboard the frigate were girls destined to be sold into slavery.

"No," Stephen said firmly. "I could not have made

155

such a mistake. They all left. And besides, if a handful of captive females were aboard the *Venture,* Tammadge would be a fool to delay sailing just so he can nab Meg and make up his numbers."

"Beggin' yer pardons, gentlemen." Meg did not look at them but at the reddish brown stain on Tammadge's handkerchief. "What if the viscount don't want me for the Barbary Coast, but for his own pleasure? Stevie, ye said as he's fond o' the razor strap an' things like that. I'd dislike havin' welts an' cuts all over me back."

Sir Nathaniel shook his head. "He won't hurt you. Not in Grosvenor Square, where screams would alert the neighbors."

"Tammadge is totally without conscience, but he is not daft," said Stephen. "Trust me, Meg. I won't let anything happen to you."

She smiled at him. "I trust ye."

He flicked open the lid of his fob watch. "I must leave, sir. I'm bidden to dine in Grosvenor Square."

"Ah! Dare we hope Tammadge will finally offer you a cut in his deals?"

"I'll be most receptive if he does." Stephen started for the door.

"Wait." Meg gathered gloves and reticule. "If ye can spare the time, will ye drop me off in Drury Lane, Stephen?"

He raised a brow. "With pleasure. But isn't it rather early for the theater?"

Her pale skin flushed pink, a phenomenon Stephen had not been privileged to observe before.

"I like ter lie on Desdemona's bed and think o' the time when I'll be leadin' lady," she said, giving him an I-dare-you-to-laugh stare.

But Stephen had no desire to laugh. He vowed, if he ever had more than twopence to rub together, he'd see to it that Meg Fletcher had proper elocution and voice training. She deserved to be a leading lady.

As they were about to leave, Sir Nathaniel issued one

more order: they must on no account show themselves at the Bow Street offices again. It now looked as though they were close to their goal, he said. Messages or reports must be sent through Samuel Crabtree or through Fletcher at the Fighting Cock to avoid any risk of being observed.

"Cor!" said Meg when they finally emerged into the street. "I won't be half-glad when my lord Tammadge stands under the nubbin' cheat wi' the noose around his neck."

"Aye."

Stephen handed her into the curricle. His thoughts were on Lady Maryann, who would be married to Tammadge in exactly two weeks, unless the viscount obliged them by abducting Meg.

Until then, Lady Maryann would meet her fiancé in the whirl of social activities. She was not an aspiring actress like Meg, or a professional who had learned the spying business during the war. She might, unwittingly, betray what she knew.

Stephen's gut tightened. He was not thinking of the possibility that Tammadge might escape justice by fleeing the country if Lady Maryann let something slip. He wondered what Tammadge would do with a betrothed who knew too much.

It had seemed like a dashed good notion when the magistrate told her of the white slavery operation. Should have scared her sufficiently to end the betrothal right then and there. But he should have known better.

And then Sir Nathaniel must needs ask her help, thus entangling her deeper in Tammadge's web.

"Bloody hell," he muttered.

"Ye're frettin' about her, ain't ye?" observed Meg as he drove off at a spanking clip. "I could tell the way ye jumped all over her an' me when I started talkin' about the viscount."

Stephen scowled. How could he not worry about Lady Maryann when he *knew* she'd exceed the magistrate's request for information on Tammadge's social engagements? He knew as surely as if she had told him, that she would involve herself deeply in the investigation. She'd—

Oh, hell! He flicked the reins and, despite the gathering darkness, feathered the corner into Russell Street. She'd be a nuisance, a millstone around his neck, while he was trying to save her. But, by Jupiter, he would handle her.

"Stephen?" Meg gave him a sly look from beneath blackened lashes. "Why don't Lady Maryann jilt the viscount?"

His temper flared. "I'm damned if I know! Silly chit should never have been engaged to the cad in the first place."

Meg did not blink or flinch at the violence in his voice. She patted his hand, clenched tightly around the reins as he pulled up near the side entrance of the Drury Lane Theatre.

"I know what's eatin' ye. It's Othello's flaw, that green-ey'd monster, jealousy."

He glared at her. "What the devil are you talking about?"

"An' I thought 'twas me who lacks book learnin'." Meg gave a sigh. "Stephen, ain't ye ever read *Othello?* I told ye—"

"I know *Othello.* I know it's the play you're doing tonight."

"I ain't in the play exactly," said Meg, honest to a fault. "I'm a dancer between acts. For now, leastways."

"I know that, too. But I *don't* know," Stephen said through gritted teeth, "what the hell *Othello* has to do with me."

"Ye don't?" She stared at him as though he had just pronounced poor mad King George sane.

"Stevie love, it's that ye're jealous! Ye want the Lady Maryann pledged to yerself."

Chapter Seventeen

Miss Fletcher's words mocked Stephen all the way to St. James's, where he had taken chambers in Ryder Street. He tried to laugh off the audacious pronouncement, shrug it off; he even startled the ostler at the livery stables where he kept a riding hack and his curricle and pair by exclaiming suddenly, "What utter rot!"

To feel jealous, to want Lady Maryann for himself, must presuppose that he had succumbed to that mawkish malady romantics called "falling in love." Hell, he had never been a romantic, and he was as far from falling in love as Lady Maryann was from being the woman to share the life of an impoverished former spy on a patch of run-down Cornish soil.

He was a man of one-and-thirty years, a toughened soldier with more than his share of amorous entanglements behind him. Lady Maryann was a stubborn, foolish society miss of eighteen, who aroused, like no one else, a desire in his breast to box her ears or shake her until her teeth rattled.

And those, Stephen maintained, were not the sentiments of a man in love.

By the time he had walked the short distance to his lodgings, the precise, logical part of his mind, upon which he had called in vain on several occasions since making Lady Maryann's acquaintance, asserted itself with odious persistence. It coldly pointed out that his flying off the handle so easily certainly presupposed a strong emotional involvement.

Stephen could not deny that emotion was at the root of mistakes and inconsistencies he had been guilty of since first setting eyes on Lady Maryann. But that was not to be held against him. When a man went out of his way to help a lady in distress, he ought to receive in return a modicum of cooperation at the very least. Since Lady Maryann was as uncooperative as she knew how, it was no great wonder he lost his temper.

The irrefutable argument should have soothed his mind, yet he could not be easy. A deep frown slashed his brow as he entered the brick-fronted building owned by a retired gentleman's gentleman, and let himself into the ground-floor flat.

Tolly had lit the lamps in the bedroom and was brushing a midnight blue evening coat. When he saw his master, he laid down coat and brush and went to the tallboy to pour out a glass of Madeira.

"Thank you, Tolly," Stephen said with a sigh of gratitude. "You always know just what I need."

Sitting on the edge of the bed, Stephen drank deeply. Disturbing thoughts of Lady Maryann receded, but the fatigue he had held at bay all afternoon returned twofold. Swallowing a groan along with a mouthful of Madeira, Stephen let Tolly, whose many talents did not include an aptitude for valeting, assist with the removal of his Hessian boots. It was the only concession to weariness he permitted himself.

While Stephen changed his raiment, he informed the butler of the latest developments at Bow Street. "And unless the *Venture* sails before Thursday," he concluded, "I'll eat my old uniform if Tammadge hasn't picked Meg for the next shipment to Algiers."

"That's all very well," said Tolly, but I've already given the uniform away. It was faded to begin with, and when the washerwoman got through with it, the tunic had shrunk to fit a lad of ten. What I want to know is how it'll help you and Sir Nathaniel if Miss Meg finds herself taken off to the Barbary Coast."

"We'll nab Tammadge when he conveys her from Grosvenor Square to Wapping. Better yet, when he takes her aboard. Caught in the act, he'll not be able to wriggle free of the noose."

Tolly sniffed. "And if something goes wrong, and the viscount gets away, the master's death will go unavenged."

Stephen turned away and poured more wine. William had appreciated a glass of Madeira before dinner. He'd laid down quite a cellar at Fant Court. But all those dusty bottles now belonged to Tammadge. Unless Tammadge had sold the Court.

He must have sold it. If the viscount hung on to estates he'd won in crooked games of chance, word of his Greeking practices must have gotten out. In the three months Stephen had been in town, he had heard no such gossip, and he could only congratulate Tammadge on his choice of man of business who disposed of the ill-gotten assets with such discretion.

Under Tolly's reproachful eye, Stephen drained the glass. "Believe me, old chap, I do partake of your sentiments."

"You should have blown his brains out, Master Stephen. And you know it."

Stephen picked up a brush from the dresser and applied it to his hair. "Mrs. Fant, if you remember, exacted my promise to go to Bow Street. I fully intended to seek out Tammadge afterwards and issue a challenge, but what Sir Nathaniel told me changed my mind. Killing the viscount in a duel would have given me the satisfaction of knowing my brother's death avenged. But Tammadge would have died a gentleman."

He swung around, facing Tolly. "When Tammadge dies," he said, his voice as hard and cold as a blade of Toledo steel, "he shall know he dies an outcast from society."

"Aye," Tolly said heavily. "And I know I shouldn't have said what I said. You did right, Master Stephen. Even a hanging is too good for the likes of him. He should be drawn and quartered, and boiled in oil."

Stephen relaxed. "I wish I could oblige. But that fate, I believe, is reserved for traitors to the Crown."

Silence reigned while Stephen struggled with a length of starched muslin around his neck. He lowered his chin, pressing down the folds of the neckcloth, and critically surveyed the results of his efforts in the mirror. It would have to do.

"And will you be taking the curricle out?" asked Tolly, holding ready the midnight blue coat. "Or shall I be calling a hackney?"

"I'll walk. I'm so damned tired, I'd fall asleep in a carriage."

"Just so long's you don't fall asleep in Grosvenor Square and wake up with a knife between your ribs," Tolly said morosely. "You should have made your excuses for tonight. Should have told his lordship you'll dine with him tomorrow."

"Oh, stop croaking." Stephen shrugged into the coat, accepted a pair of gloves, but refused the hat presented by the butler.

In the tiny entrance hall, he paused.

"Don't wait up for me, Tolly," he said, his voice gentle. "Even if Tammadge were suspicious of me — which he's not — he'd hardly kill me under the noses of a dozen or more of his servants. He'd invite me to the Fighting Cock or some such place and have me waylaid by his chums of the cudgel."

Servants would also be an impediment to an abduction, he thought as he stepped out into the night and set off toward Grosvenor Square. And yet Tammadge had invited Meg to the house.

The air, cool and invigorating, held a promise of fog or rain. Engrossed in speculation about Tammadge's methods of abduction, Stephen walked briskly and had crossed Piccadilly and passed through Berkeley Square without being aware of his surroundings. When he reached Mount Street, however, as though drawn by some secret signal, his gaze focused on the lantern-lit front of Rivington House some little distance away.

On one of the bird-nest balconies of the first story, Lady Maryann had called him a not very skillful liar.

He stood at the curb and stared.

He remembered the moment when he first saw her, flanked by Tammadge and her parents outside the ballroom. She had been looking at Woverley; she had not seen Stephen falter in his stride.

He had caught himself instantly, but he remembered thinking that now he knew how the French felt when they were hit by Winyates's experimental rockets. He remembered frowning at her, but when he bowed over her hand and looked into those wide gray eyes, he could do nothing but respond to her smile and confess that he was *enchanté*.

He had indeed been enchanted by Lady Maryann, by her pixie face, the honey brown hair bathed in moonlight on the balcony, the quaint way she had of tilting her head, the forthrightness. . . . "I always say what I mean. Don't you, Mr. Farrell?"

His hands clenched. He had lied to himself about his feelings toward Lady Maryann. He had painstakingly convinced himself that the jolt she gave him was pure astonishment at seeing youth and innocence where he expected a sophisticate, when, in fact, a bulls-eye hit of Cupid's arrow had greatly contributed to his near stumble at Rivington House.

He had told himself that his irritation and easy anger were caused only by her stubborn refusal to heed the warnings given at great risk to his mission, when, in fact, Meg's green-ey'd monster was adding fuel to the flame of wrath.

He wanted Lady Maryann to break off the engagement. He wanted her to have *nothing* to do with Tammadge.

"Sweep, sir?"

The timid voice of a shivering urchin carrying a broom too unwieldy for a lad his size, brought Stephen to his senses.

Lady Maryann might have enchanted him with the ease of a siren, but she had not enslaved his mind. He recognized his self-deception as a defense mechanism, albeit an ineffective one.

Now that he acknowledged the true state of his feelings, he'd be better able to deal with Lady Maryann—and with himself, the fool who stood in imminent danger of falling in love with a young lady way above his touch.

Stephen tossed a coin to the crossing sweep, and, without waiting for the boy to ply his trade, strode purposefully down the short stretch of Charles Street and into Grosvenor Square.

The covers had been removed. Footmen set out glasses, a decanter of port, cigars, and a bowl of nuts on the polished oak table in Lord Tammadge's ornate dining room.

"Well now, my friend," the viscount drawled when the door closed behind the butler and his minions. "Tell me where you've been hiding yourself these past four days."

Stephen had been admiring the collection of carved jade on display in a glass-fronted cabinet. He now looked into the pale eyes that had held a strange glitter throughout dinner. He had wondered if Tammadge were a trifle bosky, but there was no mistaking the watchfulness in that unblinking stare fixed on him now.

He raised a brow. "Hiding? My dear fellow, I've been laboring to mend my fortune."

"Newmarket?"

The races in Newmarket, so blandly suggested by the

viscount, were as likely a bet to win a fortune as anything Stephen could think of.

And yet, in a gut reaction, triggered by a warning system he could not explain, but which had saved him in many a tight spot on the Peninsula, he said, "Nothing so sure, I'm afraid. 'Twas a wealthy widow that drew me to Wapping."

The pale eyes rested on Stephen a moment longer, then Tammadge selected a nut and cracked it between long, white fingers.

"My poor friend," he said softly. "When I was asked what you could possibly be doing at The Grapes in Wapping, I could only surmise the tipstaff was after you and you were forced to flee town."

"It may come to that." Nothing in Stephen's demeanor betrayed tension. He pushed his chair away from the table and crossed his long legs.

"I'm surprised I was seen," he said in tones of only the mildest interest. "I was at the inn merely to purchase a small keg of rum. The widow — a captain's widow — is inordinately fond of a glass of grog."

Tammadge slid the port decanter toward Stephen. "Then you must stand in need of a decent drink. Do I congratulate you on a successful venture?"

"I'm afraid that would be premature."

Stephen filled his glass. He could not say why he was certain Tammadge's knowledge of his whereabouts was not accidental. There had been no change of expression on the viscount's face, no flicker of embarrassment, when Stephen voiced his astonishment at having been observed. Perhaps it was Tammadge's tacit refusal to disclose the source of his information that tipped him off.

Lacing his voice liberally with scorn and impatience, he enlarged on the theme of the hypothetical captain's widow in Wapping. "Even more than a young girl with her first suitor, a widow wants to be wooed. Damn her. Time and money are investments I can ill afford, but

165

no surer bet has offered itself."

"You might have applied to me if you're short of the ready," Tammadge said casually.

"Devil a bit! I haven't sunk to sponging on my friends yet."

"And I am no saphead, easily culled."

"Then why should I apply to you?"

"I might have a business proposition."

Stephen tensed, a beast of prey ready to spring. Fatigue and weariness were forgotten in a moment of unadulterated triumph. A cut in Tammadge's deals—it was what he had aimed for these past months.

Exerting an iron control over body and mind, he waved a languid hand. "I suspect a nobleman's business deals are too long on time investment and too short on returns to suit my needs."

Tammadge took a sip of wine.

"My business is illegal," he said, watching Stephen through narrowed eyes. "The profits are more or less immediate."

"Then I'm your man."

"Mayhap you are. Indulge me by listening to a word of caution before I lay the cards on the table."

"Caution! Surely you know me better than to think I'd balk at running afoul of the law?"

"If I didn't, I would not have broached the matter. No, my warning is of a personal nature."

"Speak, then." It was not difficult to show eagerness and impatience as it would be felt by the reckless, down-at-the-heels adventurer he was in Tammadge's eyes. "The sooner you're satisfied, the sooner I can rake in the blunt."

Tammadge took his time, cracking another nut and eating it. When he finally spoke, his voice was so soft that at first Stephen heard only the hiss of menace, the hint of a threat. The words themselves took a moment to penetrate.

"Keep your distance from my betrothed, Farrell. I

believe I made it clear that I do not care to have my property tampered with."

Stephen caught his breath. He thrust back the chair, toppling it as he jumped to his feet. "No doubt, my lord, you will explain yourself."

He stared at the viscount coldly—the picture of a man whose honor was questioned. But his mind cast about furiously, searching his memory for some clue where he and Lady Maryann might have been observed other than at the Crabtree rout.

If they had been seen driving to Bow Street, he did not believe Tammadge would waste as much as a word on him before making arrangements for his disposal. The visit to the Fighting Cock? There was the peg-legged soldier who had accompanied Lady Maryann and whom she had engaged to assist her impetuous young groom. But Fletcher had made it his business to examine the soldier and had declared him sound.

"Pick up the chair, Farrell. And sit down."

A man as desperate as Stephen supposedly was, would obey that implacable voice. Gritting his teeth, he stooped, reaching for the chair back.

"Be damned to you, Tammadge!" Stephen straightened and swung around to face the viscount. "I am not your lackey to order around, and never will be. I have not made overtures to Lady Maryann. And if you suspect your precious betrothed of dallying, look to yourself for the reason. I'll not be made your scapegoat."

Tammadge's face was inscrutable. "So you believe I do not please the Lady Maryann?"

"Hell, I never said so."

Stephen pulled out another chair and resumed his place on Tammadge's right. He was in the basket for sure, and the worst part was that he couldn't begin to guess whether it'd be better to clear Lady Maryann or to feed Tammadge's suspicion in the hopes of nudging him to cry off from the engagement. Once again, he could only follow a hunch, and it warned him that

Tammadge would not release the woman he regarded as his property.

"I don't even know that she's dallying. Lady Maryann has been gracious the few times we met," Stephen said, persuasive if less than truthful. "But that's no more than I expected since you introduced me to her as your friend."

"I did introduce you, didn't I?"

Absently, Tammadge refilled the glasses. Staring at a point beyond Stephen's shoulder, he sipped his port.

As the silence between them stretched interminably, Stephen had ample opportunity to curse himself for having been too cocksure and not suspecting that he was watched; for meeting Lady Maryann at all after the betrothal ball; and for not putting his foot down when Sir Nathaniel asked her to get involved in the investigation.

Tammadge set his glass on the table. "It goes against the grain," he drawled. "But I may have been mistaken. Perhaps Lady Maryann is not interested in a dalliance."

Stephen breathed easier. Whether it had been his damnable loss of temper or his attempt at reasoning, he did not care what had swayed Tammadge, as long as it had done the trick.

"She asked a great many questions about you, though," said Tammadge.

Stephen relaxed slightly. Lady Maryann's inquisitiveness! If that was all that had raised her fiancé's suspicions . . .

"Tammadge, you flatter me if you believe her curiosity stems from personal interest. We had some slight contretemps, and she probably wondered how a man of my stamp had found *entrée* into the *ton*."

"That's it, no doubt," Tammadge said blandly. "But then Rivington insisted that the marriage must take place immediately. I couldn't help but suspect the worst."

"Immediately?" Stephen deemed it best to pretend

ignorance. "You mean by special license?"

"Rivington didn't go that far. We'll wed at St. Margaret's in two weeks."

Stephen raised his glass. "Do I congratulate you, or do I commiserate?"

This drew a twisted grin from Tammadge. "I'll let you know when I find out. Now, to business. Will you stay and listen, or had you made other plans for the remainder of the night?"

"I'll listen," said Stephen, sparing a thought for Lady Maryann, who had said politely but with a militant spark in her eye that she was looking forward to seeing him later on. "I'm not showered with invitations as you are. The only gilt-edged card I received was to a ball in honor of Miss Effingham's debut."

The pale eyes narrowed. "You're acquainted with the Effinghams?"

"I wasn't, until Woverley's aunt introduced me to Lady Effingham and her delightful daughter."

Crossing his arms, Stephen leaned back in the chair. "What's the matter, Tammadge? Everything I say puts you out of temper or on your high ropes. If you're that tetchy, perhaps we should discuss business some other time. I don't mind telling you that I'm damned tired after a four-day sojourn with the lively widow."

Tammadge relaxed. "When we've come to an agreement—and I've nary a doubt you'll be a partner before the night is over—you'll not feel tired any longer."

"A partnership requires funds. As you know, I have none."

"No capital is needed. Just your time and your commitment." Tammadge drank some wine, then said, "I meant to introduce you gradually into my affairs, but with the wedding day so close, I must right away have a partner I can trust."

Stephen did not allow himself to dwell on the fact that Tammadge's wedding day would also be Lady Maryann's.

"What must I do?"

"I have a trading agreement with the Dey of Algiers, but there may be political trouble. I need someone to supervise the sale of the next shipment and to negotiate a new agreement."

Stephen's heart pounded. "Are you saying you want me to go to Algiers? When?"

"One of my ships is ready to sail as soon as the cargo for the dey is loaded. You may have seen her in Wapping. The *Venture*."

Chapter Eighteen

In the foyer of Effingham House, liveried footmen smothered yawns behind white-gloved fingers and handed hats, cloaks, and wraps to departing guests — among whom Stephen Farrell was conspicuously absent.

Maryann cast a final look over the ladies and gentlemen still remaining in the ballroom. She was angry. Farrell had particularly asked whether he'd see her at Bella's dance, but it had obviously been a ruse so he would know how to *avoid* her. He had no intention of keeping her informed, and she was burning to know what Miss Fletcher had to say about the viscount whom Farrell had introduced to the Fighting Cock. For as surely as her name was Maryann Rivington, that viscount had to be Francis Tammadge.

Pushing aside irritation at Farrell's duplicity, she took her leave of Lady Effingham, then embraced Bella.

"What a smashing success you were," she said warmly. "You'll be the toast of the town this season."

"Yes, I was a great hit, wasn't I?" Bella said with simple pride.

She drew Maryann out of Lady Effingham's earshot. "I knew Papa was wrong to want to postpone my come-out until next year. I should have been obliged to look for a husband right away. But this year — being only seventeen and having arrived rather late in town—I may concentrate on having fun."

"Having fun is the *only* thing you ever concentrate on. I shudder to think what larks you'll kick up."

Bella's dimpled smile flashed. "There are endless possibilities. And seeing you cast dark looks at the ballroom door all night cannot help but stiffen my resolve to make the most of my time before I, too, must watch for only one man. Do you mind so very much that Lord Tammadge did not come to the ball?"

"I wasn't watching for Tammadge, you goose."

"Oh? But you cannot deny you were on the look-out for someone."

"No, I cannot."

Maryann's mouth tightened as anger surfaced once again. At Bella's puzzled look she stooped to straighten a pink bow on the skirt of her friend's ball gown.

"I was not waiting for Tammadge, I promise you," Maryann said, striving for a light note. "And neither was I waiting for a secret lover."

Bella giggled. "I know that, silly. You're not the dashing, daring type."

"I may not be any good at flirting, but that is no reason to make me sound like a milksop," said Maryann, piqued. "Not dashing or daring, indeed!"

"I wager you've never been kissed. I wager that hand kiss Lord Tammadge gave you in our garden was the most ardent pledge of affection you received from a man."

Maryann gave Bella a severe look. "And since when is it a virtue to collect kisses? Besides, I wrote you that I'm not in love with Tammadge, or he with me, and that I don't expect him to sit in my pocket."

"You'd be a ninny if you expected your stiff and proper fiancé to kiss you before you're wed. And a ninny you're not," Bella conceded. "But what about a young, handsome, passionate gentleman? What about falling in love?"

"What about it?" Maryann's tone was sharper than

172

she intended. For some reason, Stephen Farrell came to mind.

But that, she told herself, was because she had been thinking about him earlier, and because she was extremely irritated with him. He certainly did not fit the picture of a young, handsome, passionate gentleman a girl would fall in love with.

He was not as old as Tammadge, but neither could he be considered young. He was attractive in a dark, rugged sort of way, but he was not handsome. And if he were passionate, it would be to threaten her with a spanking. He'd never think of kissing her.

Not that she wanted him to . . .

"This is your second season," said Bella, looking thoughtful. "You must have met someone to catch your fancy. Someone who makes your mind spin, turns topsy-turvy your notion of right and wrong. Who makes your heart beat faster, makes you feel warm and cold and shivery when he touches you."

"Fudge!" said Maryann.

But she had not forgotten her reaction to Stephen Farrell when he wrapped his hands around her arms to march her out of the magistrate's office. She couldn't precisely say he had made her mind spin, but he had certainly made her forget that she wanted to stay and listen to Miss Fletcher. He had made her want to lean back against his broad chest.

Stephen Farrell . . .

"Maryann Rivington! I demand to know who has put you in a flutter. First you look as mad as a hornet; now you blush. And don't tell me nothing is wrong, for I shan't believe you."

Maryann glanced at her mother and Lady Effingham, who stood chatting near the entrance to the ballroom that formed the west wing of the mansion's ground floor. The musicians had stopped playing, but several guests lingered to gossip or to fortify themselves with a glass of champagne before the drive home, and it looked as though Irene had decided to keep Lady Effingham company until the last straggler departed.

Desire to confide in Bella was strong. None better than her friend, who, after all, had been caught in the gazebo at midnight with a libertine, would be able to explain why simply being close to a man befuddled a young lady's mind. And how to escape that disastrous effect.

Maryann's sisters had omitted those vital bits of information when they explained about men and women and made certain she understood the act that could get a girl in the family way. Bella might be young in years, but even at fifteen, in the seclusion of a strict boarding school, she had been wise in the ways of men. Bella would fill in the gaps.

"Bella, how does one avoid feeling tingly and shivery or having one's mind befuddled?"

Bella's blue eyes opened wide. "You *don't* avoid it, silly. Since I turned fourteen, I've been passionately in love with about a dozen gentlemen and developed a *tendre* for scores more. Believe me, I know it never lasts long. You want to enjoy those heady feelings and sensations while you may."

This was not an acceptable answer. Impatiently, Maryann said, "You make no sense whatsoever, Bella. What does love or developing a *tendre* have to do with being a little confused by a man's proximity?"

"Everything," Bella declared. "And you haven't told me yet who holds the power to confuse you."

Shaking her head, Maryann said no more. She could not possibly explain that the two men who had thrown her into something very much like a flutter and had certainly at one point or the other befuddled her mind, were her betrothed and his aggravating friend.

Now that she had learned the truth about Tammadge, however, she could not recall his touch without a shudder. And the notion of forming a *tendre* for Stephen Farrell, who only made her angry, was utterly ridiculous.

"Come with me," Bella said imperiously.

She flitted to an alcove furnished with a full length mirror and a delicate piecrust table half hidden behind pale-blue draperies. When the two girls were established behind the muffling velvet folds, Bella looked expectantly at Maryann.

"Now tell me what is wrong. Do you have doubts about marrying Lord Tammadge, or are you merely in a dither because the wedding day has been set forward?"

Maryann gave a start as she recalled that she had more pressing problems to solve than the puzzle of an irrational response to Stephen Farrell's touch.

"I am not 'merely in a dither,' " she said bleakly. "I am absolutely terrified."

She hesitated, and while she searched for words, Bella said reproachfully, "You must know I'd never betray anything you told me in confidence."

"I do know. But I cannot say very much, you see. There are things *I* have been told in confidence, and they are inextricably interwoven with my problems. I will confide to you, though, that I shall not marry Lord Tammadge."

Bella's jaw dropped. "You—you've cried off?"

"No, I haven't. Everyone," Maryann said crossly, "seems to think it is a simple matter to break off a betrothal."

"Oh, no! I never thought so. A girl branded as a jilt may never find a husband. Why, even Princess Charlotte, when she threw over the Prince of Orange, did not escape criticism. But she had the people behind her because she was opposing the Prince of Wales. And she had the excuse of having formed an attachment to Prince Leopold."

"Well, I don't have that excuse. In fact," said Maryann, her good humor restored, "I don't believe Princess Charlotte would thank me for making use of her

175

fiancé to break off my betrothal—less than two weeks before their wedding."

Bella smiled, but in a perfunctory manner. "Your mama is coming this way. I daresay she's ready to leave, and we shan't be able to talk after all. Tell me quickly! Does anyone know you won't marry Lord Tammadge?"

"Mama, of course. And—and Mr. Farrell."

Bella gaped. "Farrell! The most intriguing man in town. Why, you sly thing!"

Lady Rivington's arrival on the scene put a stop to further exchanges. Maryann could only beg Bella, as she pressed her friend's hand, not to say anything to anyone.

"I promise," said Bella. "But under the condition that you tell me *all*."

The carriage, with the coachman on the box and a footman standing to attention at the door as befitting the dignity and consequence of Lord Rivington's spouse and daughter, was waiting when Maryann and Irene stepped outside.

Harv helped Lady Rivington into the coach, but as he was about to perform the same office for Maryann, he said, "Pardon me, Lady Maryann. I believe you dropped something."

He stooped, then, with a bow and a cheeky grin, handed her a piece of folded paper. It felt stiff, like a calling card, or rather an invitation, since folded it was still too large for a calling card.

Maryann had no doubt as to who had sent it and could only be thankful for the footman's cloak-and-dagger method of passing it on. As much as possible, she wanted to keep her mother in the dark about her dealings with Stephen Farrell. She had not reported the visit to Bow Street, and did not intend to do so. If Irene heard of the white slavery investigation, she'd fret herself sick.

Throughout the ride home, Maryann fingered the

card. Futile attempts at guessing what Farrell might have to say to her rekindled irritation. In order to hand the note to Harv, Farrell had to come to the Strand or to Adelphi Terrace, where the carriages were lined up during the ball. Why the dickens didn't he walk a step farther and enter the mansion on the river to speak to her, as he had promised?

She brooded on it for a minute or so, then, without a particular effort on her part, her thoughts turned to Bella's assertion that tingling sensations and a confused wit had *everything* to do with forming a *tendre* for a gentleman. She had condemned Bella's theory as ridiculous. But — her face grew warm — it was also an intriguing one.

Unlike Bella, Maryann had never been in love. And unlike her sister Elizabeth, she had no intention of falling in love and marrying a philanderer who'd make her unhappy. But it would be a sad piece of work, she admitted, if she went through her second season without once feeling her pulse race and her heart beat faster at the sight of one particular man.

Once again, Stephen Farrell came to mind. This time, Maryann explored the thought further. It would not be impossible to form a mild *tendre* for him — if only he'd remember to treat her as a woman, not a child. Other ladies indulged in flirtation. Why not she?

It was, perhaps, fortuitous that the light in the carriage was dim and that Irene was tired and disinclined to engage in conversation, else she must have noticed that her daughter was not her usual composed self. But the carriage set them down in Mount Street, and they parted company on the third-floor landing with Irene in blissful ignorance of Maryann's state of mind.

The lamps were lit in Maryann's room. Pausing only to kick off her slippers and drop reticule and wrap onto the fourposter bed, she went straight to the dresser where she was assured of the brightest light.

As she suspected, Farrell had scribbled his message

on the back of an invitation card. Lady Effingham's invitation.

Forgive me. I am too tired to go inside and seek you out. Must speak to you, though. Do you ride? I shall exercise my horse at seven near the Serpentine — until you join me, or I'm taken up by the watch for making a nuisance of myself.

Yours, Stephen.

Stephen. Not Farrell. Not Stephen Farrell. Simply, Stephen.

He asked her forgiveness. She remembered the grooves of exhaustion on his face when they drove to Bow Street. He had been without sleep for several days and nights, he had explained. She only half-believed him then, but in view of Sir Nathaniel's disclosures she did not doubt he had gone without rest, spying for the Bow Street magistrate.

A Bow Street spy. An informer.

A ferret, a snitching-rascal, as he would be called by someone of the lower orders. Maryann did not know where she had picked up the cant expressions. They were there, firmly engraved in her mind, and she still felt letdown that he had chosen such a despised profession after serving in His Majesty's army.

However, she was no longer angry that he hadn't attended the ball. His simple admission of tiredness had doused her wrath. She was breathlessly conscious of a quickened pulse when she reread his note.

Do you ride? I shall exercise my horse at seven . . .

She looked at the clock on the mantel but could not make out the time. Picking up the slim lamp on the night stand, she stepped closer and peered anxiously at the hour hand. It was almost four o'clock.

Maryann had never encouraged her maid to wait up for her, but on this occasion she regretted that Jane was not dutifully in attendance. After a ball, she'd let her mistress sleep in until eight-thirty, and that would not do at all this morning.

Short of rousing Jane now to inform her of the

changed schedule, a measure that seemed unnecessarily cruel, Maryann decided that her best course of action was not to go to sleep at all. It did not occur to her to let Stephen Farrell wait.

She disrobed and donned a riding habit. Carrying a light, she descended on stockinged feet to the first floor where a narrow chamber, referred to as the book room, was tucked away at the back of the house.

Ordinarily, Maryann read thick tomes on botany and horticulture, or accounts of travel enjoyed by daring ladies of the past. But on this night, she went straight to the low, glass-fronted bookcase beneath the window that sheltered her mother's favorite novels. Picking a volume at random, she was about to leave when she caught a glimpse of movement in the garden below.

Turning down the wick of the lamp, she stepped aside so that she would be hidden by the drapes, then looked out the window again. Save for a bright pool of light in front of her father's sanctuary, the library, all was dark. She saw no further movement or activity pointing to the presence of an intruder.

She stood a few minutes longer, almost convinced that she had been mistaken, when she heard the buzz of voices from the direction of the library. Her father must have opened the French doors. But who could be with him at this late hour?

Curious and intrigued, Maryann extinguished the light. She unlocked the window, raised the sash a few inches, and leaned against the glass pane. Moments later, her curiosity was rewarded when she saw Mr. Winsome, the secretary, step out into the light. On his frail arm hung the obviously inebriated Marquess of Woverley, Tammadge's friend with the pig's eyes.

With some difficulty, the two men negotiated the tiny terrace, then entered the dark path leading to the back gate that opened into the mews. Maryann listened for the creak of rusty hinges, yet no sound but the subdued voices from the library penetrated the night. When Mr. Winsome returned alone, she did not suspect him of tossing the portly marquess over the wall, but concluded that the hinges had finally been oiled.

During the next half-hour, Maryann watched several gentlemen leave in more or less the same state of boskiness as displayed by the marquess. Her ear became attuned to the steady hum from below. She distinguished the call of card players, a curious rattle, like a metal ball rolling around and around, and her father's voice calling out numbers and colors.

Maryann had never played roulette, but she had heard about the game and had seen the wheel in the library. Her heart hammered in her breast. Slowly, she closed the window. As she locked the latch, her last view in the pool of light in front of the library was that of her betrothed walking toward the back gate in the company of Lieutenants Wainwright and Mablethorpe, two young men very much addicted to play, and with nothing to keep their minds off cards since the victory at Waterloo.

Tammadge had visited—with two bored, reckless young men—the one room in her father's house that more resembled a gaming hell than a private chamber. And Tammadge, Rob had said, was responsible for the financial ruin of many a young blade.

For the next two hours, while Maryann sat in her chamber waiting for the hands of the clock to show a quarter till seven, the acclaimed novel *Sense and Sensibility* lay unread in her lap.

She was conscious only of an ominous echo in her ear, that of card players making their calls and the rattle of the roulette wheel in her father's library.

Chapter Nineteen

Mist hung in the air and thick black clouds kept the morning gloomy. With Robert following at a respectful distance, Maryann rode her mare Spitfire into Hyde Park. The Serpentine was still a ways off when a horse and rider detached themselves from a stand of tall beech trees and cantered toward her.

Farrell sat the powerful roan with ease and elegance. *But, then, he would,* she thought, conscious of a racing pulse. No one who wasn't a bruising rider would join a hussar regiment.

He raised his crop in a brief salute.

"Let's exercise your mare before we talk," he said with a look at Spitfire, who sidled and pranced and did her best to justify her name in a playful manner.

Maryann consented readily. They rode for the better part of a half-hour, exchanging compliments about their mounts; comparing the countryside of Kent, where Maryann had done most of her riding, with the rugged terrain of Portugal and Spain, and that of Cornwall, where Stephen owned property near Helston; or saying nothing at all. No strain accompanied the silences, each having accepted the interlude as one of neutrality.

After a brief gallop, a forbidden and therefore double-sweet pleasure for a young lady in town, Maryann reined in.

"Thank you," she said, pushing a stray curl off her forehead. "I enjoyed this more than I can say."

"So did I." His eyes laughed at her. "We did not once come to cuffs."

"A miracle. But, then, our meeting is only just beginning."

"Indeed." The laughter fled. He dismounted and, handing the rein to Robert, came around to her side. "There is much I must tell you, and none of it is good, I fear. Shall we walk?"

Maryann looked at him, the powerful arms reaching for her. Slowly, she unhooked her knee from the pommel. She leaned toward him, placing her hands on his shoulders while he gripped her waist and plucked her from the saddle as though she weighed no more than a thistledown.

How easily he could crush her. The thought was but fleeting, for she knew no fear of him. She enjoyed his strength, the firmness of his clasp as he held her suspended, then lightly set her down. And, she realized with a sense of wonder, she did tingle where he had touched her. Despite gloves, despite the layers of fabric between his hands and her skin.

They left the horses in Robert's charge and turned down one of the footpaths sheltered from curious eyes by tall hedges and budding shrubs. Farrell did not offer his arm and they walked on opposite sides of the path, with a space between them wide enough for the portly Marquess of Woverley.

"I dined with Tammadge last night," Farrell said abruptly. "I am now his partner."

Her eyes flew to his face. "Then you can prove that he is not merely a landlord but profits from the 'business conducted on the premises' as Sir Nathaniel phrased it so politely?"

"Unfortunately, I cannot. As far as Tammadge is concerned, I am ignorant of that part of his activities."

"But if he made you a partner . . . ?"

"He is too wily to entrust any one man with information about all of his enterprises and told me only about the deals with the Dey of Algiers. Someone at Whitehall let slip word about Lord Exmouth's expedition to the Barbary Coast, and Tammadge fears the negotiations with the dey will hamper his trade."

"I hope they do," Maryann said fervently. "I hope Lord Exmouth will spoil the slave trade forever."

"So do I." His steady gaze met hers across the path. "But if everything goes well, Tammadge's part in white slavery will be at an end long before Exmouth completes his mission."

"You cannot stop him *now?* Today? Is it not sufficient that he has told you about it?"

"I'm afraid not. We must wait until Tammadge gives the order to procure a shipment of young women to Algiers. Sir Nathaniel needs concrete evidence."

Maryann shivered. How cold-blooded men were. Farrell spoke of a "shipment of young women" as though it were a shipment of grain. Did he not feel the despair those girls would feel, hear the cries they would utter?

"How is it done?" she asked, curious against her will. "It cannot be without difficulty to snatch a woman off the streets. Surely she would raise an outcry."

"Tammadge has a band of footpads in his employ," Farrell said curtly. "Cutthroats who are not to be trusted to work unsupervised since they're used to maiming or killing."

"So Tammadge put you in charge of the cutthroats?"

He grimaced in distaste. "Yes."

Maryann tapped the riding crop against her skirt. She tried to imagine the scene, one of Tammadge's thugs knocking some innocent girl senseless — and Farrell standing by.

"In the past," she said, "I've been quick to believe the worst of you, and found myself put in the wrong. I

183

won't make the mistake again. I cannot, will not, believe you'd allow, even in the line of duty, that one of the young women will be hurt."

"Not if I can help it," he replied grimly.

"How far must you carry this charade? Surely you need not take them all the way to Algiers?"

"Once they are aboard Tammadge's ship, the Bow Street runners will intercede."

They had arrived at a point where the footpath joined with one of the wide carriageways and, in one accord, they turned back into the shelter of shrubbery.

"So there's still nothing to be done but wait." Maryann hoped she didn't sound as dispirited as she felt. No matter how much Farrell learned about Tammadge and his nefarious business, it would never be sufficient to arrest her betrothed before the wedding day.

"I suppose," she said, "you will receive your orders when one of Tammadge's vessels has docked?"

There was a pause before he replied. "The *Venture* lies at anchor in Wapping now."

Maryann stood stockstill.

"You must have known this yesterday," she said accusingly.

He had continued a step or two, but now he stopped and turned to face her.

"I did. 'Twas in Wapping, watching the *Venture*, that I spent the days and nights after you came to see me at the Fighting Cock. You may remember the message Miss Fletcher delivered? It was to let me know the stevedores finished loading the regular cargo."

Maryann remembered only too well Miss Fletcher's half-clad appearance in the parlor of the Fighting Cock. She also remembered her dramatic entrance into the Bow Street office. "Stevie, love!" Meg Fletcher had cried.

With an effort, Maryann banished the beautiful Meg to some deep, dark corner at the back of her mind. Stephen Farrell's dasher was none of her concern. Tammadge was.

"You did not think I might be interested in the *Venture?*" she asked indignantly. "Or in the news that Tammadge might soon be caught? Why didn't you tell me yesterday?"

"I believe that the less you know, the better off you'll be."

"So I'm still a child in your eyes," she said bitterly. "Admit! If Sir Nathaniel hadn't made it quite clear that he wants my help, you would not be speaking to me at all."

A corner of his mouth twitched. "Would I not?"

He looked at her, and a certain light in his dark eyes told her more clearly than words that he was far from regarding her as a child.

Heart pounding, Maryann held his gaze.

For a moment longer he stood, unmoving, then closed the distance between them in two long strides. She knew something was about to happen. She also knew that a sensible young lady would retreat at this point, would run for the protection of her groom, or cry out for help, or faint.

She did none of these things. Filled with curiosity and the daring of an explorer about to chart the unknown, she suffered bravely that he crushed her to his breast and covered her mouth with his.

Now Bella can say no longer that I've never been kissed, she thought. And then she could think no more.

Caught up in the heady excitement of her first kiss, she wrapped her arms around his neck and hung on for dear life as she sank into a whirlpool of pleasurable sensations.

The touch of his hands on her back made her tremble with a strange weakness while, at the same time, her muscles tensed and her body, of its own accord, pressed closer to his. His mouth, firm yet gentle, made her head spin until she was lost to all sense of time and direction.

When he pulled away, she murmured a protest. His arms tightened around her, but he did not kiss her again.

"Maryann," he said, a sound that was half groan, half laughter, accompanying the name. "You're not a pixie. You're a witch."

Her head still spun. Blinking, she gazed up into his face. "You kiss very well. You may say I'm anything you wish as long as you don't call me *Lady* Maryann again."

His insides gave a curious twist. "Are you aware," he asked gruffly, "that I am committing the ultimate folly for a man of my age and questionable position?"

"No. What is the folly?"

"I fear I am falling head over heels in love with you."

"You . . . are?" she asked, thrown totally off balance by his words as she had not been by the kiss.

His seriousness alarmed her. If she expected him to say anything at all, it was a teasing word or two about the folly of kissing in a public park. Certainly not that he was falling in love with her.

Her brow furrowed. "I wouldn't have thought it possible. With rare exceptions, you have treated me abominably."

He disengaged her locked hands from around his neck and, shaking her gently, said, "That's because I'm worried about you."

"There's no need. I can look after myself," she said absently. Strange, that she should feel rebuffed simply because he had removed her hands from his neck.

She wished she had Bella's experience. Bella would know how to deal with a situation like this, whereas she was as flustered as a schoolgirl at her first grown-up party.

"Besides," she told him in a belated attempt to appear in control, "even if Tammadge were to find out that I no longer plan to marry him, there's nothing he can do to me."

Stephen was about to contradict her when he noticed the withdrawn look on her face.

"Maryann, did I frighten you?"

"Not with the kiss." A gleam of mischief appeared briefly in the gray eyes. "I wish we could do it again."

He resisted a powerful urge to avail himself of the invitation. "But I did frighten you?"

"Well, yes. A little, perhaps."

"By admitting that I'm falling in love with you?"

With the tip of her boot, she poked at a bit of moss growing in the path. How could she explain what she did not understand herself? She felt panicked, rushed in a direction she wasn't sure she wanted to take. And it all had come about because she'd wanted to see what would happen when he embraced her. Because she'd wanted to experience a flirtation.

"It does seem to be the pattern," she said diffidently, "that a gentleman falling in love eventually wishes to make the lady his wife. But, you see, after having made such a mull of it when I planned my future with Tammadge, I am a bit leery of facing another proposal of marriage."

"Then you have nothing to worry about," he said lightly, determined that she should never know the jab of pain it cost him and equally determined to put her at ease. "I am totally ineligible to propose to you."

"Are you?"

He took her hand and, tucking it into the crook of his arm, started walking.

"I am. Your father would boot me out the door were I foolish enough to approach him. I have no title" — Hell! At present, he didn't even have his name — "no money, no land, save for that bit of farm in Cornwall I mentioned."

She should have been relieved, and was surprised that instead, she felt a sharp stab of disappointment.

"But if you're falling in love with me, who's to say I won't reciprocate? It wouldn't be the first time," she said darkly, "that a girl conceived a passion for an ineligible man and went against her father's wishes."

"No, it wouldn't."

What an odd mixture of innocent child and shrewd little baggage she was. He could not help but be amused, yet, more than that, he was touched by her self-doubt and her attempts to hint him away without hurting his feelings.

"And neither need you fear I shall importune you with further protestations of love," he said gently. "Even if *you* could, *I* would not again forget my ineligibility."

She stopped to break off a spray of blossoms from a forsythia bush. Seemingly absorbed in a study of the golden blooms, she walked on in silence. Soon, they would reach the end of the footpath where Robert was waiting with the horses.

"Stephen, why did you tell me you're falling in love with me if you don't intend to press your suit?"

"Gad! You ask the damnedest questions." He gave her a rueful look. "And I don't have an answer, save that I've broken every rule I set myself and responded to you with emotion rather than logic since our first meeting."

"How long ago that seems," she murmured, wondering if his promise not to importune her with further protestations of love meant that he would not kiss her again.

"The longest one-and-a-half weeks of my life," he said, a hint of laughter in his voice. "You'd be horrified if you knew how many times I washed my hands of you, only to turn around and seek you out again — a glutton for punishment! Each time, you were more outrageous and stubborn than the time before."

She smiled, thinking how marvelous it was that the earlier, rather awkward episode had left them more at ease with each other than they had ever been.

"You were not exactly a pattern card of politeness,"

she reminded him. "During our very first meeting, you asked what it is about me that makes Tammadge willing to jump into parson's mousetrap."

"That rankled, did it? But you know by now that I ripped up at you because you questioned my friendship with your betrothed. Any man who is not an absolute chucklehead would know why Tammadge wants to marry you."

"Fudge," she said, reminded of Tammadge leaving her father's gambling room with Wainwright and Mablethorpe. The notion crossed her mind that her father had, perhaps, blackmailed the viscount into a proposal of marriage to his daughter.

She spied a bench hidden in a tangle of shrubbery, and drew Stephen toward it. The surface glistened with moisture, but when he removed his coat for her to sit on, she laughed, only too glad to forget about her father and Tammadge.

"Put your coat back on," she ordered, spreading her skirts on the seat. "I shan't melt from a little dew, and as you can see, I don't wear velvet and lace. My habit is made of plain cloth. It won't spoil."

His heart turned over at the sight of her pixie face beneath the curly brimmed riding hat, the gray eyes bright with amusement, the soft mouth curved in a smile.

But time was running out. He must not waste another moment on such foolish dreams as kissing her again. If he wished to convince her that she must break the betrothal and have nothing to do with Tammadge, he'd have to do so now, before the clearing skies lured other riders into the park.

He stood before her, feet planted apart, his riding crop beating a rapid tattoo against the top of one boot, his jaw set.

"Maryann, at the Bow Street office, you learned about the girl that was found, battered and beaten, clutching Tammadge's handkerchief."

"Yes," she said, her smile fading.

"What Sir Nathaniel did not tell you at the time is that he suspected she was only one of several young women destined for the Barbary Coast."

She sighed. "You did say your news wasn't good. I'm not sure I want to know what you found out."

"But you must know! You must understand how ruthless Tammadge is. You believe there's nothing he could do to you if he found out you're scheming with Sir Nathaniel and me to destroy him. But a man who abducts two young girls, daughters of respectable merchants, from their own doorstep would not hesitate to ship you to the Barbary Coast as well."

Chapter Twenty

"Two girls," Maryann said tonelessly. "Is this other girl hurt as well?"

Stephen dropped to one knee in front of her. Capturing her hands in a firm clasp, he said, "We don't know yet what happened to her. Abraham Moss, the father of the girl found near Parson's Stairs, went to Bow Street last night and reported his neighbor's daughter Leah missing. Leah Goldberg and Hannah Moss were together when Hannah was abducted."

Maryann looked at him in perplexity. "I don't understand. Why was nothing said about Leah last week? Surely her parents—"

"The Goldbergs are émigrés from Hamburg. They do not trust courts or authorities. Abraham Moss went to Sir Nathaniel against the Goldbergs' wishes, and Fletcher brought me the news early this morning."

"Has she spoken about that night, this Hannah Moss?"

"No. But from her father we learned that Hannah and her friend Leah visited a third friend for a musical evening. Their street has always been quiet and safe, and as long as they went about in pairs it was deemed unnecessary to send along a servant."

"But it was not safe."

The sun broke through the clouds, yet Maryann shivered. Stephen pulled off his gloves, removed hers, and chafed her cold fingers.

"Not on that night. Hannah and Leah left their friend's house early, before nine o'clock, because Hannah developed a headache. They were not missed until ten or ten-thirty, when the rest of the musical party went home."

Maryann was silent. *Hannah and Leah.* Hannah hurt and not speaking. Leah still missing. Somehow, knowing the two girls by name made everything worse. More personal.

She was still cold. She wished Stephen would hold her.

As though he read her mind, he let go of her hands and sat down beside her on the bench. He wrapped his arms around her.

"Thank you." She summoned a smile. "I'm not usually so missish that I succumb to emotion. But this is incredible! Sir Nathaniel knows of two girls abducted by Tammadge, and yet he does nothing!"

"He can do nothing. Only a handkerchief links Tammadge to the crimes."

"Is that not sufficient evidence?"

Stephen shook his head. "Not for a conviction and a hanging. Handkerchiefs get stolen by pickpockets or are sold by laundresses."

"But if Hannah would identify Tammadge as her abductor?"

"I wouldn't count on that to happen. Her parents, I am sure, have tried everything in their power to persuade her to speak. There is the possibility that she cannot remember; she did receive a blow to the head."

"Hanging is too good for him," Maryann said fiercely, unwittingly echoing the opinion Tolly had expressed to Stephen. "Just think! Men are sentenced to hang for snaring a rabbit, and Tammadge's fate will be no worse."

Very conscious of her as she leaned trustingly against him, Stephen broached the concern uppermost on his mind.

"Maryann, you must see that you can no longer stay betrothed to the monster."

She did not seem to have heard.

"You said the *Venture* lies at anchor in Wapping. Could Leah be aboard the ship?" she asked, settling herself more comfortably.

Stephen hesitated. He should let her go, should move to the far end of the bench; yet he could not bring himself to do it. In a moment, she'd probably recall that a proper young lady did not sit with a man's arms around her. Until then, he'd make the best of it.

"Two Bow Street runners and I watched the *Venture* like hawks," he said in a deliberately brisk tone of voice and, since she made no objection to the intimacy, stroked his thumb against her slender neck just below the ear. "No girls were taken aboard."

"What is he waiting for, then?"

"Tammadge told me when I pressed him for the *Venture*'s sailing date, that he must have a red-haired girl. And from Sir Nathaniel I know that Hannah Moss has reddish blond hair."

"And Hannah got away," Maryann murmured, nudging his hand with her chin when he ceased the caress. "But why must he have a red-haired girl?"

"Apparently, Omar Bashaw, the Dey of Algiers, finds it necessary to make occasional gifts to friends lest they start thinking of assassinating him. One of those men, very hard to please, has a weakness for red-haired women."

Maryann pondered over this. "I suppose Lord Exmouth's visit to Algiers has rattled Tammadge. He's afraid to disappoint the dey."

"I wouldn't go so far as to say he's afraid. But he definitely shows concern over the situation."

They sat in silence, Stephen trying hard to remind himself of the passing time and the increasing danger of being seen with Maryann. Nannies would soon be out to take their charges for an airing; late-night revelers would ride to clear their heads. He must leave, but he could not bear the thought of parting from her.

He had believed he'd be better able to deal with Maryann once he acknowledged his feelings for her. Now he had even admitted them to Maryann, and all he'd gained was a hopeless desire never to let go of her.

"Stephen?"

Tilting her head, Maryann peeked at him from beneath long, curling lashes. It was a look that put him instantly on the alert.

"After you sent me from the Bow Street office, what did Miss Fletcher tell you and Sir Nathaniel about the viscount you introduced to the Fighting Cock? It was Tammadge she spoke of, wasn't it?"

"Yes, it was Tammadge," he said with studied indifference. "And she merely reported that he seems to enjoy the play and the company at the tavern. Nothing to do with our present investigation."

"Miss Fletcher is in your confidence?" she asked, her casualness equal to Stephen's.

"So many questions about Meg. You had better tell me what's on your mind."

"She lives at the Fighting Cock and you did say Tammadge likes the company there. Miss Fletcher has, in case you hadn't noticed, hair the color of burnished copper." Maryann paused. "Some people would call it red."

His blood ran cold. He should have known she'd hit on the obvious.

"Oh, no, my little Miss Hypothesist!" he said, tugging at her earlobe. "That's enough of speculation and conjecture. You have something more important to do."

"And what is that?" she asked, wondering if he really did not see the potential danger to his lady friend.

Or, perhaps, he was embarrassed to speak of Meg after having kissed Maryann. Gentlemen were known to succumb to the strangest scruples.

"I want you to go home and write to Tammadge," he said. "End the betrothal."

Maryann drew away a little but did not leave the shelter of his arms.

"No, Stephen."

Her tone was quiet but contained a note of implacability that dispelled any notion he might have of coaxing her into submission.

He looked at her, incredulous. "You still insist you cannot jilt him? Or that your father would not permit you to end the betrothal?"

She did not know how her father would react if she told him his prospective son-in-law was suspected of white slavery. But it did not matter; she had no intention of putting the question to a test.

Her only concern was to see Tammadge brought to justice. She would not jeopardize this end, not by crying off while her connection with Tammadge might be of use to Sir Nathaniel or to Stephen, or by speaking to her father, who might inadvertently give the game away during the viscount's next visit to the card tables in the library.

"Maryann!" Stephen shook her. Not the gentle, teasing shake he had given her after the kiss, but a harsh demand for attention.

She met his stormy look. "It has nothing to do any longer with the right or wrong of jilting a man. If Tammadge himself offered to release me, I would refuse. I want to see him caught."

"If you still entertain foolish notions of assisting Sir Nathaniel," he said curtly, "forget them. I'll not have you involved."

Her eyes widened at the peremptory tone. In her heart, she knew it was concern for her safety that made him speak harshly, and yet she could not help but stiffen against him. It was an instinctive reaction. For too many years had she fought and defied arbitrary decisions to accept his with equanimity.

"And what right do you have to exclude me?" she asked with forced calm.

His hands dropped from her shoulders. The distance between them, although no more than two or three inches, might have been an unbridgeable chasm.

"No right at all. But a responsibility."

Maryann rose. "I take full responsibility for my actions."

Stephen sprang to his feet, fear gnawing at his insides. It didn't bear thinking of what Tammadge might do to her if he suspected that she was giving a hand in trapping him.

Stephen felt helpless, balked in his every effort to separate her from the viscount. If she were a subaltern, he'd know how to handle her. . . .

"Headstrong, spoilt, and foolhardy, that's what you are, Lady Maryann! Your father did you a great disservice by not breaking you to bridle while you were young enough to benefit from a whipping."

She blanched.

"Oh, but he tried!" she shot back. "You would have been proud of him and his methods."

Stephen recoiled as though from a physical blow. "Maryann, forgive me. I spoke in anger. Misdirected anger. And out of fear for you."

Almost as pale as Maryann, he reached for her, but she stepped back, evading him.

"No need to apologize. You couldn't know."

Her shoulders drooped. She was drained of energy, the sleepless night finally catching up. She heard horses approaching and saw with relief that Robert was bringing their mounts.

"Officers from the Horseguards be comin' across the park," Robert reported. "I thought that, mayhap, ye didn't want to be seen."

"You're quite right," Stephen confirmed, silently cursing the groom and the officers for the abominable timing. He hated to leave Maryann distressed—and without exacting her promise that she would make no move against Tammadge on her own. But he must.

He retrieved the gloves from the bench and handed a pair to Maryann.

"Tammadge is not a trusting man," he said. "I know he had me watched last week, and although I'm certain no one followed me this morning, it wouldn't do if we were seen leaving the park together."

She nodded.

Accepting the roan's bridle, Stephen mounted. He looked at Maryann. "Will you think about what I said? It will be very difficult for you to meet Tammadge and not betray what you know about him. If he should suspect—"

"I know," she said quietly. "I may be in danger. But, then, you are in the same position."

His jaw tightened. He gave her a nod, wheeled the horse around, and cantered off.

Chapter Twenty-One

"And what was that all about?" asked Robert, cupping his hands to help Maryann mount.

Tearing her eyes away from Stephen's back, she turned a frown upon the groom. It took a moment to gather her wits and to realize that the question did not refer to the ache in her breast—a hurt inflicted by Stephen's wish to see her broken to bridle mixed with a hollow feeling when he rode off. No, Robert wanted an explanation of the last exchange between her and Stephen, which must have sounded cryptic as well as ominous to the groom.

She contemplated fobbing him off with some half-truths, but decided against it. Rob might refuse to drive her where she planned to go, but it was a risk she had to take. She could not, in all conscience, keep her old friend in the dark and leave him unprepared for possible danger if they ran into Tammadge.

Maryann turned her mare in the opposite direction Stephen had taken. In as few words as possible, she explained about Hannah Moss and Leah Goldberg. She was about to disclose her suspicion that Tammadge had noticed beautiful, copper-haired Meg at the Fighting Cock, when her betrothed, on a full-blooded Arabian, rounded the shrubbery ahead and trotted toward her on the bridle path.

Her hand jerked the rein. Spitfire came to a sudden

stop, looking back at her rider in hurt and puzzled inquiry.

Maryann took no notice. Gripped by revulsion, hatred, and a deep, burning anger that filled her mind to the exclusion of all else, she saw only Tammadge—the man who filled his coffers by kidnapping young women for the Barbary Coast.

And less than two weeks ago, she had believed he would make the perfect husband for her.

"Steady now, lass," said Rob, watching her face. "Ye don't want to spook him."

Maryann briefly closed her eyes. She had only a few seconds to compose herself. Then Tammadge reached her side and drew his mount to a halt.

He bowed with exquisite grace. "I stopped in Mount Street in the hopes of catching you as you set out for the Sloane Street gardens. Imagine my surprise when I was told you were still out riding."

"Yes. Indeed," she stammered, caught by surprise herself.

This was the first morning she had spent in London without so much as a thought to spare for her plants and flowers. It was no great wonder, though, after experiencing her first kiss, a declaration of love, and learning about Hannah and Leah, all in the span of two short hours.

None of this she could disclose to Tammadge, but, clearly, *some* explanation for her unusual conduct was called for.

"I had the headache a little and hoped that a ride would help," she improvised. "Perhaps I drank too much of the champagne punch at Bella's dance. Mama and I stayed quite late."

His pale eyes rested on her. "You don't seem to have benefited from the air," he drawled. "You look as if you're about to go off in a swoon."

Her hackles rose at the inflection of sarcasm in the bored voice. She had never swooned in her life and would not start now—no matter how much his company sickened her.

"You look to be in rather queer stirrups yourself," she said, scrutinizing him in turn. His lids were puffy and red, and the mouth, always thin, had a shrunken look.

"Perhaps," she added deliberately, "late nights at the gaming tables don't agree with you?"

The thin mouth tightened.

Tammadge flicked a glance at Robert. "You! Ride ahead. I shall accompany your mistress."

Noting the groom's worried frown, Maryann smiled at him. "Please do. And remember," she said, inspired by dread that Tammadge might request her company for the whole morning, "I shall need the carriage in an hour."

It would be hard to remember an order that had never been given, but Robert was no slowtop. "I'll remember," he said. "Should I send word to Lady Rivington that ye might be late?"

"That won't be necessary, I hope. Lord Tammadge will see to it that I don't miss my appointment with Madame Blanchard. He wouldn't want me to appear at the wedding ceremony in an ill-fitted gown."

Tammadge barely waited until Robert was out of earshot. "You're too familiar with the groom," he said sharply. "But never mind that now. Tell me what your remark about late nights at the gaming tables is all about."

She nudged Spitfire into a walk. "Weren't you playing last night?" she asked innocently. "To be sure, it was very dark, but I could have sworn I saw you leave our library."

"And what do you know about gambling in your father's library?" he asked, moving his mount so close that his boot brushed against the skirt of her riding habit.

"Not much." Grimly, she pulled the mare to the

200

right, as far away from him as possible. "Only that the gentlemen playing there leave in secrecy through the garden gate. I assume they also arrive that way?"

He ignored the question. "What else have you noticed?"

"That most of the gentlemen are the worse for drink."

"Nothing else?"

She thought of the roulette wheel and the screwdriver. If it had been Tammadge beneath the table with the tool in his hand, she would have instantly suspected foul play. But her father with his inordinate pride in the Rivington name, no matter how badly he wanted to win, would not take such a risk.

"Is there else to notice?" she countered. "Now you've made me curious."

He did not reply, but fell behind to allow passage for a troop of riders closing in fast. The half-dozen young gentlemen called greetings, then turned off the path toward the Serpentine.

Maryann maintained the course to Chesterfield Gate, Tammadge once more at her side.

"Your father has always held small, private card parties in the library," he said. "But several months ago, I made him a proposition. I would assist in the setup of a proper gambling establishment—which, by the by, opened formally last week—if he could persuade his beautiful and, as I was led to believe, meek and biddable daughter to marry me."

She gave him a look of loathing, quickly hidden by lowered lashes. "You must have realized by now that I am neither meek nor biddable."

"It has been brought home to me more than once."

"If you and Father . . ." Her voice trailed as the full implication sank in. Tammadge had actually bartered for her! And her father—

But it made no sense. Only a man who wanted something very badly would think of striking a bar-

201

gain over the daughter he did not want or value in the least. She would rather have expected him to offer some reward to Tammadge for taking her off his hands.

"Tammadge, why does my father want a gaming salon? And what made me particularly desirable as a wife?"

"On top of not being biddable," he said coldly, "you are also too curious for my liking."

"Are you saying we do not suit? Do you wish to end the betrothal?"

"Not at all." The pale eyes raked over her in cool appraisal. "You are still one of the most beautiful women I have encountered in a long time. I am a collector of beauty, and it is only right that my wife should be the most exquisite piece in my collection."

She swallowed a cutting reply. "Why are you telling me all this?"

Tammadge's mouth twisted in a cynical parody of a smile. "You were not impressed with my attempts at wooing, were you, Maryann?"

Memory of his embrace drove color into her cheeks. It also made her stomach churn. She did not know what to say. She had lied about a headache, about an appointment with the dressmaker; it shouldn't be difficult to come up with one small lie about her sentiments. The truth would hardly serve her purpose.

"Don't bother making up excuses," he said, uncannily aware of her thoughts. "You wouldn't convince me."

Her hands tightened on the rein. She had come to accept, at times even to welcome Stephen's ability to read her mind. From Tammadge, it was an outrage, a violation of her spirit.

They stopped at the gate where a barouche was just about to sweep into the park. Smiling and bowing from the saddle, Tammadge doffed his hat to three giggling young ladies, their pug, and a prim, elderly chaperone as they rolled past.

The interval gave Maryann time for reflection. The truth—or some of it—might be best after all, she decided.

She led the way into Park Lane. "I don't see the need for excuses, Tammadge. Neither one of us has ever pretended that ours is a love match."

"Just so. And I believe I shall yet turn you into a biddable woman by merely presenting you with a few facts."

As once before, in the Effingham gardens, she sensed some underlying menace in the softly spoken words. Uneasy, she looked toward the corner of Mount Street—so close and yet so far away.

"Your father's roulette wheel is rigged," Tammadge said. "I also know that he cheats at cards. I caught him at it a year ago."

She stared at him. She had expected—she hardly knew what, but definitely not some fabrication about her father.

"That is ridiculous! Father would not do something so stupid as cheating. He has too much pride to expose his name to scandal."

Tammadge raised a brow and said nothing.

There was no need for words. Even as Maryann voiced her protest, she remembered that she had raised similar objections when she first heard Lucy Weller's tale about Tammadge's involvement in prostitution. She had erred then; she might be wrong now. After all, she could not claim a particular acquaintance with her father in matters that did not concern his treatment of her.

They turned into Mount Street. Several hundred yards away, Rob lounged against the wrought-iron fence running along the front of Rivington House. When he saw them, he straightened.

"Where is that insatiable curiosity of yours?" Tammadge asked silkily. "Do you not want to know why I am giving away your father's disreputable secret?"

The question, and the manner in which it was delivered, put paid to the last shred of belief in her father's integrity.

"I need not ask," she said coldly. "It's what you'll hold over my head if I prove refractory."

"Clever girl."

She kept staring at Rob lest her eyes show Tammadge the disgust and animosity flaring within her. Rob had mentioned talk in a coachmen's tavern about Tammadge's gambling. . . .

"What about *your* gaming practices, my lord? I cannot get it out of my head that William Fant was ruined by play, and that his house was in *your* possession. Did he play with you? Did *you* cheat?"

His breath hissed.

She darted a look at him and recoiled from the ugly expression on his thin face. But his voice, when he finally spoke, betrayed none of the fury and malevolence she had glimpsed.

"I bought the town house from Fant's widow," he said in the bland tone so peculiar to him. "She was in desperate straits, and the males of the Tammadge family have always indulged in fits of charity. I do my best to live up to my forebears' example."

The sale of a town house should have fetched a tidy sum for William Fant's widow, yet Maryann remembered her mother saying that the young woman and her three little girls had been left penniless and had moved into her parents' house.

"I have never regretted anything so much as showing that house to you," said Tammadge, watching her through narrowed eyes. "Will you not forget about it?"

"Yes," she said slowly. "I will forget it. Matters of greater import than a town house occupy my mind these days."

"Of course. The wedding."

She nodded. *The wedding that must not take place. That*

would not take place if Tammadge could be caught in Stephen's net.

They had reached the house, and the viscount swung down to help Maryann dismount while Robert ran to the horses' heads. She stared at Tammadge, his waiting arms, and did not want him to touch her.

Irritation darkened his face. "Come now, ma'am. If you want to be on time for your fitting, you cannot afford to dally. Madame Blanchard, I understand, attends her customers strictly by appointment."

Caught by her lie! Gritting her teeth, she unhooked her knee. Perhaps, if she closed her eyes, she could pretend it was Stephen waiting to lift her down.

She was about to slide off the mare when the Arabian grew restive. Blowing and snorting, he backed his hindquarters against Tammadge, knocking him off balance.

The viscount muttered an oath. He flung around, whacked the crop against the Arabian's flank, then, white-lipped with fury, advanced on Robert, who still held both horses' reins.

"You bloody fool!"

The leather loop of the crop bit into Robert's cheek, leaving a long, red welt.

The groom stood unmoving, but Maryann screamed in outrage. Scrambling off Spitfire, she hurled herself at Tammadge, clasping his arm with both hands.

"How dare you! Accidents happen. There's no need to lay about you with a whip."

" 'Twas no accident! He did it on purpose, I say."

Tammadge tried to shake her off, but Maryann clung tight.

"Let go! Your groom must be punished."

"Robert!" She did not look at the young man, but her voice brooked no opposition. "Take Spitfire to the stables and get the carriage ready."

"Aye, my lady."

Robert was the picture of hurt innocence as he bowed his head and led the mare away. But Maryann, alerted by the meek tone of voice, saw the triumphant gleam in her old playmate's eye and knew it had indeed been no accident that the Arabian jostled the viscount just as he was about to clasp her around the waist.

She looked at Tammadge and slowly let go of his arm.

"It was no accident," he insisted.

"Whatever it was, you had no right to chastise *my* groom."

The pale eyes, neither gray nor blue, rested on her for an uncomfortably long time.

"I must change," she murmured, turning toward the front steps of the house. "Please excuse me now."

"Wait!"

Reluctantly, she faced him once more.

"When Rivington informed me that the wedding day must be set forward, he gave as the reason your mother's increasing bouts of ill health. He said the physician recommended she retire as soon as possible to one of the quieter watering places. Is that the truth?"

She feared a telltale blush was mounting in her cheeks, but she replied steadily enough. "Of course. What other reason could he have?"

"He might be afraid you'll withdraw from the betrothal, thereby endangering the partnership he and I hold."

Maryann gave a shaky laugh. How ironic! He knew her father well enough to guess the truth.

"No, Tammadge. Neither he nor you need fear that I'll cry off. You must be suffering from nerves to even think of it."

His mouth twisted in a cynical smile. "Perhaps."

She started up the front steps. At the door she remembered that she had as yet made no effort to learn about his plans for the next few days. She turned. Tammadge stood where she had left him. Fanning himself with a lace-edged handkerchief, he was watching her.

Maryann swallowed, remembering the blood-stained handkerchief on Sir Nathaniel's desk.

"Will I see you tonight at the Merriwether soiree?"

His eyes narrowed, but he inclined his head and said politely, "If it pleases you, I'll stop awhile."

"And tomorrow at Almack's?"

"I am sorry to disappoint you. I have prior engagements for tomorrow and for Thursday night."

"Indeed."

This could only mean that Tammadge was getting ready to load the *Venture* with its infamous cargo. The cad! Afraid she'd give herself away, Maryann hurried into the house.

Chapter Twenty-Two

Prior engagements.

The words haunted Maryann while she exchanged her riding habit for a gown of sprigged muslin and a spencer. If Tammadge were getting ready to load the *Venture,* not a moment must be lost. A visit to Meg Fletcher was more urgent than she had supposed.

There was so much she must do and arrange. Meg must be warned, Tammadge's implied threat to expose her father must be dealt with. And then there was Stephen, and her strange, topsy-turvy feelings for him.

He was a Bow Street spy, imperious and overbearing. Yet, at times, he could be gentle and warm and understanding. His kiss—

But she mustn't think of the kiss now, and that he was falling in love with her. She could not deal with everything at once. One thing at a time.

She looked at her hand, then resolutely picked up the ring she had stripped off before donning her riding gauntlets and slipped it on her finger. She was beginning to hate the sight of the sapphire and the circle of pearls.

Gathering gloves and reticule, Maryann composed her thoughts to deal with the most urgent of her obligations. Since Stephen had ridiculed her suspicion that Tammadge might be interested in Meg Fletcher, or rather in her hair, it behooved Maryann to deliver a warning. And never mind that she was also driven by an overwhelming curiosity to see the beautiful woman again.

She expected to leave the house unchallenged, but as she stepped into the corridor, she saw Hedwig marching toward her from the opposite wing.

"Lady Maryann!" The accented voice had no difficulty bridging the distance. "Her ladyship's been asking for you this past half-hour."

Repressing a sigh, Maryann bypassed the stairs and accompanied the maid down the hallway. "I didn't think Mama would be up this early. What is it, Hedwig? Did she have one of her bad turns?"

"Her ladyship's in a high fidget. Woke up from a nightmare and called out for you. Unfortunately, your Jane was passing in the hallway and heard the cry. And what must that flibbertigibbet do but tell her ladyship that your bed hasn't been slept in, and you nowhere to be found!"

"I only went riding."

"You tell your mother that, and be sure to calm her down so's she can get some sleep," the gaunt German woman said sternly as she opened Lady Rivington's door.

"Maryann!" Clad in a lacy robe, a becoming cap tied under her chin, Irene swung away from the window and tripped across the room to catch her daughter in a scented embrace.

"Mama, it's all right." Maryann guided her mother to a chair. "I went for a ride in Hyde Park."

Smiling tremulously, Irene wiped her eyes. "I lost my wits. So silly of me. But, you see, the nightmare — for years I dreamed that Rivington took you girls away from me. And now it's Tammadge! I dreamed he abducted you."

More than ever, Maryann was glad she had not mentioned the white slavery operation to her mother.

She talked soothingly to Irene for a little while, then persuaded her to return to bed.

"I must go out, Mama," she said, fussing with the bed cover. "Please don't worry if I'm not home in time for luncheon."

Irene noticed for the first time that Maryann was not dressed for gardening.

"Where are you going?" she asked, alarmed.

"I plan to call on a Miss Fletcher," Maryann replied truthfully, secure in the knowledge that her mother did not know who Miss Fletcher was or where she resided. "I believe she has information that will be helpful."

"Information about Tammadge? Is Mr. Farrell going with you?"

"Information about Tammadge, yes." A tinge of pink appeared in Maryann's cheeks. "But Stephen — Mr. Farrell is not aware of my plans. Robert will drive me, and I'll take Rush."

"Maryann —" Irene faltered, her shadowed eyes searching her daughter's face anxiously. "I know I promised not to ask questions and to let you go where you must, but it was with the understanding that Mr. Farrell would accompany you."

Maryann shrugged. "Surely not when I am calling on a young woman in her own home."

"I cannot help being afraid for you. Will there ever be an end to this?"

"Yes. One way or the other, it will end." *Tammadge will be caught — or left standing at the altar.*

Maryann started for the door. Glancing over her shoulder, she asked, "Mama, if you did not have Father or me to consider, where would you want to live?"

The question disconcerted Irene. "Why do you ask? What have I said to make you think I don't wish to live in London?"

"She'd want to live in some quiet place," interposed Hedwig from the corner of the room where she was folding a stack of freshly laundered garments. "God

210

knows, this racketing about town doesn't agree with her ladyship."

"Hedwig! I can speak for myself," Irene said sharply. She raised herself off the pillows and looked at Maryann. "What made you ask, child?"

"Something Tammadge said." Maryann retraced her steps to Irene's bed. "Father gave your ill health as the reason for setting the wedding date forward. He apparently told Tammadge that the physician recommended you move to one of the quieter watering places."

Once again, Hedwig made her presence known. "And so Dr. Thorpe did. Right after Lady Augusta's marriage, he prescribed a long stay in Bath. Your mother was looking forward to it, only it never suited Lord Rivington's convenience to let her ladyship go."

This time, Irene did not bother to reprimand the maid. With an attempt at humor, she said, "I told Dr. Thorpe I'd gladly follow his advice if he knew of a prescription to launch a young lady into society without the guidance of her mother. Margaret, as you may remember, had just been presented at the Queen's Drawing Room, Emily was due to come out the following season, and you, my dear, a year later."

Maryann vaguely remembered talk of postponing Emily's and her debuts by a year, but Rivington had been against it.

"My launching is ancient history by now," Maryann murmured. An idea came to her, and a slow smile lit her face.

She blew her mother a kiss and hurried from the room. A load had been taken off her mind. Tammadge, whether he became displeased with her or saw the trap closing on him, might well, in anger, expose her father and the Greeking methods practiced in the library. Maryann felt no desire to protect Rivington; but her mother, yes.

Bath was the answer. In Bath, Irene would not totally escape scandal, but she would be spared the brunt of it. Bath had its own standards and rules, and as long as a resident complied with those, the gossips had been known to turn a cold shoulder on scandal passed down from London.

She stepped outside and found the carriage waiting. Robert, a piece of sticking plaster adorning one side of his face, stood at the open door. On the box sat Rush, a fowling piece leaning against his peg leg.

"A pretty pair you make!" Filled suddenly with a sense of rare adventure, Maryann chuckled. "We'll be stopped for highwaymen unless you hide that gun, Rush."

The soldier grinned and laid the fowling piece onto the floor boards.

"Rob, are you armed as well?"

"Aye. I've got the pistol Fletcher from the Fightin' Cock gave me." The groom shot her a wary look. "And I think I'll keep it."

"*I* don't want it," she declared loftily but with a pang of regret that she hadn't thought of taking one of her father's pistols for herself. Stephen had said repeatedly that Seven Dials was a dangerous place.

She touched the edge of the sticking plaster with a fingertip. "Does it hurt badly?"

"No more'n a bee sting."

"I would have hated it if Tammadge had touched me. Thank you, Rob."

A blush stained his freckled face. " 'Twas nothin'. Where d'ye want to go? I thought, mayhap, ye might want to drive to Wapping. So I brought Rush. But goin' armed was *his* notion."

"No, not Wapping. I just want to see Miss Fletcher as fast as you can get me to the Fighting Cock."

His sandy brows snapped together. "Ye're bammin', ain't ye?"

"No, Rob." She stepped nimbly into the carriage. "You may shut the door."

He stood motionless while the frown deepened into a scowl.

"Ye never could stay out of a scrape," he muttered, shaking his head and putting up the steps with unnecessary force. "Always have to be doin' something that'll land ye in the briars. An' what Mr. Farrell will say to this, I'm sure I don't know."

Maryann's scowl was as black as the groom's.

"Robert," she said, "I'll forgive you much, including, and not limited to, disrespectful speech. But if you ever again use Mr. Farrell's point of view to show you think me foolish, I'll never forgive you. And I'll never speak to you again."

"Ye're temptin' me. Ye wouldn't be able to wind an old coachman round yer finger the way ye do me."

Reluctantly, she acknowledged that this was indeed so.

"Just don't think it gives you the upper hand," she said, turning her nose up a little. "And if you dawdle much longer, it'll be nighttime before I get to the tavern. Surely you don't want me in Seven Dials after dark?"

"Mr. Farrell ordered me—"

"You may go to the dickens, Rob," Maryann said softly. "And take Mr. Farrell with you."

The door shut with a slam. The body of the carriage rocked as Robert swung himself onto the box. A crack of the whip, and they were off.

Maryann leaned against the squabs. Far from wishing Stephen Farrell to the devil, she wished he had not ordered her to stay out of the investigation. He might be at her side this very moment.

She discovered in herself the need to explain to him why she had agreed to marry Tammadge, and why she now wanted to play a role in bringing him to justice. Never before had she wanted to justify her actions. She had done what she thought was right, and had accepted the consequences when it turned out that

213

others—her father in particular—did not agree with her.

Stephen once said that he knew more about her than she knew about Tammadge. In a sense, he was correct since she had not then been aware of the nefarious activities in which her betrothed was engaged. But whatever Stephen had learned about her, he could have no knowledge of the need that had driven her into the betrothal.

And she was curious about him—what had compelled him to accept employment from the Bow Street magistrate, whether he had family, what the farm in Cornwall was like . . . and why he had revealed he was falling in love with her. In view of the fact that he did not intend to press his suit, it seemed an impulsive act, quite out of character.

The carriage picked up speed, and when she looked out the window, she saw that they were already in the heart of the slum area. When she had passed through the filthy streets the first time she went to the Fighting Cock, she had seen mostly children, a mangy dog or two, and the men and women lolling in drunken stupor on the steps of gin houses. This morning, the streets were crowded.

A great number of men, barefoot women, and children, huddled in groups. All were quiet, but tension, so tangible that Maryann felt it inside the carriage, hung in the air. At every corner, ten, twelve pair of eyes would turn on the vehicle. No word was spoken, but anger and hatred were unmistakable.

Uneasy, Maryann withdrew from the window. She heard the crack of Robert's whip, his shout, "Hold tight!"

She had barely clasped the strap and braced her feet against the carriage floor when the horses sprang forward in the traces, and the carriage hurtled at breakneck speed through the narrow streets. Finally, they swung into the sharp turn into the courtyard of the

Fighting Cock and came to a bone-jarring stop.

"Lass!" Robert, his cap clinging precariously to the back of his head, had the door open before the vehicle had ceased rocking. "Are ye all right?"

"I would be," she said crossly. "If you hadn't decided to imitate a mail-coach driver. Dash it, Rob! There was no need to go so fast. You nearly snapped my neck with your antics."

He grinned. "Somebody's bound to snap yer neck one o' these days. Now ye know what it'll feel like."

Very much on her dignity, she alighted from the carriage only to be greeted with a scold from Fletcher, the publican, who trundled his bulk toward her.

"Whatever can ye be thinking of, my lady? Coming back here when Mr. Farrell told ye never to visit the Dials again!"

Uncomfortably aware of Rob's I-told-you-so look, Maryann said, "I must see your daughter, Mr. Fletcher. It is very important."

"Ye could have sent for Meg. To be coming here in a crested carriage when ye must know that there's riots brewing! It's madness, it is."

"But I did not know anything was wrong. What is happening, Mr. Fletcher? Why do you think there'll be riots?"

"Price o' bread's gone up again, my lady. Third time in two weeks."

"They 'ung a bloke last month," Rush muttered darkly. "A soldier he were, like me. They 'ung him acause 'e couldn't get no work an' stole a quartern loaf. Left a wife an' a quiverful of young 'uns. There'll be more 'angin's now. Mark me word."

Maryann's mouth tightened. Hung for stealing a loaf of bread! And Tammadge would be punished no more severely for stealing human beings.

"Mr. Fletcher, will you take me to your daughter, please? It is imperative that I speak with her. She may be in great danger."

A guarded look came over the publican's round face. "In danger, eh? And maybe Meg's aware of it. But since ye're here, I suppose ye might as well step inside."

When Robert showed signs of wanting to follow Lady Maryann into the tavern, Fletcher said sharply, "Are ye daft? Can't leave the carriage and horses with only one man to guard 'em."

Rob grumbled, but the arrangement suited Maryann very well. She much preferred to speak with Miss Meg alone.

As on her previous visit, the overpowering odors of ale, food, and unwashed bodies assaulted her as soon as she stepped into the dim corridor at the back of the tavern. As before, Fletcher led the way upstairs, and soon the smell of soap and beeswax defeated the rancid odors below. Again, she was shown into the neat little parlor where she had begged Stephen for help.

Fletcher knocked on the door connecting parlor to bed chamber. "Meg!" he shouted. "Lady Maryann to see ye."

There was an indistinguishable murmur on the other side of the door, but Fletcher, apparently, was satisfied.

"Meg'll be out in a trice," he said. "I'll be sending up some breakfast for her. Would ye care for coffee, tea, or a bite to eat?"

"Yes, please. Tea and toast, or whatever is available," Maryann said gratefully. She hadn't eaten since the late supper at Bella's ball, which seemed like a month ago.

Fletcher bowed himself out, and Maryann was left to her own devices. Memories came flooding back.

"Don't you trust me?" Stephen had asked when she told Rob to guard the door through which Fletcher had just left.

She had not known then that Stephen worked for the Bow Street magistrate, but she had trusted him—

despite the look of rakishness, almost dissolution, about him.

She remembered his concern when he believed Tammadge had forced his attentions on her. Only a man of high moral fiber would feel concern.

Or a man falling in love . . .

She remembered—

The parlor door and the bedroom door opened at the same time, the one to admit a young serving girl, huffing under the weight of a laden tray; the other to admit Meg Fletcher wearing a white silk robe edged with swansdown.

Chapter Twenty-Three

As in Sir Nathaniel's office, gray eyes and green met in undisguised curiosity. Neither woman spoke but waited on the maid to set the table and leave the parlor.

"What brings you back to the Fighting Cock?" asked Miss Fletcher, enunciating as carefully as though auditioning for her first leading role. "I cannot for the life of me imagine that Stephen sent ye."

"He did not. If he knew I'm here, he'd—" *He would most likely administer the spanking he promised.*

Maryann moved her eyes from the glorious hair spilling over the swansdown trim of the robe. Her face grew warm under Miss Fletcher's inquisitive stare. As on their previous meeting, she felt inadequate, a dab of a woman beside a voluptuous goddess.

"I came to warn you against Lord Tammadge."

"That's mighty generous and courageous of you." The wide smile that had been directed at Stephen in the magistrate's office, now dazzled Maryann. "Won't ye be seated? Tea and muffins don't get any tastier when they grow cold."

Miss Fletcher, sitting down across from Maryann, lifted the large green china pot and poured out two cups. "Why d'you think I need to be warned, Lady Maryann?"

Confronted by the beautiful, self-possessed woman,

it seemed she might have come on a fool's errand. Surely Stephen had seen that Miss Fletcher would be the perfect replacement for Hannah Moss.

And if he had not? If his relationship with Meg had blinded him to matters more mundane than passion?

A stab of resentment pierced her. On the previous day, in the Bow Street office, she had been unable to determine the source of her irritation. This morning, she had no trouble at all pinpointing the cause of the angry churning in her breast.

She resented that Stephen had a relationship with Miss Fletcher at all.

It was understood, of course, and nothing to be frowned upon, that a man would have a high flier in his keeping, at least until he married. Most men did, and not all gave up their inamoratas when they took a wife.

But Maryann most definitely did not want Stephen to be like other men.

She became aware of Miss Fletcher's intent scrutiny. It seemed to her that the green eyes held a gleam of understanding and, perhaps, amusement.

Maryann's chin went up. She had come all this way into Seven Dials to warn Stephen's dasher, and warn her she would.

"Do you know about Hannah Moss, Miss Fletcher? And about Leah Goldberg?"

"I do."

"Did Stephen — did Mr. Farrell tell you that Hannah has hair like yours?"

"Yes." Meg selected a muffin and passed the plate to Maryann. "Have one. Cook bakes 'em specially for me every morning."

Maryann watched Meg bite into the muffin and chew with an enjoyment that, to her, seemed out of place considering the topic of conversation and the general awkwardness attached to the situation. Her stomach, however, was of a different mind, and, after a slight tussle with her sense of propriety, she tugged off her gloves and helped herself to a muffin.

"Stephen—Mr. Farrell—" She broke off, annoyed that, for the second time, she had corrected herself. Nothing could make it more obvious that she had a rather intimate relationship with him herself than this constant stumbling over the use of his name.

"Stephen will do," said Miss Fletcher, and this time there was no mistaking her amusement. "And drop the Miss Fletcher, if you please? I'd be more comfortable with Meg."

Maryann doubted that Miss Fletcher had experienced a single *un*comfortable moment but agreed to call her Meg on the condition that her title be dropped as well.

"Knew ye was a right 'un," Meg said approvingly, the broadening of her speech indicating that now she was indeed at ease. She gave Maryann another of her generous smiles. "Meg Fletcher ter call an earl's daughter by her given name! Who'd believe it?"

"Meg, listen to me." Determined to keep her mind on the purpose of her visit, Maryann pushed aside the plate with the half-eaten muffin. "Stephen told me that Tammadge is merely waiting to capture another red-haired woman before he'll send his ship, the *Venture*, to the Barbary Coast."

Meg nodded and spread jam on a piece of toast.

Folding her arms on the table edge, Maryann leaned forward. "Tammadge has seen you here, and *he* told me he could not give me his escort tomorrow night and on Thursday because he has other engagements. I don't believe he has engagements at all. I believe he is planning to abduct you!"

Pouring more tea, Meg said cheerfully, "Aye. He'll try ter put me aboard the *Venture* on Thursday night."

Maryann had the oddest feeling, as though she stood once more in the gondola of the hot air balloon in which she had stowed away some years ago. After soaring high for many miles, the balloon had dropped suddenly. Just a few feet and, the aeronaut said, for no rhyme or reason that he could see. Maryann's stomach had flipped and she had been unable to breathe during those few seconds when it seemed the floor had dropped away beneath her feet.

She had that same breathless, hollow feeling now. Her thoughts awhirl, she stared at Meg. If Meg was convinced she'd be abducted on Thursday, then Stephen must have known about it this morning. But he had laughed when she pointed out that Meg might be in danger.

"What a fool I am," she said slowly. "Why do I always think the best of him? Why do I never want to believe that he would deliberately mislead me?"

Meg did not make the mistake of assuming "he" referred to Maryann's betrothed. She watched the young girl for a moment, then, with a small pang of regret for the wasted food, she, too, pushed away her plate. Reaching across the table, she touched Maryann's hand in a brief gesture of understanding.

"Stephen's in love with ye," she said simply.

"He told you?" Maryann asked, incredulous. She wondered why, after the many startling discoveries she had made about Stephen Farrell, she should still be surprised by anything he did or said.

"Stephen told me nothin'," said Meg. "It's me who had ter point him in the right direction. He's head over heels, but couldn't see it for frettin' about ye. You drive him near out o' his mind with yer stubborn refusal to send the viscount to the devil."

"Don't you mind? After all, you are—"

"Mind? Not a bit. I can see ye're just the lass to lead him a merry chase."

Chuckling, Meg Fletcher pushed back her chair and rose. The loose sleeves of the robe fell back as she stretched languorously. Her movements were fluid and graceful, and as on previous encounters with Meg,

Maryann felt a sharp stab of envy.

Painfully aware of her inexperience in dealing with a man's mistress, Maryann got up and started pacing. She had no desire to lead Stephen a merry chase; she felt put upon, out-of-reason cross. It was not jealousy, of course, for she was not in love with him. Besides, she liked Meg and felt that Stephen used her badly.

Calling her muddled thoughts to order, Maryann concentrated on Meg's assertion that Thursday was the day of the abduction.

"How can you be so certain that Tammadge will strike on Thursday?" she asked.

She stopped in her tracks as a dreadful suspicion gnawed at her. "Stephen planned it all, didn't he? He is using you to bait a trap for Tammadge."

Meg gave her a quizzical look. "Baitin' the trap, that's what Sir Nathaniel pays me for."

"Sir Nathaniel? But aren't you Stephen's—"

"Stephen's what?" Meg knitted her brows. "His lover? Is that what ye think?"

Meg's "Stevie, love!" was indelibly etched in Maryann's mind. "Aren't you?"

"Lord love ye! And I thought ye was bein' bashful on account of yer own feelin's for Stephen."

"My own feelings don't enter into it," Maryann said stiffly. "In fact, I don't have any."

Again, she was aware of a gleam of amusement in the green eyes, but Meg, if she held a different opinion, did not say so.

"Mind," she said, smiling softly. "I wouldn't have said no if Stephen had asked. Dashin' he is, and a real gentleman."

Maryann agreed absently. She seemed to have lost her grip on reality. Everything she had taken for fact turned out to be an illusion.

Tammadge was not the solid, upright peer she had chosen as the man to release her from her father's tyranny—or to give her the freedom she craved. He was a depraved monster, one who would lock her away on his Northumberland estate the way he locked away his priceless Oriental treasures.

Her father's pride in the Rivington name, which she had accepted as his one redeeming quality, was an illusion. His name and position could mean nothing to him if he was willing to sacrifice them to dishonorable gambling practices.

Meg, whom she had taken for Stephen's mistress, turned out to be, like Stephen, in the Bow Street magistrate's employ.

And Stephen himself—well, he was never who or what she expected him to be.

Slowly, Maryann sank onto the settle along one of the walls. Questions burned on the tip of her tongue, but she was reluctant to ask them lest she make even more of a fool of herself than she had already done.

In a whisper of silk and a gentle flutter of swansdown, Meg sat down beside her.

"Listen, dearie," she said. "I'm not Stephen's lover, nor have never been."

"I believe you." Recalling that only someone in love with Stephen Farrell would show gratitude, Maryann added hastily, "But it really makes no odds to me. I am more interested in knowing how you got involved with the Bow Street magistrate."

"Nothin' wonderful about that. I've known Sir Nathaniel since he took office in '13. Me father's a Bow Street runner, ye see."

Another illusion dispelled. Maryann was becoming inured to surprising revelations. She hardly raised a brow.

"Pa bought the Fightin' Cock as surety for his old age, but the ol' tavern has come in handy many a time. When Sir Nathaniel assigned him to the Tammadge case an' wanted my help as well, we moved in here. We kept the downstairs as grimy as any tavern in Seven Dials, an' that's where I have a small card room. When I'm finished at the Drury Lane Theatre, I come here to play. You'd be surprised to see how many gentlemen go slummin', and I'm a devilish sharp player."

"A *sharp* player? Does that mean what I think it means?"

Meg tried unsuccessfully to look indignant. "Well, I don't pink the cards," she said, chuckling. "But I'm not above usin' a trick or two if it suits me purpose."

"But you wouldn't live in the squalor downstairs," said Maryann with a glance at the silk robe of pristine white.

Meg's face clouded. "Nay. I hope never ter live in filth again. An' besides, we was hopin' Tammadge would find the tavern. He has a reputation for slummin', and I was supposed ter ask him upstairs for a private game. But he never showed. Not until Stephen brought him. 'Twas a lucky day when Stephen came to Sir Nathaniel's office." Meg nodded in emphasis. "A lucky day."

"Then it was coincidence that you and Hannah Moss have the same color hair?"

"Co-in-ci-dence," repeated Meg, savoring the word. "Well, it were and it weren't. Sir Nathaniel was told, ye see, that yeller or red hair be most appreciated on the Barbary Coast."

Maryann was silenced by Meg's matter-of-fact acceptance of the danger waiting for her.

She gripped Meg's hand. "And on Thursday? What will happen then?"

"Tammadge asked me ter play a game o' piquet and ter sup with him at his house."

"It was not Stephen's idea?"

"Nay."

Maryann breathed easier. Not that it mattered in the end who had set that particular trap. Stephen was involved and Meg was still the decoy. But at least he had not, in cold blood, sent her into the monster's lair.

Meg's next words, however, put an abrupt end to relief.

"Stephen will be there to protect me. He'll be outside with the runners, waitin' ter follow Tammadge and me to the *Venture*."

"No, he won't! He'll be out with Tammadge's thugs."

"Ah, well. The runners will be there," Meg said philosophically. "I'm glad Stephen finally got the viscount ter trust him. He's been waitin' ever so long."

Maryann set no great store in the presence of Bow Street runners. Be they ever so capable, they could not provide the same measure of protection Stephen's presence would.

If only Hannah Moss would speak up. There'd be no reason for Meg to risk captivity, no reason for Stephen to accompany a band of cutthroats while they kidnapped innocent young women. . . .

"Meg, where does Hannah Moss live?"

"I don't know." A speculative look crossed Meg's face. "I could find out. Me father should know."

"Please ask him."

A restless energy filled Maryann. She jumped up and started pacing while Meg glided gracefully from the room.

It did not take Meg long to get the information from Fletcher, but to Maryann it seemed like hours before the young woman returned with an address just off the Charterhouse Gardens.

"Let me put on a gown," said Meg. "I'll go with ye. It ain't safe for a lady to drive through the Dials district. Especially today."

"If it's not safe for me, it's not safe for you either."

Meg's throaty chuckle filled the room. "No matter what fancy clothes I wear, I'll never be mistaken for a lady. Besides, they all know me an' Pa. They know there's always a bowl o' soup an' a crust o' bread for 'em at the Fightin' Cock. So you just have yourself another cup o' tea while I change."

225

Maryann would not hear of it. She must be off without delay. "My groom is armed," she assured Meg. "As is the guard he brought along."

"Shootin' don't serve no purpose," Meg said worriedly.

"No. But if we're threatened by a mob, a shot over their heads will make them think twice about attacking."

"If ye won't take me, wait for Stephen. Me father's expectin' him in half an hour."

"No!"

The vehement refusal startled Maryann as much as it did Meg.

Stepping out into the hallway, Maryann said more quietly, "Stephen and I don't see eye to eye about my involvement in the Bow Street investigation. If I waited for him, he'd only order my groom to take me home."

"And you want ter be doin', don't ye? You want ter have a hand in catchin' that rascally betrothed of yours."

"Yes." Maryann struggled to put her thoughts into words. "I *must* take part in Tammadge's downfall. Stephen believes I'm merely stubborn and afraid of being called a jilt if I end the betrothal now. But the only time I was stubborn was when I refused to believe anything against Tammadge. I know now that I did not want to admit the future I had planned was nothing but a bubble of dreams."

"That's the worst can happen to a female," said Meg. A wistful look crossed her face, making her seem younger, more vulnerable. "I'm countin' on bein' an actress. A leadin' lady. It may be nought but a bubble o' dreams, but right now no one could possibly convince me."

Impulsively, Maryann said, "Don't let anyone talk you out of it. It is a dream that can be made into reality."

"I'm countin' on it," Meg said cheerfully, once more a self-possessed young woman. "But what about yerself? Must ye give up all the plans ye made?"

When Maryann made the decision not to marry Tammadge, she had resigned herself to years of further domination by her father and to the loss of means for the creation of a botanical garden. Questioned so bluntly by Meg, she realized that she could not — By George! She *would* not — accept such ignominious defeat.

"No," she said firmly. "I'll never give up my dreams. When Tammadge is caught and I have time to put my mind to it, I don't doubt I'll find another way to achieve my goals."

Meg nodded. "What about Stephen?" she asked casually. "Does he figure in yer plans for the future?"

"Stephen?" Maryann repeated. Her heart pounded embarrassingly hard and loud. "I think you're laboring under some misapprehension."

Meg cocked a quizzical brow. "Don't ye love him?"

Chapter Twenty-Four

"Do I love Stephen?" If anything, Maryann's heart beat faster and louder than a moment ago.

She shook her head in vehement denial. "Of course not! I'd be the most foolish chit on earth, wouldn't I, to love a man who only makes me angry?"

"And anger's the only feelin' he awakens in ye?" asked Meg, not hiding her disbelief. "Think on it, dearie."

Maryann did, remembering when Stephen had lifted her off Spitfire. When he had kissed her.

Her face grew warm. She cast a harried look at the stairs — a way of escape from uncomfortable questions. Really! Meg should know better than detain her with absurdities.

Memories, once stirred, would not be stilled. They traveled back further, to that moment of silence after she told Stephen she didn't believe in knights coming to a lady's rescue. For the span of a heartbeat, they had looked at each other and she had known that Stephen would act her knight if the need arose. She had felt safe — and cherished.

She remembered her feelings when she saw him the very first time. And she recalled how often he was on her mind.

"Well?" Meg demanded imperiously.

"No," Maryann admitted reluctantly. "It's not only

anger he stirs in me."

Meg smiled.

"It's not love, though," Maryann assured her earnestly. "I admit I am intrigued by Stephen. I even admit that, at times, I like him prodigiously. I may be in the throes of what everyone calls 'developing a *tendre.*' But it is not the same as falling in love."

"Bless ye," Meg said, amused. "I didn't think anyone could be that naive. Not even a sheltered lady of quality."

Maryann glowered. There it was again, that hateful word *naive*. Stephen had applied it to her, as had Tammadge. Now Meg.

"I must go." Clasping gloves and reticule to her breast, Maryann turned away. "Thank you for the tea and muffin."

Meg's rich laughter followed her down the stairs.

"And I say ye're as much in love with Stephen as he's with you! Only you're afraid to admit it."

Afraid to admit it. Afraid . . .

Meg's voice still echoed in her mind when Maryann reached the dim entryway. Picking up her skirts, she ran across the courtyard to the waiting carriage.

"What's wrong?" Rob's hand closed over her wrist while he looked her up and down as though he expected to find some dreadful injury. "Knew I should've gone in with ye. A tavern like that ain't no place for a lady."

She gave a shaky laugh. If she had been assaulted by one of the tavern's patrons, she could not be more unnerved than she was by Meg's assumption that she was in love with Stephen.

"Rob, I'm all right. Just in a hurry, as usual. I want to go to Wilderness Road off the Charterhouse Gardens. Do you know the direction?"

"Aye. An' what might ye be wantin' there? It's a fair way out, I warn ye."

"Number thirty-one, Wilderness Road. That's

where Hannah Moss lives. The girl who escaped Tammadge. Let's go, Rob. I want to see if I can coax her to speak about that night."

Still watching her with concern, he handed her into the carriage. Within seconds they were on the way.

Maryann tried to keep her mind on Hannah Moss and what she would say to the girl, but with no one to reprimand her if her thoughts strayed, she was soon mulling over Meg's words.

They were nonsensical, of course. She was *not* in love with Stephen Farrell. Surely, she'd be the first to know if she were?

After a moment or two of pondering, Maryann admitted she had no answer to the question. Her meager knowledge of the mysteries of falling in love was gleaned through observation, not experience.

She had watched her sister Elizabeth lose her heart. For Bess it had been love at first sight. She was still in love with her husband, but starry-eyed, glowing happiness had turned into tears and bitterness soon after the wedding.

Bella tumbled in and out of love the way a puppy tumbled in and out the shallow waters of a creek. It was not a prospect to inspire confidence in the lasting power of love.

And Stephen—if it were love that made him warm and tender one moment, autocratic and overbearing the next, then love was an uncomfortable companion, a burden rather than a joy.

Even those glum observations would not, however, stop her from admitting she had fallen in love if that were the case. She feared dark, locked cellars and, perhaps, just a little, Viscount Tammadge. She was *not* afraid of loving a man.

Deep in thought, Maryann paid scant attention to the streets they traveled or to the screams and shouts that had accompanied her journey for several minutes. But when the progress of the carriage was reduced to jerky stops and starts, once almost tumbling her off the seat, she could no longer turn a deaf ear on the clamor.

Cautiously, she looked out. Her eyes widened at the sight of the tattered crowd surging around the carriage. Most of the men and women paid no heed to the vehicle. Intent on their purposes, they forged noisily ahead toward Holborn, the same way the carriage was going. For the most part, the shouting was indistinguishable, but now and again Maryann caught the cry, "Bread! We wants bread!"

From the corner of her eye, she saw a handful of ragged men dangerously close to the carriage and the spinning wheels. She started to call a warning, but the words stuck in her throat when more men closed in, shaking scrawny fists at her and yelling abuse.

Heart pounding, she sat back from the window. It did not matter that she understood only one word out of ten. Anger and hatred could be conveyed without language.

She heard the crack of Robert's whip at the same moment as something hard hit the carriage door. A second missile hit the glass pane, cracking it. Trembling, she pressed into the corner of the seat while stones and refuse hailed on the coach.

"My lady!" Above the rattle of the speeding vehicle, Rush's call through the communications panel was all but lost. "Are ye hurt?"

"No. But let's get away from here. Fast! Before you or Rob are hit."

She heard the horses neigh. Rocking violently, the carriage came to a stop, throwing her off balance. Her fumbling hand missed the leather strap affixed to the carriage roof to prevent just such an ignominious topple as she suffered, falling across the seat and knocking her head smartly against the armrest.

But the throbbing in her head did not matter. All she could think of was the gray-faced, angry mob outside. What would they do to her? What would happen to Robert and Rush? Why did the two men not fire their weapons?

Cautiously, she sat up. She was about to adjust her hat, whose brim had, somehow, come to rest on the tip of her nose, when a pistol shot rang out—too far distant to have been fired by Robert. A hush fell over the street, and Maryann sat motionless.

One man's voice, startlingly familiar and yet alien with its broad accent, rang out loud and clear.

"Guards! T' Guards, they be comin' down Holborn!"

An instant of silence reigned, then the shout of "Guards!" was taken up by dozens of voices, male and female. Shod feet stamping, bare feet slapping on the cobbles told Maryann that the crowd was dispersing in all haste.

She had time only to shove her hat back before the door opened.

As always, Stephen was hatless. His hair stood on end as though he had repeatedly run his fingers through it. His face under the Peninsular tan was pale, the dark eyes raking her with painful intensity.

"Maryann!" Stephen's voice was hoarse with concern. He swung himself into the carriage and gathered her in his arms.

Safe and cherished.

She hid her face against the broad chest so invitingly close. If her heart had pounded with apprehension before, it now hammered because Stephen's appearance had set her spirit soaring.

She was grateful he sent the crowd running; that was understood. But more than that, when he flung the carriage door open, she had realized that there stood the man of her secret dreams. He was with her and nothing else mattered.

Not even the question as to whether or not she was falling in love. . . .

For now, at least, it did not matter.

Slowly, she pulled out of his embrace. She wanted to see him, make certain he was flesh and blood, not the shadowy figure that had haunted her dreams.

He saw the look in her eyes, a dawning awareness, and every intention of not pressing further demonstrations of love on her went the way his former resolves not to see her again had gone.

"My little madcap. My love!"

Her face was close, her lips parted invitingly. He did not try to resist the temptation, but covered that soft mouth with his. When she made no demur, he drew her closer, enfolding her once again in his arms.

Despite her small stature, she fitted against him perfectly, as the tiny dwellings of the Pyrenees fitted against the side of the mountains — snug and secure, meant to weather a lifetime.

But he mustn't think of a lifetime with Maryann. He must be content with today and tomorrow. And today Maryann returned his kiss with an ardor that set his pulse racing and his blood coursing hotly.

Stephen gave himself up to the fire and the innocence of her kiss, to the warmth and softness of her slender body. Nothing, not thoughts of a questionable tomorrow or knowledge of a bleak future, must spoil this moment.

But something, someone, did. All of a sudden, Stephen knew they were no longer alone. Someone was watching. Silence hung over the street, but his neck prickled, and his back, exposed to the open carriage door, felt vulnerable.

Cupping his hands around Maryann's face, he slowly pulled away.

"It's only Rob," she murmured before he could turn around. "He won't tell."

"In that case—" A gleam lit his eyes. "Shall we do it again?"

A mischievous look crossed her face, but she shook

her head and turned to the groom.

"What happened to you and Rush?" she asked, hoping the breathlessness inflicted by Stephen's kiss was not too obvious. "I was worried when neither one of you fired your weapon."

"Aye," Rob muttered, looking from her to Farrell. "Mighty worried ye was."

She tried to look severe. "You're being impertinent. Tell me! Why didn't you fire a shot over their heads when they threw stones?"

" 'Cause I had me hands full with the horses. An' Rush, the ol' fool, stood up to fire the fowlin' piece an' got knocked over. Dropped the gun right unner the horses' hooves. It's a wonder it didn't go off."

"We had best get going," Stephen broke in. "There's no telling how soon the crowd will be back once they realize none of the Guards are anywhere near."

"Aye, sir! We'll be off afore the cat can lick her ear." A wide grin split Rob's face. Saluting military fashion, he shut the door.

Settling herself on the forward seat, Maryann shot a covert look at Stephen, who had taken the seat opposite her. He had kissed her again—and that after discovering her in just the sort of danger he had warned about when she ventured into Seven Dials the first time.

She did not think he had changed his mind about keeping her out of the investigation. And yet, so far, he had said nothing.

But he had kissed her.

"Do you know, then, that I am going to see Hannah Moss?" she asked once they were under way.

Stephen took due note of the demurely folded hands, the lowered lashes and, very much at odds with this picture of meekness, the tilt of her chin and the firm set of the mouth that had, moments ago, been soft and pliable under his.

His gaze traveled to her disheveled curls, the wide-brimmed hat clinging raffishly to the back of her head just behind one ear. She looked like an urchin. An adorable, exasperating pixie.

"Meg told me. Also that I had missed you by a scant five minutes," he said. "I knew you'd have trouble getting through to Holborn. There's a bakery there, you see."

"So you left your curricle at the Fighting Cock and went after me on foot?" Resolutely, she put the kiss from her mind. A note of defiance crept into her voice. "Well, don't think you can make me change my mind about going to see Hannah."

"No." Stephen looked at her pensively. "I don't think I can."

Her eyes widened. "You are *not* ordering me home?"

"Would you stay at home?" he countered. "I think not. And since I planned to see the Moss family sometime today, I may as well go now and keep an eye on you at the same time."

The scheme itself suited her very well. But his reason for giving her the pleasure of his company was enough to cast her into the dismals—or to raise her hackles. It could not be said of Stephen Farrell, she thought resentfully, that he wore his heart on his sleeve.

To complete her confusion, he reached over and untied the ribbons of her hat. It was an intimate gesture, and quite disturbing.

Adjusting the frivolous piece of head covering to a more suitable angle, he said, "Most women would have heeded my warning not to return to the Dials. You were also warned by Fletcher and Meg."

"Don't forget Rob," she cut in. Taking the ribbons from him, she deftly tied the bow. "He was most concerned about what you'd have to say to the exploit."

Stephen was not diverted. "But you're not like most women, are you, Maryann? What drives you to fly against common sense, against the conventions? You cannot convince me that it is considered suitable for a young lady to visit the back slums."

"Don't you see, Stephen?" She was no longer defiant or resentful but looked at him pleadingly, seeking his understanding. "I got myself into this—this imbroglio. If I cannot extricate myself under my own power, I am not fit to live the life of independence I dream of living."

"A life of independence?" he repeated, startled. "Who ever heard of it? You could never live alone without incurring censure. You'd have to surround yourself with simpering companions and starchy chaperons."

"But Stephen—"

"You wouldn't like it at all," he assured her. "You had much better marry some young fellow you can wind around your little finger."

She had been amused by his depiction of her independent life, but the last statement snuffed all desire to smile.

"I don't want to be married to some spineless gaby," she said crossly. "I'd much rather live with a simpering female companion."

"Nonsense."

For a while, only the rattle of carriage wheels and the clatter of horses' hooves broke the silence while Maryann looked pointedly out the window and Stephen contemplated a loose thread on the index finger of one of his gloves.

An unraveling thread was a minor, unimportant matter, but it was something concrete on which to focus a mind that had the regrettable tendency to dwell on a kiss and the foolish hopes it had raised in his breast.

As though drawn by a lodestone, his gaze shifted to Maryann. A life of independence—what utter rot! She might believe she could extricate herself from the mess

236

she'd landed in, but *he* knew better.

Or did he? Maryann was stubborn. Indeed, she was mulish. She was naive, but she was far from being a feather-brained widgeon. She *must* recognize the danger of the situation, must know he could not allow her to run the risk of getting hurt. And yet she persisted in involving herself. . . .

Maryann turned from the window. She already regretted her childish outburst and was astonished and not a little relieved to find him studying her in puzzlement when she had expected anger.

"I did not mean I wanted to live *alone*," she said.

And suddenly it was not at all difficult to explain to him about her father's tyranny, about her desire to get away from Rivington and her dream of designing a botanical garden.

"Gardens to be visited and enjoyed by Londoners who day after day live in gray houses, gray streets," she said, her eyes aglow with enthusiasm. "Don't you think that gardens, somewhere near Seven Dials for instance, might help just a little?"

"They would," he said, his gaze tender. "On Boxing Day, my mother's baskets for the villagers always included seeds, and not just for onions, carrots, and turnips. Flower seeds as well. 'Flowers are a luxury most of them cannot afford,' she used to say. 'But they're a luxury all of us need.' "

Her face fell. "A botanical garden is a luxury I must postpone."

"Because you won't have the money Tammadge was willing to settle on you? Maryann, I apologize for accusing you—"

She interrupted him. "Of being a mercenary harpy?"

He took her hand, raising it to his lips. "I apologize most humbly."

She smiled, and he once more caught the pixie look that never ceased to touch his heart.

"But you were quite correct, Stephen. I was mercenary. I wonder, though, how you found out. You said you didn't question our staff."

"*I* did not." He inserted a finger behind the collar of his shirt and tugged. "But my man Tolly did."

She looked hurt, but said, "It doesn't matter. And I shan't ask you to divulge which one of our servants is a gossip."

"I had no call to throw the marriage settlement at your head, even though I did not know then to what good purpose the money was to go."

Maryann blushed. "Dash it, Stephen! I'm no saint. I had selfish motives for everything I did. You see, I did not want even my husband to hold me in his power. If I had my own money, I believed, I'd be totally independent."

"You did make a mull of it, didn't you?" He grimaced wryly. "Tammadge is not the man to give his wife free rein."

"I know." She hesitated. Sending him a sidelong look, she added, "I met him in the park after you left me."

"The devil you say! What did he want?"

"I don't really know." She frowned. "He said he wanted to see me before I set out for Sloane Street, and then we talked about so many things, I never did get around to asking why."

From the tail of his eye, Stephen saw they were passing the chapel and the west front of the boys school located in the Charterhouse. There was little time left before they'd reach Hannah Moss. Time he'd rather spend discussing Maryann's gardens and life of "independence" than asking about Tammadge.

The devil fly away with Tammadge!

"What did he have to say?" he inquired with more reluctance than he cared to admit.

Dutifully, she reported that the viscount would be at the Merriwether soiree that night and that he had engagements, the particulars of which he had not disclosed, on Wednesday and Thursday. She paused, giving Stephen every opportunity to inform her of the role Meg was to play on Thursday night.

He did not, and she told herself not to be a ninny. She had not really expected it and had, therefore, no reason to feel disappointed. And if she happened to plan on being in Grosvenor Square that night, *he* would have no cause to fly up into the boughs and rake her over the coals.

After some thought, she told him about the gambling salon in the library of Rivington House and the cheating her father was involved in.

Stephen's face tightened and she fell silent, believing it was disgust at her father's disgraceful activities that gave his features the hard, chiseled look.

"Tammadge told you about your father to show you're in his power," Stephen said harshly. "And he a cheat himself! That's why I approached Sir Nathaniel originally. Tammadge is the man who ruined my brother."

Chapter Twenty-Five

"Stephen, I am sorry. Will he come about, your brother?"

"He is dead."

Maryann caught her breath. The second death connected to gambling and Tammadge.

But, perhaps, she was jumping to conclusions. Perhaps Stephen's brother had died of an illness, or in an accident.

She was about to ask when she noticed the bleak look in his eyes. Shifting to the seat beside him, she took his hand and pressed it.

"We will catch Tammadge, never fear."

Stephen shook off the dark mood. This was not the time to be thinking of William, or to let bitterness push him into disclosures about himself and William that might be a source of danger to Maryann if Tammadge found out. Much better wait until Thursday night, when the viscount's game would be finished.

"I'll nab him all right," he said, making it a vow.

"*We* shall," Maryann corrected automatically, her mind on what Stephen said earlier. "Are you not in Sir Nathaniel's employ, then? You said *you* approached the magistrate—about Tammadge's cheating."

He raised a brow. "Does it matter whether or not am paid for what I'm doing? I am still a Bow Street spy."

To her, it did matter.

The carriage came to a stop in front of Number thirty-one, Wilderness Road, one of a row of plain, narrow, two-story houses with dormer attics. Doors, all made of some dark wood with a polished brass knocker in the center, were lined up side by side along the street, as were the scrubbed front steps of white stone.

A clean, quiet, respectable, safe neighborhood patronized by craftsmen and shopkeepers. The street where Hannah Moss and her friend Leah had been abducted. It was incredible. Footpads did not usually frequent districts where they'd be easily spotted.

Maryann's mouth felt dry when she accompanied Stephen to Hannah's door. An hour or so ago at the Fighting Cock, it had seemed perfectly reasonable to visit Wilderness Road. But now she felt like an intruder, calling on a family who'd be preoccupied with the injury to their daughter.

Stephen let the knocker fall against the brass plate. As though sensing Maryann's reluctance, he said, "If Hannah does remember something and can identify Tammadge, I won't have to submit five or six young women to the indignity of being abducted by Tammadge's thugs."

Maryann nodded. Neither would Meg have to go into Tammadge's house.

A young serving girl opened the door a crack and peeked out. When Stephen told her that he and Lady Maryann Rivington wished to see the master and mistress, her dark eyes widened. She darted a look at the crested carriage standing at the curb, and flung the door wide.

"Please ter step inside," she murmured. Wiping her hands on the large apron that enveloped her skinny person, she led the way to a room at the back of the house, then scuttled off.

"I don't think anyone has used this parlor," whispered Maryann, staring at the pristine condition of furniture, rugs, and draperies. "Every chair lined up just so. Not a worn spot on the upholstery."

There was a twinkle in Stephen's eye when he replied, "It's only the nobility who take pride in the display of worn upholstery and threadbare rugs and curtains. Shabbiness has no place in Mrs. Moss's parlor, which is undoubtedly reserved for the grandest of occasions."

She heard footsteps in the tiled hallway and could only frown at him reprovingly before a slender man of some fifty-odd years and a woman, several years his junior, hurried into the room.

The woman stopped just inside the door and Maryann's attention was caught by her hair. Covered by a small square of white veiling, the braided tresses, too, seemed white at first glance. A second look showed that they were a very pale blond.

The man's hair was dark, his sidelocks streaked with gray yet thick and glossy as a youth's, as was the hair on the crown of his head covered by the *yarmulka*. The tails of his frock coat flapping, he rushed to shake hands with Stephen.

"Mr. Farrell! Welcome. I am Abraham Moss," he said, slightly out of breath and not very successful at hiding his agitation. "I received your note but a few minutes ago and did not expect to see you until much later."

When Stephen explained that the early call was due to Lady Maryann's desire to see Hannah, Mr. Moss nodded, but the look of worry on his face deepened.

"Hannah won't speak."

The woman by the door said, "Abraham, dear. Will you not introduce me?"

He spun around. "My love, forgive me. I did not mean to ignore you."

"It matters not." Her accent was like Hedwig's, but her voice was softer, in keeping with her gentle features and the slight roundness of her figure.

Mr. Moss introduced her as Hester, the beautiful wife he had met in Flensburg, a port on the Baltic Sea where the Prussian province of Schleswig-Holstein bordered against Denmark. He had traveled extensively in his younger days, he explained, as he owned an import business with warehouses in St. Catherine's Street.

"That is very close to the docks," said Stephen. "Did your daughter visit you at the warehouses?"

"Nearly every day our Hannah went to help her papa with keeping the books," said Hester Moss, her eyes filling with tears. "She was such a clever, lively girl. And now—"

Maryann exchanged a look with Stephen, and knew he was thinking exactly what had occurred to her. Hannah's visits to her father's waterfront offices had not gone unnoticed. And when the order had come from Tammadge to kidnap a red-haired girl, his cutthroats had known where to find her. In quiet Wilderness Road, where girls were allowed to walk unaccompanied, even at night.

Hester Moss dried her eyes. "Come, Lady Maryann. I will take you to Hannah. But not Mr. Farrell. And I will stay in the room. I hope you do not mind."

"No, of course not."

If truth be told, Maryann was relieved that Mrs. Moss would stay with her. Beset by doubts about her ability to achieve success where Hannah's parents had failed, she followed Hester to the second floor.

Blinking, she stood in the door to Hannah's room. A dozen lamps, all lit despite the brightness of the day, bathed the chamber in a strange yellowish light. A huge fire roared in the hearth, and before it, staring into the flames, sat Hannah in a wing-backed chair that dwarfed the slender body. She wore a bandage around her head and sat as lifeless as a doll.

Compassion smote Maryann. Hannah Moss was

even younger than she. A pretty girl, if rather color-less. Brows and lashes were barely noticeable against the blanched skin, and her long hair, a pale reddish-blond, could not compare with Meg's fiery curls.

"I fear you will be uncomfortable," said Mrs. Moss, drawing a chair for Maryann to the fireplace. "Hannah is always cold, and she screams when the room is dark. We leave the lights burning day and night. Her screams are worse than the silence."

Hester Moss sat down by the window and picked up a piece of tatting from a small table. Judging by the length of the lace, she had sat there many hours and worked while keeping her daughter company.

Feeling awkward and ill at ease, Maryann started talking to Hannah. She told her who she was and why she had come to Wilderness Road.

Hannah gave no indication that she heard, or that she was aware anyone had entered her chamber.

Maryann spoke of Leah and the abduction, but still there was no response from the girl.

After a while, Maryann slipped into German. She had no reason to suppose Hannah was familiar with Hester's native tongue; she did it merely to change the pattern of their one-sided conversation. Suddenly, however, she was aware of tension in the room. Tension that did not come from her or Hester Moss, but from Hannah.

Again, this time in German, she spoke of the abduction and of Leah's disappearance.

The tension in the room grew so strong, it was a tangible thing. Maryann sat on the edge of her chair. Hester Moss laid down her tatting and stared at the two girls.

Hannah did not move or speak.

Disappointed, Maryann rose. Gently touching the young girl's shoulder, she murmured, *"Auf Wiedersehen,* Hannah. I must go now, but I hope to see you again soon. May I come back?"

There was no response.

"She and Leah spoke German always," Mrs. Moss said with a sigh. "The Goldbergs have come eight or nine years ago from Hamburg, and Leah preferred to speak the old tongue."

She got to her feet. "Come, Lady Maryann. I shall take you downstairs."

The two women had reached the door when Hannah moved her head.

"Ja, bitte komm wieder," she said softly.

Please come again, Hannah had said.

Encouraged by Hester Moss and—to her astonishment—by Stephen, Maryann returned to Wilderness Road on Wednesday and Thursday afternoon. Each time, she went with high hopes of coaxing the girl to talk. Each time, she left disappointed.

Hannah no longer was a lifeless doll. On Maryann's second visit, the young girl studied her, at first covertly, then with open curiosity. When Maryann told her about the Sloane Street gardens and her dream of having her own botanical gardens, Hannah's brown eyes lit up, and she smiled. But she did not speak. And when Maryann mentioned Leah, she withdrew into her shell of obliviousness.

On Thursday, Hannah's reaction to Leah's name was quite the opposite. She became agitated, thrashing her head and muttering incoherently.

Maryann was convinced that, during her absence, Hannah had been thinking about her friend and the awful night when they were captured. She felt that a break was imminent in Hannah's resistance to remember, but Hester Moss feared her daughter would work herself into a fever. She begged Maryann to be careful and not to persist with questions.

"The blow to the head," Hester said tearfully, "it was meant to kill Hannah. But that night, she has braided her hair and pinned the braids to the back of her head. It saved her life, the physician said to Abraham and me. If she did not have the braids, the blow would have broken her skull. He says our Hannah is fine, but he worries about a fever."

Maryann was in a quandary. It was late Thursday afternoon. That night, knowing Tammadge planned to take her aboard the *Venture,* Meg would have to go to Tammadge's house—unless Hannah could identify the viscount as her abductor. But looking at the girl's ashen face, the eyes moving erratically behind closed lids, Maryann could no more persist in questioning her than she could have pulled a kitten's tail.

She gave Hester Moss a reassuring smile. "I shan't disturb her any more."

Turning to Hannah, she said, "Please, don't fret yourself. If all goes well, I shall have good news tomorrow, and you need never again think of that horrible night. *Auf Wiedersehen,* Hannah. *Bis morgen.*"

Determined to be in Grosvenor Square that night, Maryann left the Moss's house. She had no notion what she could do if Tammadge drove off with Meg and the Bow Street runners did *not* interfere. She might have to follow Tammadge to the docks, a prospect that sent a chill down her spine. If he discovered her—

She pushed the thought aside. There was no point in borrowing trouble. Everything would work out all right. She must believe that.

While Robert drove her home, she tried to relax. It was a longish ride, as long as an hour if they encountered lumbering drays or carrier carts, and should have provided ample opportunity to rest before she reached Mount Street. But her mind would not be still; Hannah's distress gave her no peace.

When she reached Rivington House, James, on duty in the foyer, informed her that Lady Rivington had already gone upstairs to change for dinner. Wearily, Maryann entered her own chamber to bathe and don a lavender silk gown, which, she believed, made her look older than her years and was just the thing to wear to the musicale she meant to attend.

The evening would be a penance, but in order to catch Tammadge, she'd gladly suffer worse.

She had seen him briefly at the Merriwethers' soiree on Tuesday, after her first visit to Wilderness Road, and she'd had the dickens of a time stopping herself from hurling the betrothal ring at his feet and denouncing him then and there. She was grateful she did not have to face him on Wednesday, or this evening.

But she also would not see Stephen. He'd be occupied supervising Tammadge's cutthroats while they captured a half-dozen girls.

Stephen . . . who had played knight to her damsel in distress in Seven Dials, who had kissed her and, instead of scolding and ordering her home, had taken her to see Hannah Moss. Much against his better judgment, she did not doubt.

Her heart warmed and the heaviness lifted from her mind.

Sitting at her dressing table, Maryann caught her reflection in the mirror. She saw the blush on her cheeks, the wide, shining eyes.

Blushing and starry-eyed — like Elizabeth when she fell in love.

The thought, fleeting as it was, startled and disturbed Maryann. She was pensive and distracted when she joined her mother for dinner, a fact that did not long escape Irene's notice.

Having received disjointed replies to several questions, she signaled to the butler. "That will be all, Melville. You may serve dessert in half an hour."

When the butler had departed, she directed a thoughtful look at her daughter. "Dearest, ·if you do not wish to converse with me, just say so. But please don't assure me you'd like nothing better than go to Mrs. Webster's musicale when I ask you about the Sloane Street gardens."

Startled, Maryann laid down her fork. "But I am certain you asked if I had changed my mind about attending the musicale."

"That, my dear, was at least fifteen minutes ago, and you muttered something about lilies of the valley blooming in a se'nnight. You're so scatterbrained, if I didn't know you're deeply involved in extricating yourself from a betrothal, I'd suspect you were in love."

Maryann was conscious of a surge of warmth to her face.

She gave her mother a rueful look. "I don't know what I am or how I feel, and it is not a comfortable state of affairs," she confessed. "Less than two weeks ago, I was self-assured, knew exactly what I wanted and how I felt. Now, it seems, I'm caught in a perpetual game of blind man's bluff."

Observing the flushed face, Irene raised a brow. "Maryann, dear. If you're speaking of feelings, you need only stand still long enough to take off the blindfold and examine them closely. Infatuation is easily mistaken for love."

"I know that. Bella is the perfect example."

Irene remembered the talk she'd had with Maryann on the night of the betrothal ball, her daughter's refusal to let love enter into a decision about marriage.

"By the same token," she said, helping herself to a sliver of game pie and a spoonful of barberry preserves, "I know an overcautious young lady who might not acknowledge that she has fallen in love for fear of getting hurt — as one of her sisters has been hurt."

Absently, Maryann traced the leaf pattern woven into the damask cloth. Meg had accused her of being afraid; now her mother said more or less the same.

But she was *not* afraid. Not in the sense Meg or Mama implied.

"I'd be willing to run a few risks," she said, her eyes on the tablecloth. "If only I could be certain I can trust my own judgment. I have erred so often—"

She looked up. "Mama, how will I know I'm in love and not merely infatuated?"

Irene's gaze was unfocused, and she appeared to be looking deep inside herself. The corners of her mouth curved upward in a slow, tender smile.

"Child, I cannot tell you *how* you will know," she said, meeting Maryann's troubled look. "I can only assure you that, when you are ready to give your heart, you will know *without a doubt* that you have found your love."

"Mama, did you ever fall in love? You said—"

Maryann broke off, annoyed with the butler who entered bearing a dish of syllabub, a great favorite with Irene, and exasperated with Harv and James following in Melville's wake to clear the table and sideboard.

Throughout the dessert course, her mother appeared to be in a state of confusion, her color fluctuating between a delicate blush and an intriguing pallor. Maryann was burning to get an answer to her question, but there was no further opportunity to be private until they entered the carriage for the short drive to Mrs. Webster's house—in Grosvenor Square.

Mrs. Webster's neighbor on one side was Viscount Francis Tammadge, and it was Mrs. Webster's kitchen maid Lucy Weller who was walking out with one of Tammadge's grooms.

Harboring the vague notion of enlisting Lucy's assistance, Maryann had approached her mother on Tuesday and had volunteered to accompany her to Mrs. Webster's musicale, but it was not surprising that Irene asked if she had changed her mind. Maryann detested the harp and song recitals rendered by Mrs. Webster's uppity nieces.

At the moment, however, fear of musical torture

was far from her mind. She was intent on pursuing the question she had posed at the dinner table.

To avoid crushing the lace of her mother's gown, Maryann settled herself across from her facing the rear of the carriage.

"Mama, do you remember what I asked you when Melville interrupted us?"

Irene met her daughter's eagerness with composure.

"Child, in your eyes I may be old and feeble, but let me assure you I'm not yet in my dotage. I remember very well what you asked me. Every single one of your questions! And I mean to find out who has put you in such a flutter that you don't know your own mind. An unprecedented occurrence!"

For a moment, Maryann said nothing but marveled how neatly the tables had been turned on her.

"Maryann, dear. I am waiting for an answer."

Only one of the lanterns inside the carriage was lit, and Maryann took care to keep her face in the shadows lest Irene observe the same telltale signs of confusion she had seen in her mother at the dinner table.

She took a deep breath. "It is Stephen Farrell."

Having said the name, Maryann relaxed. She felt absurdly relieved — as though she were a child again and had confessed to some misdeed that had been plaguing her conscience.

Chapter Twenty-Six

"Well!" said Irene. "I shouldn't be surprised, I suppose. If it had been one of the young men you met while you were in my company, I must have noticed. But Mr. Farrell—my dear, what do we know about him?"

"Nothing much," Maryann admitted. *There's a bit of farmland in Cornwall, and he had a brother once—a brother who was ruined by Tammadge.*

"Tammadge thought highly enough of Farrell to include his name in the list of guests he wished me to invite to the betrothal ball," said Irene. "But that, you must agree, is not a recommendation."

"Stephen had his reasons for befriending Tammadge."

"I don't doubt it," Irene retorted with a rare show of dryness. "Nevertheless, I think I'll have a word with Agnes Crabtree. Farrell attended her rout, and she would not invite anyone—"

"Don't, Mama!" Maryann interrupted hastily as the carriage came to a halt in front of Mrs. Webster's porticoed mansion. "It's not as though Stephen had proposed or . . . or *anything*. He says he is totally ineligible."

Irene raised a brow but said no more.

Harv opened the door and let down the steps. Moments later, the two ladies entered a foyer the size of a large drawing room, the floor laid in an intricate pattern of colored marble tiles, and the high, vaulted ceiling supported by five fluted pillars. Several ladies and a small number of gentlemen were gathered in the foyer, most of them near the open door of the music room directly across from the front entrance.

One man stood apart, a tall man of muscular build, a shoulder propped against the central column, a hand stuffed carelessly into the pocket of his midnight blue evening coat.

Irene said something, but Maryann did not hear. She was aware only of a racing pulse, a surge of pure joy, at the sight of the familiar male shape. She did not see his face; it was turned away from her. But she could not mistake the dark brown hair with its lighter streaks bleached by the Spanish sun, or the tautness of the powerful body that, even in a negligent pose, seemed to be on the alert.

Joy turned to dismay. He was supposed to be with Tammadge's cutthroats! Stephen himself had told her that he'd be sent out to capture a shipload of young women once Tammadge had found another red-haired girl.

He turned his head and caught sight of her. If she had not been watching closely, she might have missed the flicker of surprise—or annoyance—that crossed his face.

Without consideration for decorum or her mother's presence, she hurried to Stephen.

"What happened, Stephen? Where is Meg? Isn't she next door? And why aren't you—" She broke off, uncomfortably aware that, but for Meg's frankness, she shouldn't have known of the trap set for Tammadge this night.

Frowning, Stephen completed her question. "Why am I not out with the thugs?"

She nodded.

He pushed away from the pillar. "Now why did I

252

think you might be ignorant of the plans?"

"I wouldn't know." She met his frown with a wide-eyed stare. "May it serve to teach you a lesson."

"I wish it might," he said after a moment's pause. "It's a devilish hard lesson. In fact, I find it impossible to ignore orders given by my instinct. And it tells me in no uncertain terms to keep you out of this mess."

"I am too deeply embroiled." That, if nothing else, she *had* learned from Tammadge Tuesday morning.

"Maryann, I have no right to expect anything of you, but I wish you'd permit me to—"

"To do what?" she asked suspiciously. "Take me home?"

"I would have phrased it less bluntly." His expression softened. "I would have said, 'Allow me to slay your dragon, dear lady.' Or, 'Permit me to wear your colors, and I'll fight your battles for you.'"

"You have much to learn about my daughter, Mr. Farrell."

Two astonished faces turned to Irene Rivington. Neither Maryann nor Stephen had noticed her joining them.

She smiled, holding out her hand to Stephen, who took it and raised it to his lips.

"I doubt Maryann believes in knights," Irene said quietly. "She has always fought her own battles, no matter what the cost. You cannot expect her to change overnight."

"In truth, Lady Rivington, I do not know which of us should change. Perhaps it is *my* attitude that is at fault."

"Indeed, it is!" said Maryann, but neither her mother nor the man who had told her only a few days ago that he was falling in love with her paid the slightest heed.

Irene asked, "What *is* your attitude, Mr. Farrell?"

"There you have me, ma'am. I'm dashed if I know! Since I met your daughter, my heart and my mind have been at loggerheads. In my heart, I admire her spirit, her intrepidity, and I cheer her on. But my mind tells me she must not be permitted to engage in reckless exploits. She must be sheltered, protected."

"Perhaps," Irene suggested gently, "you are confusing heart and mind? Or, perhaps, it is your heart that speaks both times, in which case you ought to be able to find a compromise."

His eyes met Irene's and held them. "Ma'am, you are very wise."

"Stephen!" said Maryann, and her imperious tone gave not a hint of the breathless interest evoked by the exchange with her mother. "Does that mean you'll finally tell me what is going on?"

His gaze shifted to her, then back to Irene. "Lady Rivington? Will you entrust your daughter to me for a few minutes? I shall take the greatest care of her."

"I do not doubt it, Mr. Farrell. And I hope, for your sake and hers, that Maryann will learn to distinguish between tyranny and chivalry."

Irene's attention was caught by a stir at the door. "Oh! There is Agnes Crabtree. Maryann, I hear the harp being tuned. I'll go in with Agnes. Join me soon, will you?"

She hurried off, and Maryann, recalling that her mother intended to question Mrs. Crabtree about Stephen, watched with mixed emotions as the two ladies greeted each other, then strolled arm in arm toward the music room. For two pins, she'd run after them. But—

Turning to Stephen, she encountered a quizzical look.

"For a moment, I thought you might follow your mother," he said. "I wondered if I had given you the faith to believe, if not in knights generally, at least in *this* knight. But you *don't* trust me to go after Tammadge by myself, do you?"

"I do trust you, Stephen." It seemed to her that the

hammering of her heart was louder than her voice. She swallowed and said firmly, "You must believe that."

He nodded rather curtly.

The buzz of conversation in the music room dimmed, and a complacent female voice bade the company enjoy her niece's rendering of *Hachas and Pavane*, a Spanish composition for the harp. A footman hurried to close the ornately carved mahogany door on musicians and audience.

"What you want to know will not take long to tell," said Stephen. "You won't miss much of the performance."

"As though I cared about that! I merely accompanied Mama to be near Meg."

"You don't say."

The wry tone drove warmth into her cheeks. "Don't tease me, Stephen. Tell me why you're here and not out with Tammadge's cutthroats to arrange for a shipment of girls."

"I had no orders from Tammadge, it's as simple as that."

"No orders! Stephen, he must have changed his mind about sailing the *Venture*."

Depression settled on her. If Tammadge had changed his plans, it meant he would not be caught that night. It meant a continuance of the betrothal. For the first time, she doubted her ability to keep up the charade.

"Meg's engagement with him was not cancelled," said Stephen. "She's with him now."

"Do you think he had news from Algiers?" she asked, trying for a hopeful note. "That, for some reason, he plans to send only Meg?"

"I don't know. Like you, I came to check on her."

"But you can see nothing from here! How will you know—Oh!" she interrupted herself. "How stupid of me. I forgot about the Bow Street runners."

He raised a brow but made no comment on her intimate knowledge of the arrangements.

"Yes," he confirmed. "Three runners are hidden in that bit of garden in the middle of the square and three more are posted in the mews where Tammadge has his stables. I'll be notified when he makes his move."

"*If*," Maryann corrected him. "Without the other girls—" She shrugged and said no more.

"Maryann, we don't know for certain that his thugs are not roaming the streets at this very moment—or did so last night—to snatch a half-dozen young women. Tammadge may have decided I cannot be trusted after all."

"You said in the park that he had you watched. Do you think he knows of your visit to Hannah?"

"Only if he has you watched as well. I am sure I wasn't followed to the Fighting Cock, and afterwards I rode in your carriage."

"But he wouldn't—"

She remembered Tuesday morning when she had encountered Tammadge after her meeting with Stephen, remembered his suspicious questions and his threats, and she could easily believe that he would have her watched.

A chilling thought, one that raised goose bumps on her arms and back, and, judging by the tight set of his jaw, was just as abhorrent to Stephen as it was to her.

An arm length apart, they looked at each other. Neither heard the applause greeting the end of the harp solo. Neither noticed the footmen's interested stares.

"Maryann, I love you."

Stephen's voice was low and husky and stirred an answering chord in her blood. He made no attempt to close the distance between them, but it did not matter. He had broken the cold grip of apprehension. She felt enveloped by the strength of his love.

It was then that she realized how much his regard, his caring, meant to her. There was no need to keep her own feelings under lock and key, no need to be afraid to trust her judgment. She had made grave errors in the past weeks since the fatal decision to marry Tammadge. This time she could not go wrong. She had the evidence of her heart to rely on. "You will know without a doubt," her mother had said.

"Stephen," she whispered, her feelings mirrored in her eyes.

He caught his breath sharply, wanting yet not daring to believe. But when she stepped toward him, her hands outstretched, he knew no hesitation. He clasped her hands firmly, possessively.

The door to the music room opened.

"Confound it," he muttered, releasing her.

Confound it! Maryann echoed silently.

Footsteps whispered across the marble tiles. Maryann did not need Stephen's "Miss Bella!" to alert her to her friend's approach. She was only too familiar with the eager, I-must-not-miss-anything pace of the slippered feet.

"Maryann!" Bella came to a breathless halt. "And Mr. Farrell!"

Her blue eyes darted from one to the other, and Maryann could almost hear her thoughts: *I said you were a sly thing, Maryann. But this time, you won't escape me. I want to know all!*

Directing a dazzling smile at Stephen, Bella said, "I have strict orders to take Maryann into the music room."

"Orders from Lady Rivington?" he asked. "That, of course, explains why you raced into the foyer as though pursued by a tiger. She is *such* an ogre."

Maryann's mouth twitched, but on Bella the irony of Stephen's words was lost. Bella heard only what she wanted to hear.

"And I must say, Mr. Farrell," she continued

257

blithely, "when I learned that Maryann was out here for the length of that drea—delightful harp recital, I had to agree with dear Lady Rivington that you have monopolized her quite long enough."

This was too much for Maryann. "Bella, you are a fibster! Mama would never say anything so rude."

Stephen took her hand and under Miss Bella's widening gaze dropped a kiss on her wrist.

"Go with your friend," he said quietly. "I have told you everything I know, I promise you."

"No, Stephen! Please let me stay with you."

"Dash my wig!" exclaimed Bella, in her astonishment parroting one of her papa's favorite expressions. "I have stumbled onto an intrigue. I would never have believed it of you, Maryann!"

They paid her no heed.

"Stephen, don't send me away." Maryann was calm but determined. "I couldn't bear not knowing what is happening. And I promise I won't ask you to take me along if you get word that—"

A thunderous knock on the front door drowned the rest of her promise. Stephen, tense and alert, watched an indignant footman stalk to the door and fling it open just in time to receive a smart rap on the chest with a metal-topped walking stick that had been used in lieu of the knocker.

"No offense, my good man." The burly individual on the stoop swept off his curly brimmed beaver hat. "I beg yer pardon, but I'm in a devilish hurry to speak with one Stephen Farrell. Bow Street business."

Before the footman could draw breath, before Maryann could say anything, Stephen was at the door.

"What happened, Simms?"

"It's Miss Meg. She's just—"

The Bow Street runner, with Stephen's hand on his back, found himself inexorably propelled down the marble steps, and the rest of his explanation was lost to Maryann.

She hurried to the door. "What did he say?" she asked the footman. "The Bow Street runner — Mr. Simms — what did he say?"

The footman huffed, his face red, his eyes glaring. " 'No h'offense,' 'e said! 'No h'offense!' "

"Yes, yes," Maryann said impatiently. "And I am very sorry that you got hit. But what did he say to Mr. Farrell? About Miss Meg?"

"I wouldn't know, my lady."

Maryann stared out into quiet Grosvenor Square. Where was Stephen? Where had he disappeared so fast? She should be able to see him still. Many of the houses were lit, and tall gaslights spread their bright glow on street and sidewalk.

"Maryann! What is going on? I demand to be told!"

Bella. Her untimely appearance may have been a blessing in disguise.

Maryann swung around and grabbed her friend's arm. "I want to go for a short walk. Will you come with me?"

Bella's eyes glistened with excitement, but she held back. "Not unless you tell me why. You promised to tell me *everything!* But you never came to see me."

"I cannot say anything. Not now. And if you won't go with me, I'll take the footman."

One look at Maryann's face, and Bella wisely refrained from further badgering.

"Of course I'll go, silly! But it mightn't be a bad notion to take the footman, too. It's dark outside."

Thus it was that two young ladies, followed by a stately figure in a magnificent purple-and-crimson livery, set out for a stroll in Grosvenor Square some time after ten o'clock at night.

Stepping out of Mrs. Webster's house and walking past Tammadge's home, Maryann felt as self-conscious as a fox in front of the smoke house. She almost expected Tammadge to jump out and seize her, but nothing happened. In fact, she thought, looking back

259

at the house, Tammadge might not have been home at all that evening, for none of the windows facing the square showed a light.

Where the dickens was everybody?

Despite Bella's protest and the footman's groans — he suffered from bunions and pinching shoes — Maryann increased the pace. She had not heard or seen a carriage since the Bow Street runner had fetched Stephen, but, on the other hand, neither Stephen nor Tammadge would have their conveyances waiting in plain sight in Grosvenor Square. She'd just peek into Lower Brook Street, perhaps walk past the fenced garden in the center of the square, and —

A screech from Bella made her jump.

"How much farther do we need to go, Maryann? You said it'd be a *short* walk. And this is the third time I stepped on a pebble!"

Maryann gave Bella an exasperated look. She, too, had stepped on pebbles but had ignored the discomfort. After all, evening slippers with their thin soles and crisscross ribbon ties were not meant to be worn in the pursuit of kidnappers. Neither were her lavender silk gown and Bella's gossamer-thin white muslin.

The thought gave her pause.

Slowing down, Maryann looked at Bella and herself and questioned the wisdom of her impetuous act. She realized that there was nothing at all she'd accomplish by traipsing around the square. She could not help Stephen, even if she knew what he was up to.

On the contrary. If something were afoot, if Tammadge were engaged in transporting Meg to the docks, the appearance of his betrothed accompanied by a friend and a footman must present a serious handicap.

She'd be a hindrance rather than a help, Stephen had told Sir Nathaniel when the magistrate asked her to assist them. The last thing Maryann wanted to do was prove the bitter denouncement true.

Glancing around the quiet square, she prayed she hadn't already done so.

Resolutely, she stopped.

"Let's go back, Bella." She gave her friend a mischievous look. "With any luck, Mrs. Webster's nieces will have finished by now, and we can enjoy Caroline Hawthorne's performance on the pianoforte."

Chapter Twenty-Seven

Maryann was not destined to experience enjoyment of any kind for the remainder of the evening. After being thoroughly catechized by Bella about her betrothal to Viscount Tammadge and her relationship with Stephen Farrell, she had to endure a homily from Mrs. Webster. The widow took it as a personal affront that Maryann had come to her house "only," as she phrased it, "to snub her nieces by avoiding the music room during their performances."

Upon returning home, Irene added to Maryann's discomfort by gently pointing out the impropriety of leading a younger friend astray and appropriating the services of a footman not in their employ. Irene, it appeared, had come in search of her errant daughter and the young lady sent to fetch her, and was dutifully informed by the second footman stationed in the foyer that Lady Maryann and Miss Bella Effingham had "gorn fer a walk."

Chastened, Maryann retreated to her chamber, but her ordeal was far from over. As soon as she found herself alone and undistracted by scolds or questions that could not be fully answered, she fretted about Stephen and Meg.

Stephen had expected to be called by the Bow Street runners when Tammadge made his move, but the few words of Simms's message she had overheard were ambiguous and confusing. "It's Miss Meg. She's just—"

Surely, if Meg had been carried off to the *Venture,* the runner would have been more specific? But against this argument spoke Stephen's quick disappearance, which pointed to hot-footed pursuit.

Worried and miserable, Maryann got ready for bed. Pulling off the betrothal ring and thrusting it among an assortment of baubles and trinkets atop her dresser, she berated herself for parading in the street at a time when she might overset Stephen's arrangements to catch Tammadge. The next moment, she regretted that she had not persisted and completed a full circle around the square.

Anything could have happened, and she wouldn't know until Stephen sent word.

She huddled under the covers, wishing it were morning and wondering how early she might expect to hear from him. Stephen had a servant, Tolly. He might send him as soon as he had taken the shaving water to his master.

Or Stephen might personally call on her, taking the front steps two at a time, his hair windblown, for he'd be hatless as always—some time, when she had nothing else to worry about, she must ask why.

She pictured stately James opening the door, Stephen giving the footman an impudent grin or a wink and demanding to see her to make his report about the evening.

What the news would be, became less important than the man who'd bring it. Her mind refused to worry and speculate any more—as though it had been waiting for the moment when she would focus her attention on Stephen and herself.

Her heart started to pound and a warm glow spread slowly, deliciously, from her head to her toes. She knew exactly how it would be when they'd meet face to face in the morning. Many a time had she lived a moment like that in her secret dreams. Only this time, it would be no dream. It would be no faceless shadow who took her into his arms.

Stephen would embrace and kiss her. Again and again, he'd assure her of his love. And she would tell him that she loved him. . . .

When Maryann awoke in the morning, her first thoughts were of Stephen and that she would see him before long. Even the uncertainty of Meg's fate could not dim the glow in her eyes or stop the singing in her heart.

She did not go to the Sloane Street gardens, nor, despite her promise, did she make plans to visit Hannah Moss. She installed herself in the small downstairs parlor where she could hear any carriage that stopped, or, if a certain gentleman happened to be walking, she'd be the first to hear the knocker.

As the day progressed, the look in her eyes became harder. Surely he must know that she was anxiously waiting for news. How dare he let her stew and worry! And if he did not have time to spare for the woman he said he loved, a brief note would do as well as his visit.

A note, of course, would not do half as well as a personal appearance, but by the time the butler came into the parlor to light the lamps, Maryann would have settled for anything, any kind of message that assured her Stephen was safe. If Tammadge had discovered the trap . . .

It did not bear thinking of, yet try as she might, she could not give her thoughts a different direction. She pictured him captured and bound aboard the *Venture*. She pictured him slain, his body tossed into the river by Tammadge's cutthroats.

Twice within the hour, she sent word to the stables to have the horses put to. Twice, she countermanded the order, afraid Stephen would come, or a message would be delivered while she was off on a wild goose chase.

She stood beside the fireplace and was about to tug the bellpull once again when she heard the door open. She whirled, her mind so totally focused on Stephen that she expected to see none but him.

It was Irene who stood in the doorway, one hand pressed against the jamb as though she were in need of support.

"Rivington wants to see you, Maryann. In the study."

Maryann did not move or speak immediately. The appearance of her mother when she expected Stephen, and her father's command, had snapped the tension pulling her taut as a fiddler's bow. Her legs turned to jelly and her mind felt numb.

Slowly, she crossed the room. She had not seen her mother since luncheon, and although she had been preoccupied with her own thoughts, she *had* noticed that Irene was looking quite chipper at that time. The change was startling. Irene's face was pinched, and her eyes had the strained look that presaged a severe headache.

"Sit down, Mama. You look about to swoon."

"No, I am to return to the study immediately." Irene lowered her voice. "I came to fetch you myself because I wanted to give you warning. Tammadge is there."

Maryann blinked. "Tammadge in the study," she repeated blankly.

Her stomach knotted. Since Tammadge was free, Stephen had failed. Or there had been no abduction at all. Or Stephen and Meg were both—

"And . . . and he brought a young man."

"Stephen?"

She knew it could not be Stephen before she finished saying the name. And yet, she must have cherished a forlorn hope, else the expression on her mother's face would not have had such a damping effect.

"No, oh no! Not Mr. Farrell." Irene's voice shook. "But I mustn't say any more. Rivington will explain."

Clasping her daughter's hand, Irene started down the hallway where the study was located next to the library-cum-gambling salon.

"Don't tarry, child. You know how cross he gets when he is made to wait."

"Mama, I am no longer a child who must be led by the hand. And I shan't run away, I promise you."

A horrifying thought occurred to Maryann. "Or is it that you're holding my hand because"—her voice caught—"because you know I will need your comfort? Does Tammadge bring bad news about Stephen?"

Irene came to a stop a short distance from the study. She cast a harried look at the closed door, then at her daughter. It was difficult to think or to focus on anything; the vise around her head was tightening unmercifully.

"Maryann, this has nothing to do with Mr. Farrell. It concerns you alone. Your life. Your future."

The study door opened. The Earl of Rivington stuck his grizzled head into the hallway and bellowed, "Dammit, Irene! Didn't I tell you to bring the chit immediately? That I would talk to her myself?"

Irene flinched at the loud voice, but Maryann raised her chin and straightened her shoulders.

"In a moment you may tell me anything you like, Father. Just let me take Mama upstairs. You must see she's not well."

"I'll stay," said Irene and walked past her husband into the study.

Maryann measured her father with a look that would in the past have earned her a box on the ears. But although his face turned a mottled purple, sure mark of a mounting ire, his eyes did not meet hers and with a jerk of the head, he indicated that she was to follow her mother.

Without looking right or left, Maryann swept into

the narrow room that held her father's desk, several straight-backed chairs, and cabinets containing ledgers and business papers.

Quite often, Rivington's secretary could be found working at the desk, but on this day Mr. Winsome was apparently closeted in his own dingy office next to the basement stairs. Instead, Maryann saw a youth standing at the window, his back to the door. A blue coat, padded at the shoulders and nipped at the waist, and a pair of tight, canary yellow pantaloons proclaimed an aspiration to dandyism. Unfortunately, the fashionable raiment also stressed and drew attention to the stockiness of his build.

As she took a seat beside her mother in front of the desk, the young man turned his head, watching her over his shoulder. She judged him to be about her own age, although a sullen look about the mouth made him appear younger and distorted his features, which, she believed, might be rather pleasant when he smiled.

At first glance he looked familiar, but she did not recall having seen him before. She acknowledged him with a nod; he answered with a scowl, then turned back to what must have been a most absorbing view of the flagway leading to the service entrance of the neighbor's house.

Maryann gave a mental shrug and angled her chair so she might observe Tammadge leaning against the mantelpiece on her left. It took willpower, almost more than she possessed, to train her gaze on him.

How she despised him, loathed him, now that she knew what dirty business schemes were conceived behind that high forehead! There was no doubt in her mind, however, that whatever Rivington planned to tell her was connected with Tammadge. She wanted to see his eyes, the only feature that might give away his true feelings.

"Good evening, Tammadge." It might not be a wise

267

thing to do, but she could not stop herself from taunting him. "You must have entered via the mews and Father's, uh, library. For I did not hear the knocker on the front door."

"How observant you are." At his blandest, he bowed, then resumed his former casual pose, one elbow resting on the mantel shelf, legs crossed at the ankles.

She wanted to scream at him, ask what he had done with Stephen. With Meg. But she could not be certain that he had indeed discovered Stephen's involvement with the Bow Street court, and she must dissemble. She must be the actress Meg wanted to be.

She didn't trust her voice, not yet, and merely leaned back in the chair, her arms crossed over her breasts.

Expecting that her father would settle himself behind the desk, she was surprised to see him join the youth at the window. The earl looked at Tammadge, as though asking permission to speak.

Barely noticeable, Tammadge shook his head. "Since it was I who brought young Master Reginald to town, permit me to smooth your path just a little, my dear Rivington."

Against her will, Maryann's interest was piqued. Every other Rivington male carried the name Reginald, including her father and the cousin who had beheaded her favorite doll and would some day inherit the title and the estates.

"Do I have a cousin I have not yet met?" she asked, looking at the youth in a different light.

She could still see only his back, but it did seem to her that there was a resemblance to the executioner Reggie in the young man's square shoulders and short neck. And, perhaps, a resemblance to her father's beefy shape as well.

Her gaze shifted to Rivington, whose face had once more turned a mottled purple. His jaw worked furiously, but he spoke not a word.

"My dear Maryann," Tammadge said silkily. "Three days ago, you asked why your father wanted a gambling salon so badly that he would agree to a partnership with me."

Maryann tightened her arms over her chest lest he see her shiver. He *knew* she did not trust him. She shouldn't have flung her suspicion in his face — suspicion that he had gambled with William Fant, and cheated.

Collecting her wits, she said coldly, "I do not see what the gambling salon has to do with Master Reginald."

Tammadge raised his hand and gently fanned himself with his handkerchief.

"Don't you, my sweet, innocent Maryann?"

She heard the soft hiss of her mother's breath, her father's snort, and a sound from the young man at the window that was a mixture of a sob and a choke of laughter.

The truth hit her in the face.

Reginald spun away from the window, facing her with features that were the younger version of her father at his most belligerent.

"I'm your brother, Lady Maryann. Your father's bastard."

"Yes," she said slowly. "So I gathered. How do you do, Reginald?"

He sneered. "You *didn't* know. You had no notion until I told you. Confess it!"

"I could dispute with you, but I shan't," she said. "What's the point of brangling?"

Her heart hammered. She *had* realized who he must be before he had spoken. What she did not know was how she felt about the young man — her brother. Half brother. He seemed so much like her father, and yet there was something in his face that her father's had never shown. Vulnerability.

269

She glanced at her mother's pale face. No matter how disastrous the marriage, how disliked the husband—a sudden confrontation with Rivington's son by another woman would be a harrowing experience. And that Irene had not until this day known of Reginald's existence, Maryann did not doubt.

But why had Tammadge taken it upon himself to thrust Rivington's illegitimate son under their noses? And what did the establishment of a gaming hell in the library have to do with it all?

She sensed Tammadge's eyes on her, and knew without being told that he was well aware of the questions buzzing in her mind.

She'd be dashed if she asked.

For the first time since she had entered the study, Irene spoke up. "Reginald, you must be very hungry by this time. I believe, up in Oxford, they feed you boys at six o'clock."

"Yes, ma'am." He hesitated, then bowed awkwardly. "I'm devilish sharp-set. Lord Tammadge did not think it necessary to stop, save to change teams. And then I had time only for a sandwich or two."

"In that case you must certainly eat something to tide you over." Irene, distressed though she was, smiled kindly at the young man. "I'm afraid dinner will be rather late tonight."

She looked at her husband and issued the first order she had ever given him. "Ring for Melville and tell him to look after the boy."

Rivington's eyes bulged and his color came and went in a most alarming fashion. He looked about to explode, but Irene did not lower her gaze or, Maryann noted proudly, show in any way that she was intimidated.

Finally, Rivington stalked to the desk and tugged the bellpull on the wall behind it.

When, presently, the butler had borne young Master Reginald off, Irene said in a tone of voice that reminded Maryann strongly of her German grandmother, "And now, I think, we shall have no more theatricals. It is time that Maryann be told what this is all about."

She measured Tammadge, then her husband, with a scathing look. "Rivington, will you tell your daughter what you explained to me earlier? Or will you leave that up to my lord Tammadge as well?"

And just as though it had indeed been the indomitable Baroness von Astfeld und Hahndorf who had spoken, Rivington received the rebuke in silence.

Tammadge waved his handkerchief. "Rivington may have the honor. Though I don't doubt," he added softly, "but he'll make a mull of it."

Maryann looked at her father. "Why does Tammadge know about your son, but, apparently, no one else?"

"He found out because he set his man of business to snoop on me," the earl barked, then, with a look at Tammadge, closed his mouth tightly.

"Is he blackmailing you?"

Rivington sank into the deep leather chair behind the desk. Leaning back, his fingertips beating a tattoo on the armrest, he glared at his daughter.

"I'll have no more impertinent questions from you, gal! Tammadge tells me you've shown signs of wanting to draw back from the engagement. I'll have none of that, I tell you! Tammadge is my partner. He laid out his blunt. Still does, as a matter of fact, for wine, food, etc. And I—"

"You, sir," Maryann interrupted, "staked your daughter as surety against his money."

Rivington's massive body shot forward. He leaned across the desk, his bloodshot eyes narrowed. "You said yes quickly enough when you found out he'd settle a fair share of that money on you!"

Maryann blanched. The argument was irrefutable. The generous settlement had indeed been an incentive

271

to accept Tammadge's proposal. Her shame and regret were no less bitter for knowing that she had been duped, had been made to believe she entered the marriage contract of her own free will when, in fact, she would have been given no choice had she shown herself reluctant.

She spoke with forced calm. "I want to know why you're gambling and cheating when you've always stressed that no slur must be cast upon the Rivington name. And how your—that young man ties into it."

"He is my son!" Rivington shouted. "The only son I'll have. And I can give him nothing but the money I make gambling!"

"But you're wealthy. The estates—"

Rivington's fist slammed on the desk. "Do you know what it takes to maintain a house in London? Do you know what it costs to dower five daughters? And when I'm gone, the estates and the title will be your cousin's!" Bitterly, Rivington added, "There'll be nothing for my son."

Maryann unfolded her arms. Although she was certain she knew the answer, she had to ask one more question.

"And if I do not marry Tammadge?"

Rivington drew a shuddering breath. "You *will* marry him. Lest you want to see me arrested for debts and for cheating, and your mother turned out into the streets!"

Chapter Twenty-Eight

Maryann got to her feet. Hands clenched, she advanced on Tammadge.

Rivington set up a roar, ordering her to sit down.

"Quiet, Rivington!" Tammadge barely raised his voice, yet the unmistakable command was instantly obeyed.

"I find that, after all, a rebellious spirit appeals to me more than meekness. If your daughter wants to slap me, she may do so with my goodwill."

"Blackmailer!" Shaking with revulsion and anger, Maryann shoved her hands behind her back. "I would not touch you did I wear gloves."

He did not move a muscle, his casual pose by the fireplace portraying infinite boredom. Only a sudden icy glint in the pale eyes betrayed that he was not as indifferent as he'd like to pretend.

"Aren't you just a trifle overdramatic?" he drawled. "Blackmail—what a distasteful word—does not enter into the picture. I clearly remember that you assured me neither Rivington nor I need fear you'd break the engagement."

She gritted her teeth. It seemed that everything she had said and done since Tammadge offered for her hand was coming back to haunt her.

Tammadge raised one pointed brow. "Am I wrong?"

"No."

273

She *had* told him she would not cry off. But how different the situation looked then. There had been no threat of having her mother turned out into the streets. She had not known then of a sullen youth — a half brother — dependent on Rivington's support.

Maryann felt trapped. The image of hounds closing in took possession of her mind, as once before, when she believed herself rejected by the one man who could help her find the proof of Tammadge's misdeeds.

Stephen.

She looked at her mother, who had assured her that Tammadge's presence and Rivington's disclosures had nothing to do with Stephen.

How wrong! He was committed to destroy Tammadge.

Yet, how could she let him do it — or continue herself to work toward that end? Tammadge's destruction would bring about her father's ruin, which, in turn, would mean impoverishment for her mother.

But she must not think of that now. And she must put Stephen from her mind until she was out of Tammadge's sight — lest she betray her fear for Stephen's safety.

Irene's eyes met hers with a silent plea. Her mother was at the end of her strength.

Summoning a smile, Maryann said, "If we want to give dinner to that hungry young man, we had best go and change."

Rivington thrust back his chair. "Not until I have your word —"

"Rivington!" Irene interrupted. "Don't harass Maryann. You will just have to trust her to do what is right."

To do what is right. The words burned in Maryann's mind.

Drawing Maryann with her, Irene swept out the door held open by Tammadge. The burst of energy lasted until they reached the half landing on the stairs

274

and Irene knew herself unobserved from the study. Leaning on Maryann's arm, she finished the climb to the third floor much more slowly.

"Thank you for your championship," Maryann said when she had made her mother comfortable on the day bed. "I never doubted you had pluck, but it takes a special strength to face down Father and Tammadge. I know the appearance of the boy must have been a shock to you."

Irene clasped her hand and pressed it.

"Now it's up to you, child. You must do *your* part."

Maryann nodded. She had been tempted to share her troubled thoughts, to ask her mother's advice. But no longer. She had always fought her own battles, made her own decisions.

She understood now what Irene had meant when she said, "This has nothing to do with Mr. Farrell. It concerns you alone. Your life. Your future." Irene might have added, "Neither has it anything to do with me or with young Reginald."

For it was Maryann who had to live with the consequences of whatever decision she made.

To do what is right.

But *what* was right?

"Mama, before you fetched me to the study, did you learn anything about that boy—about Reginald?"

Irene was reluctant to speak about Rivington's son, but Maryann persisted. She did not wish to distress her mother, but she must have all the facts before making a decision. And she would not go to her father if she could help it.

After a while, it became evident that Irene was not so much upset or embarrassed as she was afraid to rouse pity in Maryann's breast for her half brother.

The boy's mother, she finally admitted, had died when he was still in leading strings. He had been fostered by various women of respectable background, and by no means had he been mistreated or neglected!

By some lucky chance, Rivington had contrived to enter his "ward" at Harrow when Reginald was about eleven or twelve years old, and then, later, at Christ Church in Oxford.

Reginald Makepiece was a very fortunate young man, Irene assured Maryann, his future taken care of if he applied himself to his studies and learned to nurture friendships with those of his fellows who might, later on, assist him in procuring a lucrative post.

Maryann agreed absently.

Reginald Makepiece. Not Reginald Rivington. She remembered the sullen look on his face, the choke — half sob, half laughter — when he said, "I am your brother. Your father's bastard."

"How old is he, Mama?"

"He told me he'll turn eighteen in October."

Born ten months after Irene had presented Rivington with his fifth daughter . . . Maryann.

Her thoughts churning, Maryann remained only a few minutes longer, then sought refuge in her own room.

The lamps had been lit. No matter that both Hedwig and Irene called Jane a flibbertigibbet, the girl never forgot to light the lamps well before evening shadows in the room might remind her mistress of dark cellars. Maryann appreciated the gesture, but this evening she thought not of her own fear of the dark, but of Hannah Moss's.

She had promised Hannah another visit, and even though she could not be certain that the girl had listened, she must keep that promise — no matter what her decision about Tammadge would be.

First, however, she must see Stephen.

A drawer fitted behind the ornate front of a console table held everything she required: ink and pens in a leather case designed for travelers, and a stack of writing paper.

Her hand shook a little as she wrote, and when she

finished and looked at her handiwork, she was tempted to do it over. But even eight words — *Dear Stephen. I must see you. Yours, Maryann* — were too much effort to copy.

Resolutely, she folded and sealed the missive. At least she had not let the stupid, self-pitying tear that got away smudge the ink.

Harv would take the note to Stephen's lodgings in Ryder Street. He might, she thought with a surge of hope, bring back a reply.

But hope would not achieve as much as action. Her hand steadier, she pulled out a second sheet of paper and addressed it to both Meg and Fletcher at the Fighting Cock. Rush must deliver that one. And if neither was at the tavern, he must take it to Sir Nathaniel Conant in Bow Street. Somehow or other she would find out what happened the night before.

Anticipation of hearing from either Stephen or Meg carried her through dinner. She had been half-afraid Tammadge would insist on taking his potluck with them and was relieved to see that he had not. Even so, the meal was a horrid affair such as she prayed she'd never have to endure again.

Her mother looked far from well and hardly spoke at all, but Maryann knew better than to suggest she retire. A certain glint in the shadowed eyes when they rested on Rivington told Maryann that Irene would not leave.

Rivington, who never dined at home unless they were giving a formal dinner, had canceled an engagement at White's in honor of his son's presence and harped on the shortcomings of daughters in general, and Maryann in particular.

Reginald, when addressed, was either sullen and taciturn to the point of rudeness, or he lashed out with cynical, snide remarks. He indicated that he expected an invitation to stay in town for a few days and, in the same breath, professed a burning desire to escape all

Rivingtons and return posthaste to Oxford.

Maryann did not know how she felt about the moody young man. She imagined herself in his place . . . Rivington's son, but no right to the name or the advantages and privileges that went with it . . . and was torn between pity and exasperation.

But those were superficial emotions. What she felt deep in her heart was less easily defined, and at the moment, until she had news from or about Stephen, she did not even want to try to examine her feelings.

When she and Irene finally withdrew from the dining room, Harv was waiting in the hallway. Maryann's blood quickened with excitement. To ignore Harv was harder than sitting through the dinner had been, but she accompanied Irene and deposited her in Hedwig's tender care before flying down the stairs again and pelting the footman with questions.

"What did Mr. Farrell say, Harv? When is he coming to see me?"

Chapter Twenty-Nine

"I'm sorry, Lady Maryann, but nobody was home at all. Not even Mr. Farrell's man."

"Not at home," she repeated tonelessly, her hopes dashed. Apprehension gripped her with renewed force. "What about my note?"

"On the hall table in Mr. Farrell's flat. The retired gentleman's gentleman as owns the building didn't think nothin' of unlocking the door and adding it to all the other notes. It seems Mr. Farrell is gone quite often."

"Thank you, Harv." She had to clear her throat before asking, "Has Rush returned?"

"No, Lady Maryann."

"Please send him to the book room as soon as he comes in."

Huddled in an old, worn armchair, her feet drawn up under her skirts, and surrounded by Irene's novels and her own favorite volumes on botany and horticulture, she hoped to forget her problems and hold at bay her fears—for a little while at least.

She looked at etchings and pencil drawings of the flowers and plants she loved, and imagined herself in her own gardens . . . breathing the sweet smell of honeysuckle, the perfume of lavender and roses. As they would in a real garden, the freshness and beauty of her dream garden soothed her mind. For a little while. When she was obliged to turn a page, her anxious thoughts immediately jumped to Stephen.

He and the Bow Street runner had left Mrs. Webster's house and disappeared almost immediately. Had he followed Tammadge and Meg? Had he been discovered?

She started to shake as earlier fears reawakened. She was cold and sweaty at the same time, and knew she must stop anticipating the worst. It was possible that there had been no abduction at all, and that Meg and Stephen were closeted with Sir Nathaniel to devise a new plan. She would know as soon as Rush had tracked them down at the Bow Street magistrate's office — or wherever they were meeting.

The thought of Stephen at work on a new trap for Tammadge brought no peace of mind either. Not when she kept hearing her father: "You *will* marry Tammadge . . . lest you want to see your mother turned out into the streets!"

With great concentration, she was able to keep her attention on the drawings. She flipped the pages faster to avoid getting sidetracked.

Until she came upon the colored sketch of a posy of violets.

She stared at the delicate flowers, remembering the wilted posy Stephen had offered her on the way to the Sloane Street gardens. The day she wanted to hit him because he called Tammadge a perverted sadist.

It seemed like a year ago, yet less than two weeks had passed. In that time, Stephen had sunk in her eyes from a spy-hero to a cad and a defamer, then had risen from a Bow Street spy to the man she trusted implicitly.

And now she loved him. Foolishly, no doubt. Hopelessly, perhaps. But that was something she did not want to think about. Not now.

She wanted to think about Stephen and what he might have said and done if Bella had not interrupted them. She wanted to anticipate the moment she would see him again.

Her eyes on the violets, she finally relaxed, even dozed a little, and, as on the night before, allowed herself to daydream about Stephen. Fear and apprehension had no place in this dream world, only warmth, tenderness, and the sweetness of love.

On and off, she was aware of faint sounds, a footstep, a voice, in the garden below. They did not bother her. She knew they must be her father's gambling friends sneaking into the library. Her father and his disreputable enterprise did not belong in her dream world either.

Only Stephen. His arms around her, his mouth trailing kisses on her brow, her temple, her cheek, the corner of her mouth.

The warmth of his body against hers, the slight abrasiveness of his face . . . it was so real . . . so much more satisfying and, at the same time, more tantalizing and intoxicating than anything she had imagined before.

"Stephen," she murmured, placing her hands behind his neck and burying her fingers in the crisp hair.

Crisp hair! Her eyes flew open.

"Stephen!"

She snatched away her hands and tried to get up, but he was perched on the armrest of the chair and gently pushed her back.

"What an abandoned little pixie you are." There was laughter in his voice, laughter dancing in the dark eyes. "Cuddling up to anyone who awakens you with a kiss."

"I believed—never mind what I believed." She gave up struggling against the restraining hands, but succeeded in putting her feet on the floor.

"Stephen, what the dickens happened last night? Where have you been? Where is Meg? I've been out of my mind with worry!"

"Nothing happened. Tammadge didn't take the bait." He looked at her, conscience-stricken. "I thought you knew."

Nothing happened. Weak with relief, she leaned her head against the back of the chair. But not for long.

Eyes kindling, she asked, "And how, pray tell, should I have known? Did you send me a note? Did you call on me to lay my fears at rest?"

"I thought you must have heard Simms report that Meg had left Tammadge's house."

"I heard just enough to make me fear the worst. I went outside, but you weren't there. No one was there! Where were you?"

"Simms and I accompanied Meg to Upper Brook Street through the garden enclosure in the center of the square. That way, we would not be observed by Tammadge."

"Or by anyone else."

Her mouth tightened. Upper Brook Street, by Jove! On the opposite side of Grosvenor Square where she and Bella had walked toward Lower Brook Street.

Stephen said nothing. His dark eyes rested on her with a quizzical look, and vexation melted. How could she stay resentful when he was safe, when he was with her? It was her dream come true.

"Stephen, who let you in? I did not hear a knock announcing you. How did you find me?"

His impudent grin flashed. "I was in the gambling room. I met Wolversham, you see, and when he said he was going to play at 'Rivington's Club,' as he called it, I could not resist tagging along. I wanted to see you."

One of his arms enfolded her shoulders, one lay across her breasts. It was a most delicious imprisonment.

Maryann had more questions, but for the moment she abandoned them. She had only to raise her face a very little before his mouth claimed hers, gently at first, then more demanding.

She responded naturally, without hesitation, opening herself to him as a flower would unfold its petals under the kiss of the sun. This might be the last time he kissed her, the last time he held her close. Once she told him—

She thrust the thought away, abandoning herself to the bittersweet rapture of love just found and soon to be given up. She wanted to be close to him, and when his arms suddenly shifted, clasping her around the hips and sweeping her off the chair, she flung her own arms around his neck and clung to him tightly.

For a while he held her thus—her heart beating against his, their mouths locked in a kiss. Then, slowly, he set her down.

"Maryann, tell me," he demanded. "What I read in your eyes last night—is it true?"

She needed no time to think, did not have to ask what he meant.

"Yes, Stephen. I love you."

"And I love you."

The face that could be so harsh and unyielding was filled with tenderness when he bent to kiss her once again. It was a kiss of sweetness, a silent avowal of love; a kiss that demanded nothing, only gave.

With a groan half-stifled, he put her from him.

"I must go, Maryann."

The words hit her like a spray of cold water. She remembered her fears, her father's demand. Tammadge's blackmail.

"Stephen, no! We must talk."

"Tomorrow, my love." He touched a finger to her cheek. "Can you meet me at Hookham's? I understand it is usually deserted at noon."

Her eyes widened. "You must be mad! We cannot meet in a lending library. Tammadge—"

"The devil fly away with him! Maryann, I must not linger. I only left the gaming room 'to blow a cloud' in

283

the garden."

"Very well. We'll talk tomorrow." Perhaps it would be easier then to tell him of her father's demand. Perhaps.

"Stephen, at least tell me where you were all day. And all evening. I sent a note to Ryder Street. You weren't there. Were you hiding from Tammadge?" she asked, once more afraid for him. "Is he suspicious of you?"

"Not at all. I called on him—rather, I tried to. I was told he had gone up to Oxford for the day."

"Yes, he—never mind." Tammadge's travel to Oxford had to do with *her* problem, not with Stephen's.

"I must go, love." He turned abruptly and walked to the door. "I am to take Wolversham's place at the whist table. He's losing heavily and wants out."

She knew it would be foolish if he lingered, but she did not want to let him go. Something might happen to prevent another meeting . . . he might be detained, or . . .

"Stephen, don't go! I have this strange feeling about tomorrow—oh, I cannot explain!"

"I know exactly what you mean. It's intuition, premonition, or whatever you want to call it. But nothing will happen tomorrow. *My* feelings tell me that we *shall* meet."

He opened the door. "By the by, I have a message for you from one of your footmen who caught me climbing in a kitchen window. He's not certain how much longer you want him to wait up for Rush."

"Harv! So that's how you knew where to find me. You made him tell you."

Stephen grinned. "What's your pleasure, my lady? It's one o'clock or later. Footmen—and even pixies—should be in bed by now."

A knot of apprehension twisted her stomach. She had not realized it was quite so late.

"Tell him to go to bed. But, Stephen, listen!" She followed him out into the hallway. "I sent Rush to the

Fighting Cock, and he has not returned!"

"I wouldn't worry. A tavern is a tempting place for a soldier."

If she were not familiar with every nuance of the deep voice, if she were not sensitive to the slightest change of expression or stance, she would have accepted the explanation without reservation. But she knew him too well.

Something about Rush's tardiness — or the fact that the peg-legged soldier had gone to the tavern at all — had put Stephen on the alert.

"What if Meg wasn't there, Stephen? At this time of night, she would not be at the theater. Are you quite certain she is all right?"

"Meg?" One foot on the stairs, Stephen looked back at her. "Didn't I tell you? She's probably celebrating. She was in high croak last night after fleecing Tammadge at piquet. Won fifty pounds."

Chapter Thirty

"But why, if Meg is all right, didn't Rush return with a message from her?" Maryann asked when, contrary to her fears, she and Stephen met without a mishap at Hookham's lending library in Old Bond Street.

They were as private as they could wish to be, sheltered from view among the stacks and too far in the back of the library to be overheard by the bored clerk perched behind his tall desk, or the elderly lady flipping through periodicals in the reading area. Taking no chances, though, they spoke in hushed tones.

"Because he's still at the tavern. Drunk as a brewer's horse."

"Oh."

So it had been nothing but the truth when Stephen said the night before that a tavern was a tempting place.

"Thank you for checking on him," she said.

Stephen nodded. "Fletcher is letting him sleep it off. No doubt you'll see a very sorry soldier this afternoon."

Absently, she agreed.

"What will happen now, Stephen? Is Sir Nathaniel giving up?"

Stephen's face hardened. "No! It's the devil of a coil, I admit. We were so certain Tammadge would take Meg to the *Venture* and we'd nab him — and then, nothing! But we won't give up. We'll think of something."

"Perhaps Tammadge never intended to take Meg.

What does she think?"

Stephen placed two of the steps used to reach the highest shelf close together and offered one to Maryann as a makeshift bench.

Seating himself, he said, "She's as much in the dark as Sir Nathaniel and I are. All she had to report was that the servants, save for Tammadge's valet, had been given the evening off and that, after several games of piquet and a 'scrumptious supper,' she was asked to come back next Thursday. Tammadge made no demands of her or said anything that would imply he might do so next week."

"I am glad. I don't want her hurt in any way."

Stephen looked at Maryann. He forgot anger and frustration over his failure to catch Tammadge as his heart swelled with love—and pride.

Her kisses had shown her innocent of passion or lust; the wide gray eyes were clear and guileless as a child's. Yet she showed an understanding and generosity of spirit for Meg's situation that many a mature woman would have been unable to offer.

He wanted to pull her into his arms and—"

"Ha!" Maryann exclaimed and immediately looked guilt-stricken. "I'm sorry. I didn't mean to shout. But I believe I may have hit on something."

He was still thinking about what he'd like to do if his situation were different. If he didn't live under a false name—or, at least, had told her who he was—if he still had his investments, he might forget that Maryann was above his touch. He might ask her to marry him and grow flowers in Cornwall. . . .

Her next words caught his full attention.

"This coming Thursday is the second day of May, Stephen. That evening, Princess Charlotte will marry Prince Leopold."

"By Jupiter! If I didn't forget." He was about to slap his thigh when he recalled their surroundings. He lowered his voice. "There'll be so much celebrating in the streets, Tammadge could abduct every woman and child in town and no one would take notice."

He saw her eyes widen, her face turn pale. With an effort, he suppressed the excitement surging in him. He reached over to press the hands clasped tightly in her lap.

"I know that's taking us too close to your own wedding day. May the sixth. I'll never forget how you flung the date at my head at the Fighting Cock. But remember, Maryann! You will *not* marry Tammadge."

"I may have to," she whispered.

"No!"

Two large tears fell.

Within the airless confines of the high stacks, Stephen felt cold. He got off the steps.

Raising her hands to his lips, he vowed, "I'll do *anything* to keep you away from Tammadge. If Thursday turns out to be another blind, I will call him out."

"You don't understand."

Her hands clutching his, she rose. "Stephen, circumstances have changed. I am totally in Tammadge's power."

Baldly, without mincing words, she told him of the summons from her father, of Reginald, of Tammadge's blackmail. She did not cry any more, but her eyes, which had always before held a glint of determination or rebellion, or a spark of mischief, had the dull look of hopelessness.

A vise gripped his gut and tightened unmercifully as he listened and began to foresee the inevitable conclusion of the sorry tale.

"If anything happens to my father, Mama will have nothing but debts. She won't be able to move to Bath, where she'd escape the brunt of the scandal. She—"

Her voice broke. She withdrew her hands from his grip, fumbled in her reticule for a handkerchief, and blew her nose.

To Stephen, it was a valiant gesture that gave him

hope. She might think herself lost, doomed to martyr-
dom. But her spirit was not broken.

When she looked at him again, though, he could not
like the bitter twist of the mouth he had kissed only a
few hours earlier. He stepped toward her to wipe out
the bitterness with the tip of a finger, but she drew
away.

"I shan't have a dowry," she said. "Mama cannot rely
on me to contract another advantageous marriage and
offer her a home — even if I were willing to consider
such a step once more. As father said, she'll be out in
the street."

"Your sisters —"

"Not one of my worthy brothers-in-law would allow
his wife to associate with Mama," she said bitterly. "Not
if the Rivington name is tainted by scandal.

"And then," she added after a pause, "there is Reginald."

"With the education your father has provided, the
boy is well able to take care of himself. He is eighteen,
you said. Not a helpless infant."

"But what is there for him to do? Clerking?"

"There is nothing wrong with clerking."

"He wants to read law. As long as my father provides
for him, he can stay at Christ Church. Stephen, I cannot forget that he, but for the mischance of being born
illegitimate, would be the future Earl of Rivington."

"That is to be laid at your father's door. *You* can do
nothing about it." Stephen gave her shoulders an exasperated little shake. "And neither need you feel guilty."

He saw the stubborn tilt of her chin and realized that
her unbroken spirit could work against him as much as
it could against Tammadge. Right or wrong, she felt
responsible for her mother and the boy Tammadge had
thrust under her notice.

And he unable to help.

Stephen had been bitter about William's suicide, had
raged at William's cowardice, but not until now had he

wanted to curse William for gambling away not only his own property, but Stephen's as well.

"I had much time this morning to think about the decision I must make," said Maryann. "If I defy my father and Tammadge, I will condemn my mother to penury. But if I marry the monster, I'll be going against all principles I hold dear."

"I told you!" he said with a harshness stemming as much from frustration at his helplessness as it sprang from apprehension of what she'd say next. "I shall not let you marry Tammadge. He will be arrested and convicted. Or he shall die at my hands."

She was so pale, he could see the veins beneath her skin.

"Stephen, it is too late. I must ask you to let Tammadge go."

He flinched.

He'd had ample warning of what she would ask, yet he was not prepared. The wrench at his heart was infinitely worse than the physical pain he'd suffered when, climbing the Pyrenees, he had been kicked by a mule.

"Don't ask me that! You must know I cannot back out of my commitment."

"Yes, I know." Her shoulders drooped. "But I had to ask anyway. Good-bye, Stephen."

She turned, stumbling blindly into the steps behind her, but was caught by Stephen. With her back toward him, he pulled her into the shelter of his arms, fiercely determined to protect her, to save her from Tammadge and her own misguided sense of obligation.

One of the feathers on her hat tickled his nose, and he had to twist his head to speak around it.

"Before you go," he said hoarsely, "let me tell you again that I love you."

A tremor ran through her slight frame. She drew breath, like a sob barely stifled.

"I love you, too."

The words were almost inaudible, but he heard.

He tightened his hold on her. "If you will but trust me, I'll see to it that nothing happens to your father — provided he gives up the gambling salon."

For an instant, she yielded against him, and his spirits rose. Then she stiffened.

"My father is over his head in debts. So far, his name and position have kept the creditors at bay, but *one word* against him will send them scurrying to our door. He'll end up in debtor's prison." *And Mama — on the streets.*

"I'll make certain Tammadge will have no chance to say that word."

"How?" she asked sharply. "By killing him?"

Yes, by killing him.

He did not say it aloud. He did not need to.

Maryann turned in his arms. Her hands frantically clutched at the lapels of his coat.

"You mustn't kill him! I forbid it. Do you hear, Stephen? You must not kill Tammadge. I could not live with myself if you were arrested for murder."

"Shh!" His voice was rough, hiding the tenderness welling in him. "You'll have the clerk on us if you don't take care."

"I don't give a straw! Promise me, you won't call him out!"

He looked into her eyes, and, seeing her fear, he grew calm.

He wanted Maryann's happiness more than anything in the world. And he wanted Maryann.

But he was committed to go after Tammadge — committed personally for the sake of his sister-in-law and his young nieces, and bound by pledge to assist the Bow Street magistrate in ridding society of a canker.

Desire and obligation — a chasm gaped between the two. But he had overcome obstacles far more difficult and deadly.

"Promise, Stephen!"

The stakes were high, but never were they more worthwhile.

"If *you* promise not to marry him."

They stared at each other in a silent battle of wills. Stephen forceful, demanding. Maryann pleading.

Again he felt her tremble. She slumped against him, hiding her face against his chest. And the dratted feather tickled his ear.

"I cannot bear to marry him," she admitted.

Stephen gave the hat a nudge, tilting the nuisance of an ornament to a more accommodating angle. One hand cupping her cheek, the other stroking her back, he held her against him. He did not allow himself to feel relief. Maryann was a woman. She might well give in to the pressure of what she perceived as obligation and duty, and change her mind.

And he knew better than to press his luck by insisting on a promise when he knew that he would never make the vow she demanded.

"Are you planning to see Hannah again?" he asked.

Her face still rested against his chest and her answer was muffled. "I must. I told her I would."

Satisfied, he said no more. As long as Maryann saw Hannah and was reminded of the viscount's trade, there was a good chance she'd stand firm.

For some time, Stephen had been aware of movement in the front of the library. Twice, he had heard the door open and close, and he knew that they must soon be discovered.

Gently rubbing her temple with his thumb, he said, "Won't you let me look at you once more before I must send you home?"

A tentative smile greeted him when she raised her face. Consigning to perdition anyone who'd dare spy on them, he traced the curve of the smile with his mouth.

"You had better go now," he said reluctantly. "I hear someone coming this way."

Looking dazed, she drew away. "You go first. I'll select a few books. One of us should give the poor clerk

292

some business after sheltering us for so long."

He adjusted her hat, then looked deep into her eyes. "That's better," he said. But he was not speaking of the hat.

Maryann watched him go, and when he disappeared around the stack into the main aisle, she slowly followed. Surely there was no harm in looking after a very handsome man. Many girls did so.

She stepped out into the aisle and came face to face with Mrs. Webster. Maryann curtsied; the widow nodded and swept past her. She had not forgiven the slight to her nieces.

The snub did not greatly disturb Maryann. She was absorbed in watching Stephen. She had convinced him she wouldn't marry Tammadge; she was sure of it. But she had promised nothing.

A tightness in her chest made breathing difficult. He had passed the reading area where three elderly ladies now sat with newspapers and periodicals. In a moment, he'd be gone.

She saw him nod to the clerk, heard him say something about coming back to look for a military history book when he had more time at his disposal.

He was almost at the door when it was opened from outside and a young gentleman, fashionably attired in a fawn-colored double-breasted coat of superfine, off-white pantaloons, and glossy Hessian boots, entered the lending library. Catching sight of Stephen, the young elegant stopped in his tracks, his face breaking into a wide smile.

Stephen, too, came to an abrupt stop. Maryann could not see his face, but, judging by the stiffness of his back, his reaction to the fashionable gentleman was anything *but* pleasure.

The young man snatched off his hat. "By Jupiter!" he exclaimed. "I couldn't have wished for a better sight on my first day in town. How do you do, Major Fant?"

Chapter Thirty-One

In the sudden silence after the boisterous greeting, Maryann's gasp was clearly audible to anyone in the reading room.

Major Fant. Stephen Fant.

William Fant . . . his brother?

Stephen's head jerked. He looked at her, and the expression on his face was all the confirmation she needed.

She could not move, simply stood in the middle of the lending library and stared at him.

A look of pain crossed his face. He turned to the newcomer and, clamping his hand around the young man's arm, propelled him outside.

The snap of the door shutting exploded like a pistol shot in Maryann's ears. She gave a start, instantly aware of four pair of eyes on her.

Five pair, for Mrs. Webster had returned from the back of the room and stood at her side.

"Are you quite well, dear?" the widow asked. "I heard you gasp. Are you in pain?"

"I am perfectly all right," Maryann lied. She hurt badly. Her chest, her throat, her head, everything felt tight, sore.

Stephen Fant . . . whose brother shot himself. It explained so much.

But he had not trusted her sufficiently to tell her.

Not even after he had fallen in love with her.

Maryann heard Mrs. Webster offer the use of her carriage, heard herself declining politely but firmly. A few more civilities were exchanged — she was not certain what she said, but she must have made the correct responses, for Mrs. Webster remained quite affable. Presently, Maryann curtsied and took her leave.

Outside Hookham's, Stephen waited for her. Alone. He was as pale as the day the mob stoned her carriage in Seven Dials.

Bitterness welled in her. Concern, remorse, were no good *after* he had broken her heart. She didn't think she could speak to him now — save that she wanted to know *why* he had carried on the deception when he should have trusted her.

He offered his arm. She accepted. In silence, they started to walk.

A short distance ahead, Rob was driving the carriage toward Piccadilly. Around them thronged a busy crowd — ladies shopping, gentlemen on the strut, maids, footmen, delivery boys.

It seemed to her that there were two Maryanns. One was wrapped in pain, oblivious to anything but misery; the other stood apart, watching with a disinterested eye and making certain that the conventions were observed — an acquaintance acknowledged, a smile maintained, for a lady must not wear her heart upon her sleeve.

"Maryann."

She felt Stephen's eyes on her and, despite the low tone, heard the urgency in his voice. But she did not turn her head.

"I'd give anything if I could change what happened. That you needn't have heard it *this* way — by accident."

She looked straight ahead, saw her carriage check at the corner, then sweep into the flow of traffic in Piccadilly.

"It wouldn't have happened! Not if *you* had told me. Stephen, why didn't you? Why didn't you trust me?"

Beneath her hand, the muscles of his arm tautened. He was silent.

"Why, Stephen?"

If only she did not love him so much, the pain in her heart might be bearable. Bewildered, angry, and very hurt, she finally looked at him.

"You said you love me. Doesn't love include trust?"

He slowed his steps. His eyes never left her face.

"I trust you. But there are some things a man must keep to himself, especially if he falls in love at a time when it's most important that he remain aloof and objective."

"Are you saying that falling in love was . . . ill-timed for you?"

"Very." His look was rueful, tender, apologetic. "Bear in mind that the object of my love was, and still is, betrothed to the man I swore to deliver to the Bow Street court."

The words stung. "I would not have betrayed you!"

"You misunderstand," he said quietly. "It was recognition I feared — sudden exposure, as it happened today — and that Tammadge would discover your knowledge of my deceit. Maryann, even before I knew that I loved you, I wanted to protect you."

He was so calm, as though they were discussing the advantages and disadvantages of the use of lime in an asparagus bed! A bitter retort sprang to the tip of her tongue, but something in his look gave her pause. He believed sincerely that she would understand his reasoning.

Yet, she did not.

"I daresay it's because I don't have much experience with being protected that I cannot help but be hurt by your silence," she said. "There have been so many things you did not tell me . . . that you worked with Sir Nathaniel, that one of Tammadge's ships had already docked in Wapping, that a trap was set for him with Meg as bait."

They turned the corner of Piccadilly. Rob had stopped the carriage some distance ahead, in front of a tea chandler. When he saw them, he flicked the reins and drove on.

Bitterness suppressed but a moment ago flared hotly. "Is it also for my protection that you ordered *my* groom to keep his distance? No doubt he'll speed away if I try to enter the carriage before it suits you."

She thought she saw his mouth twitch ever so slightly, and felt like the child he often called her. But his gaze was somber.

"Maryann, do you want to leave? You need only say the word, and I'll hail Robert."

Quieter, she said, "I don't want to leave just yet. I want to know why you did not tell me that your brother was the unfortunate William Fant."

Stephen came to a sudden stop. He was oblivious to stares and mutterings of passersby who had to step into the street to get around them.

"You know? About William's . . . suicide?"

She had finally pierced that calm front, but the knowledge gave her no satisfaction.

Drawing him into the doorway of a glover's shop, she said, "Lady Oglesby, your brother's sister-in-law, is a neighbor at Rivington Hall and a very dear friend of Mama's."

Mouth set grimly, Stephen was looking at her, but there was an expression in the dark eyes that made her wonder what he actually saw. It certainly was not her.

"You thought him a coward," she said intuitively.

"I cursed him for his cowardice. He wrote to me, explained that Tammadge had threatened his wife and daughters. But even when I learned from Sir Nathaniel about the white slavery operation, I did not fully understand William's despair. Not until I met you."

She was no longer in doubt that Stephen saw her.

The look in the dark eyes pierced into her soul. It numbed the hurt and dulled the sharp edge of bitterness.

"Maryann, that was when I grew afraid."

"You? Afraid?"

He gave a harsh laugh. "Scared stiff! I had Susan and my little nieces to protect. I was beginning to understand William's hopelessness, for nowhere could I see a way to get proof of Tammadge's crimes. And there you were, at first bound and determined to marry him, then threatening to bring about exactly what had drawn Tammadge's vengeance on William's head. Exposure of his evilness."

A gentleman approached the doorway, his step hurried, his face set in disapproving lines. Stephen clasped her elbow, and they moved on before the glover's prospective customer could reproach them for obstructing his path.

"Maryann, I love you. Can you understand why I wanted you to do nothing but end the betrothal?" Stephen's grip was as tight as his voice. "Why I tried to keep you out of the investigation and, when that was not possible, told you only what I believed would frighten you into giving up your plan?"

"You were afraid for me. Concerned for my safety."

She was subdued. She *did* understand. When she had believed Stephen in danger, she had been distraught with worry.

But she had kept nothing from him, or only irrelevant bits and pieces of information, and only in the beginning of their acquaintance when she'd had to remind herself that she should not trust him because of his friendship with Tammadge.

Again she caught sight of Rob tooling the carriage at a sedate pace.

As so many times before, Stephen knew her thoughts, anticipated her wishes. He gave a whistle, and Rob pulled to a halt. By the time they reached the vehicle, the groom had opened the door and returned to the box.

Stephen bowed over her hand.

"I love you, Maryann," he said softly.

She could not speak over the lump in her throat, only looked at him with her heart in her eyes.

"You still hurt," he said.

"I do. A little," she whispered. "I love you, Stephen."

It looked as though he were about to speak again, then changed his mind.

Pressing a kiss onto her wrist, he handed her into the carriage. "Shall I tell Robert to take you home?"

"To Wilderness Road. A visit to Hannah is long overdue."

The visit with the silent girl sitting before the blazing fire in an overbright room did nothing to lighten Maryann's mood. Returning home in the late afternoon, she did her best trying to understand Stephen, telling herself that he had done no more and no less than adopt the strategy she had taken with her mother.

But the dull, persistent ache, the disappointment, would not go away. Being kept in the dark about his identity by the man she loved was *not* the same as a daughter sheltering her mother from anxieties that would bring on a severe headache.

Deep in troubled thoughts, Maryann entered the house and found Rush waiting in the foyer. The peg-legged soldier stumbled in his eagerness to apologize. He was abject and remorseful and begged her not to cast him out, but to give him another chance at serving her.

She was distracted and dealt with him briefly, reading him a scold, then sending him off to the kitchen for a meal.

Although she had noticed that his tattered clothing

299

was in worse condition than ever, she had asked no questions. If he had been engaged in some mill or a bout of fisticuffs, she did not want to know.

She forgot about his sorry looks as soon as he was out of sight, but she could not as quickly forget that Rush had been unable to look her in the eye. He was not cocky like Robert, but in their brief encounters he had always faced her squarely. Except this time.

It was embarrassment, she told herself. He'd get over it.

She had too many things on her mind, too many things to do during the next days, to spare another thought for a man who neglected his duties and imbibed so much that he ended up—as Stephen had phrased it—drunk as a brewer's horse.

Stephen. He was constantly in her thoughts. She recalled their meetings trying to determine when she had begun to fall in love with him, but could not. It might have been when he drove her to see Sir Nathaniel and she read in his eyes that he would come to her aid, would act her knight.

Unfortunately, their concepts of a knight were as different as buttercups and bluebells. Stephen would slay the dragon *for* her. She wanted him to slay it *with* her.

And, remembering the very first time she set eyes on him, she admitted the possibility that she had fallen in love with him right then and there. But too many things happened too fast, always with Stephen seeming to be a villain, until she had been convinced that her first impression of him was totally false.

She caught herself looking for Stephen in the next few days. Everywhere she went, her eyes searched for the tall, straight figure, the dark, sun-streaked hair—at Lady Effingham's rout on Saturday, while she walked with Bella in Hyde Park on Sunday afternoon, at Lady Jersey's soiree on Monday night.

But Stephen did not appear. Apparently, he was

taking no chances of being recognized once more.

It was Tammadge she saw — too often for her taste. She avoided direct contact as best she could, unblushingly soliciting the help of her mother and Bella. But the pale eyes pursuing her in Lady Effingham's drawing room and in Lady Jersey's salons were almost as hard to bear as the encounter in the park when he insisted on walking between her and Bella, a young lady on each arm.

And then there was Reginald. The youth would remain with them until the following Tuesday, Rivington coldly informed Maryann. The day after her marriage to Tammadge.

The reminder of her wedding day, Monday, May the sixth, sent a shiver down her spine. Resolutely, she put the date from her mind while making an effort to get to know her half brother, but, although not openly hostile, Reginald made it clear that he preferred Irene's company to Maryann's.

On Monday night, just one week before the day set for the wedding, Irene asked Maryann to come into her room on their return from Sally Jersey's soiree.

"My love, I'm worried about you," she said, quite uncharacteristically pacing the way Maryann usually did. "You have been subdued, distracted — and, worse, you have not said a word about your and Mr. Farrell's progress in getting the proof of Tammadge's crimes."

Arriving at the dressing table, she swung around to face her daughter on the day bed.

"In fact, you have not mentioned Mr. Farrell at all since the day after Mrs. Webster's musicale. What's wrong, Maryann? You're in love with him, aren't you?"

"I am."

Irene studied her daughter's pale face, the shadowed eyes, the melancholy droop of the mouth. "When he spoke to me at Mrs. Webster's, I gathered that he is deeply in love with you. Was I mistaken? Does Mr.

Farrell *not* love you?"

"He is not Mr. Farrell, Mama! He is Stephen Fant. Maj. Stephen Fant. Only he never told me. I found out by accident, because someone recognized him."

Irene sank onto the stool in front of her dresser. "William Fant's brother. Well! And Lady Oglesby thought he was in Paris!"

"Mama, he did not trust me with his name! How can he say he loves me?"

"Child, what are you saying?" Irene crossed the room and sat down beside her daughter. "Did you quarrel over this?"

"N-no. I was too hurt to think of pulling caps. I only wanted to know *why*. He said it was for my protection."

"But you, I daresay, don't think that justifies deception. Well, if *he* could not convince you, I shan't waste my breath on arguments."

Irene clasped Maryann's hand. "But I will say this! Love is precious. Don't let it escape. You don't know how lucky you are to have found the man you love before you were irrevocably tied to Tammadge."

Maryann's attention was caught. "Is that what happened to you? That you fell in love *after* you married Father?"

Irene's eyes had a faraway look. "Yes, I fell in love."

"And what happened?"

Irene smiled, but the smile held a hint of sadness. "Nothing happened. It was too late for Pierre and me. I was married. Gussie had just turned one, and Margaret was on the way."

"Pierre, a Frenchman. One of the émigrés?"

Irene nodded.

"Did he not fight for you, this Frenchman? Try to persuade you to run away with him?"

"He was married also."

"Star-crossed love."

Irene's voice became brisk. "But yours is not. That's

302

why I told you about Pierre and me, to show you that some obstacles are insurmountable; others, like hurt feelings, even blackmail, can be overcome."

"Can they?"

"Child, don't throw away your happiness, your love. Fight!"

Chapter Thirty-Two

Maryann left her mother and went to her own room. She looked at Tammadge's ring on her fourth finger. Slowly she stripped it off.

In the back of a drawer in her dressing table, she found the box in which Tammadge had carried the ring. The sapphire and the pearls looked beautiful against the burgundy velvet lining. Much better than on her finger.

She closed the lid and set the box on the mantel shelf. She was done with the ring.

Despite her admission to Stephen that she could not bear marrying Tammadge, she had not been certain at all about what she *should* do. But no longer was she undecided.

Fight for love and happiness.

If her father ended up in debtor's prison, and she and Irene penniless, she could always hire herself out as a gardener and support her mother. And Mama had the seven hundred pounds sent by *Grossmutter*. It wasn't much, but it would tide her over until Maryann could provide for her.

No matter what the cost, Tammadge must be punished. Hannah must see justice done. And so must Stephen.

In two days, the fight against Tammadge would be over. She did not allow herself to doubt. If Tammadge was serious about sending a shipload of young girls to the Dey of Algiers, he would do it on the day of Princess Charlotte's wedding when the streets would be noisy with celebrations.

Two more days and she would see Stephen. And if she was not certain yet whether she would overcome her hurt feelings, she knew she did not have to confront the question immediately.

Fight for love and happiness.

It was a good thought to go to sleep on.

Tuesday morning, to the neglect of the Sloane Street gardens, Maryann decided to drive out to Wilderness Road. She was surprised to see that Robert was accompanied by Rush, but made no comment. If it was one of Rob's dictatorial whims, she did not want to enter into an argument. And if it was Rush's notion of making up for his slip from grace, she wouldn't want to snub him with an order to stay at home. The soldier's reluctance to look at her seemed to confirm the latter theory.

When she arrived at the Moss's house, Hester asked her to go upstairs to Hannah while she settled an argument between her cook and the butcher. Maryann had not been alone with Hannah before, and to her dismay, the girl started to cry when she entered the light-flooded room.

But then Hannah spoke.

"I'm so glad to see you! I was afraid you wouldn't come any more."

Maryann sat down in a chair beside her. "But why, Hannah? When I left Saturday, I said I'd be back."

"You promised last week to come on Friday. But you did not. And on Saturday you said nothing about that man you call Tammadge, or told me the good news you said you might have. And you didn't ask questions . . . about . . . about Leah and that night. As if . . . as if you wanted to forget all about it."

Maryann's heart raced with excitement. Hannah *had*

been listening, and now — bless the girl! — now she was coming out of her shell.

"Forget, like you, Hannah?" she asked, her voice gentle.

The pale face puckered. "I want to forget. But I cannot!"

"Why don't you tell me about it?"

Tears streaming, Hannah cried, "I cannot! I cannot!"

Hester Moss followed by Abraham rushed into the chamber.

"Lady Maryann," said Hester, wrapping her arms around her daughter. "I beg you to remember that Hannah must not be upset."

"She spoke!" said Mr. Moss, his voice unsteady, his eyes suspiciously moist. "Hannah spoke! It is a good sign. The wound on her head is healing well, but when she has talked about that night, she can heal inside as well."

Over his wife's protest, he allowed Maryann to put more questions to Hannah. The girl shook her head and cried harder. She cried as if her heart were breaking, but she did not scream or thrash her head or show any of the signs of rising hysteria that had marked her earlier reactions to Leah's name.

Maryann looked at Abraham Moss.

Running his fingers through his graying sidelocks, he said, "Perhaps we should let her rest. If Hester agrees, you might return tomorrow."

"Yes, I agree." Hester smiled at her husband. I have thought about the matter, and as always, you are in the right. It will be good for Hannah to speak about that awful night."

Maryann left the house in Wilderness Road in a buoyant, hopeful mood. The decisions she had made the night before were the *right* decisions. If she had needed proof, Hannah's improvement had supplied it. Soon, the girl would be able to speak about the night she was found unconscious, clutching Tammadge's handkerchief.

For the first time ever, Maryann felt truly in control of her life. One by one, she was finding solutions to problems that had seemed insurmountable a short time ago. One by one, she would overcome difficulties and obstacles ahead, like the hurt that still plagued her when she remembered Stephen's deception.

She was determined not let it come between them. She loved him. She missed him with an intensity that was frightening and exhilarating at the same time.

Two more days without seeing Stephen.

Taking refuge in daydreams about the life of a farmer's wife in Cornwall, growing vegetables and flowers to sell — part of the money to be used for Irene, the rest saved for the botanical gardens she would some day design near Seven Dials — Maryann arrived in Mount Street with her cheeks flushed and her spirits high.

She entered the house and was greeted by James with the intelligence that young Mr. Makepiece was desirous of having a word with her. Mr. Makepiece, the footman informed her, could be found in the book room.

Stopping only to deposit her hat and gloves on the hall table, Maryann hurried upstairs. A request from Reginald to see her was unusual, to say the least.

He was sitting in the worn leather chair she had occupied the night Stephen surprised her with a visit, but he rose as soon as he saw who entered. This exhibition of politeness did not surprise her. She had believed him rude when she first met him, but a few nights of his company at dinner had taught her that his manners were extremely nice, if, at times, a trifle awkward.

He blushed easily, and did so now, a youthful trait that could be endearing. Unfortunately, the dull red of his face, the stance, head slightly lowered and pushed forward like a bull ready to charge, reminded her of her father. She knew the comparison was illogical, and she was ashamed of the negative reaction it precipitated.

Perhaps he sensed that brief flare of antipathy—had always been aware of it and had, therefore, avoided her. She was certain he had noticed it this time.

The look he gave her betrayed anger, she thought, and defiance. But also hurt.

Her face burning with shame, she took a chair near his. "Please sit down, Reginald."

After a slight hesitation, he complied. "If this isn't a convenient time for you," he said quite civilly, "I apologize. I don't, however, want to postpone what I have to say."

"I promise to give you all the time you need, but before you speak, allow me to say something."

"Very well. It's not as though *I* had anything pressing to do. Lord Tammadge was in such a hurry to get me to London, I didn't even have time to pack my books."

She would have liked to pursue the topic of his studies, but knew that it was only an excuse to avoid the subject she *should* be discussing with him.

"Reginald, I owe you an apology. I fear I have allowed antagonism toward my father to spill over into my treatment of you."

He turned as pale as he had been red a moment ago. His eyes were hard and bitter.

"Then I didn't imagine that you don't like me! Well, it wasn't to be expected that the legitimate daughter would meet her father's bastard with anything but contempt."

"Oh, no!" Maryann was horrified that he had misconstrued her explanation. "My contempt and dislike are for my father, not for you. He has caused my mother, my sisters, and me more pain and heartache than any man has the right to do."

Reginald stared at her.

"I used to think him a great gun," he said hesitantly,

as though feeling his way through unexplored thoughts. "He always gave me what I wanted, quite unlike the fathers of other boys I knew. Most boys get regular whippings. He whipped me only once — years ago. I wasn't even in Harrow then. But he'd heard me brag that he's my father, and I wasn't supposed to ever say that. I am his 'ward,' you see."

"Yes, I see." Hoping she was better at hiding pity than she had been at hiding shameful, unjustified antipathy, she asked, "Do you still think him a great gun?"

His face hardened. "No. Mind you, I didn't want to admit at first that he isn't the gentleman I believed him to be. After all, he's the only kin I have. But I'm not green or stupid! I can see what's going on in this house and how he's getting the blunt to pay for my schooling."

He rose and stood before Maryann, his feet apart, hands behind his back. He looked determined, firm, but not intimidating. The eyes meeting hers were hazel, not the pale blue of her father's eyes.

"Somehow or other I mean to become a barrister. I'd do just about anything to achieve that end, but I won't accept money gained by cheating men too drunk to see which card they are playing."

"You won't?" she asked faintly. Obviously, not only were his manners nicer than she had supposed but also his notion of propriety. "Have you told Father?"

"Of course."

"And? Did he have nothing to say about it?"

A shadow crossed his face. "He threw a royal fit. But I care nothing about that. I also told him —"

"What?"

He gave her an uncertain look. "I had no right, I suppose, for it's none of my business. But I told him I don't want my sister to marry a man she hates, so that my father can continue in his dishonorable ways."

Speechless, Maryann looked up at him.

He held her gaze. "That's all I wanted to say," he said gruffly. "Thank you for your time."

"Thank *you!* Reginald, I am truly grateful."

He shrugged and started to turn away. " 'Tis nothing. If I cannot be a nobleman, I shall at least be a gentleman."

"That you are! Who—no, I need not ask. It was my mother who told you about Tammadge's blackmail, wasn't it?"

"Yes." He gave her a fierce look over his shoulder. "For two pins, I'd call him out!"

"Don't!" Maryann hastily got to her feet. Gripping his arm, she said, "Tammadge isn't worth the shot. Reggie, promise me not to call him out or even speak to him about it!"

A strange expression crossed his face, softening it, making him look younger than his years. Again Maryann noticed how different he was from Rivington.

"No one's called me Reggie since my mother—"

His mouth compressed. He looked at her hand on his arm, but made no attempt to remove it.

"Don't fret yourself," he said with studied indifference. "I already gave Lady Rivington my word. She said everything would work out. That you'll marry someone else."

And Maryann knew she would. If and when Stephen asked her. She'd marry him, and never again show him that he had once hurt her very badly.

"Yes, I will."

"That sounded like a vow," said Reginald. "You ought to save that for your wedding day."

She smiled, finally at ease with him—her half brother.

"It's a vow I don't mind making over and over. But I'll wait until Stephen can hear it."

Together, they left the book room and joined Irene for luncheon. The change in their relationship was obvious. Irene watched them with a look of puzzlement that slowly turned to one of satisfaction, but she made no comment.

They were having coffee when James entered the dining room and announced that Miss Fletcher was asking to speak to Lady Maryann. He had taken the liberty, he said, of showing the young woman into the front parlor.

Wavering between pleasure at the unexpected visit and apprehension about the meaning of it, Maryann murmured an excuse and hurriedly joined her visitor.

"Meg! Do you bring news?"

"Aye, indeed."

Meg's generous smile allayed any fears that the news might be bad, and a certain gleam in the green eyes raised hope and expectation in Maryann's breast.

"Tell me!" she demanded. "Is it a message from Stephen?"

Meg laughed. "Such eagerness from the lass who vowed she ain't in love!"

"Much has changed since we met." Maryann pressed her hands against her burning cheeks. "I am no longer afraid to admit that I love him."

"It's *you* as has changed," Meg said wisely. "Ye're a woman now."

Maryann frowned at the implication that she had not been a woman but a girl, a child, until now. But, for once, she swallowed a heated denial. Neither did she show again her impatience to hear Stephen's message.

"Please sit down, Meg. Would you care for coffee, tea? Perhaps a glass of sherry?"

"Nay, lass. I thank ye, but I ain't got the time. Must be at the theater at three for rehearsals. I only stopped by to warn ye that both Stephen and Tammadge will be at some do tonight. Some chit's come-out ball."

"Caroline Hawthorne's?" Maryann asked faintly. It was the ball she and Irene planned to attend.

"Aye, that's it. Stephen seemed to think ye mightn't want to go if ye knew he'd be there."

With her long, graceful stride, Meg walked to the

311

door.

"But I know better!" she tossed over her shoulder. "Ta ta, dearie. And good luck!"

Maryann saw them enter the ballroom together. Tammadge was speaking, and Stephen thrust back his head and laughed.

Superb actors both. The one hid behind pale, bored eyes and a bland smile the mind of a fiend; the other cloaked with great skill his determination to trap the fiend.

Maryann gripped Bella's wrist and drew her away from a knot of giggling young ladies who were using the time between dances to catch up on gossip. Behind a screen of potted plants and silk flower garlands, she stopped.

"They are here, Bella!"

"I would never have guessed it. Look!" Indignantly, Bella showed her a wrist marked by fingernails.

"I'm sorry," Maryann said absently.

She peeked through the garlands. "They're turning the other way, toward the punch bowl. Remember now! Be subtle if Tammadge is still with him. I depend on you."

Forgetting her injuries, Bella squeezed close to Maryann and took a peek herself.

"Stop fretting. I have great experience in luring a man to a secluded chamber without attracting notice." Bella sighed. "Oh, but he *is* handsome, your Stephen. Even from the back."

Maryann nudged her toward the ballroom. "Go now. With Tammadge you never know how long he'll stay. And if he leaves, I'm sure Stephen will have to go with him."

"I just wish you'd tell me—"

"You'll be the first to hear it all, I promise."

Bella grimaced wryly and flitted off.

Maryann had no idea how long it would take Bella to separate Tammadge and Stephen, but she suspected it wouldn't be too long. She lingered awhile, then, as the violin quartet struck up a country dance, slowly moved around the potted plants.

She had taken but a few steps toward the door when a softly insinuating voice to her right made her start.

"My dear Maryann," Tammadge drawled. "I am, as always, delighted to see you. I only wish I were not the harbinger of bad news, for I would dearly like to ask you for this dance. Alas, it must not be."

Maryann had listened with irritation and impatience at first, but now she asked apprehensively, "What bad news? Is it—"

The pale eyes rested on her. "Now I wonder what you thought it was that made you break off so abruptly."

"If you will come to the point, my lord," she said coldly, "I need not engage in guessing games."

Withdrawing a handkerchief from a pocket of his coat, he fanned himself languidly. "I'm afraid Lady Rivington was overcome by the heat. Our hostess—"

"Where is my mother?" Maryann interrupted, looking around the ballroom with an anxious eye.

"As I was trying to tell you, our hostess has taken her upstairs. She asked me to fetch you."

Without ado, Maryann placed her hand on the proffered arm. Stephen must wait until she had seen that her mother was all right.

Tammadge led her out into the hallway and to the stairs going up to the second floor, the same way she would have gone to meet Stephen.

She went with Tammadge unhesitatingly. But when he stopped before the door to the small sitting room that was supposed to be her rendezvous with Stephen, she hung back.

"Where are you taking me? I should have thought Mrs. Hawthorne would let Mama rest in one of the bedrooms."

"The sitting room has a comfortable couch. And it meant only one flight of stairs to climb instead of two."

It made sense, yet she shivered when he opened the door and motioned her to enter.

She could see only one half of the dimly lit room, the fireplace, several chairs drawn up before it — but not the couch.

Even as she reached out to push the door wider, she felt his hand against her back propelling her inside. She had a good view of the couch then. A beautiful, upholstered couch with velvet-covered cushions. Unoccupied.

She whirled in time to see him shut the door.

"How dare you! You lied to me." She was not afraid, only very angry. "Let me out at once."

Tammadge smiled.

She recoiled, her stomach knotting.

The door was behind him. She was *not* afraid. She had only to step past him, to open that door and walk out.

Slowly, he came closer.

Her gaze riveted to his face, she backed farther into the room. Still he advanced. Still she retreated, until, finally, there was nowhere for her to go. She had backed against a wall.

Nearby, to her left, stood the couch. At some distance to her right was the fireplace, and far away, across the room, was the door.

"Let me out," she repeated, but her voice was barely audible.

Still smiling, he took her hand and raised it. Not to his mouth as she half-feared, but to look at it.

"I see you're not wearing my ring."

Chapter Thirty-Three

Heart pounding, Maryann snatched her hand away. "I shall *never* wear your ring again."

Tammadge's eyes narrowed.

"My dear Maryann," he said silkily. "A lady should not allow anger to betray her into rash speech."

She swallowed. How she hated it when he called her his dear Maryann in that detestable way. The endearment mocked and taunted; the possessive "my" held the conviction, the threat, that she would inevitably be his.

Fear tightened her throat. She told herself she had no reason to be afraid. Tammadge was powerless. He could not force her to wear his ring, or to marry him, or even to stay in this room. She had only to walk past him.

"I did not speak rashly, my lord. I took off your ring last night. It is safely stored in its box and shall be returned to you in the morning."

"So I misjudged you again." His mouth twisted. "I thought you a dutiful daughter. How unwise of you to disillusion me."

Having known him to move only in a languid manner, Maryann was unprepared for the swiftness of his attack. He seized her around the waist, lifted her off her feet, and flung her down upon the velvet cushions of the couch. The weight of his body, the iron-hard mouth pressing against hers, cut off the scream rising in her throat.

Sickened and panicked, she grasped his hair and pulled with all her might to end the repulsive kiss.

She felt him shift, his legs and torso pinning her down, and felt his fingers close around her neck. She felt the pain . . . her senses swimming.

But the loathsome mouth no longer violated hers.

She clawed at his hands. To no avail, they held like steel manacles.

Stephen! she screamed silently. *Stephen, help me!*

"I won't hurt you," said Tammadge, his voice soft, even gentle, in chilling contrast to the cruel clutch on her neck. "I never damage beautiful things. But you're unlike any other of my possessions. You have a will of your own."

His grip loosened, and Maryann drew breath in painful gasps.

"I was prepared to overlook your aversion to me, was prepared to tolerate, even enjoy, your rebellious spirit." Menace crept into his voice. "But I will not tolerate rejection."

"I'll never marry you." She wanted to scream the refusal, but the words came out as a hoarse whisper. Tears of impotent rage blurred her eyes. She could not move, could not even scream for the pain in her throat.

"Never," she repeated defiantly.

"Oh, but you will." His thumbs caressed her throat, his voice coaxed and promised. "I'll make sure of it."

The fingers extended their exploration to her bare shoulders, the swell of her breasts. Her skin crawled under the touch. Blindly she lashed out, clawing at his face, his hands.

She heard the rip of lace and silk the same moment she heard the opening of the door and Bella's voice, cut off in mid-sentence by a screech.

Then Stephen's deep-toned drawl: "It seems, Miss

Bella, that the private spot you spoke of is not as private as we could wish."

Muttering an oath, Tammadge released Maryann. He wiped his chin where one of her fingernails had drawn a drop of blood, then scrambled to his feet with undignified haste.

"Farrell, what the devil do you mean by barging in?"

"I beg your pardon, Tammadge. Lady Maryann."

Trembling with relief, Maryann sat up. Stephen had come—her knight.

His voice and demeanor were cool, as though it meant nothing to him that he had found her pinned helplessly beneath the man he hated and despised. But she saw the granite hardness of his eyes, the hands clenched so tightly at his sides that the knuckles showed white.

Tammadge, composure regained, walked toward him. "You are *de trop,* my friend. If you take Miss Bella three doors farther down the hall, you'll find a couch that equals this one in comfort and softness."

Stephen did not move from the doorway, and Bella still stood motionless, her mouth half open as though she were about to scream again.

"Lady Maryann." Stephen made a slight bow in her direction. "I do believe you've torn the lace on the neck of your gown."

Blushing hotly, she covered the gaping tear with her hands.

Stephen kept looking at her, his eyes, his frown, clearly conveying some message. She was shaken, though, and slow to get his meaning.

"Oh, what a shame!" cried Bella, emerging from the unusual bout of silence and immobility. She ran past Tammadge and sat on the couch with her arms around Maryann.

"Your favorite gown!" She turned innocent blue eyes on the viscount. "Did you try to pin it, Lord Tammadge? I fear you must have pricked yourself. There's blood on your chin."

Tammadge dabbed the scratch with his handkerchief. His pale eyes moved slowly from Bella to Maryann to Stephen.

"A woman's touch," he said, his face and voice expressionless. "I cannot compete with that when it comes to the pinning of torn laces. Farrell, my friend, shall we leave the ladies to enjoy a moment of privacy?"

"But of course." The tone of Stephen's voice rivaled Tammadge's in blandness.

He allowed the viscount to precede him out the door, then said over his shoulder, "Ladies, we'll be waiting to escort you to the ballroom."

He disappeared from view, and Maryann leaned her head against the cushions. She felt safe, protected. Stephen would see to it that Tammadge had no further opportunity to be alone with her.

She heard Bella mutter, and slowly sat up. Her friend was rummaging in the tiny reticule dangling from her wrist, and, after a prolonged and frantic search, withdrew a paper of pins.

"I am sorry," Bella whispered. "I should have known he'd seek you out. But he said he was going to speak to Mrs. Hawthorne, and I believed him. So I didn't particularly hurry to get Mr. Farrell here. I was never more shocked than when I opened the door and saw—"

"It does not matter that you were late. I am grateful you came at all. And more than grateful that you took the hint about torn lace. I could not think properly and didn't realize what a good excuse it made to keep you with me."

Maryann was beginning to relax. She took a pin from Bella's shaking fingers and inserted it in the gaping neckline of her gown, then took another pin.

She frowned at her handiwork. "But how am I going to speak with Stephen?"

"I'll think of something," Bella promised. "I botched your rendezvous. I'll make it up to you—if I have to swoon at Tammadge's feet!"

"Don't be silly." Having pinned the lace and silk of the bodice, Maryann rose. "Better ask him to dance."

"All right." Bella was not one to quibble over minor details, but she looked rather dubiously at Maryann's gown. "The rip is still showing. I don't think you ought to go downstairs like the ravaged heroine in a gothic novel."

Maryann gave a choke of laughter. The sound was not quite steady, nor was it totally joyful, but it was laughter nonetheless.

"*You* are the heroine, Bella. If I hadn't been so shaken, I'd have gone into whoops when you asked if he had pricked his chin." She peeked at the bodice of her gown. "Let me have one of the flowers in your hair. That should fix it."

With a silk rose pinned over the rip, Bella's hand supportively in hers, Maryann left the sitting room where she had spent the most harrowing minutes of her life—worse, she acknowledged, than a day and a night in a windowless cellar.

Tammadge and Stephen were waiting by the staircase. She did not look at Tammadge; if she did, she might not be able to go on. Instead, she kept her eyes on Stephen as she walked toward them, gathering strength from the warmth of his gaze, the nod of encouragement.

"Remember," she whispered to Bella. "A dance with Tammadge."

But the ruse was not needed to separate Tammadge from Stephen. The Marquess of Woverley trundled his portly shape up the stairs. His gait was unsteady, the red face covered with a sheen of perspiration. The pig's eyes stared dully.

"Tammadge," he croaked before he had reached the

top step. "I'm damned near ruined! Run off my legs!"

"Steady, old fellow," said Stephen, a hint of steel in his voice. "There are ladies present."

Woverley paid him no heed. Swaying drunkenly, he said, "Did you hear me, Tammadge? I said I'm all to pieces! Dropped a bundle at Rivington's Club. And signed more vouchers than I can afford."

"Rivington, eh?" Tammadge shot an unreadable look at Maryann, then took Woverley's arm, turned him around, and started him down the stairs.

"To tell the truth, Woverley, it doesn't come as a surprise to me. You see, Rivington is not above—" Tammadge broke off.

Looking over his shoulder, he said, "Farrell, give me a hand. I'm afraid Woverley is too drunk and too stout for me to manage."

"Gladly. Allow me to escort the ladies to the ballroom first."

Offering an arm each to Maryann and Bella, Stephen swept them past Woverley and Tammadge to the floor below. Just outside the ballroom doors he stopped.

"Maryann!" Without regard for Bella's presence, he clasped her hand in both of his. Concern deepened his voice. "Are you all right?"

She nodded. "I don't think I was in any danger. He only scared me a little."

His eyes searched her face. "There is so much I want to say, but we have only a moment. I must go with Tammadge lest I want to rouse his suspicion. Tomorrow, he'll introduce me to his thugs. And on Thursday, with the early evening tide, the *Venture* will sail."

"Early? But—but what about Meg?"

"She'll receive a note, bidding her to Grosvenor Square Thursday afternoon instead of evening."

Bella cleared her throat. "A commotion on the stairs!" she warned. "I think Tammadge has grown impatient waiting for you, Mr. Farrell."

There was no time for a prolonged farewell, no time for what they wanted to say to each other—none of it having to do with Tammadge or the arrangements to catch him.

Stephen pressed a kiss into Maryann's palm. She whispered, "I love you." Then he was off to assist Tammadge with the inebriated Marquess of Woverley while Maryann, hurried along by Bella, slipped into the ballroom.

And that was the moment that stayed in Maryann's mind. When she returned home with Irene, she would have been unable to say, if asked, whether or not Caroline Hawthorne's come-out ball had been a success. Even the horror of Tammadge's attack had faded. All Maryann remembered was the feeling of loss, of desolation, when Stephen left her.

She should have said more, should have assured him that she was grateful for the rescue, for his protection—that she had realized the withholding of his name from her had indeed been a protective measure, not a sign of mistrust.

They had so much to discuss, but no time or opportunity to do so. She knew he loved her. She did *not* know whether her earlier rejection of his protectiveness had convinced him she would not make the right wife for him.

She slept restlessly, awaking and sitting up with a start several times. It seemed to her that she could hear voices and the crunch of footsteps in the garden below, something that had not happened before when she was in her room. Unlike the book room, her bedchamber was three floors above the gardens, and unlike the book room, it was in the opposite wing from her father's library. But then, on other nights she had not been restless. And neither had she had her window wide open.

She slept and woke and slept again. When she sat

up in bed for about the dozenth time, she thought at first it was the silence that had awakened her. A hush hung in the air, a stillness that was as jarring as — as the sound that had roused her. She remembered it now.

A shot.

Male voices raised in indistinguishable shouts started up as she thrust back the covers. She did not stop for a light or slippers or even a wrap, but ran from the room, down the corridor and three flights of stairs, and she did not slow until she reached the library door.

Breathless, she pushed down the handle. The door was locked.

The shouting had quieted to a mutter. She heard a sound like a piece of furniture being dragged. Then a thudding noise — but no! That was her heart.

For a moment, she stood motionless in the grip of apprehension. She spun and ran toward the green baize curtain that concealed the back stairs. Through the sculleries and kitchen she hurried, out the back door, and into the garden.

Dew dampened her nightgown as she brushed past shrubs and bushes. Gravel bit into her bare feet until she reached the terrace outside the library.

She came to a stop, her eyes on a knot of men all talking at once to a portly figure standing alone in the middle of the terrace. The Marquess of Woverley.

One pistol dangled from his right hand, another was held in his shaking left hand which pointed the firearm every which way. Woverley looked dazedly from one man to another.

"He should have met me," he mumbled. "Shouldn't have ignored my challenge. Not the thing to do, ignore a gentleman's challenge."

The men fell silent and exchanged looks. Maryann recognized two, silver-haired Sir John Lewis and Mr. Winsome, her father's secretary, whose dry cough seemed worse than ever.

Woverley swayed. The pistol in his left hand pointed at Mr. Winsome. The frail little man blinked red-rimmed eyes and jumped aside.

Maryann shivered. The scene on the terrace was a macabre play, one that would be over any moment. The curtain would fall, and there'd be applause to break the tension.

The pistol wavered on. One of the men surrounding Woverley told him not to be a fool, to put the weapons down, but no one went up to him and took them away.

Woverley's voice rose to an angry shout. "He cheated, dammit! Tammadge said so. Rivington cheated me, and that's why I called him out. Offered him one of my Mantons, but he wouldn't take it."

Again, the pistol in his left hand pointed at one of the men.

"Rivington laughed! You all heard him. He cheated me and then he laughed at me. Damn his money-grubbing soul! That's why I shot him."

is all ... [illegible faded text] ... as the crack of a fire pistol's
discharge ... as well.

"Sir John ... Pay got a witness. I mean, I think that
... his own ... there's no one present. Hm ..."

Chapter Thirty-Four

The Earl of Rivington was dead.

Maryann saw him stretched out on the faro table which someone had dragged against the wall by the French doors.

She felt nothing.

At three-thirty on the morning of Wednesday, May first, she rang the bell summoning the servants to the library. She sent Harv for a surgeon and, on the suggestion of Sir John Lewis, for the constable as well.

"It's merely a question of formality," Sir John assured her. "We all can attest to the accidental firing of the weapon."

Maryann stared at him. She had known the silver-haired gentleman since she first came to town with her mother and sisters. She had walked in the park with his granddaughter. He sat in Parliament, she knew, and was a justice of the peace in his home county.

"It is best, Lady Maryann." He spoke with quiet authority. He did not try to avoid her eyes but watched her with grave concern. "For everyone, including you and Lady Rivington."

Accidental death — no trial, no scandal or very little.

Maryann thought of the alternative — a charge of willful murder against Woverley, the trial exposing the late Earl of Rivington as a gambler and a cheat, her own testimony about what she had heard on the terrace in all likelihood dismissed as the ravings of a distraught daughter.

"Sir John, since I was not a witness, I suggest that you or one of the gentlemen present at the time of the . . . accident speak to the constable."

He bowed. "I agree, Lady Maryann. It is not necessary that he should bother you at all. I shall also have a word with Woverley. His mind, I fear, is sadly addled from shock. Travel abroad and a prolonged stay in warmer climes will be just the thing for him."

Maryann watched Sir John pass through the French doors onto the terrace, where the Marquess of Woverley sat in solitary splendor. He had finally given up the pistols in favor of a bottle of cognac and was fast drinking himself into a stupor.

Turning to the stunned servants hovering in the doorway, she ordered coffee to be served to the gentlemen in the library and told Hedwig to go to Irene and to keep her upstairs.

She went to her room to dress, then spent a few moments with her mother, who had heard the news from Hedwig. Irene was pale but quite composed. Spectacles resting on the tip of her nose, she was compiling a list of mourning apparel to be ordered from Madame Blanchard.

"Mama?" Maryann said hesitantly. "You are all right?"

Dipping the pen in the ink stand, Irene looked at her daughter. "I do not feel like mourning, but the proprieties must be observed."

"Yes, of course."

A bill more or less would make no difference. And later —

Maryann closed her mind to whatever might happen later, when all her father's debts were disclosed. She returned to the library, where she calmly accepted the condolences of the surgeon when he had completed his examination of the still figure on the faro table.

She felt nothing.

She spoke with Reginald, answered his questions as best she could, and, when he suggested that it might be better if he left immediately, convinced him to stay a few days. There would be much that needed to be done, and, although she had Mr. Winsome to help her, she'd rather have a brother at her side while she faced brothers-in-law, her father's friends, his heir—and his creditors.

Her mind functioned like the wheels inside a wellmade clock. She knew it would not be long before merchants, tailors, and bootmakers gathered at the door, and instructed Mr. Winsome to bring her father's account books into the front parlor where she might study them.

Looking at the sums Mr. Winsome pointed out to her—most of them on the debit side, something stirred in her. Concern for her mother. She wondered how Irene would hold up under the strain of the next days or even weeks, worried how to make provisions for her.

And she thought with longing of Stephen, who would not be able to come to her until Thursday night.

She was relieved to find that not all her feelings were frozen. Her father was dead, shot by one of his gambling companions. And she felt nothing about his death. Not regret, not relief. Nothing.

At eleven o'clock that morning, she heard the knocker on the front door. The sound was strange—dull and lifeless. Someone had, apparently, wrapped the brass fixture in black crepe. However dull the sound, from that time on it did not cease. Some of the callers only left cards, others, friends and well-wishers of Irene, or the morbidly curious, asked to be admitted.

On Mr. Winsome's insistence that he was well able to deal with creditors until the arrival of the new Lord Rivington, Maryann assigned him the use of her father's study and went upstairs to join her mother in the drawing room.

The first person she saw, and who saw her when she entered the crowded room, was Tammadge.

He stood alone by one of the windows and immediately started toward her. Grim faced, she watched him. Indeed, her feelings were not dead. Anger and revulsion flared hotly in her.

Impetuously, she met him halfway. "How dare you show your face!"

One pointed black brow rose. "I have come to condole with you on your sad loss and to assure you that Lady Rivington will never suffer from want. As my wedding gift to you, I have made over to your mother a lifetime annuity of two thousand pounds."

Rage blurred her vision. She had to take several deep breaths before she could trust herself to speak without screaming.

"My father was killed because you told Lord Woverley about his cheating," she said, her voice low, throbbing with anger. "No doubt you believe you have me cornered, that, faced with penury and debts, I'll change my mind and marry you."

"You will certainly change your mind."

She drew another deep breath. "You miscalculated, my lord! *I* shall provide for my mother. And you may go to the devil!"

White faced, his eyes narrowed, he stepped so close that his breath stirred tendrils of her hair. "Just wait until word of your father's activities is out, and you and your mother find yourselves ostracized."

The close contact made her skin crawl, but she did not retreat.

"Lord Tammadge," she said icily. "You will give the word at your peril."

"And just what do you mean by that?" An ugly look crossed his thin face. "What has your father told you about me?"

She measured him from head to toe, then turned her

back on him.

Seeing the butler hovering near the door, she said, "Melville, Lord Tammadge is leaving. Please fetch the box on the mantel shelf in my room and give it to him. He will not be calling again."

She did not check to see what effect her words had on her erstwhile betrothed, or whether others had heard her, but crossed the room to her mother's side.

It was obvious that her confrontation with Tammadge had not been noticed here at the back of the large chamber. Both her mother and Lady Effingham, who was seated beside Irene, smiled at her.

"My love, you ought to change," Irene said gently. "Madame Blanchard sent two gowns for you. Jane took them upstairs."

Maryann left without protest. Like her mother, she did not feel like mourning, but the proprieties must be observed.

Cousin Reggie, who had once executed her favorite doll and who was now the Seventh Earl of Rivington, arrived in the afternoon. He was curt and wasted no breath on sympathy, but after an hour spent with Mr. Winsome, he joined Maryann in the front parlor in slightly better humor.

"It's not as bad as I feared," he said bluntly. "Your father was a wastrel, but with some wise investments— I'm not exactly a pauper, you know— and a little economy, I shall have the estate back in shape in a year or two. It'll be a drain on my finances to settle his debts— gad, you wouldn't believe the amount he owes at Tattersall's!"

"Five thousand pounds," said Maryann. "I saw the books this morning."

The new earl hunched his shoulders and lowered his head in a manner reminiscent of the late earl. "But I'll settle. Can't have it said of me that I cast off my aunt and cousin."

Family pride, thought Maryann. She hoped it

wouldn't lead him down the road her father had taken. She prayed that, for his sake as much as her mother's and hers, a scandal over her father's death had been averted by Sir John Lewis's action.

"There won't be any money for you or Aunt Irene. Not even a dowry for you," the seventh earl said gruffly. "But the dower house belongs to your mother. If she does not want to live near Rivington Hall. I'll make arrangements to lease it. The rent should cover the cost of simple lodgings and her upkeep."

"Thank you."

Relief brought tears to her eyes. She had told herself she could provide for her mother, but deep in her heart she had doubted her capabilities.

She blinked the suspicious moisture away and left the parlor before she could disgrace herself with a fit of weeping.

With the intention of gathering her wits and her strength, Maryann sought refuge in her room. She lay down on the bed, but had barely closed her eyes when her maid opened the door and peeked in.

"What is it, Jane?"

"There's a note, my lady." Eyes bright with curiosity, Jane approached the bed.

Stephen! was Maryann's immediate thought, and her pulse started racing.

But it was not the bold writing that had covered the reverse side of Lady Effingham's invitation and bade her come to Hyde Park.

Her gaze skipped to the signature: Hannah Moss.

This was unusual enough to temper disappointment. With growing excitement, she read the long, meticulously written note.

Hannah begged Lady Maryann to come to Wilderness Road the following day. She had made up her mind to visit Parson's Stairs, where she had been found unconscious. She wanted to see if the location would help her remember details about the abduction. At present, she was aware only of blind horror and fright.

She did not want her parents to know about this since she feared her mother would forbid such an undertaking, and asked that Lady Maryann call at ten o'clock when Hester and Abraham would be at synagogue.

And would Lady Maryann please come disguised as a servant girl? A lady would attract undue notice in a part of town that consisted mostly of warehouses and shipping offices.

"Jane, when was this delivered?"

"Just now, my lady. The girl as brought the note is waitin' fer an answer."

"Where?" Maryann rose hastily. "I'll speak to her."

"In the entrance hall, my lady."

The young maid who had admitted her to the Moss's house blushed and curtsied awkwardly when Maryann approached.

"M'lady," she stammered. "I'm sure Miss Hannah wouldn't have bothered ye if she had known about yer father. But we hadn't heard, an' when the footman told me, I didn't know what ter do."

"What you must *not* do under any circumstances is tell Miss Hannah. I don't want her upset."

"Yes, m'lady."

Maryann hesitated. "How is Miss Hannah? Has she spoken again?"

"Oh, yes! She's gettin' ter be the way she was afore she was kidnapped. But she's frettin' about not r'memberin'."

"Then tell her, please, that I will call for her with my carriage at ten o'clock as she requested."

The maid beamed. "Yes, m'lady. I'll tell her. It'll make her ever so happy!"

After seeing the girl off, Maryann sent word to the stables that she would require the carriage with Robert and Rush in attendance at nine o'clock the following morning for a visit to Wilderness Road.

Back in her room, she inspected the gowns she wore to the Sloane Street gardens. Choosing a simple cotton print, she wondered what else she could do to make herself look like a maid. A maid on an outing with a friend, she reminded herself. Perhaps celebrating Princess Charlotte's wedding.

What she needed was one of Hedwig's caps.

It took repeated explanations of the reason for the masquerade and assurances that Robert and Rush would be with her at all times, but finally Hedwig was persuaded to part with one of her cherished caps.

"Mind you," she said, hiding concern behind teutonic gruffness, "if you're not back by afternoon, I'll send the runners after you."

"Whatever you do, don't tell Mama!"

"*Niemals,*" Hedwig promised.

Having made her preparations, Maryann should have been able to relax, but with every minute ticking by, her excitement grew.

Unlike last Thursday, she had made no plans to assist in Tammadge's capture on the morrow. She had been willing to leave everything in Stephen's hands. But now an opportunity had been handed to her.

If her action helped Hannah remember, if the girl accused Tammadge, the Bow Street magistrate would be able to have him arrested before he abducted Meg. Before the cutthroats forced young girls aboard the Venture.

There were many ifs to contend with, but to have played a part in Tammadge's downfall would give her great satisfaction.

From her window, Maryann watched evening shadows creep across the garden. Time dragged unbearably slow. If only it were morning. . . .

Jane came to light the lamps and pull the drapes across the window. There was nothing left to do but pace the floor . . . until dinner . . . until morning.

Somehow, Maryann got through the evening, even

through dinner which the new earl took with them before retiring to a hotel. He had given permission, graciously to Irene and Maryann, and reluctantly to Reginald, to stay at Rivington House until after the funeral, which he had instructed Mr. Winsome to arrange for Saturday.

"Your wedding will have to be postponed, of course," the earl told Maryann gravely as he took his leave. "I hardly think Tammadge would be satisfied with a small, private ceremony."

"Tammadge and I have decided that we do not suit."

He frowned. "Is that how it is? No doubt he found out about your father's debts. Well, well! I wouldn't have taken Tammadge for a man who looks to his bride's dowry."

Maryann did not disillusion him.

"What about that boy — gad, why must your father have given him a family name? Reginald! Pshaw!"

Maryann waited.

The earl collected hat and gloves from the hall table. "I cannot be expected to provide for your father's bastard."

"If he weren't the bastard, you would not be the earl, Reginald!"

She saw his face turn a dull red. More quietly, she said, "But no, you need not be responsible for him. If I find the money to pay the fees, would you speak to the dean at Christ Church to make certain he won't be kicked out for lack of connections? He is known there as my father's ward."

After some thought, the earl said reluctantly. "I daresay I could do it."

"Thank you."

She accompanied her cousin to the door, and, when she closed it after him with a sigh of relief, found Harv waiting for her.

Looking as important as only he knew how, the footman said, "There's a gentleman waitin' for you, Lady

Maryann. Knocked on the back door, he did. Said he wouldn't come in."

Stephen! It simply must be Stephen.

Her heart raced faster than her feet as she hurried down the back stairs and into the kitchen. Robert was rolling dice with Rush and James at the scrubbed table. Before they could scramble to their feet, she had flown past them, opened the back door, and stepped into the darkness of the garden.

Strong arms wrapped tenderly around her. A broad chest waited for her to lean against it. The cloth of his coat felt rough against her cheek, and he smelled of the cheroots she had sometimes seen him smoke, but she did not mind. Tenderness and strength; roughness and a manly scent. They were Stephen.

And he was with her.

The thought filled her mind and her heart. She had no wants, no needs, save to be held by him.

"My love," he murmured, burying his face in her hair. "I only just heard the news or I would have been with you sooner."

She pressed closer, reluctant to speak and spoil the sweetness of the moment.

"Woverley himself told me," said Stephen. "What an awful thing to have happened!"

Clinging to him, she raised her face. Stephen at least must know the truth.

"Are you aware it was no accident?"

"It was not? I suppose I should have known."

The light from the kitchen windows was not sufficient to show the expression of his face, but she felt his tension, heard the tight note in his voice.

"Tammadge put Woverley up to it," she said. "He believed my father's death would force me to marry him."

"Never shall you marry him! You are mine."

Stephen tightened his hold possessively. "The devil fly away with eligibility! You'll wed me and no one

333

else."

Her heart swelled with joy and love.

"Yes, sir," she replied instantly and with becoming meekness.

He was quite still.

The tension flowed out of him. He shifted his hold. His hands clasped her waist. Sweeping her off her feet, he held her suspended.

"She says she will!" he shouted, swung her in a circle, then set her down.

Before she could catch her breath, his mouth covered hers, stifling any admonitions she might have been inclined to utter. But she had no such inclination. Locking her hands behind his neck, she returned his kisses with ardor and devoted herself to convincing him that he would never regret his impetuous offer of marriage.

A long time later, he asked, "You won't mind not having a botanical garden?"

"I shan't mind not having it immediately."

It was difficult to think of anything but his hands moving up and down her back and making her skin tingle. But she did remember a daydream of growing flowers in Cornwall and selling them to support Irene and to finance her own gardens some day.

The daydream she'd indulged in after her last visit to Hannah.

"Stephen, I have such news! Hannah Moss is coming out of her shell. She has asked me—"

"Hannah speaking? But why haven't you told me?"

"It only happened yesterday. She did not say much, but she—"

This time, Stephen had not interrupted her. She had stopped herself, realizing that she could not tell him about the planned excursion to the waterfront with Hannah.

There was no danger involved during the morning hours of Princess Charlotte's wedding day, with a stalwart groom and a soldier dodging their every step. But she knew instinctively that Stephen would worry anyway. And tomorrow, of all days, he must have a clear mind.

No, she would not tell him. She finally understood why some things were best left unsaid, even if one loved and completely trusted another.

"But what?" Stephen asked. "What did Hannah do or say?"

"She said she'd like to forget about that awful night when she and Leah were abducted." Which was the truth, after all, except that Hannah had admitted she could not forget.

"Kiss me, Stephen," Maryann demanded. "We'll have more than enough time to talk while we till your fields in Cornwall. Tonight, I want only your kisses."

Chapter Thirty-Five

Robert pulled on the reins and stopped the carriage in a warehouse yard.

"This be it, ladies," he said through the communications panel. "As close as I can take ye to Parson's Stairs."

Maryann took Hannah's hand and squeezed it. The girl looked pale, her brown eyes enormous beneath the frill of a mobcap that hid most of her hair and the bandage on her head.

"We don't have to do it," she said after a painful struggle between compassion for Hannah and desire to contribute to Tammadge's downfall. "Whether you remember your and Leah's abduction or not, by tonight Tammadge will be in Newgate."

"But I must remember! I must know what happened. I have so many nightmares about dark, cold places, about running and yet not getting away from whatever it is that threatens me."

Robert opened the carriage door. With an air of resolution, Hannah rose and stepped out onto the cobbles.

"And," she said when Maryann joined her, "I must remember for Leah's sake."

Maryann placed an arm around Hannah's waist. They walked briskly, Robert and Rush following at some distance as Maryann had instructed them to do before she set out to fetch Hannah. Presently, they reached St. Catherine's Street crowded with carts and wagons, sailors talking and joking with each other in different tongues, clerks hurrying to and fro, women with shopping baskets on their arms.

No one paid them much attention, and Maryann silently blessed Hannah for thinking of dressing up as servant girls. They blended right in, she felt, with their simple gowns of printed cotton, their shawls and mobcaps.

Here, she need not think of black crepe on the front door, or callers who condoled and asked prying questions about the "accident" in her father's library. She felt at liberty to enjoy the warmth of the sun, the breeze off the river, the air redolent with the smell of tar, the scent of exotic spices stored in the warehouses.

If she could have shared the experience with Stephen, her contentment would have been complete. As it was, she must take consolation from the thought that soon she would share her life with him.

Intrigued by the bustle around her, she kept eyes and ears wide open. She cast surreptitious glances at sunburnt men in varied garb but all moving with the same slow, rolling gait that tagged them as sailors. She caught snippets of gossip: talk about a tavern brawl; about a fire in one of the breweries nearby; overheard a woman trying to talk a friend into going to Clarence House that night to see Prince Leopold off as he set out for the wedding at Carlton House.

Mention of the royal wedding brought her own to mind. Her marriage to Stephen.

As Cousin Reggie had pointed out, a wedding during the year of mourning must be a small, private affair. It was all she wanted, as long as she could be Stephen's wife immediately. St. Margaret's was reserved for Monday, May the sixth, just four days off . . . but the banns had twice been read for Maryann Rivington and Francis Tammadge. It was not likely that the parson would agree to substitute Stephen Fant as the groom's name on the third reading.

Perhaps a special license?

So absorbed was she in her thoughts that she gave a start when Hannah stopped suddenly.

"Parson's Stairs," the young girl said, staring across the street toward the riverbank where a set of shallow steps led down to the water. "I don't remember anything about being here. What shall we do?"

Firmly, Maryann directed her attention to the problem at hand. They had come here for a purpose, not to daydream or to sightsee.

"Sir Nathaniel Conant said you were found on the waterfront near Parson's Stairs. That does not necessarily mean on the riverbank itself, but it would give us a place to start."

Maryann cast a look over her shoulder to make certain Robert and Rush still followed. Seeing the busy waterfront area now, she no longer thought of spices and goods stored in the warehouses, but of Stephen and Tammadge's cutthroats. They might be right here, looking for a likely prey.

Watching for a gap between lumbering wagons and the smaller carts whose drivers had a tendency to whip up the horses and unexpectedly speed past slower-moving vehicles, she said, "Shall we cross?"

"Wait." An intent look sharpened Hannah's delicate features.

"If we went west on St. Catherine's Street and crossed Pillory Lane," she said, "we'd eventually reach my father's warehouses. I know our warehouses like the back of my hand. And Father has a night watchman, whom I know quite well."

"And if you were running away from someone," said Maryann, picking up Hannah's train of thought, "you would not run away from the watchman who could help you, but toward him!"

Excitement gripped her. They were on the track.

"Where does St. Catherine's Street lead going east?"

"To the docks, to Wapping."

"We'll go that way."

Hannah reached for Maryann's hand and held it tightly. In silence, they started walking east.

Presently, the character of St. Catherine's Street changed. There were fewer warehouses, the long brick buildings often separated by stretches of rubble and charred ruins. No pedestrians crowded the street. Only carts and wagons still rattled to and fro between the docks farther east and the city to the west.

"Warehouses seem to attract fires," said Hannah, looking at the jagged remnants of a brick wall.

Grass sprouted in the cracks, even a bright golden buttercup or two. The sun shone as warmly as before. Yet Maryann was glad of the shawl around her shoulders.

Hannah increased her pace. "My father says all this will be rebuilt some day. There are plans afoot for the construction of new docks right in this area."

She seemed to derive comfort from thinking about Abraham Moss and made several more remarks prefaced "My father says," but at the sound of a man's heavy tread approaching rapidly behind them, she broke off with a shrill cry and would have run had Maryann not held her hand.

"It must be Robert," Maryann said as much to reassure herself as to comfort Hannah.

A quick look over her shoulder confirmed it was indeed the groom who was trying to catch up. The sight of his freckled face cheered her immensely.

Still, she could not help wishing he were Stephen.

She stopped. Rush, she saw, was lagging some distance behind. "What is the matter with him?" she asked Robert. "Does his leg bother him?"

"So he says," Robert muttered, his eyes on the soldier hobbling slowly closer.

"What do you mean? Don't you believe him?"

The groom shrugged. "Can't say as I do, and can't say as I don't. In any case, I could have driven ye in the carriage if I'd known ye were plannin' to traipse along St. Catherine's Street. But ye said ye were goin' to Parson's Stairs."

Maryann made no reply. She, too, was watching Rush. She had hired him because he had begged for work and had assured her that his peg leg was no handicap. She had seen him move as fast as any other man, although, of course, he could not run. But since the bout of drunkenness at the Fighting Cock, a change had come over Rush.

"M'lady," the soldier said breathlessly. "Ye shouldn't be out this way. It ain't safe."

Pity stabbed her. His face was pale and contorted with pain. Sweat glistened on his brow. No matter what Rob believed, he was not pretending to be in pain.

"I must go with Miss Hannah, Rush. Why don't you sit down on that bit of wall and wait?"

He looked at her, an expression in his eyes that was a mixture of anguish and gratitude. Slowly he turned and started to hobble toward the bit of ruin Maryann had indicated, but after a step or two, he swung around.

"Don't go, m'lady!"

A knot of apprehension twisted her insides. "Why, Rush?"

"That Lord Tammadge, 'e had me beaten an' he said he'd cut off me other leg if I didn't tell him where ye was goin' an' who ye was seein'."

Muttering an oath, Robert jumped on the soldier and knocked him down.

Sharply, Maryann called the groom off. She felt sick.

She looked at Hannah, but the girl was lost in thought, staring intently at a barely visible footpath that led past one of the few warehouses still serving its purpose, up a grassy slope, and disappeared in a tangle of wild rose bushes and hawthorn.

Maryann turned back to Rush, who was slowly picking himself off the ground. Fear cut through her as she remembered that he had been in the kitchen when she met Stephen outside the back door.

"What else have you told Tammadge?"

"Nothin', m'lady. I swear! An' I only told 'im about ye 'cause he—"

"Lady Maryann!" Robert cut in sharply. "Miss Hannah, she's wanderin' off!"

Intuitively, Maryann's eyes went to the path. Hannah was walking past the warehouse toward the gentle slope with the tangle of shrubbery at the top.

"Rush, if you endangered Mr. Farrell, I will—I will turn you over to the Bow Street magistrate," she vowed.

Followed by Robert and by Rush's protestations of innocence and helplessness, she hurried after Hannah. The girl had slowed, her steps faltering, and Maryann caught up with her in no time.

"There's a dead house up there," Hannah muttered. "My father says it used to be an ice house, but now it's a dead house for the drowned. There's no mortuary nearby, so the coroner comes to the dead house to examine the bodies."

"Hannah, for goodness sakes!" Maryann stared at her. "Whatever are you talking about?"

"I remember the wild roses and the hawthorn. They caught at my gown. But that's where we were taken, Leah and I. To the dead house. It was cold there. Cold and dark."

"Lady Maryann." Robert's freckles stood out on his blanched skin. "Let's turn back. Ye don't want to go inside a dead house. Ye never know how many bodies be lyin' around."

Maryann looked at the thicket of shrubs and bushes ahead. Barely visible above straggling branches was the flat, creeper-covered roof of a small square building.

She shivered.

Hannah kept walking, and Maryann fought to shake off a strong reluctance to follow.

"Come along, Rob. The dead don't hurt anyone."

Hurrying to catch up with Hannah, Maryann saw her disappear among the bushes that grew taller than a man's head. She started to run, but a scream, high-pitched with terror, stopped her in mid-stride.

"Turn back, lass!" Robert pushed past her on the narrow path. "I'll see to Miss Hannah."

She watched him disappear as well, and cast a longing glance at St. Catherine's Street where a wagon trundled slowly in the direction of the docks. Perhaps she should go for help.

She plunged into the thicket.

Her shawl caught on the vicious spikes of hawthorn and was torn off her shoulders. She did not stop to free it, but thrust forward until she burst into a small clearing with a square, creeper-covered brick building in the center. The dead house.

She saw Hannah no more than ten paces away, limp in the grip of a scar-faced man; saw Robert strike the man down with a blow to the head, only to be felled himself when the cudgel of another hit him between the shoulder blades.

And, apparently, there was a third man. Cruel hands grabbed her arms from behind, twisting them. She gasped in pain and stumbled forward.

Her eyes stung, but she had no difficulty recognizing Tammadge when he stepped out of the narrow doorway of the dead house.

Or Stephen behind him.

Chapter Thirty-Six

Maryann bit her lip to stop herself from crying out to Stephen. Rush had spoken the truth. He had not betrayed him. Stephen was free. Safe. But only as long as she preserved silence as well.

Across the clearing, their eyes met.

Shock held Stephen motionless. Maryann was the last person he expected to see, wanted to see, in this place of death that served, until the tide was right, to hide the young women Tammadge planned to ship to Algiers.

"My dear Maryann," Tammadge drawled. "It gives me great pleasure to welcome you. But please, won't you step a little closer?"

She did, forced by the unseen captor at her back, who once more twisted her arms.

"What? Have you nothing to say?" Tammadge asked mockingly. "And why the masquerade? Did you think I would not recognize you if you concealed your hair beneath that ridiculous cap?"

Contempt and loathing sharpened her voice. "I don't give a straw whether you recognize me or not. It's *you* I want recognized."

She looked at Hannah, who stood staring at the viscount, her eyes wide, nostrils quivering like a deer who smelled danger.

"Hannah, do you know Lord Tammadge?"

Tammadge flicked an uninterested glance at the girl.

"Yes. No." Hannah shook her head despairingly. "I just don't know! My head hurts. I cannot think."

"Hannah, take off your cap," said Maryann.

Stephen groaned. His love was fast plunging them into total disaster.

He shook off stupor and moved to Tammadge's side. "What is this?" he asked sharply. "Why is Lady Maryann interfering in our business?"

"Lady Maryann is not interfering," Tammadge said silkily. "She is contributing. She'll make a delectable gift to the Dey of Algiers."

"You're jesting." Holding his temper on a tight rein, Stephen wondered frantically whether Sir Nathaniel's men delegated to dodge his steps had seen the two girls and the groom.

Trying to gain time, he said, "If you no longer want the Lady Maryann, give her to me."

"No." Tammadge glanced at Hannah, who was slowly pulling off the frilly cap. "You may have the other one, scrawny though she is—"

His eyes narrowed at the sight of the long, reddish blond hair, then widened as recognition dawned. "So you're not dead. How careless my men are becoming."

He pulled out a handkerchief and fanned the lace-edged square of lawn in front of his face.

Hannah screamed.

"The handkerchief!" she cried. "The fanning! You did that while your men tried to push us into the carriage that was to take us from here to the docks. The coachman had a lantern and I saw the handkerchief. And when Leah was hurt, you tossed it to me. You told me to wipe off the blood. You didn't want her face marred."

"Quiet!" Tammadge strode up to Hannah and slapped her. "It matters not whether *your* face is marred. In less than two hours, I will personally deliver your replacement to my ship."

But Hannah, once started, could not stop giving voice to memories.

"I whispered to Leah that the men were busy with the other girls. We should flee. She moved her head, and I thought it meant yes. I ran. I expected her right behind me, but when I looked back, I saw one of the men pursuing me. I ran fast, so fast I could not breathe. But I kept running. I saw the light at Parson's Stairs, and then—"

Tammadge raised his hand to slap her again, but Stephen was quicker. Clasping Tammadge's wrist, he bore the arm down.

"No more!" he said icily. "And tell your thug to let Lady Maryann go."

"You dare order me?" said Tammadge, his face distorting. "You are but my lackey. Dispensable."

Maryann's stomach knotted with fear. Stephen watch out! she wanted to shout. Don't give yourself away.

She looked at Rob. The fingers of one hand twitched, but he was still unconscious. He would be of no help.

Hannah cried, "What did you do with Leah? Where is she?"

Maryann struggled to free herself, but her captor's grip was too strong. In desperation, she kicked a foot backward, using the heel of her half-boot as a weapon.

The heel struck. Yelping, the man let go of her arms.

She reached Stephen and Tammadge just as the man who had knocked Robert down dragged Hannah off to the dead house. The girl screamed when he pushed her through the narrow doorway. Maryann wanted to comfort her, but for the moment Hannah must fare alone. Stephen needed her.

Stephen, she feared, was being quite reckless. He still gripped Tammadge's wrist, and he looked about to lose his temper. He'd give away the game—and where the dickens were the Bow Street runners who were supposed to have followed him and the thugs?

"Maryann, go to Hannah," said Stephen, a wary eye on Tammadge's men as they crept closer.

"*Maryann*," Tammadge repeated hoarsely. "So that's how it is."

"That's how it is," Stephen said deliberately.

He'd end the game now. Alone. The runners, if they were nearby and had seen the two girls, would have interfered by now. He must assume they had lost the trail between the Covent Garden market, where the thugs had captured three young women, and this dreadful spot.

He let go of Tammadge's arm. "Maryann has done me the honor of accepting my proposal of marriage."

Tammadge sneered. "I must congratulate you. I fear, however, that your betrothal to her will be of even shorter duration than mine."

"Indeed. I plan to wed her without delay."

His every sense alert, Stephen took note of the two footpads' positions. They hung back, waiting for a sign from Tammadge.

A glance at Maryann convinced him that a second command to leave would be a waste of breath. He knew that look of determination only too well.

"Maryann is a mulish chit," Tammadge said maliciously. "I'd wish you joy of her, but she insulted me once too often. She will be imprisoned in the dey's harem."

The pale eyes resting on Stephen held an evil glint. "And you, Farrell, will be slave to some Barbary pirate."

"The name is Fant. Stephen Fant."

Tammadge blanched and took a backward step.

"Fant." Droplets of sweat appeared on the high forehead. The handkerchief moved with unusual ferocity. "Brother, I assume, of the foolish William?"

346

Stephen's hands clenched, but he kept his temper under control. He heard Maryann's cry, "No, Stephen. Don't!" as though she knew what he was about to do.

His eyes never strayed from his brother's tormentor. "Francis Tammadge, I arrest you in the name of the law."

The handkerchief fluttered to the ground. Tammadge's hand dove into the pocket of his coat. He pulled out a small pistol.

Stephen lunged.

Maryann gasped. A fist pressing against her mouth, she stared at the two men locked in a deadly embrace.

Tammadge held Stephen in a tight clutch around the waist while Stephen hooked an arm around Tammadge's neck, pressing the viscount's face into his shoulder. His left hand gripped the wrist of the gun hand, forcing it down until it rested against Tammadge's side.

But the pistol, she saw with horror, pointed its muzzle at Stephen.

Her breath caught when the two men teetered drunkenly. If they fell, surely the gun would go off.

If only Robert would come to! From the corner of her eye, she risked a quick look at the groom and saw him sitting up and pointing the pistol Fletcher had given him first at one of Tammadge's cutthroats, then at the other. The scar-faced man on the ground was stirring; obviously Robert had his hands full.

Fighting despair, she again turned her attention to Stephen and Tammadge. The viscount had let go of Stephen's middle and grasped an ear. He gave a vicious yank.

Maryann winced, feeling Stephen's pain. His grip on Tammadge's neck loosened for an instant, then tightened again. But during that instant, Tammadge forced his gun hand between their bodies.

Fear squeezed her heart. Above the scream thrusting past her fist, she barely heard the report of the pistol, muffled as it was by the two bodies.

But she saw them fall, saw Stephen lie motionless atop Tammadge.

"No!"

Pain such as she had never known ripped through her. Stephen could not, he must not be hurt! Or worse.

As she started toward Stephen, the burly Mr. Simms in his frock coat and beaver hat, followed closely by five more Bow Street runners, burst into the clearing.

Too late! Too late, her heart hammered.

The distance was only a few paces, yet it seemed to take an eternity before she reached Stephen's side. She dropped to her knees, tugging at his shoulders, crying his name.

Stephen turned toward the beloved voice. He shook his head, fighting the numbness that had gripped his mind and limbs when, just before they hit the ground, Tammadge's body had twitched like a puppet's whose strings were pulled too hard.

A face, a pixie face with fearful gray eyes and a tremulous mouth, bent over him. The sight quickened his pulse and filled him with elation. It was over. Tammadge was dead. Maryann safe. His brother avenged.

"Maryann. Love! Stop shaking me. How do you expect me to get up with you rattling the teeth in my head?"

The mouth curved in a smile. Joy lit the expressive eyes. Joy and love.

"Stephen! You are all right!"

Someone out of his range of vision cleared his throat. "Pardon me, Mr. Farrell. We'll be takin' the females to the carriage. D'ye want us to haul those thugs to Bow Street, or would ye be wantin' to do the honors yerself?"

Stephen got to his feet. His arm wrapped around

Maryann, he faced the Bow Street runner.

"Simms, you rascal. What the devil took you so long?"

The man's color rose. "We lost ye," he admitted sheepishly. " 'Twas at Billingsgate. One moment we was right behind ye, and the next we was followin' a cart filled with stinkin' fish. Then some peg-leg limpin' down St. Catherine's tipped us off to this place. But ye did all right, I see. Got Tammadge."

"He's dead," Stephen said quietly.

The Bow Street runner did not bother to look at the viscount's still form.

"A hangin' would have been too good for him," he said and turned away.

Stephen looked at Maryann.

She was pale, but when their eyes met, she smiled. "It is over," she said, unconsciously echoing his own thought.

She clasped his hand and drew him away. "We shall forget Tammadge," she said firmly. "Let's go quickly and take Hannah home. She'll want to be with her parents."

"As will Leah."

Following Stephen's gaze, Maryann saw seven young women emerge from the dead house. Hannah, her arms around a dark-haired girl, was the last. The glow on her face confirmed Stephen's words.

"You found her!" Maryann turned shining eyes on Stephen. "How wonderful."

"Nothing wonderful about it. Leah and two others were already in the dead house when we got here. When Hannah ran away—and Tammadge thought she'd been killed—he simply locked the other girls up again and had Scarface guard them."

The mention of Tammadge's name raised goose bumps on Maryann's skin, but then Stephen drew her against him. Immediately she felt warm and protected. Tammadge was dead, and she need not think of him again. Not ever.

Stephen kissed her forehead. "Shall we go?"

"Oh, yes! And when we've taken Hannah and Leah home, we must find Meg and tell her that she need not go to Grosvenor Square."

Epilogue

Champagne flowed from bottles and fountains. Glasses were raised in celebration of the royal wedding. "To Princess Charlotte and Prince Leopold!"

Inside the Effingham mansion, the ballroom was lit by hundreds of candles in chandeliers and wall sconces. Outside, a dainty paper lantern thoughtfully provided by Bella shed a feeble glow over one corner of the terrace. Stephen and Maryann stood well beyond the circle of light.

He raised his glass. "To you, my love. May you never regret taking on this worthless, impoverished—"

She stopped him with a finger pressed against his mouth.

"To us. To our love. Our dreams."

He swept her into his arms. The chink of two glasses shattering on the pavement was the only sound to break the stillness of the night until the lilting tune of a waltz stole through the closed French doors.

Maryann listened wistfully. How she longed to dance the waltz. Her father had never permitted it, and now she was in mourning.

Gently, she pulled out of Stephen's arms. "Would you think me outrageous if I asked you to waltz with me?"

He drew her close again. "No, love. You are courageous and without pretense. You'll worry me and drive me to distraction with your expectations of independence, but nothing you do will be outrageous."

"I daresay you're right." A gleam in her eyes belied the primness of her mouth. "Nothing could be more outrageous than the way you arranged our marriage."

His mouth brushed her hair. "It's the way knights work. Swiftly and efficiently. Besides. I didn't dare give you time to change your mind. I knew it'd be best if I sent word to Sir Nathaniel last night, immediately after you said yes, to arrange for the special license."

Nestled in the curve of his arm, she danced the waltz. The touch of his hand caressing the nape of her neck spawned the strangest notions. So she could not be outrageous? If he but knew of the awakened desires and longings, he would speedily be undeceived.

She smiled. Or, perhaps, he would not. He always seemed to know her most secret thoughts and to anticipate her every wish. Hadn't he arranged for Mama and Reginald to witness the wedding? And for Bella and Meg to be bridesmaids? And within the hour they'd start on their wedding trip. To Cornwall. To her new home.

Her hand, which had, very properly, rested lightly on the sleeve of his coat, slid up his arm, across his shoulder, a move that inspired more outrageous notions. The smile deepened. How far, she wondered, would they drive before they stopped for the night?

Her fingers touched the crisp, dark hair. The golden glow of the paper lantern highlighted the sun-bleached streaks, as had the candles in the small chapel where they were married.

"Stephen?"

"Hmm?"

His mouth claimed hers, distracting her from the question she had been about to ask. It hadn't been all that important. But some day, she thought, losing herself in a whirl of pleasurable sensations — some day, when she had nothing else to think about, she'd ask him why he never wore a hat.